# Hatchet Island

# Hatchet Island

Paul Doiron

MINOTAUR BOOKS
NEW YORK

Published in the United States by Minotaur Books, an imprint of St. Martin's Publishing Group

HATCHET ISLAND. Copyright © 2022 by Paul Doiron. All rights reserved. Printed in the United States of America. For information, address St. Martin's Publishing Group, 120 Broadway, New York, NY 10271.

www.minotaurbooks.com

Designed by Jonathan Bennett

The Library of Congress has cataloged the hardcover edition as follows:

Names: Doiron, Paul, author.
Title: Hatchet Island / Paul Doiron.
Description: First edition. | New York : Minotaur Books, 2022. | Series: Mike Bowditch Mysteries ; 13
Identifiers: LCCN 2022009055 | ISBN 9781250235138 (hardcover) | ISBN 9781250235145 (ebook)
Classification: LCC PS3604.O37 H38 2022 | DDC 813/.6—dc23
LC record available at https://lccn.loc.gov/2022009055

ISBN 978-1-250-23515-2 (trade paperback)

Our books may be purchased in bulk for promotional, educational, or business use. Please contact your local bookseller or the Macmillan Corporate and Premium Sales Department at 1-800-221-7945, extension 5442, or by email at MacmillanSpecialMarkets@macmillan.com.

First Minotaur Books Trade Paperback Edition: 2023

10  9  8  7  6  5  4  3  2

*For Vicki and David Henderson*

All photographs are memento mori.

—SUSAN SONTAG

# Prologue

Every night, no matter how many drinks he'd had or joints he'd smoked, he would awaken to the screams of birds. For an instant, he would think he was back on the island. Then his hand would find the lamp beside the bed and the light would expose the messiness of his dorm room.

The odd thing was he'd never had trouble sleeping on Baker Island, where the chatter of gulls and keening of terns had lasted from dusk to dawn. The night terrors had only started afterward—once he'd returned to the mainland. Now insomnia was short-circuiting his central nervous system.

Through the fall and winter, he'd shuffled around campus until the administration and his mother had decided it would be best for him to return home to Maine. He had pretended to agree with their judgment, but the truth was he had lost the will to fight.

Then one morning in March, for reasons he could only guess at, he awakened to find that he'd slept through the night. He'd risen with a clear head and an appetite for real food, and now he was driving north on Route 1 with the window cracked and music blasting. Someone on the Maine birding listserv had reported a rare boreal owl in Bar Harbor, he'd told his mom, and he had decided to "twitch" it in the hopes of getting photographs.

"What time will you be home?" she asked, thrilled to see him showered and dressed in clean clothes.

"That depends if I see it!"

"Before dark?"

"It depends, Mom."

On the passenger seat beside him was the expensive camera she had given him for Christmas: a Nikon D5 with a Nikkor super-zoom telephoto lens. It amused him to think that the setup was worth more than his beater Subaru with its leaking head gasket.

One reason he felt better was because he'd finally replied to Maeve. Since well before Thanksgiving, she had been sending emails pleading with him to return to Baker Island for another summer internship. The woman was, if nothing else, relentless, and the seabird colony was, without question, his favorite place on earth. Maeve understood he wasn't himself but swore everything could be cured by holding a puffin chick again in his hands.

The weather was also acting as a balm on his spirit. Maine was enjoying one of its freakish thaws that make March such a roller-coaster month. Officially, spring was still a week away, but with the streams choked with runoff and pussy willows budding, a person could fool himself into believing winter had been banished and it would never snow again.

He'd been watching for early migrants, as he always did behind the wheel, but had seen nothing of note. The most interesting thing, from an ornithological standpoint, was a lone raven lingering beside a massive bloodstain in the road, the remains of a deer or possibly a young moose whose carcass had been crushed to bonemeal. Ravens weren't usually so bold as to scavenge in traffic.

He'd taken the coastal route from Brunswick to Belfast, thinking it would afford him good views of the sea, forgetting that the road consisted mostly of commercial strips between gray stretches of woods. Occasionally there would be a seaside village, still hibernating. Lots of "see you in the spring" notices on signboards. He'd desperately wanted to see the ocean again and felt cheated.

He was trying not to think of Maeve or the refuge, but the scenery wouldn't permit him a moment's peace. Every few miles, he would pass another random business named for the comical little bird she had helped bring back to Maine. Puffin Plumbing, Puffin Pizza, and most absurdly, the Huffin' Puffin cannabis dealership. He used to find these things funny.

Past Belfast, dark clouds spread across the sky, and he found himself fidgeting, unable to get comfortable in his seat. Wasn't that the same black BMW behind him since Rockland? It was March, there was almost no traffic on Route 1, and how many black BMWs were there with tinted windshields and Maine plates?

In the distance now, he glimpsed the two towers of the Penobscot Narrows Bridge rising above the evergreens. But his gaze kept returning to the mirror. The BMW wasn't tailgating him exactly, just keeping pace. When he sped up, it sped up. When he slowed down, it slowed down and refused to pass. After the morning's reprieve, he felt the familiar anxiety returning like someone had cranked up the voltage in his nerves.

If he could just get across the bridge, he would be safe, he thought. What story did that come from? The one with Ichabod Crane. If he could just get across the bridge, he would be safe from the Headless Horseman.

He saw a sign for a scenic turnout ahead and made his decision. Without signaling or slowing down, he turned sharply into the unpaved pull-over. The driver of the BMW kept going straight without a single beep of his horn.

Meanwhile, his heart was throbbing, and he felt dizzy enough to pass out. He tasted bile in his throat. He threw open the door and leaned against the car until he could recover himself. While he'd been driving, the wind had turned, or maybe it was because he'd stopped on an exposed hillside above the Penobscot River, frigid with snowmelt. But it felt as if winter had returned with full force.

He waited for the BMW, but it didn't reappear, and, shivering, he made his way to the information kiosk at the head of the turnout, mostly because he had never stopped here before. A weathered sign advertised the observatory atop the western tower, but the viewing platform was closed until June, just his luck. He leaned down to read the smaller print that explained the spectacle before him:

> The only observatory bridge in the Western Hemisphere and the tallest in the world . . . the observatory is, at 420 feet, 42 stories, the tallest occupied structure in Maine. The design

of the obelisk towers pays homage to the local granite industry which harvested granite from—

He could read no more. He tore his eyes away from the sign to
the man-made cliff blasted in the bedrock across the road. The rock
was jagged and orange with iron oxide, as rusty as the western face
of Ayers Island, where it looked across the sea at Baker.

Again, he felt dizzy.

"Excuse me. Would you mind taking our picture?"

It was an older woman, somewhere between his mother's age and
Maeve's, and a silent, uncomfortable-looking man who kept his
hands in his pockets and had to be her husband.

Virginia license plate. Tourists. What were they doing in Maine
in March?

"Sure," he said. "Happy to."

She handed him a smartphone that had been state of the art a
decade earlier. He coaxed them into position against the backdrop
of the bridge as if portraits were his passion instead of wildlife photography. And he snapped three photographs to be safe.

"That's so sweet of you. You're so sweet to do this for us," the
wife said with a slight drawl.

People always called him *sweet*. People always called him a kid.
Because he had a baby face. Because, even with blond stubble on his
chin, he looked like a high school freshman.

Now he was back in the car and heading north again. There was
a stoplight before the bridge. There were just two lanes separated by
a concrete barrier in the center where the suspension cables held the
structure aloft and a pathetic four-foot-tall rail on the sides above
the water. He idled at the stoplight, staring down the long, straight
chute before him. When the light changed to green and he didn't
move, the trucker behind him leaned on his horn, and he started to
laugh.

He had just remembered the lie he had told his mother. There
never was a boreal owl.

He stamped on the gas and drove halfway across the bridge. Then
he hit the brakes just as hard, forcing the box truck behind him to

do the same. Leaving the engine running, he swung open the door and got out, looking downstream at the river and the bay and the vast ocean beyond.

He felt well again. Better than well. Ecstatic.

He would have no need of his grandfather's revolver, hidden beneath the passenger seat.

Behind him, he heard a man speak. It must have been the trucker. "Kid? Kid? Don't do it, kid."

Then other voices from the vehicles behind the box truck.

"No! Please! Don't!"

But he was already vaulting the rail.

With cries of horror in his ears, he spread his arms like wings, taking flight.

# I

The sound of a gunshot will travel miles over open water—especially when the bay is as calm as it was that morning.

"What was *that*?" Stacey said.

She paused in her paddling and let one blade hang above the surface, trailing a reddish-brown tendril of rockweed. The length of her tanned neck shone with perspiration although we'd only left East Boothbay twenty minutes before. She had managed to stuff most of her hair under a faded Red Sox cap and had secured her ponytail through the adjustable fastener. There was gray in the brown now, just a few strands of spider silk.

"Probably a lobsterman shooting a gull," I said.

"It's a little early for an execution, don'tcha think?"

An effervescent mist that was already burning off in the July heat was all that separated our kayaks. I had to dig in hard with my own paddle to prevent a rear-end collision. Our seagoing boats were sixteen-foot Lincoln Seguins and not made for tight turns.

My momentum carried me forward. As I slid alongside her, Stacey took hold of the grab-handle on my bow to keep us from drifting apart. I caught a whiff of coconut-scented sunscreen from her outstretched arm. The rising sun was a pale smudge behind her, like a yellow thumbprint left by a painter on a wet gray canvas.

"Didn't you used to shoot gulls when you were an intern on Baker Island?" I asked. "Because that's where it sounds like the shot came from."

"Yeah, but we had a dispensation from the feds. It was the only effective method we had to protect the puffin and tern chicks from predators. We all hated it. The gulls were just doing what they evolved to do."

"Maine lobstermen believe their dispensation comes from a higher authority."

As if on cue, we slid past a fluorescent yellow buoy. The float was attached by a groundline to a lobster trap—or possibly a string of traps—that was resting on the bottom, fifteen fathoms below. It was just the suction of the outgoing tide, but the buoy seemed to be straining to pursue us the way a leashed dog might follow you on a sidewalk.

Near the Thread of Life Ledges, a sloop, running on its engine because there was no breeze, overtook us. A young family was on board. Stacey waved to a little girl, four or five years old, sitting beside her dad at the tiller, and she called back in a squeaky-toy voice.

"We're going *sailing*!"

"You're going to have so much fun!" Stacey replied as the boat's wake sent us rocking.

I knew how nervous she was—about where we were going and what we might find there—and I admired how she'd been able to fake cheerfulness for the little girl's sake.

"What did Kendra say exactly in her email?" I asked. "Tell me again."

Kendra Ballard had been Stacey's college roommate, and they had also worked together on Baker. She served now as Dr. Maeve McLeary's project manager, overseeing the Maine Seabird Initiative's restoration efforts on Baker Island. She collected the survey data, managed the project's two interns, and almost never left the island between May and August, after the birds migrated offshore.

"It was short," Stacey said, then recited: "'*Stevens, I don't know what to do. Maeve has gone missing. She's been away for two nights, and we have no idea where she went or why she isn't checking in. Other weird shit is happening, too. Some lobstermen who were hassling us are getting more aggressive. Can you please come out here tomorrow with Mike? Make sure he brings his badge and gun.*'"

The fact that she had memorized the email told me how rattled she was.

"Did you try calling her to find out more?"

"Baker Island is in a dead zone. On clear days, the researchers can sometimes get texts or send emails, but you know how spotty coverage is offshore. The nearest cell tower is on Ayers Island, but there's a hill in the way and no line of sight."

"The researchers don't have a satellite phone?"

"Maeve must have taken it. Otherwise, Kendra would have used it to call."

"But there's a marine radio?"

"I tried to raise the island last night on my neighbor's VHF, but Kendra and the others must have already turned in. The staffers sleep on tent platforms scattered around the cookhouse. I thought it would be easiest to head out at dawn and see the situation first-hand."

"Maybe we should have taken my boat."

"We had the kayaks all packed for our camping trip, and I'd reserved our site on Spruce Island. The irony is that I'd already been thinking of stopping at the seabird colony on our way out. I must have had a premonition that we would be needed on Baker."

The statement would have sounded silly if it didn't happen all the time. I had never believed in clairvoyance until I'd met Stacey Stevens and her mother, Ora.

"Did Maeve ever do anything like this?" I asked. "Did she ever disappear the summer you were an intern?"

"No! She was super-conscientious and hands-on. I guess you'd call her a micromanager, but I was nineteen and didn't mind being bossed around for the cause. She was the most brilliant person I'd ever met. Steve Kress rightfully gets the credit for bringing puffins back to Maine, but Maeve McLeary established a larger colony, using different methods. The big-name ornithologists said the birds would never breed as far south as Baker Island. But she proved those men wrong."

Another gunshot echoed across the water.

Trying to see through the mist was like peering through layers of gauze. The indistinct shape of a forested island loomed ahead and to port. The big ball compass on my deck said we were headed southwest, which meant that vague mass of land was Ayers Island since we'd already passed Thrumcap. Sounds do strange things at sea, but my meager powers of echolocation told me the shooting was coming from the seabird colony on Baker Island, two miles farther south.

"It has to be a lobsterman shooting gulls," said Stacey, but with diminished conviction.

"Why do you say that?"

"Because Maeve McLeary had a rule that we couldn't commit 'the daily murder' until the last puffin-watching boats had left for the day. She didn't want us to be photographed killing gulls."

"But Maeve isn't there, according to Kendra."

Stacey had no answer except to increase her strokes until she had once again pulled ahead of me.

The wind was forecast to rise later, turning onshore in the afternoon, but so far, the air remained breathless. The sea was a sheet of hammered platinum. Every stir of my paddle brought the fecund smell of the ocean into my nose and mouth. It was as if I could taste the teeming life in the depths: the phytoplankton and the zooplankton, the oyster beds, the shoals of mackerel, and the deep-diving seals. The sensory stimulation left me feeling intoxicated.

It wasn't just the sea air, either.

Despite all odds, I'd found myself back together with Stacey Stevens after more than two years apart. Our break, when it occurred, had seemed irreparable, absolute, and it had shattered the hopes of her parents, Charley and Ora, who were mentors and friends to me. Now the wheel of time had come full circle, and somehow, I was again courting the woman who had been my live-in girlfriend and almost my fiancée. From my perspective, our relationship was simultaneously thrilling, familiar, awkward, and terrifying. We had become different people during the hiatus. Intimate strangers.

We'd been planning this kayaking trip for weeks. I had thought it would give us the chance to take our relationship to the next level. But that was before Kendra called for our help.

The sound of a motorboat, approaching us at a high speed in the fog, caused me to sit upright, which in turn caused the kayak to wobble. I steadied myself by pressing my hips into the seat and bracing my paddle against the water.

"They're in a godawful hurry," I said. "They must be going thirty knots. I'm glad we're not in the channel or they might run us over."

"*Godawful?* You've been spending too much time with my dad. Fortunately, Parson's Ledge is between us and the boat lane. But their wake is definitely going to drench us, so get ready."

Just then, the bow of the boat broke through the fog, a hundred yards to starboard. Strangers to Maine might have mistaken it for the working lobsterboat it had once been. But the white paint job was too perfect, and there were no traps stacked on the deck. Mainers called these remodeled vessels *picnic boats* because their owners took them island-hopping for lunches and cocktails. This one was towing an inflatable dinghy that was practically skipping like a stone across the water.

I got only the briefest glimpse of the speeding boat before it lost all detail in the haze. Because of the windscreen, I couldn't make out the foolhardy person at the helm other than that she seemed to be a woman. But I did catch the name of the vessel on its transom.

*In this fog, at that speed, they might kill someone,* I thought.

"Get ready!" said Stacey. "Turn your bow into the wave or you'll be swamped."

We watched the massive wake crash over the barnacled peaks of Parson's Ledge, the sound as loud as a thunderclap.

Soon Stacey's kayak began to rise and fall on the approaching swell. Then I felt a stomach-lifting sensation as I climbed my first real wave of the day. The front half of the boat seemed to hang suspended for an eternity, then it went crashing down into the trough. Icy water washed up the spray skirt all the way to my chest. I pushed with my left foot on the pedal that controlled the rudder until the wake had moved past.

"Thanks a lot, *Selkie,*" I said.

Stacey whipped her head around. Polarized sunglasses hid her jade-green eyes, but I could feel the alarm that had come into them. "What did you say?"

"The name of that boat was the *Selkie*."

"Are you sure?"

"Yes. Why?"

"Because the *Selkie* is Maeve's boat."

"You mean we found her?" I said, incredulous. "That was easy."

"It would be if we had a clue why she isn't answering Kendra's hails or where she's heading at warp speed."

# 2

The sea was a chameleon; it changed color as the mist lifted. It had been a leaden gray when we'd pushed off from the boat launch. Now in the fullness of the sunlight, the water above the shoals was transmuted, as if by alchemy, from metal into turquoise. Out in the open ocean, it changed again, becoming as hard and blue as sapphire.

"Where do you think Maeve was going in such a rush?"

"In that direction? She could've been headed anywhere from Pemaquid Point to Maritime Canada."

"That narrows it down," I said, smiling because I wanted to reassure her. "At least we'll be able to tell Kendra that Maeve hasn't died in a shipwreck—yet."

Ayers Island rose to our left now: forested and stone-faced. The cliffs were gouged as if by some great sea monster that had tried to claw its way out of the deep. Gray schist glinted with mica crystals. Water, tinted rust red by iron oxide, dripped down the cracks like trickles of blood.

"I thought Ayers was made of granite."

"You're thinking of Hatchet Island," said Stacey, reaching to open her forward hatch. She brought out a water bottle. "That's where the old quarry was. You can't see it from here, but it's just behind Ayers."

I followed her example. It was hot, and my lips tasted of dried salt from when I'd been splashed with seawater.

"There's a fault running between the two islands," she said, between sips. "That's where Ayers Village is—along the channel. It's very shallow there. We can circle around tomorrow on our way home and see the Ayers Island Lighthouse, but Clay Markham is notoriously private, so we won't be allowed ashore."

The mention of Markham's name made me frown.

"My mom had one of his photographs in our house. It gave me nightmares."

"Let me guess. The one with the big wave?"

I could see the image as clearly as if I were standing in the hallway outside my bedroom.

The photo was titled *Shipbreaker,* and it showed a fishing boat on a storm-tossed sea. A wall of water thirty feet high hung over the wooden vessel. The photo must've been taken mere seconds before the rogue wave came crashing down. My first response to seeing this image was always wonderment: How puny and insignificant the man-made object looked before the power of nature. Only by looking closer did I notice the two doomed men on board the boat. Then my awe gave way to disbelief, confusion, and horror.

We were drifting now, letting the falling tide pull us out to sea.

"Does anyone know when or where that picture was taken?"

"Markham won't say, but his biographer thinks it was off Kamchatka, based on where he was traveling that year."

"I don't see how he can keep something like that secret."

"He took that picture back in the sixties, Mike. There wasn't social media or internet detectives back then."

"I was obsessed with those two fishermen," I said. "My mom told me they had to have been rescued. Because the photo wouldn't have become so popular if it showed two people about to die."

"Markham is such an amazing talent," said Stacey as if she hadn't heard the irony in my voice. "I'd cut off my pinkie to talk photography with the man for an hour."

Her admiration was so innocent, I decided not to say what was on my mind: that before I'd ever heard of a snuff film, I'd encountered its photographic equivalent in *Shipbreaker.*

My gaze moved to the photographer's island. Along the tops of the cliffs ran a seemingly unbroken hedgerow of beach roses and barberry. Even if you happened to find finger- and toeholds up the rock face, you would still have had to pass through a thorny fence before you could enter the coolness of the forest. I saw no sign of human habitation. No cottages, no shacks, not even indications of a path.

"Wasn't Markham involved in some sort of scandal?"

"He did an exhibition of photographs a few years ago of live children posed as corpses."

"Sounds charming."

"It got a bunch of people riled up, as you might imagine. Markham couldn't have paid for better publicity. It ended up being the biggest show of the year at the Museum of Modern Art."

"The thing I'm remembering was sexual."

"Markham and his wife supposedly hire handsome young men to work on their estate. A former employee came forward with an accusation, but nothing was ever proven. The poor guy had a history of drug abuse and was basically painted as a pathological liar. He overdosed before he could tell his story to the district attorney."

"That was convenient."

"Not every death is a murder, Mike."

The remark reminded me of a question I'd been meaning to ask. "Why do you think Kendra wanted me to bring my badge and sidearm?"

"You're a game warden," Stacey said. "Baker Island belongs to the state. It falls under the domain of the Department of Inland Fisheries & Wildlife, even if they've handed it over to the Maine Seabird Initiative to manage. Visitors are prohibited from trespassing on the island. Maybe she thinks you might have to arrest someone."

Kendra had mentioned that some of the local lobstermen had become increasingly hostile. While it was true I had police power on the island, the job of enforcing laws among Maine's fleet of unruly commercial fishermen fell to the Marine Patrol. I certainly wouldn't be chasing any lobsterboats in my kayak, I knew that much.

The breeze carried the aromatic sweetness of the balsam firs down to us from the island. A song sparrow announced itself from the flowering roses. Few land birds bred on these offshore refugia. I wished I could wander in the coolness of those green woods.

Stacey had secured her forward hatch and was ready to go. "We'd better get a move on if we want to land on Baker at mid-tide."

The waves began to build as we left the protection of Ayers. From a mile out, Baker Island took the shape of a green crown above a circlet of pink boulders. I needed to point the bow into the line of approaching whitecaps to avoid being broadsided.

Stacey let out a whoop.

A puffin had come streaking in from behind us like a thrown pass. It was a football-shaped bird with a parrot bill flying low and very fast on whirring wings. I looked up at its white breast and tuxedo of black feathers, and then it was gone.

"It didn't make a sound," I said.

"They're not exactly songsters. But in their burrows, they make funny snoring noises."

Baker Island was taking on definition as it emerged into the full sunlight. It was ridge-backed and ringed with granite ledges, the lowermost of which were shaggy with rockweed and glistening from the falling tide. Above the island, a living storm was raging. White shapes spiraled skyward like pieces of paper blown aloft, and from the cloud of seabirds came a cacophony of barks, shrieks, cackles, and screams. Half a dozen species giving voice to their alien, unknowable emotions.

Just then, I felt a chill go through me.

I share my home with a 145-pound wolf hybrid. His name is Shadow, and living with him has taught me that the superstition is true: the experience of being secretly watched, especially by a predator, really can induce a physical sensation of fear.

I let the pounding waves turn the kayak counterclockwise until I was facing Ayers Island and saw a gray figure standing motionless atop the cliff. From this distance, I couldn't tell if it was a man or a woman—or even if it was a human being. It might have been a driftwood scarecrow meant to frighten off curiosity seekers.

"There's another puffin in the water ahead," Stacey called.

I took my eyes off the figure. A puffin floated in the chop. It bobbed for a moment like a hunting decoy carved out of cork. Then it burst free of the grip of the sea and beat its wings fast, flying low toward the distant colony.

When I turned my attention to Ayers again, the scarecrow had vanished.

## 3

There were birds everywhere. Birds on the water. Birds in the air. Birds headed out to sea, and birds returning, their bills shining silver with fish to fill the mouths of their insatiable young.

Drawn by the sight, Stacey had quickened her strokes until she'd opened another gap between us. My left wrist was beginning to ache. I'd dislocated it over the winter—or rather someone had dislocated it for me—and I had only recently completed physical therapy to regain a full range of motion. Even healthy, though, I wouldn't have been able to keep pace with her.

In addition to being a bush pilot, a biologist, an emergency medical technician, and a gifted photographer, she was a kayaking guide, too. Stacey Stevens was so good at so many things it made lots of men feel inadequate. I found it sexy as hell.

Half a mile from the island, the air bloomed with a musky odor that managed to be both pleasant and nauseating, like the perfumes one encounters in certain church pews.

"What am I smelling?"

Stacey threw a word over her shoulder that sounded like *petrol.*

"It's not gasoline."

"Not *petrol,*" she answered with a laugh, "*petrels,* as in Leach's storm petrels. They spit out this funky-smelling oil to waterproof their feathers. Predators hate the taste, too. Maeve used to joke that if we ever got lost in the fog, we could find our way back to Baker by following the smell of the petrels."

Now I could make out one of the observation blinds planted on a slab amid beach peas and bayberry bushes. It looked to be little more than an upright plywood crate, scarcely big enough to hold a single adult. The top half was open to the air on three sides so the researcher could watch the birds from a place of concealment. I thought I discerned the shape of a silhouette.

"Are those bullet holes in the wood?" asked Stacey.

Before I could answer in the affirmative, a woman emerged from the box with a shotgun in her hands.

She had strawberry-blond hair and an impressive tan you don't often see in people with her coloring. She wore a stained T-shirt that clung to her abdomen, denim cutoffs that exposed bronzed thighs, and rubber boots that extended to her knees. A pair of heavy-duty binoculars hung from her neck.

The shotgun was a Remington V3 Sport. The improbably beautiful young woman didn't point it at us, but the careless way she let the barrel wander made me uneasy. As a game warden, I had dealt with too many jittery, impaired, and untrained gun handlers.

"We come in peace!" said Stacey, raising her voice to be heard above the seabirds.

"Oh, I'm sorry!" said the woman, who looked genuinely abashed. For a moment I thought she might even drop the gun. "I hope I didn't frighten you!"

"Were you scaring away gulls?" I asked. "We heard two shots on our way out."

Under the circumstances, I decided *scaring away* was a better turn of phrase than *killing*.

Her nervous smile dropped. "No, not gulls."

"I'm Stacey Stevens, and this is Mike Bowditch."

The young woman shaded her eyes from the sun to study us. "Did you paddle out to see the puffins? We don't get many kayakers this far from shore. There are some in the water behind you, and they roost near their burrows. The nests are all numbered on the rocks."

"Actually, we're friends of Kendra's. She asked us to come out here this morning. Didn't she tell you to expect us?"

"She didn't say a thing to me." Her offense showed so clearly in her expression. The barrel started to drift again. It wasn't that she didn't know how to handle the gun; the problem was she didn't respect it. "No one is allowed to come ashore on Baker Island without permission."

"Yes, we know," said Stacey with more patience than I was feeling. "I was an intern myself here about a thousand years ago. And Mike is an investigator with the Maine Warden Service. What's your name?"

"Hillary Fitzgerald."

She had a budget walkie-talkie, a Motorola Talkabout, clipped to her low-riding cutoffs, I couldn't help but notice.

"Hillary," I said, "maybe you can radio Kendra and tell her we're here."

"What's this about?"

"It would be better if Kendra explains," said Stacey.

I wondered if she saw herself in the intern; Hillary was probably the same age she'd been when she'd worked for Maeve McLeary.

"Can you wait here while I call?"

"Of course."

Hillary Fitzgerald wandered off behind her observation blind, setting the shotgun down casually on the flat, guano-stained roof.

I brought my kayak alongside Stacey. "What do you make of Kendra not telling her about us?"

"There's a good reason for it, I'm certain."

*She doesn't trust her own intern*, I thought.

"If Hillary wasn't shooting gulls, what was she shooting at?"

"I have literally no idea."

The current was carrying us toward the granite berm that served as a buttress around the island. The ebb tide had raised up a few boulders, shaggy with ocher rockweed, into the open air. More boulders shimmered, out of focus, through the green water beneath our hulls.

I couldn't hear anything Hillary was saying into the radio, but the way she was gesticulating told me the conversation with her supervisor was not pleasant.

"Is there a pocket beach where we land?" I asked.

"No."

"How do the researchers get ashore?"

"There's sort of an oblong boulder over there." She gestured to the west. "We used to call it Plymouth Rock. Maeve and her crew tie up the *Selkie* to a mooring in the cove and use a skiff to row in. If the tide is right—which it isn't—you can nudge your kayak in next to Plymouth Rock, but you need someone to pull your bow out of the water."

Successful seabird nesting colonies are characterized by their inaccessibility. But I couldn't believe this one rock was the only place to gain access to Baker Island.

"Is it really the only landing?"

"Not if you believe Maeve," Stacey said. "She claims to have been alone here one night and woke up to see a strange man outside her tent. She chased the intruder, she says, but lost him in the fog. Maeve McLeary is the most fearless woman I know."

The waves were nudging me toward the rocks. I back-paddled to hold my position. "I'm surprised you didn't go looking for the secret landing when you were an intern."

"I did look for it! One afternoon, I spent a couple of hours circumambulating the island. There's an abandoned lifesaving station at the south end—built during the age of the dory men—but its pier burned a long time ago. I couldn't figure out how you could safely land a boat there now."

Hillary snatched the shotgun from the observation blind and approached the edge of the rock wall again. "You need to wait here. Kendra's on her way."

"Can't we just paddle over to Plymouth Rock?" Stacey asked.

"I'm sorry," said Hillary, "but I'd prefer you didn't move until we get this straightened out."

We bobbed in the water. The young woman watched us. None of us spoke.

At last, Stacey decided to make another attempt at winning over the suspicious intern. "How many nesting puffin pairs do you have this year, Hillary?"

"Six."

Stacey looked like she'd been gut-punched. "We had twenty-seven the summer I worked here."

At the moment, a short, muscular woman came limping up the path. She was clutching what looked like an antique walking stick, carved from some twisting black tree.

Kendra Ballard had cropped hair that looked like it had been dyed with India ink. She was wearing dusty zip-off pants and a faded T-shirt from the Pogues' reunion tour. Her gray-tinted sunglasses were too large for her small, cleft-chinned face. Kendra was not unattractive, but she seemed to belong to a different species (as did we all) from the redheaded sylph.

"Stacey, thank Goddess! I wasn't sure you got my message."

"Kendra, what's going on?"

"I'd like to know myself," Hillary said acidly.

Her supervisor ignored her, choosing instead to address us. "Paddle around to the cove and clip up to the mooring ball. I'll have to pull you ashore in the skiff since the tide's wrong for the kayaks."

Hillary started gesticulating again. "You don't have the authority. Maeve is the only one who can approve visitors."

"But Maeve isn't here," said Kendra. "Which is why I called my friends. We need their help, Hillary. You know how desperate the situation is. Please cut me some slack. I'm clutching at straws."

The younger woman's face fell. "Why couldn't you have just trusted me?"

"Because everything's gone to shit, and I'm not thinking clearly."

At last, Stacey spoke. "If it's any consolation, Ken, we brought four pints of Ben & Jerry's for you in our cooler."

"Chunky Monkey?" said Hillary, beaming for the first time since we'd arrived.

"And Cherry Garcia for Kendra."

Her friend seemed to be blinking back tears. "Stevens, you beautiful bitch. Come ashore so I can kiss you."

# 4

On the outdated map I had consulted of the Maine coast between the Kennebec River and Pemaquid Point, Baker Island appeared triangular. It was flat on its north end, and long on its eastern and western shores, narrowing to a wedge where it jutted into the Atlantic. In area, it measured a mere eleven acres. Its highest point was a central ridge that rose all of ten feet above the peak of the spring tides. The only permanent structure was the run-down lifesaving station near the southern tip.

As we paddled round the northeast point of the isosceles, Stacey gestured at an unoccupied mooring. It resembled a floating volleyball that was chained to a concrete block on the sea bottom. Nearby, a wooden rowboat rode the chop at the end of a long rope tied to a boulder onshore.

"I've never seen Ken that agitated before." Stacey's tone was solemn. "Whatever's going on here is worse than I imagined, Mike."

"It all comes back to Maeve," I said.

"How can you say that?"

"Because she's the one who's missing."

Kendra made a bullhorn of her hands. "Tie up your kayaks to the mooring, and row the skiff to the landing."

"You're not calling it Plymouth Rock anymore?" Stacey said.

Kendra flopped a hand at her young intern. "Hillary unilaterally canceled the Pilgrims."

"That's not true!"

A laughing gull began circling us. It was sleek and black-headed.

23

Suddenly, it let loose with a maniacal cry. Random laughter always makes me think of the criminally insane. I had to remind myself that the gull wasn't crazed, but it took some doing.

We grabbed our dry bags, rafted up our Seguins, and clipped them to the mooring chain beneath the "volleyball." Kendra hauled the skiff within reach. The researchers used an impressive "clothesline" system to bring it back and forth to shore and keep it from drifting off in the night. The entire boat was whitewashed with bird droppings: slimy, oozing, and rank with the smell of digested fish.

"Be careful. You don't want to fall in," called Kendra.

"Poor Garrett fell in his first day," said Hillary, whose entire manner had changed with the promise of ice cream. "We should have seen it as a bad omen."

Garrett, I gathered, was the name of the Maine Seabird Initiative's third staffer. Stacey had said there was always at least a trio of researchers on Baker Island in addition to Maeve McLeary.

Carefully, we climbed out of our kayaks and into our private ferry.

"The currents around the island are deceptively powerful," explained Stacey.

"That's the worst thing about being here," said Hillary, "not being able to swim on hot days."

"You can swim all you want," said Kendra, beginning the work of hauling the rowboat hand over hand to the landing. "You're just not guaranteed of making it back."

When the skiff bumped the rock, she gave us each a hand up.

Up close, she smelled of peppermint—she must have used Dr. Bronner's soap to bathe and launder her clothes—with the faintest hint of marijuana. She stood all of five feet tall. Maybe five feet one. Her black dye job was growing out, revealing lighter roots. In one nostril, she wore a steel ring. Her face was prematurely weathered, a side effect of a decade working in the sun and wind.

"The facilities are on the way to the cookhouse if you need to use them," said Kendra, who seemed to appreciate how long we'd been stuck in our boats. "We have a state-of-the-art outhouse now with a composting toilet and everything. Maeve spared no expense in building our commode."

The last line struck me as the telling one—a jab at Maeve Mc-
Leary's spendthrift ways?

Kendra was paying out the algae-slick rope that she'd gathered.
When the skiff had drifted thirty yards, she knelt and made the line
fast to a rusted cleat hammered into the granite.

Stacey shrugged off her personal flotation device.

I got my life vest off and unfastened my dry suit and stepped out
of it. Underneath, I wore a black T-shirt with a warden badge em-
broidered on the chest and soft-shell pants. Under the hem of my
shirt, inside my waistband, was the belt and the concealed holster in
which I carried my off-duty gun: a Beretta PX4 Compact.

"Thanks for this," said Kendra, accepting the cooler from Stacey.
"But we've been especially well supplied with ice cream and beer
this summer, thanks to the siren of Baker Island."

"I wish you wouldn't tease me," said Hillary. "It's not like I en-
courage them."

"Oh, please. You know those lobstermen are all coming here to
see you. Don't try to deny it."

"I'm not!"

"In your email, you said the lobstermen were hostile," I said.

"Oh, they hate the rest of us," said Kendra. "It's Hillary they're
sweet on. We even have a lovestruck Marine Patrol officer this year.
Except he brings us doughnuts instead of PBR."

"Rick is obviously going through a midlife crisis," said Hillary.
"His wife is divorcing him and taking the kids. What am I supposed
to do? Besides, we might need his help."

"Is his name Rick Spinney?" I asked.

But none of them seemed to have heard me.

Kendra leaned on her black walking stick. "Hillary, shouldn't you
be finishing your shift?"

"I want to hear why you called them," the intern said with an
honest-to-goodness pout. She had large hazel eyes with red lashes
and naturally bee-stung lips. "I have a right to be part of the conversation. There's something you're not telling me."

Kendra burst into laughter. "There's a *shitload* I'm not telling you.
But I promise we'll discuss it over lunch. Cards on the table. I swear."

"Mmm," said Hillary.

"She can't possibly be that naive," said Stacey after the intern had left.

"Don't be fooled by the little-girl act," said Kendra. "Hillary is as smart as Garrett, and they're both smarter than I am. She's an honor student at Cornell and a champion downhill skier, and yes, she did some modeling when she was younger. My theory is that Hillary Fitzgerald is a celestial being from another dimension sent here to remind me of life's essential absurdity."

"What about this Garrett?" I asked. "What's his story?"

Stacey raised her index finger. "I want to talk about Maeve first. In your message, you said she was missing."

Kendra cast a glance up the grassy bank as if she feared being overheard.

"She's been gone two nights. We tried radioing her and texting when we could get a signal. My next step was trying a carrier pigeon. Or a carrier puffin, I should say."

"Well, we know where she is or was," I said. "Half an hour ago, she nearly ran over us in the *Selkie*. She had the throttle wide open, and we barely got aside in time. She was headed northeast. I hope she didn't take out a paddleboarder in the fog."

"Fuck," said Kendra.

"She didn't stop here first?" asked Stacey. "When she was so close to Baker? I assumed she must have."

It was a good thing Kendra had a stick to lean on because she seemed suddenly unsteady. "No."

"Do you know where she might be going?" I asked.

"In that direction? I don't have a clue."

Stacey put her hand on her friend's shoulder. "What's wrong with her, Ken? Why is she acting this way?"

Kendra glanced again at the hummock above the landing. "I know this will sound melodramatic, but I think Maeve is going nuts. I don't mean she's old and losing her marbles. I mean she's going batshit crazy."

## 5

Kendra wanted to tell us about Maeve in private, behind four walls. Baker Island didn't seem short on privacy to me. But the way she leaned on that gnarled black staff, I figured she needed to sit down for this conversation.

Birds began dive-bombing us on our way to the cookhouse. The terns were content to shriek from the air, but the laughing gulls came swooping in, close enough that one knocked my cap off my head.

"Christ!"

"You learn to duck working here," said Kendra. "Steve Kress, who started Project Puffin, wore a tam-o'-shanter so the gulls would peck at the pompom rather than his head."

Stacey reached her fingers under the brim of her faded Red Sox cap. "I still have a scar on my scalp. You can see it when my hair's wet."

I bent to retrieve my cap from a cluster of goose tongue. Stacey and Kendra kept on walking, without breaking stride.

Just beyond the rise, I saw the antenna of the marine radio atop the cookhouse before anything else. Then, as I crested the lip, I heard a screen door slam, and the research station itself came into view. It occupied a small dell and a southwest-facing hummock. In addition to the main building, which seemed the only communal structure and storm shelter, there were a few sheds and outbuildings, including the luxury commode, as well as assorted tent platforms, four of which had tents with tarps on them.

I entered the dimness of the cookhouse and found Kendra sitting alone on a threadbare couch with her tanned legs stretched across the coffee table. She kicked aside a dog-eared paperback with the title of *Murder with Puffins* on the cover to make more room.

"Stacey needed to make a pit stop. There's water over there if you need some."

She pointed me to the makeshift kitchen and a shelf lined up with five-gallon jerricans. I took a mug down from a hook, unscrewed the spigot from a jug, and tilted the heavy container forward until water splashed into the stained cup.

I did this several more times.

As I drank, my gaze drifted around the room and settled on the marine radio on a shelf in the corner. It was a Raymarine with a black handset and a red LED display that glowed like devil eyes. Without a satellite phone, the VHF was currently their sole reliable connection to the mainland.

I noticed a small, ragged hole in the wall facing the ocean. I plotted the trajectory in my head and crossed the room and found a timber with a deep divot from where someone had carved out the bullet.

I pointed at the ragged hole. "Is this why you asked me to bring my badge and gun?"

"It's more in case we have uninvited visitors."

"Do you have many?"

"Every day, but I want to wait for Stacey before I start running through the signs of the apocalypse."

"Do you have any coffee?"

She was aghast. "In this heat?"

"It's a game warden thing," explained Stacey, peering in through the screen door. "They'll drink coffee anytime, anywhere."

The shelves in the kitchen were crowded with cans of soup, diced tomatoes, and black beans; bottles of hot sauces, olive oil, and balsamic vinegar; packets of ramen; boxes of sesame crackers and Girl Scout cookies; bags of tortilla chips and cheese popcorn. Mesh bags dangled from the ceiling. One contained onions, another limes, and a third bananas. I felt like I had wandered into the galley of some modern-day man-of-war setting out for the Spice Islands of the East Indies.

I busied myself at the linoleum counter, finding a can of coffee and a filter and filling a scorched carafe with water. I heard the springs in the sofa groan as Stacey settled down beside her friend.

"What's been going on, Kendra? We want the full story. Why do you think Maeve is going crazy?"

"It began last summer. We had only nine pairs of puffins nesting, the lowest until this year. The Gulf of Maine is getting too warm for them, and the population is collapsing. It sent her into a horrible depression. Then a rumor started going around that Maeve was part of the cabal who had pressured the feds to close part of the gulf to lobstering to protect endangered right whales."

"Was she?" I asked.

Kendra grinned. "Yeah, but she thought she'd kept her participation a secret. That was when the threats started in any case. Maeve comes out to the island in the off-season just to commune with the place. She found that someone had shot up the observation blinds and, as you noticed, Mike, even some of the buildings from the water. Maeve camped out here in January hoping the sniper would come back so she could confront him. She had a friend drop her off so it would look like no one was on the island."

"I told you she was fearless," Stacey said to me.

"More like borderline suicidal," said Kendra.

The walls of the cookhouse were decorated with a hodgepodge of documents and images: a detailed map of the island with burrows and nests marked with flags; a contemporary nautical chart of the local waters that showed how deeply it dropped off along the east side of the island. Mostly, though, there were photographs, nearly all of them showcasing Maeve McLeary. In the oldest images, her signature ponytail was almost sable colored. Then it became streaked with gray. Eventually, it turned to pure silver.

Her eyes were closely set, unblinking, and intense like those of a night heron. The island weather had taken a harsh toll on her face. It didn't surprise me that recent photos showed bandages and scars from spots where basal cancers had been excised. In all the pictures, she was dressed in the same outfit: chambray shirt, denim pants, and Bean boots. She was one of those eccentrics who insisted on wearing a personal uniform.

"Next came the plague of weasels," said Kendra. "When Maeve visited the island in February to see if there had been more vandalism, she saw an ermine."

"How can that be?" Stacey asked. "Short-tailed weasels don't swim in salt water."

"Some asshole brought them here," said Kendra.

"Why?"

I already guessed the answer. In Europe, short-tailed weasels are called *stoats* (or *ermines* when their coats turn white during the winter). They are deceptively small predators, measuring less than a foot from nose to tail, and weighing not even a pound, and like most mustelids, they can be almost sadistically vicious. I'd heard stories of short-tailed weasels tearing out the throat of every hen in a henhouse without eating a single bird.

"It had to be more retribution for Maeve's involvement in the whale stuff," I said. "The hope is that the weasels will wipe out the entire seabird colony."

"That's one of the sickest things I've ever heard," said Stacey.

"It explains what Hillary was shooting at this morning," I said.

"You're never going to get rid of weasels by shooting them, Ken." Stacey rose to her feet and stood over her friend to emphasize the point. "You need a professional trapper out here."

"I know, I know," said Kendra, letting her gaze rise to the uninsulated ceiling. "But it doesn't matter to Maeve. We've put out rat traps, but it's not enough. She wants us on weasel patrol, too. I told you she was losing her mind."

"There's something else you're not telling us," I said.

Kendra looked at me with surprise. "Why do you say that? How did you know?"

"Because everything you've told us happened months ago. It doesn't explain why Maeve would disappear now, at the peak of the nesting season. Why would she be racing around the islands without telling you what she was doing?"

Kendra glanced at her friend. "It's kind of spooky how he puts this stuff together, Stevens."

"He's almost as scary as my dad that way," said Stacey.

Kendra spread an arm across the top of the lumpy sofa where the imprint of Stacey's body still showed. "You're right, Mike. There is something else. You must remember Mrs. Werner, Stevens. The masking tape heiress? She passed away last month. Parkinson's."

"That's so sad," said Stacey. "She was such a nice, down-to-earth woman."

Kendra ran a hand through her spiky hair. "More importantly, she was our second-biggest donor."

"Who's the biggest?" I asked.

"*Anonymous*," said Stacey and Kendra at the same time.

They couldn't help but laugh at that.

"Maeve has some rich patron whose name she won't disclose," explained Kendra, still smiling. "I've been her project manager for years. I have a right to that information."

"Didn't Mrs. Werner leave funding for the initiative in her will?" Stacey asked.

"Alas, no. She wanted her sons to endow their own charities. Unfortunately, they'd prefer to fund frivolous causes like removing land mines and eradicating polio."

"No wonder Maeve is freaked," said Stacey.

I drank the last of my coffee. "Isn't there government money for seabird restoration?"

"There is," said Stacey. "If you're willing to do things the government way. But that's never been Maeve's style. She's always at war with the U.S. Fish and Wildlife Service and your agency, Mike. She's even alienated National Audubon over the years."

"We assumed Maeve had gone inshore to make some development calls," said Kendra. "We thought she'd hit up some donors and prospective donors. But then when she didn't come back or call, we began to worry. When I saw her off, she looked so red-eyed and haggard."

"Oh, Ken, I'm so sorry for you guys. And for her."

"I forgot to mention that her weekend gin and tonics have become her nightly gin and tonics. She recently got plastered and started wailing how everything was her fault. Like she was responsible for the island being cursed."

As I was returning to the coffeepot to refill my mug, I noticed a lonely photograph tacked above the sink. The picture occupied a place of honor—you couldn't wash a dish without seeing it.

The portrait showed a delicate teenage boy with oversize blue eyes like a woodland creature from a Disney film and a cleft chin with blond stubble that made him look silly instead of rugged. In the picture, he was wearing a blue polo shirt and shorts and holding a camera with an enormous telephoto lens. The backdrop was a wall of out-of-focus evergreens. There were no trees on Baker Island, so the photograph must have been taken elsewhere.

"Who is this?" I asked.

The room fell silent—or as silent as was possible on this island of harpies.

"That was our dear Evan," said Kendra at last. "He was in high school when Maeve brought him out here. It was because he was a prodigy, the best young birder in the Northeast. And one hell of a photographer, too."

Her use of the past tense interested me. My neck began to tingle. *He's dead, this kid.*

"What was his last name?"

"Levandowski."

"When was this picture taken?" I said.

"Last summer," said Kendra and her voice cracked with emotion. "Maeve took it. What does it matter? Why are you asking me these questions?"

The walkie-talkie on Kendra's belt chirped. She pulled it loose and spoke into the mic. "What's up, Garrett?"

A fuzzed voice came through the speaker. "The creep is back."

Kendra groaned. "What's he doing this time?"

"Same thing as always."

"We'll be right down." She looked at me through watery eyes as she rose from the couch. "You asked why I wanted you to bring your gun. This is why."

# 6

We followed a trail along the ridge. The ground was strewn with pebbles that crunched underfoot. There was just a thin layer of sand for plants to spread their roots. The higher ground, thick with bayberry, raspberry, and poison ivy, was where the laughing gulls chose to nest. We spooked dozens of them into the air. They cackled madly at us before beginning their strafing runs. We increased our jog to a sprint.

Ahead I saw another blind, outlined against the deep blue ocean. The plywood structure was about the size of a box in which you might receive a new refrigerator. It alone among the blinds I'd seen had received a fresh coat of paint. Taupe with a lemon-yellow trim.

A husky man emerged from the shadows of the blind as we approached. I felt embarrassed at my surprise to discover that Garrett Meadows was Black.

"Hello?" he said, looking shy and confused. "I didn't hear we were having guests today."

His skin was tawny with a mask of reddish freckles around his eyes. His hair was cut very short but still wanted to curl, and there were hints of auburn in his beard. He wore glasses with serious lenses. Among the Baker crew, he was the only one dressed in clean clothes: a khaki field shirt, canvas work pants, and neoprene-topped Muck boots. A floppy, wide-brimmed hat hung from a cord down his neck. He clutched his Motorola Talkabout as if afraid to drop it.

"This is Stacey Stevens," said Kendra. "She was an intern with me my first summer. And this is Mike Bowditch. He's an investigator with the Maine Warden Service."

"Garrett Meadows. Pleased to meet you." He had a deep voice that rolled up from the diaphragm. "Listen, I hope it's not bad manners, Warden, but since you're here, maybe you can help us with this creep."

He gestured out to sea. My focus shifted to a motorboat idling seventy yards off the western tip of the island. It was a Chris-Craft 25 GT launch: one of the new models with all the bells and whistles.

"He refuses to answer my hails," Garrett said.

"Maybe he's not receiving them."

"Oh, he's receiving them just fine." He lifted the microphone to his mouth and clicked the button. "What's going on, *Spindrift*? Anything wrong out there?"

The breeze was light enough that we could hear Garrett's words coming through the stranger's VHF and floating back to us across the sea.

There was no response from the *Spindrift*.

"Is he harassing the birds?" I asked.

"He's harassing us," said Kendra, raising her walking stick.

"He's just taking pictures," added Garrett.

I pushed my cap back from my forehead. "Doesn't a puffin cruise come here every afternoon to do the same thing?"

Garrett Meadows studied me. "Everyone else who comes out to Baker focuses mostly on the birds, but our friend ignores the birds like they're not even here. The man is our own personal paparazzo."

"He's our own personal *stalker*," added Kendra.

I reached out my hand. "Let me have a few words with him."

Smiling broadly, Garrett passed me the walkie-talkie.

"*Spindrift, Spindrift,* come in, *Spindrift*. This is Mike Bowditch with the Maine Warden Service calling from Baker Island. Are you in need of assistance, *Spindrift*?"

My voice returned from across the waves like a false echo.

There was no reply from the boat—although the silhouette seemed to shrink farther beneath the sunshade that covered the helm.

"All right, *Spindrift,* I'm going to assume you can't answer because your radio isn't working. I'll put in a call to the Coast Guard to send out one of their response boats. I'll also hail the Marine Patrol. They may have an officer who's closer."

I'd barely finished the last sentence when the launch's engine roared to life.

I had forgotten my binoculars in my kayak, but I have better than average vision, and I could read the name *Spindrift* painted on the transom.

The Chris-Craft had a hardtop sunshade that cast a shadow on the boat's console. A lone man stood at the wheel. He was slender, possibly tall but maybe just lanky, and wearing a cap with an unusually long bill. It might have been a swordfisherman's hat like the one Hemingway favored in Cuba. The stranger's face, unfortunately, remained in darkness beneath the overhead screen.

I handed Garrett back his walkie-talkie. "There you go."

"Thank you, but he'll be back later, I'm afraid."

Kendra waved away a wasp circling her head. "Tell him what you saw last week, Garrett."

"I was out here early, before sunrise," he said, stroking his beard. "I wanted to record the Leach's storm petrels returning to their burrows. They're nocturnal, unlike the other species that nest here. The moon was up and three-quarters full, casting a lot of light on the water, and I saw that man rowing his dinghy *away* from the island."

I glanced at the vanishing boat. "Do you think he'd come ashore somewhere?"

"If he didn't, he was looking for a place to land."

"But you didn't see him actually set foot on the island?"

"Does that matter?"

"We need proof that he was trespassing."

Kendra began growing red beneath her tan. "The fact that the asshole is taking pictures of us isn't a form of criminal harassment?"

"The problem," I said, "is that there's no law against making someone uncomfortable by taking their photograph in a public place. His behavior has to escalate before we can legitimately inter-vene."

"What are you saying?" said Kendra. "That I have to wake up some night to find the creep outside my tent before the cops will do anything?"

"Maybe you should all get shotguns?" Stacey said.

I knew she was joking, but her humor was lost on the others.

"Absolutely not!" said Garrett. "I can't believe we're even dis-cussing this subject. I already get nervous the way Hillary handles that thing."

Kendra extended her twisted black stick. "I'd offer you my shille-lagh, Garrett, but I'm still dealing with this ankle sprain."

"I never expected I'd need a weapon on a puffin island off the coast of Maine," said Garrett. "Frankly, I find the whole situation absurd and troubling."

"He won't be back tonight at least," said Kendra. "The latest forecast says we're getting two inches of rain and gusts up to twenty miles per hour. You guys are welcome to camp on one of our plat-forms."

I had the feeling she wanted me (and my firearm) to stick around, but I'd been looking forward to having a private night with Stacey. On the other hand, it felt callous to abandon these fright-ened, vulnerable people.

"You're talking like you still haven't heard from Maeve," said Garrett perceptively.

"No, but our friends here saw the *Selkie* on the way out. Maeve nearly swamped their kayaks."

"Where did she seem to be headed?"

"Northeast," I said. "We lost sight of her in the fog."

"Isn't there anything you can do about our stalker, Mike?" asked Kendra, putting her weight on her walking stick again. "We need some relief from this shit."

"When I get a signal, I'll make a call to the Coast Guard to find out who owns the boat," I offered. "I can't pinch him for harass-ment unless he's been warned to stay away from you and defies the order. And I can't pinch him for trespassing if there's no evidence he's landed on the island. But I can send him a message that I'll be closely monitoring the situation and he'd better not test my patience."

"Pinch him?" said Garrett, pushing his glasses up his nose. "That's a colorful turn of phrase."

"It's old police lingo."

"Is it Maine lingo?"

"I don't honestly know."

"I'm curious, because, in case you haven't guessed, I'm not originally from around these parts. I need to learn the local patois if I'm going to blend in with you Mainers."

I had only known Garrett Meadows for five minutes, and I already liked him.

# 7

When he learned this was my first time on a puffin island, Garrett invited me to join him in his blind. "There's only room for two. Unless you'd like to relive old times, Stacey, in which case I can go."

"Thanks, but I've counted enough terns to last the rest of my life."

"I thought as much," he said with a smile.

It was settled that Garrett and I would meet the women back at camp for lunch in an hour. He opened the door of the blind as if I were a guest at his home. I had to duck and felt bad about taking the only chair, but he said he'd happily crouch. "I've been sitting all morning and need to get the blood pumping in my quads."

Before she left, Stacey leaned in through the open door. "Don't get lost coming back, Mike."

"He'll have me as a guide," said Garrett. "I would also guess the warden knows a thing or two about orienteering."

"Don't leave the path is what I mean. The military used Baker Island for target practice during World War II, and there is still unexploded ordnance."

I hit my head on the low ceiling as I rose from my seat. "How have I never heard this?"

"If you'd downloaded an up-to-date nautical chart instead of using a map from the FDR administration, you would've seen the warnings."

"There should be a sign!"

Garrett already felt comfortable enough with me to pat my shoulder. "There is a sign—a big sign—on the southern tip of the island. Most boaters come that way from Boothbay Harbor. The state placed the billboard there so no one would miss it."

Kendra squeezed her head in beside Stacey's. "The unexploded bombs and shrapnel were supposedly removed, but there was a big boom ten years ago no one could explain. Maeve thinks a mink set it off. One had swum over from Ayers and was raiding nests."

I thought it sounded like another campfire story.

"It must've been an obese mink to detonate a buried bomb."

"Laugh if you want, but Maeve never saw the mink again."

Then she closed the door, leaving Garrett and me alone in the intimacy of the observation blind. His skin smelled of mosquito repellent, which I took as a warning of biting insects to come. I noticed he'd patched the bullet holes in the blind with duct tape. And a can of taupe paint in the corner showed he'd attended to the exterior restoration personally.

"Why don't you try out my binoculars, Mike? What I like about Swarovskis is they have a superior field of view and better color fidelity than their competitors."

They must have cost $3,000 at least. Some little old Austrian had probably spent a year of his life grinding and polishing the lenses. I have twenty-ten vision, but the binoculars made me feel like a peregrine falcon.

I focused first on the distant island to the northwest where Stacey and I planned on spending the night. Spruce Island was easily accessible from Boothbay Harbor and a popular camping destination, but we had a secluded site reserved. I was still hoping for a romantic evening, and as for the rain in the forecast, I never would have become a game warden if I minded sleeping out in foul weather.

Garrett surprised me with a question. "How long have you known Kendra?"

"Five years, give or take."

"Has she always been wound so tight?"

"I'd better plead the Fifth."

"I thought as much. Well, she certainly has cause to be stressed, dealing with our esteemed boss. Maeve McLeary is proof of the old adage 'Never meet your heroes.'"

It was cool in the shade and even relaxing if you could block out the constant cries of the birds, which I found myself hard pressed to do. Garrett asked how much I knew about seabirds, and when I said, "Not enough," he gave me a quick tutorial in differentiating the three tern species on the island: common, arctic, and roseate.

Some razorbills were hopping about the boulders—majestic black-and-white birds related to puffins—but I found myself training the Swarovskis on the boats visible on the water beyond.

I scanned the lobsterboats and counted six. Sunlight flashed off the nearest ones as if they had mirrors for hulls. Most of the fishermen were busy hauling traps, meaning their boats were unanchored and often idling; but I managed to read four names. There was the *Centerfold* and the *Bonnie,* both out of Boothbay Harbor, the *Guttersnipe* out of Damariscotta, and the *Frost Flower* out of Ayers Island.

All but the *Frost Flower* had the same bumper sticker on their transoms:

## FUCK THE WHALES

"The birds here are also of interest," said Garrett with a sly smile.

"Watching boats is a game warden thing. Sorry."

He removed his glasses and held them up to the sunlight, then went to work on the dusty lenses with a microfiber cloth.

"No apology needed. You don't have an accent, but I get the sense you're a Maine native."

"Right again. Where are you from, Garrett?"

"Most recently, the University of St. Andrews in Scotland where I'm getting my MSc in biology with a focus on ornithology. But I'm from West Philly originally. I did my undergraduate work at UPenn."

"How did you end up here, if you don't mind my asking?"

"I attended Germantown Friends on a scholarship, and they took us on a field trip out to Cape May, New Jersey, during fall migration. The hawk watch counted two thousand falcons that day, and when I came home, I knew what I wanted to do with my life. My mom did not approve until I showed her how much professors at elite universities could earn."

One of the tuxedoed razorbills hopped to a nearby boulder. He was so close I could have reached out and touched him.

"But how did you end up on Baker?"

Garrett moved to a kneeling position. "I had lined up another position in the UK, but it fell through, and I didn't know what to do with myself. Then I saw a posting from the Maine Seabird Initiative. The project had an unexpected opening. I knew I'd earn next to nothing, but Dr. McLeary is a legend in the field, and I had never been to New England. Only after I accepted did someone tell me Maine is the whitest state in the nation!"

I didn't know how to respond to this.

Instead, I readjusted my ass on the frayed chair and turned my binoculars to the creatures around me, reminding myself that birders came from far and wide to see these beautiful rarities and I should seize the opportunity to appreciate them.

I spotted seven species of seabirds perched on the rocks or in the surf offshore. Laughing gulls occupied the highest boulders. The confusing tern species mingled below. The puffins hung together on slabs crusted with orange lichen. In the water, a raft of eiders drifted past while a lone cormorant dove deep and surfaced after what seemed like half an hour with a tinker mackerel.

Captivated by the birds, I was startled when Garrett spoke. "Not these two again."

I let the binoculars fall against my sternum and saw a lobsterboat sliding into view from the south. Its engine was off, and it was drifting past on one of the powerful currents that surrounded the island and made it so dangerous.

The boat was larger than most of the vessels I'd been watching: thirty feet from stem to stern. It had a blue hull and a white cabin. A blaze orange buoy hung from the canopy so that their competitors would know the men aboard were pulling only their own traps. Its other signature features were two flags flying from the sides of the cabin. One was a pirate sigil: the skull and crossbones. The other was the battle flag of the Confederate States of America.

I slumped back against the chair and turned to Garrett. "You're fucking kidding me."

"I wish I were."

"They do this often?"

He blinked repeatedly, telling me how nervous he was. "Every damned day."

Two men were aboard the boat, a captain and his mate, a position known in Maine as a sternman.

Physically, they couldn't have been more different.

The sweaty-faced captain was dressed in a size XXXL tie-dyed shirt. His muscular chest merged seamlessly with his beer belly above faded orange Grundéns fishing pants. He wore those multihued, wraparound shades favored by Major League Baseball players.

The sternman, by contrast, seemed made entirely of bone and sinew. I could have counted every rib in his rib cage, traced every vein along his forearms. He wore only board shorts and rubber boots.

Even from a distance, I could tell there was something wrong with his profile. I zeroed in the binoculars and saw that he was disfigured: the lower half of his otherwise handsome face was seamed with red and white scars. His head was shaved up the back and around the ears, but the hair on top was long and fell to one side in golden-blond locks.

As soon as they got within shouting distance of the blind, the captain turned on a radio and cranked up the music. Suddenly, the speaker mounted inside the cabin started blasting an obscene rap tune. It was Sir Mix-A-Lot expressing his honest admiration for women with well-developed gluteus muscles.

I pushed open the door and sprang into the dazzling sunlight.

"Turn it off!" I shouted above the music and the birds.

The speaker went silent.

I peered into the cabin and located what I expected to see: a marine shotgun with a corrosion-resistant barrel mounted above the dashboard. The captain had only to swing around to grab the gun.

"Who the fuck are you?" the mutilated sternman called.

"Not the person you were expecting?"

The boat's captain leaned his top-heavy torso over the gunwale. He was wearing a cord necklace with a shark's tooth pendant: a great white shark. "Where's my brother Garrett?"

Like a genie summoned, the researcher emerged from the blind. "Hey, guys."

"There he is!" said the captain. "The man himself. How's it hanging, my brother?"

My temples began to throb. "What's the deal with that flag?"

"We're pirates," said the sternman, thinking he was clever.

"I'm talking about the other one. Don't pretend you don't know what it means."

The captain peered slowly at the Confederate flag, rippling in the sea breeze. "It's just a symbol, dude. It can mean whatever you want it to mean. There's not one interpretation."

"Like hell there isn't," I said.

I couldn't tell if he was stoned or just stupid.

"Ever hear of free speech, asshole?" said the sternman.

The captain flashed me a dumb grin. "I know what you're thinking, dude, but we're just having fun with our boy, Garrett. When we're passing by the island, we like to play tunes to remind him of the hood."

I glanced at Garrett. "The hood?"

"It's nothing," he whispered. "I'm used to this shit."

"This isn't a racial thing," said the barrel-chested captain with the sincerity of someone who believes his own bullshit. "We're all brothers under the skin. Right?"

I became aware of two gulls scrapping over a starfish. Their laughter was the humorless din of an asylum.

"You never answered my question," snarled the sternman. "Who the hell are you anyway? I haven't seen you around before."

"Police." I held up my badge so that it caught the sun. I didn't want to confuse them by specifying that I worked for the Warden Service, especially since I had the same arrest powers as any other cop. One of the first things they teach you at the criminal justice academy is to always maintain a command presence. "How about you shut up with the wisecracks and give me your names?"

The sternman was having none of it. "How about you—?"

Fortunately, the captain possessed a teaspoon of good sense. "Whoa! Whoa! Whoa! Take it down a notch, Chris."

"You're such a fucking pussy, Bear."

"Maybe, but it's my boat, and I pay your wages. Lower those flags."

"For fuck's sake!"

"I said take them down, dude."

The sternman brought out a Bic lighter and a crushed pack of cigarillos. He lit one. He was thinking it through. After a tense moment, he reached for the pirate flag and ripped it off the pole.

"And the other one!" I said.

The man named Chris was gentler with the Stars and Bars; he even folded it respectfully in a triangle.

The captain pushed his shades atop his head to be sociable. "I'm Bear Goodale, and this is my *homme de stern* Chris Beckwith. I didn't get your name, Officer?"

"It's Bowditch. Where do you guys fish out of? Boothbay? Damariscotta?"

"We're over on Ayers," said Goodale amiably. In his mind we were all friends now that the flags were down.

"Maybe I'll stop by later since I'm in the neighborhood."

"You ain't allowed, asshole," said Chris Beckwith, exhaling smoke as if he'd swallowed burning coals. "The island is private property."

"The man's law enforcement, Chris," said Goodale. "He can go where he pleases. Nothing much to see on Ayers, though. Listen, we should really get back to hauling."

"Not without an apology," I said.

"Absolutely," said Bear. "We are one hundred percent sorry. We totally respect the badge. Blue lives matter."

"Not to me, to Mr. Meadows here."

Garrett pressed against my shoulder, whispering, "I appreciate what you're trying to do, but it's not necessary."

Bear extended his arms in a world-embracing hug. "Garrett, brother, we're sorry if anything we did crossed the line for you. You know we mean well, and it's all in good fun."

"Can't take a fucking joke," muttered the sternman, Beckwith.

"It's OK, guys," Garrett said with such friendliness he almost convinced me. "We're cool."

Goodale gave us a thumbs-up as he started the engine. "Take care, Garrett. You too, Officer."

Beckwith flicked his cigarillo into the sea. A gull made a dive for the butt, thinking it might be a snack. The bird had the sense to spit it out.

As Bear Goodale brought the boat around, I read the name on the transom.

*Persuader.*

# 8

I tried to get information from Garrett about the harassment he'd been experiencing from the men aboard the *Persuader,* but he said it was no big deal and not worth discussing. His friendly manner was gone, and I felt that he was seeing me as a police officer who had not yet earned his trust.

He secured his floppy hat by tightening a chin strap. "I think I'm going to head back to base camp."

"I'm going to stay a little longer if it's all right."

"I promised Stacey I'd guide you safely home."

"I'll try not to step on any bombs."

I felt bad that I'd let righteous anger get the better of me. The next time Goodale and Beckwith returned, Garrett Meadows would have to face them alone. I hoped I hadn't created problems for him by my combative attitude. I worried that I had.

As the breeze died, it sucked the oxygen from inside the observation blind, and the box began to bake. I pressed my face to one of the openings. The air shimmered above the sun-scorched rocks, and the smell of guano became overpowering. Buzzing flies found me in the blind and settled on my exposed skin to lap at the salty sweat.

I had lost my desire to watch birds.

Hunched to avoid aerial attacks, I made my way along the central trail. Chicks peeped unseen from the cover of the raspberries and beach roses. Fewer adult birds were around to harass me, and I assumed it was because they had flown out to sea to fish.

I paused at what seemed to be the highest point on the island. I wanted a 360-degree view of this cursed place. To the southeast, I could see the abandoned lifesaving station—a white building with a red roof—across a rippling field. To the southwest, I could see the backside of a billboard. It must have been the sign Garrett had mentioned, the one warning boaters not to land because of the unexploded bombs.

A flurry of gulls was swirling over the base camp. The birds weren't diving but turning in tight circles as they do above a crowded beach.

Stacey and the researchers were gathered at a picnic table on which they'd stretched a plastic gingham tablecloth. There were plates with sandwiches and a big pitcher of lemonade that was drawing yellow jackets desperate to drown themselves in the sugary water.

"Hillary's made her special lobster rolls," Kendra said.

As a native Mainer, I was a snob when it came to lobster. I took a tentative bite of the sandwich Hillary put before me.

"This is the best lobster roll I've ever had!"

Stacey covered her mouth because she couldn't stop chewing to speak. "What's crunchy in it?"

"Crushed salt-and-vinegar potato chips. It's my secret ingredient."

"Eat up," said Kendra. "We have lobsters coming out our ears. Luckily, there are a few fishermen around who like Hillary more than they hate Maeve."

"Enough, Kendra," said the intern. "Enough, OK?"

Garrett seemed to be holding himself above the bickering. He had made himself a peanut butter and jelly sandwich. "Unfortunately, I'm allergic to seafood," he explained. "That's another thing I should've considered before taking this job."

"I'm allergic to cats," said Kendra.

"Cats won't kill you," said Garrett between bites of his PB&J.

"You've obviously never lived with a cat," said Stacey.

I wiped my mouth with my napkin. "Where's the best place if I want to try to send a text?"

"The highest spot on the ridge trail," said Kendra. "You just came that way."

"Mike's worried about his wolf." Stacey knew me too well. "He's having separation anxiety."

"You own a wolf?" said Hillary, hazel eyes widening.

"*Own* is the wrong word."

Stacey threw her elbows on the table. "You should see him, Kendra. Shadow is this beautiful, powerful animal with a flawless black coat. Aside from Mike, I'm the only one he lets touch him."

Garrett pretended to choke on his sandwich. "*Shadow?*"

"I didn't name him," I said quickly. "I confiscated him from two meth-heads who'd traded drugs for him. He lives in a wooded pen behind my house."

"A cage, you mean?" said Kendra.

Too late, I remembered Stacey telling me that her roommate had been a militant animal rights activist at the University of Vermont.

"I let him inside occasionally," I said, hoping that would placate her, knowing it wouldn't.

"They're buddies," said Stacey. "Shadow slept in the bed one night and pushed Mike onto the floor."

"Wolves are wild animals," said Kendra, sounding like she was back at a campus protest march. "It's a mistake to treat them like domesticated dogs."

"I couldn't agree more," I said.

"Then why is he your house pet?"

"Ask fate."

Garrett angled his upper body across the picnic table the way a chess player might lean across a board. "Now that's an intriguing comment."

"Fate brought Shadow and me together. I can't explain how or why. All I can say is he's *supposed* to be in my life."

"Show them some pictures, Mike," said Stacey.

I got out my cell, pulled up my photos, and passed the phone around.

"He's beautiful!" said Hillary. "Oh my God, I want one."

The sight of the wolf affected me with worry. I hadn't left Shadow alone for the night since December. Logan Cronk, the son of my friends Billy and Aimee, was watching him for me. I always had misgivings, leaving the animal in the boy's care.

Kendra scowled across the table at me.

Hillary rose and began collecting plates and cups.

"Let me help you," I said.

Inside the cookhouse, Hillary was quiet, maybe because she was still smarting from Kendra's jibes. In the awkward silence, I couldn't help but become aware of the screaming gulls outside.

"Stacey told me the birds keep up that racket all night," I said, drying the dishes after she washed them. "It would drive me insane. How did you get used to it?"

"Earplugs."

"I can't sleep with them. I feel like I'm making myself vulnerable. I need to be alert."

"Like your wolf?"

Kendra's disapproval had made me disinclined to discuss Shadow. "I understand you're studying ornithology at Cornell, Hillary."

"I was," she said. "But I'm switching majors."

"Oh?"

"It was so romantic being out here last summer, on this beautiful island with all these incredible birds. And Evan. But I was naive about a lot of things. I guess I don't want to end up miserable like Maeve or . . ."

*Kendra.*

"'There is no path to happiness. Happiness is the path.'"

She stopped rinsing a bowl. "Who said that? You're quoting someone."

"Stacey's mother."

"Really? That's so wise."

I let out a laugh. "She was quoting Buddha, I think. But Ora Stevens is one of the wisest people I know."

After we'd finished the dishes, I drifted outdoors again, expecting Hillary to follow, but she remained inside, pretending to neaten the shelves. I sensed she wanted space from Kendra. Maybe space from all of us.

"I almost forgot," Stacey was telling Kendra and Garrett. "On our way out, we saw a puffin flying in with butterfish in its bill."

Kendra groaned.

"What's wrong with butterfish?" I asked.

"It's a southern species that's been moving into the Gulf of Maine due to global warming," Garrett explained. "Puffins evolved to eat skinny fish like herring and sea lances. Butterfish are shaped like silver-dollar pancakes. The chicks can't swallow them, and consequently they starve."

"I'm telling you, Stevens, the end is nigh," said Kendra.

Hillary came rushing out the door, letting it slam behind her. She appeared flushed.

"Maeve just called on the radio. She said she's heading back to the island later this afternoon. She wants to beat the rainstorm. You know how she hates driving in the rain or dark."

"Did she say where she is?" Kendra asked.

"No. Just that she was heading back."

"Well, did she say what she's been doing?" Stacey asked.

"Running around the state, meeting with people, trying to raise money. She said she thought we knew. She said it never occurred to her that we'd be worried."

"That's bullshit," said Kendra.

"How did she sound?" I asked. "Matter-of-fact? Impatient? Anxious?"

Hillary brought a hand to her mouth and spoke through her fingers as if she hoped not to be heard. "Tipsy."

"This evening should be fun," said Garrett, sighing as everyone rose from the table.

I expected a wisecrack or a lament from Kendra, but she didn't speak as she pulled the cloth from the table and shook off the crumbs. She wadded the plastic under her arm and stalked off toward the laundry shed. She limped slightly without the help of the black walking stick.

Stacey made a pained face. I heard a series of big waves break hard against the boulders behind us. Then the gulls descended.

# 9

Garrett left for his observation blind. Hillary excused herself next, saying she wanted to change clothes before her afternoon shift. I was struck by how the mood had altered with the news that Maeve McLeary was returning to the island. They had panicked over her absence; now they dreaded her return.

"We should be going, too," Stacey said to my relief.

"I wish you wouldn't." The pleading quality in Kendra's voice was more than mere politeness. "But Maeve is so unpredictable these days, especially when she's been drinking. She might hug you as a long-lost daughter or launch into a tirade because I let you on the island without her permission."

"You'll make it through, Ken. You've only got another month here."

"And then what?"

"You'll figure it out."

We walked down to the landing formerly known as Plymouth Rock and waited while Kendra hauled in the skiff through the creaking pulleys. The tide had risen above the seaweed-clad rocks. Waves bubbled over our shoes. We were a week from a full moon, so the tide was running high. In six hours, it would, correspondingly, be running lower than normal.

"You need to call me the next time you come inshore," Stacey said. "We'll get together over nachos and margaritas and talk about happier days."

"It'll have to wait until we've closed everything up for the winter."

I began putting on my dry suit and life vest. "Maeve doesn't give you a day off?"

"She might if I asked. But to be honest, I'm worried that everything would go to hell if I left. I feel like Prometheus chained to the rock. Except I have gulls eating my liver out instead of eagles."

The bow of the skiff bumped the boulder, but instead of making the line fast around the rusted cleat, Kendra continued holding it taut.

"Spruce Island is about two miles northwest," she said. "It's actually closer to Ayers than it is to Baker as the gull flies. On clear nights, we can see the campfires there. But not in the rain. Still, I'll be happy to think of my friends close by even if I can't see you."

The college roomates embraced each other.

Stacey and I climbed into the rowboat. The paddles knocked loudly in the oarlocks as I lifted them from the bottom of the skiff and fitted them into place and began to row. The currents were as strong as they had described, and I had to exert myself.

We climbed into our kayaks.

"I love you, Ken," Stacey called. "Take care of yourself and be safe. Nothing matters more than your well-being."

Kendra managed a smile. "Not even the puffins?"

"Not even the puffins."

"Maeve McLeary just felt someone walk across her grave!"

We began to paddle. In the distance, I saw the puffin tour boat out of Boothbay Harbor motoring toward us, a brown cloud of exhaust trailing behind. Nearer, a Friendship sloop bobbed off the eastern side of the island. The noonday sun was bringing out the sightseers.

The voices of the people on the sailboat carried across the water.

"Which of them are puffins?" a woman asked.

"The black ones with the red feet," a man answered.

"Should we tell them those are guillemots?" I said to Stacey.

But she wasn't paying attention; she was staring back at Plymouth Rock. Kendra had already disappeared from the landing. With no one visible, you could have believed the Maine Seabird Initiative was already gone, resigned to the island's history like the ruined lifesaving station.

There was a steady breeze now, blowing from the southwest: a harbinger of the approaching thunderstorm. The wind whipped spray into our faces as we paddled, and the salt water clouded the lenses of my sunglasses. I didn't need a barometer to know that the atmospheric pressure was dropping.

"What did you and Kendra talk about while I was with Garrett?"

"That kid mostly, Evan Levandowski."

"He's dead, isn't he?"

"I won't even ask how you deduced that," she said. "He killed himself this spring. Three weeks before he was supposed to return to Baker Island, he jumped off the Penobscot Narrows Bridge."

I remembered the story now. The Maine media has an unofficial policy of not reporting the details of suicides. But when a promising young man swan dives off the Penobscot Narrows Bridge, it is undeniably news.

"Do they have any idea why he killed himself?"

"Kendra thinks something happened to him at the end of his internship or maybe just after he got home. When she saw him at the traditional Labor Day party at Mrs. Werner's house, he barely said a word to anyone. She said he looked shell-shocked."

"With teenagers, it's not always a single incident that drives them to suicide."

"True."

"Does Kendra know if he left a note?"

"No, but she says Maeve was in contact with him the morning he killed himself."

That detail struck me as more important than she realized.

"I couldn't help noticing in the photographs posted around the cookhouse how Maeve always had her arms around her beautiful interns, male and female."

My words seemed to shock her. "You're not suggesting she sexually harassed him?"

"It would explain some things."

"Maeve has always known where the line is, even when she's half in the bag. Maybe she's walked up to it, but she's never crossed over. Kendra would've told me if she had suspicions."

Two great black-backed gulls crossed our bows, heading toward the island. They belonged to the largest and arguably the fiercest species of gulls in the world. Even bald eagles didn't tangle with them. The predators were headed to Baker to hunt chicks. It was telling that Stacey paid the birds no notice.

"I'm sorry not to have met Maeve," I said.

"Maybe it's for the best," she said. "Last night, I felt this overwhelming sense of nostalgia, thinking back to the summer I worked with Kendra. We were so young and had this shared sense of purpose. And Maeve seemed so wise and strong. She was my first real mentor, the person who inspired me to devote my life to protecting wildlife. I hate to say it, but I'm glad she wasn't there today. I would've hated to see what she's become."

We were fighting the obstinate southwest wind. It felt like we weren't getting anywhere.

"I doubt I'll ever come back to this island," she added.

"You never know."

"I mean, I doubt I'll want to."

"Do you mind if we make a short detour before we go?"

Helped by the waves, I used a couple of sweep strokes to bring the bow of the kayak around until I was looking back at Baker Island. At the southeast end, I saw the billboard rising above the blush-colored boulders and, farther away, the crimson roof of the lifesaving station.

I didn't need binoculars to read the warning on the sign.

DANGER

UNEXPLODED ORDNANCE

ISLAND CLOSED

# IO

Because it was the height of summer and Spruce Island was less than seven nautical miles from Boothbay Harbor, I had worried that we would find it overrun. That I might even have to chase squatters out of our reserved campsite.

As it happened, the dire weather forecast turned out to be a godsend. We seemed to have the island to ourselves.

Spruce was two or three times larger than Baker with basalt outcrops the color of cast iron and a handful of pebble beaches. Most of the narrow island was covered with namesake spruce and firs, and some of the trees ventured so close to the water their roots twisted from the undercut banks like emergent tentacles. The campsites were easy to spot because of the drag marks where previous visitors had hauled up their kayaks and dinghies, as well as the charred driftwood where they'd made their beach bonfires.

I used the paddle to brace myself when I stepped out of the Seguin. The knee-deep water was so frigid it made my shin bones ache. The gravel rolled under my water shoes as I took hold of the grab handle and walked the bow into the shallows, then hauled the kayak high up the beach beyond the wrack line.

We spent twenty minutes bagging the trash we found: soda cans and beer bottles, a couple of loaded diapers, dirty white wads of paper used by adults for the same bodily functions, assorted snack bags.

Stacey had an empty hold in the stern of her kayak and agreed to stuff the garbage there.

When the site was clean, we unloaded our gear. The place where we chose to pitch our tent was a patch of bare earth that had been raked and leveled until it was almost perfectly flat. We hung up a line between the nearest spruces to dry our wet clothes. I noticed that the lower branches of the trees had been snapped or sawed off, and I couldn't help laughing out loud.

"What's so funny?" she said.

"These are cat spruces. I'm just imagining people throwing these sticks into the fire and wondering why their campsite suddenly smelled like cat piss."

The heat hadn't broken, despite the gusting wind.

I wiped my forehead with a bandanna. "What do you want to do?"

"Swim!"

"The water is freezing."

"I thought you were a Mainer."

There were plenty of boats in view, and no doubt many of the boaters had binoculars and cameras, but Stacey stripped herself naked, except for her sneakers. She had inherited a gene from her father that kept her from gaining weight no matter how much she ate. I could see her stomach muscles outlined above a triangle of brown hair.

Before she could tease me again, I unzipped my dry suit and pulled the T-shirt over my head, feeling a twinge in what I was coming to think of as my bad wrist. The day's exercise had vanquished the deodorant I had applied that morning.

I watched Stacey run naked to the waterline. As I slid down my underwear, I felt self-conscious about my erection, but my plunge into the icy sea took care of that.

I came up blowing. "Jesus!"

"Give it a minute," she said, swimming on her back away from the island. "You'll get used to it."

I pursued her with long strokes—she was right about me being a powerful swimmer—and when I caught up, I wrapped my arms around her, holding the both of us above the water with my kicking legs. Then I kissed her. First on the mouth, then behind her ear, and then along her neck beneath her wet hair, tasting the salt.

"Let's go up on the grass," she said.

I stared into her eyes. The brightness of the afternoon had made her pupils contract, and her green irises appeared enormous. Despite the coldness of the ocean, I felt blood returning to my groin. "Are you sure?"

"I'm ready."

"You're not afraid of how you'll feel about us afterward?"

"I already feel it, Mike."

We made love on a bed of moss at the edge of the clearing. Neither of us cared that we might be seen by someone spying from one of the boats. In our minds, we were the only two people on the earth. We made eye contact and smiled shyly at each other until the intensity of our lovemaking overwhelmed us.

She finished on top of me, and then I rolled her onto her back. I wrapped my left arm around her and grabbed her hair with my right and kissed her hard, making eye contact the whole time, until I could no longer contain myself. Afterward, she stroked my head and sweaty shoulders, but we didn't disengage from each other. When I finally raised myself up on my arms and looked into her eyes, I knew that I had never stopped loving her while we'd been apart.

It had always been Stacey. It would always be Stacey.

Her smile became mischievous.

"What are you thinking?" I asked, still breathing hard.

"That I need another dip in the ocean."

"That's all?"

She touched my cheek. "No."

I rolled off her and stared up at the aqueous light in the interlaced boughs of the trees and the sun still sparkling above everything. Stacey rose to her feet, and for a moment, I felt the coolness of her shadow before she sprinted down the beach.

A winter wren was singing his heart out from inside the toy forest. The kaleidoscopic light in the spruces held me spellbound. I listened for the splash when she dived in again. And I knew, for the first time in a long time, that I was happy.

That afternoon, as the sky darkened, we explored the trails that connected the three campsites. Stacey brought along her camera to take pictures of the thick carpets of sphagnum moss and the Indian cucumbers pushing up through the matted soil.

The other sites were as litter-strewn as the one we'd chosen. The largest seemed to be the most heavily used. It was situated on a cove that looked west toward Damariscove. The grass was trampled and dead in the rectangular patches where people had pitched their tents. The grill over the firepit was so black with creosote it should have come with a cancer warning.

"It looks like they tried burning their Budweiser cans in the fire," I said.

"I'm surprised it didn't work. The melting point of aluminum is only twelve hundred degrees."

"How do you know the melting point of aluminum?"

"Doesn't everyone?"

Cabbage white butterflies flittered in the beams of sunlight shafting through the trees. Stacey found an edible bear's tooth mushroom growing on a lonely birch. She had learned foraging from the most knowledgeable woodsman of my acquaintance, so I tended to trust her when she said it wasn't poisonous.

We carried driftwood up from the shore to the ring of stones. When I reached into my backpack, three disposable lighters fell onto the grass, along with a ferro rod and striker.

She nudged me. "Are you sure you have enough lighters?"

I'd had a rough night in the woods at Christmastime. After my Jeep had been forced into a frozen river, I'd needed to make a fire to save my life and had found myself, it's fair to say, underprepared. Never again.

When we'd planned this trip, before we'd heard from Kendra, I had assigned myself the job of making supper. After years of subsisting on microwave burritos and pizza slices, I had decided to improve my diet. I had no aptitude for cooking, but I was learning that quality ingredients can overcome mediocre preparation. I had packed venison tenderloins wrapped in bacon; four ears of sweet corn from Billy and Aimee's kitchen garden; and strawberries and biscuits for shortcake. Stacey suggested we sauté the bear's tooth mushroom in the cast-iron pan.

"We'd better get a move on," she said. "See how dark those clouds to the south are?"

"I guess we won't be sleeping under the stars."

Stacey sat on a log and crossed her sand-flecked ankles. She stared at Baker Island, already no more than a shadow along the horizon.

"I can't help worrying about Kendra and the rest of them. Maeve, too. I have this feeling of doom."

"The climate is changing. Baker Island might not be a place for puffins anymore. The Maine Seabird Initiative might have run its course."

She let out a sigh. "You're such a man."

"What does that mean?"

"It means, for a person who's otherwise so perceptive, you can be really obtuse about things. But I don't want to talk about Baker Island anymore. I want to enjoy our evening."

Supper was fantastic, more because of the freshness of the food than my culinary ability. It helped that we were both famished. I had planned on boiling hot water for coffee but decided to give my stomach a break. It would have been just for me, anyway. Stacey rarely consumed caffeine after noon.

She yawned into the back of her hand.

"How are you sleeping these days?" I asked.

"Better."

"You always had such a hard time when we were together before."

"Not sleeping must have made me a real joy to be around," she said. "When I was a kid, I always slept like a stone."

"What happened?"

"My mom's crash. I had nightmares about it for months afterward. And then I couldn't fall asleep for fear of the nightmares."

When Stacey was in college, her dad had decided to give her mom flying lessons. As a lifelong pilot, Charley Stevens lived in the air. The sky was his natural element, and he wanted to share his joy with his wife. He was normally a thoughtful man, but he missed the signs that Ora was just humoring him.

They were returning to Flagstaff Pond with Ora at the controls when the plane came in inches too low. Charley, in the back seat, was momentarily distracted by the autumn color on Bigelow Mountain and didn't grab the stick in time. The Cub clipped the top of a tree and hit the water at a bad angle. Ora severed her spine, broke multiple bones, and suffered a serious concussion, while Charley emerged with just a fractured tibia.

Stacey saw it all from the dock.

"I would've had nightmares, too," I said.

"I was so angry at my dad for pressuring her," she said. "But I was a pilot, too, by that point and kept telling her how great flying was and how she needed to learn. She did it to please me as much as him, and I couldn't deal with my complicity."

I felt a raindrop hit my forehead. But I didn't move.

"I took my rage and guilt out on my dad first," she said. "We'd always been so close. Then when my mom was out of the rehabilitation center, I found myself getting angry at her, too. I wanted her to blame my dad for the crash, but she just accepted the reality of her condition.

"Anyway, I started acting out—because I was mad at him, mad at her, mad at myself. Of course, they understood what was really going on. Every time they forgave me, I behaved worse. That's why I left New England to go to grad school out west. I thought I could outrun my pain by moving to Colorado. I did the same thing to you when I hightailed it to Florida."

I squeezed her hand. "How come you've never told me this before?"

"I was in denial."

"What changed?"

"A friend in Florida suggested I start seeing a therapist. My counselor was a recovering drug addict, and she had all these sayings that drove me nuts. Like once we were talking about how I needed to make peace with my dad, and she said, 'Acceptance is when you stop trying to change your past.'"

"That's a good one."

"That wasn't my favorite line of hers, though. The one that really changed my thinking was: 'You're not really an adult until you've stopped blaming your parents for all your problems.'"

A rumble of faraway thunder told me to stop wasting time.

"Would you care to join me in the tent?"

"I don't know if I have it in me to do it again, Mike. I'm more exhausted than I have any right to be."

"It was emotional, visiting Baker again," I said. "Not to mention the fact that we paddled a half marathon. Why don't you get ready for bed while I clean up."

"I want to help you."

"Let me do it. Please."

While she brushed her teeth, I rubbed sand against the cast-iron skillet and the enamel plates to scrape away the grease. Then I filled the folding camping bucket with seawater. I paused beside our kayaks at the top of the beach, looking east toward Baker Island, but saw only blackness.

The fire went out with a satisfying hiss when I dumped the bucket on it. The rain began almost immediately after I had kicked sand and dirt on the embers that had refused to dim.

When I crawled into the tent, where we'd zipped together our sleeping bags, I found Stacey already asleep.

I stretched out beside her in my underwear, and she slid her back against me without waking so I was spooned around her body. I listened to the rain pouring on the tarp and the waves running up the beach. And then I was asleep.

# II

I awoke twice in the night.

The first time was scarcely an hour after I'd drifted off—10:17, according to the luminous hands of my watch—when I heard a motorboat idle up to the opposite side of the island. The rain was still coming down, although not as hard as before.

So much for having Spruce Island to ourselves. I expected to hear a commotion as the late arrivals came ashore and tried to make camp in the rain and the dark, but they must've decided to sleep on board, which suggested the boat was large enough that it had a cabin. Except for the engine and the splash of the anchor, I heard nothing, not even a voice.

Instinctively, I felt for my Beretta alongside the sleeping bag. There had been a time when I slept fitfully if I didn't have a firearm within reach of the bed. I thought I'd outgrown that paranoia, so common among law enforcement officers, but the brutal attack I had suffered over the winter had scraped the skin from my nerves, and the wound still hadn't healed.

Stacey didn't stir. In time, I fell back asleep.

Hours later, I awoke in total darkness to the sound of a distant gunshot. At first, I thought I had dreamed it. But this time, Stacey had heard the sound, too, and clutched at me.

"What was that?"

"A gunshot."

I had closed my hand around the grip of my sidearm. The breeze was up again, and raindrops were pattering the tent tarp. We listened and listened, but there was no second shot.

"It sounded close," she said, sitting up to light the lantern.

"I don't think it was," I said. "I was asleep, but my gut tells me it came from Baker."

"Maybe one of our friends saw a weasel."

Stacey switched on the camping lamp suspended on a hook from the top of the tent. It swayed when she let go; the shadows swung back and forth, before coming to rest. My diving watch, my stepfather's old Marinemaster, gave the time as 3:42.

"Kendra knows to fire three shots as a signal, right?" I said.

Three of anything—whistle blasts, mirror flashes—were the internationally known sign for distress.

"What makes you think something's wrong?" she asked.

"Just a feeling." I pulled my T-shirt over my head. "There was such a bad vibe there."

She buttoned up her shirt. "What do you want to do?"

"Go back."

"Now? In the darkness?"

"We'll have to wait for first light."

She reached for her cell phone. "No service, of course. I wish we had a marine radio."

"We may be in luck." I slid the sleeping bag down my legs to pull on my pants. In the shaky lamplight, the four-inch scar from my recent gunshot wound appeared bloodred. I kept waiting for it to fade. "A boat came in while you were sleeping. I heard the engine and then the anchor being lowered. But no one came ashore. I'm thinking they decided to sleep on board rather than trying to pitch camp in a downpour."

"I'm coming with you," Stacey said, struggling into her long pants.

"I was hoping you would. On a night like this, being hailed by a woman is less threatening than having a strange man calling at your boat from the shadows."

"Especially when he has a gun in his hand."

I had picked up the Beretta without thinking. I unzipped the flap and ducked outside the tent. As I stood upright, I tucked the hand-gun in the back of my waistband. The rain was becoming a steady drizzle. Mist steamed from the ground, and the air was heavy with the smell of the sea. The storm had churned up the waves, and we could hear them crashing against the beachhead in the dark.

Stacey crawled from the tent with her high-powered headlamp already fastened over her ball cap. I settled for the handheld flash-light I'd kept beside my sleeping bag. It was a three-thousand-lumen Fenix capable of throwing light a third of a mile in clear conditions.

She started through the woods without waiting.

Stacey had always been as quick and agile as a deer, but I had to watch where I stepped. Spruce roots twisted up through the thin layer of humus and dead needles, and the exposed rock was slick. She reached the other side of the island while I was still dodging branches.

"Hello!" I heard her call. "I'm sorry to wake you. I know it's late, but it's urgent. Hello! We're wondering if you could call someone on your radio for us. It's urgent."

I pushed through some soaked bushes and saw her standing above a steep gravel beach. The light from her headlamp was fuzzed with rain and mist. The beam died over the water before it could touch anything resembling an anchored boat.

I added my own high-powered flashlight to hers, but the fog that had followed the heavy rain was impenetrable.

"Are you sure you heard a boat?" she said. "You didn't just dream it?"

"Listen!"

Now in the dark there came a definite sound. Someone was stum-bling around the deck of a boat.

Stacey tried again. "Hello!"

Our silent visitor refused to answer. I had the sense they might even have frozen, so as not to give themselves away again.

"Please! We need your help!"

Then we heard the metallic clatter of an electric winch pulling up an anchor chain, and a big engine roared to life. Too big for a sailboat motor. I caught another noise, too: an electric whine that pierced the air for five seconds, then stopped.

"Please! Don't go!" Stacey said. "We need your help!"

The idling engine shifted gears, and I could smell its exhaust. A red glow appeared in the fog—a navigation light on the port side of the bow. As the boat turned away, we saw the white running light centered on the stern. It faded, then disappeared as the boat retreated from the island.

"Maybe you should've told them you're a game warden," Stacey said.

"You don't think they were scared enough as it is?"

"Scared of what?"

"Maybe they thought we'd caught them trespassing."

"Come on, Mike. Provided you're not blocking a navigation channel or don't steal someone's mooring, you can anchor wherever you want. Every gunkholer knows that."

The term was Maine jargon—or maybe just wharf-rat jargon— for a boater who wanders around the islands and peninsulas, stopping in coves and sheltered inlets for the night.

"What do you want to do?" I said.

She turned to me again. Her headlamp was blinding. Illuminated shapes like protozoa swam across my field of vision.

"Pack up, I guess, and be ready to head out as soon as it's light."

"We're going back to Baker, then?"

"Unless you think that gunshot came from somewhere else."

# 12

An hour before dawn, the fog invaded the island. It crawled up the beach and slithered between the tree trunks, and we heard water dripping from the evergreens so that it still seemed to be raining in the forest.

We dressed in the dark, both of us adding layers against the cold we were sure to encounter at sea. Then I started a fire in the circle of wet stones and made breakfast while Stacey took down the tent. I fried eggs and bacon and grilled biscuits in the bacon fat. I dropped the eggshells in the coffeepot to settle the grounds and make cowboy coffee.

Neither of us said much while we ate and warmed our hands around the steaming mugs.

The wind had died, as it often did before sunrise, and we heard the tolling of a distant buoy, rocked by waves that were the remnants of the night's storm.

We knelt over Stacey's navigation chart and discussed how to make the crossing in the fog. The firelight gave the laminated map a reddish sheen.

"We can't take sight bearings, so we'd better hope the ball compasses on our boats are accurate."

"I checked mine yesterday against my Suunto."

I tugged a lanyard out from under my shirt collar and showed her the field compass. I had attached it to the braided cord on which I wore my dead father's dog tags, the ones he'd come back with from

Vietnam. Strange that I considered them good luck charms, considering what a sad and misfortunate life he'd led.

Stacey drew a line with her finger across the chart from Spruce to Baker Island.

"If it were flat calm, we could just power over, keeping to our heading, and I wouldn't worry about us drifting. But we've got a rising tide; plus, the winds will pick up after the sun rises. The last forecast I saw was for southwesterly winds around fifteen knots, and there are sure to be stronger gusts out on the blue water."

I felt so much out of my element here. In the North Woods, I could find my way blindfolded, spun around three times, with my shoelaces tied together. But the ocean was another kind of wilderness. I was grateful to have a kayaking guide with me as experienced and levelheaded as Stacey.

"Dividing two point two miles by a paddling speed of four knots means we should reach the west side of Baker in thirty-three minutes," she said. "On my own, I could go faster. Just so you know, the pace I plan to set is going to challenge your abilities. But I think we're less likely to get off track if we go hard."

"You don't need to worry about me."

"Do you know how many times female kayak guides hear that from their male clients?"

"I'm not your client, Stace."

She leaned across the map and kissed me. "No, you're not. You're the most relentless person I've ever met. No one else I know could have survived some of the things you have in the woods."

"But we're not in the woods."

She smiled as she picked a coffee ground off my bottom lip. "To be safe, I'm also going to aim off twenty degrees to the northwest. I'd rather miss Baker and run into Ayers, than find ourselves past the Brigands with nothing but two thousand miles of open ocean between us and Spain."

"I heartily endorse that plan." I rose to my feet. "It'll take me five minutes to put out the fire, and then I'll be ready to go."

"No," she said, "we're going to sit tight."

"What about Kendra? And the others?"

"It'll be bad enough in the fog, trying to maintain our direction. We don't need the darkness slowing us down, too. Trust me on this, Mike."

"I do."

I kept myself busy washing and storing the camp cooking gear. Then I cut off a spruce bough from a dying tree and used it to brush the tent site clean. The needles that had fallen during the storm clung stubbornly to everything, including my sandy pant legs.

Even before the sun rose, the fog became suffused with a faint light. Somewhere offshore, herring gulls began to quarrel. I felt anticipation building as if I'd been injected with adrenaline.

Finally, Stacey judged it safe enough to shove off.

She ran her kayak out from the beach and hopped into the cockpit with such practiced ease. Momentum carried her into the cottony fog. Her forward strokes were so clean and rhythmic she scarcely made a sound, sliding across the surface.

My own launch was less graceful. I slid into my cockpit before I was clear of the shallows. The boat scraped along the submerged gravel before I was free.

She was waiting offshore, with her spray skirt already buttoned up around her torso.

"You're going to want to put yours on, or your boat will fill up from the spray and surf. I can hear the waves thundering out there. We're in for a wild ride. Are you all right following me?"

"Did you know ego is the number one cause of death among males? I read it in the *Journal of the American Medical Association.*"

She threw back her head and laughed. "Don't fall too far behind."

The ball compass on my foredeck showed us headed northeast, as Stacey had planned. I put my upper body into my strokes to keep sight of her boat's yellow stern. She left such a slight wake I couldn't just follow her slipstream.

At first, the sea was the color of mercury, but as we paddled farther from the island, the wind picked up and the water turned slate gray. A light froth began to bubble around my stern, and I started getting sprayed in the face as I cut through the chop. Soon we were surrounded by whitecaps.

"The seas are running heavier than I'd expected," Stacey called. "I'm going to adjust course a bit to head north."

The one positive thing I could say about the wind was that it tore occasional holes in the sheets of fog.

A fluorescent-orange lobster buoy appeared out of nowhere to my right. It was so bright I couldn't imagine how I'd gotten so close without seeing it. Lobstermen are required to display their floats so that their rivals could tell they were hauling their own traps. I remembered an orange buoy hanging from the cabin of the *Persuader*. This was one of Bear Goodale's traps.

My shoulder muscles began to burn. I needed to practice more; I needed to suck up my pride and let my girlfriend give me a few lessons.

When I lifted my head, I realized I'd lost sight of Stacey's kayak. Nor could I detect even a faint wake.

"Talk to me."

If she answered, I didn't hear her voice. The waves were knocking so hard against my hull.

As a veteran warden, I was an expert on the mental errors people make when they begin to fear they're lost. Self-doubt becomes the catalyst to a series of bad decisions. What ends up killing people is that they don't stick to the plan.

Heading north, I began to dig in hard with my paddle. I breathed in through my nose and out through my mouth. Blood thumped in my temples.

Suddenly, a whistle pierced the mist.

The noise came from behind and to the right. I raised the paddle to a horizontal position and saw Stacey emerge from the fogbank with her signal whistle clenched between her teeth. The current carried me toward her kayak. She was holding in place with a combination of forward strokes and back strokes. In my sprint, I had passed her without even realizing it.

My voice came out ragged. "I thought I'd lost you."

She let the whistle drop from her mouth. It was attached by paracord to her life vest.

"Never," she said. "I won't let it happen."

"Any idea where we are?"

"More than halfway there. We're being swept along faster than I'd estimated, even after I adjusted our heading. But we're fine."

"I wish this damned fog would lift."

"Mike, I'm going to have you go ahead of me the rest of the way. It'll be slower with you leading, but we won't get separated again. Just keep an eye on the compass. Keep yourself pointed north. I'll be right behind you."

"Wait a minute," I said.

"What?"

I inhaled deeply. "Smell!"

She filled her lungs, then shook her head. "Sorry, but I don't know what you're smelling."

"Petrels! Leach's storm petrels from the island! You told me that Maeve used to joke about following the smell of the birds if she ever got lost in the fog."

"Your senses really are superhuman, Mike. Are you sure you're not part wolverine?"

"Part wolf, maybe. I've inhaled so much of Shadow's hair it's mutated my DNA."

"As much as I'd like to tell you to follow your nose, I'm going to put my faith in the compass. Set a new bearing for twenty degrees."

"Twenty degrees it is."

Occasional gulls and terns began drifting past in the water. Then we found ourselves amid a vast raft of eiders. The ducks, normally so skittish from being hunted, didn't even flush as we filed through their congregation. The oily funk of the petrels filled my sinuses until Stacey said she could smell it, too.

The first boulders appeared out of the fog, wet from the rain. Above the nearest ledges was a jumble of granite stones streaked with running guano. And above that erratic wall towered a white billboard that warned in bloodred letters of dangerous bombs waiting to explode.

# 13

A tern was perched on the flat roof of Garrett Meadows's blind, watching us with eyes as soulless as black beads.

"Would the staff be in their blinds in this fog?" I asked.

She didn't answer but quickened her strokes, making for the north end of the island and the research station.

A quick-walking plover caught my eye, traversing the boulders, plucking scuds from the bladder wrack. It wasn't even the middle of July, but the bandit-masked shorebird had already raised its young in the Arctic and was migrating to its winter range in the Caribbean.

My reverie didn't last twenty seconds. Stacey let out a single blast on her whistle. The piercing sound caused the nearest birds—puffins and razorbills, mostly, but also the plover—to take flight.

"That'll wake them." I tried to keep my tone light.

But she wouldn't be reassured. "Now I'm worried, Mike."

"Give them a minute to answer."

There were no noises except for the caterwauling of the birds and splashing of the waves against the rocks.

Stacey blew three blasts on the whistle now: *emergency.*

She began paddling before the last echo died. This time, I had no trouble keeping pace. My adrenal glands were working overtime.

We rounded a buttress of granite boulders and came upon the mooring ball bobbing in the chop.

The skiff was gone.

I glanced at Plymouth Rock and saw that the rope was still knotted around the rusted cleat. The limp line disappeared into the gray-blue water.

"Maeve never returned last night," Stacey said. The certainty in her voice was eerie.

"You said she didn't like making the trip in the rain."

"And that gunshot we heard—it wasn't one of them firing at a weasel."

"We can't know until we go ashore."

"I'm afraid to, Mike."

"Do you want me to?"

"That's not what I mean. I'm going with you. I just don't know if I can bear to see what's up there."

"Don't get ahead of yourself, Stace. There are lots of innocent explanations for this."

"I can't think of a single one."

We'd gotten lucky with the tide. I took the initiative to land first.

With several sprinting strokes, I managed to power the bow of my kayak into the wedge between Plymouth Rock and its neighboring boulder. Keeping my center of gravity low, I pushed myself up from the cockpit and crawled forward over the deck. I felt my handgun on the belt beneath my dry suit. The weight pulled against the synthetic fabric. Then I was ashore.

As I straightened up, I gave a glance to the path leading up the grassy lip above. Between Stacey's whistle and the racket I'd made exiting the kayak, I half-expected to see someone standing there in the mist. But I saw no one and heard nothing but birds.

"Hurry, Mike."

I took hold of the grab handle of my kayak and dragged the boat up until it caught in the grass.

Behind me, I heard the smack of a paddle hitting a rock and then the grinding sound of Stacey driving her own boat into the narrow opening between the boulders. By the time I turned around, she was already scrambling on hands and knees across her deck. She sprang clear of her boat and landed on the shore.

She was in too much of a rush to worry about it drifting off. She didn't even remove her life vest.

As she shot up the trail, calling the names of Kendra, Hillary, and Garrett, I took a moment to yank her kayak above the high-water line. We didn't need to risk losing a boat.

Stacey had already disappeared into the fog. I could no longer hear her calls above the shrieking birds. In this heart-thumping moment, they really did sound like winged terrors sent by vengeful gods.

I was halfway up the slope when a question occurred to me.

I turned and made my way down the oblong boulder until I came to the rusted cleat. I reached my hand into the water and pulled up the slimy rope. I retrieved about twenty feet of line before I found the newly frayed end. It had been cut.

*Someone was in a hurry to leave. Or to keep someone from leaving.*

I dropped my personal flotation device beside my Seguin, partially unzipped my dry suit, and removed my firearm from its holster. I chambered a round and began making my way through the weeds parallel to the trail.

Stacey, unfortunately, had sprinted up the muddy path. The treads of her Chuck Taylors obscured whatever footprints hadn't melted in the rain. I hoped her haste wouldn't prove to be something we regretted.

*I'm already treating this as a crime scene,* I realized.

*Fuck.*

I made for the cookhouse and the circle of tent platforms around it. I found Stacey emerging from Kendra's tent, her eyes wide, her face ashen.

"She's not here. None of them are."

"Stace, I need you to slow down. We can't go trampling over the ground. We can't contaminate the scene."

Her gaze got stuck on the Beretta in my hand. "Where are they, Mike?"

"I don't know. But we'll find them."

Bending over the ground, I began to inspect the grass. It was impossible for me to tell if the worn area around Kendra's tent showed anything beyond the constant tread of feet back and forth between the platform and the little paths leading to the outhouse, the cookhouse, and the larger trails crisscrossing the island.

"Come toward me. Follow your own footprints. That's good."

When she reached me, she pressed herself against my chest and looked up into my eyes. "Where could they have gone?"

"The skiff line was cut. The end was frayed."

"That boat isn't meant to be rowed back to the mainland with three people aboard, especially in a storm. They would've had to be desperate to attempt that crossing. What happened here last night?"

"Do you notice anything different from when we left?"

Stacey grabbed my shoulder. "There!"

She was pointing at a yellow piece of plastic stuck in a bayberry bush ten yards from our position. It was a spent shotgun shell. The casing might or might not relate to the gunshot we'd heard, but I had a feeling these committed environmentalists didn't leave litter around, least of all highly visible shotshells.

I blazed a path across a patch of creeping juniper that clutched the granite slope with its tough roots. The low-growing evergreen showed no sign of having been stepped upon. I crouched near the spent casing, trying to get a sense of where the shooter had been standing when the hull was ejected from the receiver.

"We need to use their radio to call in to shore," Stacey said.

After her initial bout of nerves, she was thinking clearly. She was ahead of me in remembering the radio. It felt like having another warden at my side.

"I'll go in first. But you need to be right behind me."

"Why?"

"Because you're more likely to spot anything out of place." I handed her my little Fenix flashlight. "We have to be careful. I don't know who or what we might find inside. When we go through the door, I'll go left, and you go right. Understood?"

I didn't expect to find an armed stranger inside the shack. But I was past the point of pretending there were innocent explanations for the ominous situation.

"Hello?" I tried to sound friendly. "It's Mike and Stacey. Is anyone there?"

No answer.

Through the screen, I could smell the ripening bananas hanging in the mesh bag and the acrid smell of a recent fire in the cookstove.

"Kendra? Hillary? Garrett?"

I stood to the side of the door as I pulled it open. I stepped inside and to the left, keeping my back to the wall. It was very dark and very quiet.

Stacey moved right as she entered, just as I'd told her. She swept the room with the flashlight beam.

Dishes were drying beside the sink. The same ceramic vase of fading flowers stood at the center of the dining table. The room looked almost exactly as it had the day before.

There were only three exceptions. The door to the upright gun locker hung open. A short-tailed weasel with a bloody face was glaring at us from under the couch. And someone had taken a club to the expensive marine radio, smashing it to pieces.

# 14

The weasel shot across the room and disappeared under the propane stove. There had to be a hole to the outdoors down there, amid the cobwebs and dust bunnies.

"Who would have smashed the radio?" Stacey said.

"Someone who didn't want it to be used. Right now, we need to find a way to contact the Marine Patrol."

"But how?"

I held the door so she wouldn't touch the handle as we left the building.

"We're going to the high spot on the ridge trail. That's where Kendra said they got the best reception, although I can't imagine we'll find a signal in this weather."

She peered into the fog. "Shouldn't I keep looking for them while you call for help?"

"Not while there's a shotgun unaccounted for. Whatever went down here, I need to contact the cops."

"It can't have been one of the crew," she said. "Whoever destroyed the VHF, I mean. That's not who these people are. They're researchers."

"We don't know them, Stace."

"I know Kendra."

Once, maybe. But that was many years ago. And what had happened to her friend in the interim, working for a demanding egomaniac like Maeve McLeary, living among strangers on a remote island where the constant cries of birds were like the lacerating voices inside the mind of a paranoid schizophrenic?

"Maybe we'll luck out and get a cell signal," I said.

As I spoke, my gaze drifted toward Hillary's platform on the hillside above. The zipper of the tent was down, causing the front to gape. The tarp had also come loose from one of its tie-downs and was rippling in the faint breeze. I spotted something else, as well: a small orange object lying in the wet grass below the platform.

"Hold up," I whispered. "I want to look at Hillary's tent first. You need to walk exactly where I walk. OK?"

The orange object revealed itself to be a foam earplug. I wore similar ones to protect my hearing when I went target shooting. Hillary had told me she used them to muffle the raucous birds and sleep through the night.

Two steps closer and I saw the drag marks. A limp body had been pulled through the weeds and puddles, leaving parallel tracks from the unconscious person's feet scraping the vegetation and mud.

Stacey saw them, too. "Oh, God."

"She was dragged from her tent. There's blood on the ground in front of the platform. And boot prints. See?"

The tracks were large for a man and very large for a woman. They had a raised heel and a minimal tread not fit for hiking. If I had to guess, I would have said the prints had been left by boots commonly worn by commercial fishermen.

"I should look inside," I said.

Again, I blazed my own path through the trailing juniper to avoid stepping on evidence.

A fist-size stone lay beside the steps. It appeared to have been recently dropped based on how it rested in the grass.

I angled the flashlight beam inside the yawning tent. The light found a red pool. The blood was darkening and becoming tacky as it congealed.

Hillary, or whoever had been in her tent, was almost certainly dead.

"She's not here," I said.

"Do you think there's a chance she's still alive?" Stacey asked, choking on her words.

I didn't answer.

We walked parallel to the path the intruder (as I'd begun to think of him) had used to drag Hillary's body. The footprints took us in an unexpected direction. Not toward Plymouth Rock and not toward the trail leading to the south end where Garrett had seen the man from the *Spindrift* rowing away from the island. Instead, the intruder had made for the outhouse at the edge of camp.

Stacey clutched my shoulder. "Her sweatpants!"

They had been pulled off and tossed in the bayberries outside the latrine.

I saw that the legs of the pants were muddy, especially along the backs and bottoms. In my mind, I saw an anonymous man shuffling backward with his arms hooked under the armpits of the limp intern.

The intruder had made no effort to hide his boot prints. The impressions were stamped into the older tracks left by the researchers coming and going. One clear set led away from the building, meaning the intruder had left his burden behind. A forensic technician would get an excellent set of casts.

The stench of human waste was strong, despite the installation of a composting toilet.

I maneuvered into position on the left side of the structure so I could throw the door open with my left hand and then angle my body to face the interior. Action movies have popularized the center-axis relock—a shooting stance meant for close-quarters combat—but it had its uses at times like this.

This time, I didn't announce myself. I inhaled deeply, tasting all the foulness in the air, then let out half my breath.

In one motion, I pulled the door open and stepped forward, blading my body, holding my firearm close to my chest with the barrel at a slight diagonal.

Whatever I had expected, the sight was even more horrifying.

Hillary was there.

Her murderer had propped her corpse on the toilet with her head tilted carefully upright against the wall. She was wearing a faded Cornell T-shirt and no underwear. The fatal wound on her temple was hidden beneath a crimson mass of blood-thickened hair. Death had robbed her beautiful face of her tan; she had become unrecognizably pale. An orange earplug still protruded from her left ear.

Her eyes were wide open. The son of a bitch must have pried the lids fully apart with his fingers. Her pupils were different sizes. At an autopsy I once attended, the corpse had worn the same aspect. The state's scandal-plagued medical examiner, Dr. Walter Kitteridge, had described the dead eyes as having "attained a cadaveric position."

I heard Stacey choke on her breath. She had pressed herself against my shoulder for a closer look.

The murderer had done one more thing to complete the degradation and desecration of Hillary Fitzgerald. He'd hung a pair of binoculars on a strap around her neck. She sure as hell hadn't gone to sleep wearing them.

*Why would he do that?*

It was Stacey who interpreted the grotesque tableau for me.

"He posed her that way, Mike. He posed her in order to take a fucking picture."

## 15

We found Kendra's body behind the cookhouse. She was lying on her back on a bed of creeping juniper. Her top was off, but her sports bra remained in place. She was still wearing the cotton shorts in which she slept, but her legs were parted, and her bare feet were muddy and cut where she must have run across the ledges and through the spiny ground cover.

A red mark that, had she survived, would have become a gruesome bruise disfigured her left forearm. It was possible the radius had been broken beneath the whitening skin, Stacey said. Her knuckles were scuffed, too.

These were defensive wounds.

Kendra's sightless eyes stared up at the gray void. Her killer had posed her with the shotgun she must have used to defend herself. Her dead hands held it across her body in a port arms position that made me wonder if her murderer was ex-military.

Like Hillary, she seemed to have been killed by a blow to the head. Multiple blows, I deduced. One to the forehead to knock her down, another to the left temple to deliver the coup de grâce. The murder instrument appeared to be the butt of her shotgun, based on the blood and hair on the stock. Her attacker had wrestled it loose from her hands and then slammed it repeatedly into her skull.

She had been killed after Hillary, I conjectured. The Cornell student had been ambushed while sleeping in her tent. I hoped she had died without ever awakening.

It was likely Kendra had heard something and managed to outrace the intruder to the cookhouse, where she'd armed herself from the gun locker. I wanted to believe that the shot we'd heard had been Kendra firing the Remington in self-defense. I wanted to believe she'd wounded her assailant. Without handling her corpse or otherwise disturbing the scene, I had nothing to go on but suppositions.

Using my phone, I snapped photos of the body from several angles, as I had with Hillary. My cell was down to a 10 percent charge. I'd forgotten to plug it into the portable power bank I brought everywhere I went in the outdoors.

Stacey had taken a seat in the muddy path below me. She leaned forward with her bare arms between her legs and her head bowed. She was not sobbing, but I could see the movement of her rib cage as she took hyperventilating breaths. In the end she had been unable to maintain her impartial EMT composure. I couldn't blame her.

"Kendra died fighting, Stace."

When she raised her head, I saw tears streaking down her cheekbones, making rivulets in dirt she'd managed to get on her face.

"What difference does it make? She's still dead."

"There's a chance she managed to wound the guy before he got the gun away from her. For all we know, he's bleeding out somewhere nearby."

"No, he isn't."

I couldn't determine if this statement was an expression of grief or something else: an occult pronouncement.

"The shotgun is accounted for at least. I wish I could lock it up again instead of leaving it there, but the state police evidence technicians won't want it disturbed."

She raised her bloodshot gaze. "Where's Kendra's shillelagh?"

"Do you mean that walking stick?"

"It's a blackthorn Maeve brought back from Ireland when she was working in the Skellocks. She gave it to Kendra as a gift. She's been using it as a cane after twisting her ankle, she told me."

"It's probably still in her tent." I hesitated, unsure of how to phrase the question that had arisen as soon as we came upon the second corpse. "You don't think Meadows could have—?"

"Absolutely not."

"Me, neither."

We listened to the birds for a while.

"Where is he, then?" I said at last.

"Posed somewhere in the fog with a noose around his neck, I'm sure. A faux lynching would fit this asshole's style."

"It's possible Garrett managed to escape on the skiff."

"He didn't get far in that case."

"Why do you say that?"

She pointed down the slope to where the boulders made their encircling wall around the island. The vague shapes of perched birds, including one cruciform cormorant, drying its wings, showed in the mist. The fog was no longer an opaque barrier but more like a translucent film. Through it, I saw birds in the water. And something else as well.

A floating oar.

"I think we'd better find that spot where they could send and receive messages."

"Let's hope we can get a signal to call the authorities," she said in a flat voice. "Because I can't sit around waiting for the fog to clear. I don't have your patience."

It was a surprise to be praised for a virtue no one else thought I possessed.

At what seemed to be the highest point on the island, we both tried our phones. We performed a series of lame pantomimes—waving the cells overhead—hoping it would gain us a signal. Nothing worked. An indicator on my screen showed my charge had dropped into the single digits.

"I've come up with a plan," said Stacey finally.

"You have?"

"I'm paddling my kayak over to Ayers Island. Maybe I'll get a signal from its tower before I make it across. Or I might meet a lobsterboat with a VHF. In any case, I should be able to call from the village."

I didn't like the idea of us splitting up. But I recognized the reasoning behind her plan. I could have offered a counterargument—what if the murderer was lying in wait offshore?

"I have a flare gun in my hold," she said. "I bought it for a trip I was supposed to lead for some at-risk girls. It's still in its packaging. I'd forgotten it was there."

"A flare gun isn't much of a weapon."

"Not against a firearm, maybe."

"Which the killer might have."

"If he was armed, why did he bludgeon Hillary? Why didn't he shoot Kendra before she got a shot off herself? Why didn't we hear more gunfire?"

"Those are all good questions. But we can't assume anything. For all we know, we may be dealing with more than one intruder."

"You're the footprint expert. How many sets have you seen?"

"Just one."

"Me, too."

I had momentarily forgotten what a good tracker she was. But of course she'd been paying as close attention as I had been to the trails. "What's your plan for me?"

She offered the saddest of smiles. "You don't need my advice, Warden Investigator Bowditch."

"I would still appreciate your thoughts."

She pulled her fog-soaked hair away from her face. Her cheeks had flushed in the cold and wet.

"Search the island. It's possible Garrett is hiding somewhere. There's a good chance you're going to hear a fishing boat soon. They're usually out early. Maybe you can find one of the Motorolas the staff was using. They have no range, but you should be able to raise a passing boat. You can always signal with your pistol."

"All right," I said. "You've convinced me."

"I hope so! It's a good plan."

We made our way in silent procession to the landing. At Plymouth Rock, Stacey zipped up her personal flotation device.

"Do you want to take any of my gear?" I asked.

"I have what I need. And it's a short paddle to Ayers as the puffin flies."

"I've been thinking about how the killer posed Hillary and Kendra for pictures."

"And how Ayers Island just happens to belong to a photographer known for his macabre images? It was where my mind went, too. But I don't see Clay Markham cruising over here in a thunderstorm to commit senseless murders, do you? The guy must be close to eighty, among other things. It's more likely whoever killed them wanted to point a finger in his direction."

I found it hard to smile after the horrors I had seen. "That's good detective work. Maybe you should stop looking for jobs as a wildlife biologist and consider a job in law enforcement."

"Thank you, Mike."

"For understanding?"

"For trusting that I am up to this. For not trying to persuade me to stay behind while you went for help."

"You're the superior kayaker, Stace."

"Lots of guys wouldn't admit that."

"Lots of guys are idiots. Would you be offended, though, if I ask you to take extra care? We have no idea what might be waiting out there."

"No offense taken, babe."

When she looked up to be kissed, I saw tears sliding down her face again. But she brushed them away and hardened her expression.

The tide had risen slightly while we'd been on the island. After she'd climbed back into the cockpit, I pushed the bow of her kayak loose from where it was wedged between the rocks.

"I'll be right back," she said.

"See you soon."

Clear of the island, she swung the boat around and turned to the northeast, following her compass. I stood at the end of the boulder, watching until her yellow Seguin vanished in the mist.

Baker Island was home to thousands of shrieking, wailing, laughing birds.

I felt very much alone.

# 16

The best use of my time, I decided, was to search for Garrett Meadows.

I couldn't assume he had tried to flee the island in the skiff. The intruder might have been the one to cut the line. And there was no saying how that oar had fallen into the water.

I remembered what Garrett had said about the silent man in the swordfishing cap: "Everyone else who comes out to Baker focuses mostly on the birds, but our friend ignores the birds like they're not even here. The man is our own personal paparazzo."

Photographing the researchers without their consent was one thing.

Sneaking into their camp to bludgeon them to death was another level of messed up.

The best place to look for signs of Garrett Meadows was in his tent, of course. So that was where I began.

While the risen sun yet remained hidden, the mist had become permeated with ambient light. In the yellow-gray glow, I could now see blades of grass without the help of artificial illumination. I followed my own footprints back to the base camp and then down to Garrett's tent, which was the closest to the water.

I nearly stepped on a pair of glasses in the weeds.

Had he dropped them in flight? Did he have another pair? How well could he see without their assistance?

On the edge of the platform were two slip-on mud shoes, the

kind worn by backyard gardeners, arranged side by side. I squatted and inspected the wet ground and found the prints of two bare feet. A set of tracks led through the mud toward the shore path before disappearing into the juniper. The spiky plant would have cut up his feet, and sure enough, I soon found blood, ten yards in.

There was no sign of the intruder anywhere around Garrett's tent.

*Interesting that the murderer didn't make the tent of the only man on the island his first stop.*

I hadn't yet met a violent criminal with a degree in gender studies. Males were the protectors. Females were the protected.

*Unless our guy knew Kendra was the one most likely to fight back or be armed. Which means he had personal knowledge of the staff.*

I jumped onto the platform, landing to one side of the yawning tent. Peering in with my flashlight, I saw that a sleeping bag was bunched as if he'd kicked it off his legs. Otherwise, everything was clean and orderly. The tent looked and smelled new, as if he'd bought it on his drive up the coast. The women's tents had been unswept, strung with drying socks, and littered with used mugs and half-read books.

*What am I not seeing?*

*A flashlight.*

Surely, Garrett had kept a light source nearby in the event he had to go to the outhouse in the dark. I didn't have to return to the other tents to remember that Kendra had a camping lantern within reach of her sleeping pad and Hillary had a headlamp.

I didn't want to get ahead of myself, but indications pointed to Garrett having heard something—a scuffle, a shot—at which point he fled in a panic. He must have known he'd dropped his glasses but had been in such a hurry he didn't dare hunt for them in the dark. My bet was that he'd made directly for the landing.

I relocated his bloody tracks in the mud on the far side of the juniper patch but lost them again where he'd crossed an exposed ledge. The pounding rain had washed the stone clean. But I suspected he'd continued toward the landing after he'd hit the shore.

We'd seen no sign of him when we'd arrived at Plymouth Rock, but I took another look between the half-submerged boulders that flanked the launch and was relieved not to stumble on yet another corpse.

Someone had either taken the skiff or cut the line so that it had drifted off. My money was still on Garrett. There was zero evidence to confirm my hunch. But losing an oar in a desperate attempt at escape was consistent with what I'd heard about his lack of boating experience.

I checked my watch and realized I'd been ashore less than an hour. The slowness with which time seemed to move here reinforced the purgatorial impression I had formed of this forsaken place.

On a whim, I tried my cell phone, but there was still no signal.

Every now and again, a seabird would materialize and dematerialize in the fog like a winged apparition. And I thought of Stacey out there alone. Her odds of getting her phone to work were probably no better than mine.

I decided to make another attempt to raise help.

Taking a shortcut, I waded through a swath of tall grass that smelled pungently of storm petrels. Baker was home to two species, Stacey had said, neither of which were in evidence. The nocturnal ones were all sleeping in their burrows while the diurnal ones must have been hunting at sea.

Next, I entered into the domain of the terns. The sharp-winged birds rose up shrieking from their hidden nests. For the life of me, I couldn't understand how anyone could get accustomed to the cacophony of Baker Island.

Turning inland, I followed a thin path, more like a crease in the bushes, up to the ridge. I moved slowly, my imagination filled with images of wartime munitions lurking everywhere about me, hidden beneath a scrim of pebbles. I had trespassed into the nesting grounds of the laughing gulls. They began their aerial assaults. I covered my head with my hands and received a cut along a knuckle from one of their beaks.

The insane cries of the gulls were so earsplitting I didn't hear the boat engine at first.

I turned in a full circle, until I could locate the direction of the sound.

The invisible boat was approaching at an idle from the north—it was headed to the mooring.

Careless of unexploded bombs, I took off at a sprint toward camp. I wanted to believe Stacey had already found a lobsterboat and directed it to the island. But I couldn't assume the visitor was friendly.

To be safe, as I topped the hummock above the landing, I threw myself down behind the boat shed where the researchers stored ropes, life vests, folded and unfolded tarps. I wished I'd brought along my binoculars.

Circles of illumination floated like will-o'-the-wisps in the fog. The vessel slowly took shape, then gained definition. The white bow belonged to a former lobsterboat that had been remodeled for a second life as an inshore runabout. It was towing an inflatable dinghy on a polyester line.

Just as the name *Selkie* came into view on the prow, a female voice exclaimed, "What the fuck?"

It was Maeve McLeary.

It occurred to me that I shouldn't make my presence known immediately. Better to observe the ornithologist's reaction to the missing skiff if she didn't know she was being watched.

"Where's the goddamned rowboat?" She brought the *Selkie* in a circle around the volleyball. "What the hell is going on?"

I saw her now: a skinny woman dressed in yellow oilskins. She wore a khaki cap with the puffin logo that was the Maine Seabird Initiative's insignia. A silver braid hung down the back of her rain jacket. I couldn't make out her wrinkled features, but my imagination could supply them from the shrine of photographs inside the cookhouse.

"How the hell did they lose the rowboat?" She had a very loud, although not unpleasant voice.

The water churned up behind the boat was aquamarine with white bubbles. Billowing exhaust fumes added a purplish tint to the fog. McLeary was obviously a skilled boat handler, moving easily around the deck to secure the *Selkie* to the mooring. She pulled in the dinghy, then began rowing ashore with economical oar strokes.

Only now did she catch sight of my Seguin hauled up above the tide line. I was puzzled she hadn't seen it sooner.

"Whose kayak is this?"

I almost waited too long. I tucked my Beretta inside my dry suit where she wouldn't see it and advanced down the trail.

"Mine."

She paused in mid-row and let the plastic oars hang dripping as if she hadn't entirely heard me. She squinted up the hill. The sight of me, a stranger, provoked instant rage.

"Whoever you are, you're trespassing on my island. Are you responsible for my missing skiff? Where the hell is my crew?"

Before I could answer, she'd begun rowing back to the *Selkie*.

"Dr. McLeary! My name is Mike Bowditch. I'm an investigator with the Maine Warden Service."

It was my impression, based on the quickness with which she tied up the inflatable and scrambled aboard the *Selkie,* that she hadn't heard a word I had said.

"Dr. McLeary!"

As she turned the engine key, there was a momentary whine from some petulant warning indicator. With her other hand she grabbed the mic attached to her VHF radio.

"Mayday, Mayday, Mayday!" she shouted into the hand unit. "This is *Selkie, Selkie, Selkie*. This is *Selkie*. Position is Baker Island, north end. One adult on board. Reporting an unauthorized intruder in restricted area. Male, early thirties, six feet plus in height, approximately one hundred and ninety pounds, dressed in olive-and-orange dry suit. Island research staff won't answer hails. Repeat: no response from research staff. Intruder used red Lincoln Seguin to access restricted area. Requesting response boat. *Selkie* is thirty-two-foot cruiser, white hull, white deck. Over."

I produced my badge and held it out. "I'm a game warden, Dr. McLeary. My name is Mike Bowditch."

A voice came through the overloud speaker: "*Selkie, Selkie,* this is Coast Guard Station Boothbay Harbor. Message received. RP-M on the way."

I had reached the terminus of Plymouth Rock. Still clutching my badge, I raised my hands above my head as if surrendering to over-whelming force. But Maeve McLeary glared at me from the safe distance of her picnic boat.

She must have had clout with the Coast Guard if she could per-suade an E-3 to send an armed boat to her rescue without explana-tion. Hopefully, when the Coasties arrived with their M4 carbines and M60 machine gun, they would be willing to listen to me before they opened fire.

# 17

After the Coast Guard had assured and reassured Maeve Mc-Leary that a response team was en route, she emerged from the cabin with an orange flare gun pointed in my direction.

It was hard to predict what might happen if she pulled the trigger. Odds were that she would miss hitting me altogether. The short barrel hadn't been designed for accuracy since flares are meant to be fired high into the air. If it did hit, the incendiary might simply bounce off my body, causing a bruise at best, internal bleeding at worst. There remained the real possibility, however, that the projectile, loaded as it was with strontium nitrate, potassium perchlorate, and hot-burning magnesium, might set me afire. Since I had no desire to become a human torch, I kept my hands raised above my head.

"Who are you?" she shouted again.

I used my calmest voice. "My name is Mike Bowditch. I'm a warden investigator with the Department of Inland Fisheries & Wildlife. This is my badge in my hand."

She cupped her left ear. "Who?"

Maeve McLeary, I realized, was hard of hearing. No wonder she hadn't responded to anything I'd said before.

"A game warden! Here's my badge!"

She'd understood me this time, but my answer didn't help her make sense of the situation.

"Where's my crew?"

"I'll explain. But can you lower the flare gun first, please?"

This time, she did as I asked. The haze was thin enough that I could see her face clearly. She looked significantly older than she did in the photos, but that wasn't surprising. People keep their best pictures and discard the unflattering ones.

"Where's my crew?"

I debated what to do.

No law enforcement officer wants to give a death notification. It is the worst part of the job. But the unenviable task is made even worse when uncertainty hangs over the scene. Unlikely as it was, I had to treat McLeary as a potential suspect for the time being.

"I am afraid I have very bad news."

"Damn it! Hang on."

She disappeared into the cabin again and reappeared fiddling with what must have been a pair of hearing aids. She'd thrust the flare gun into the front of her rain pants in case she needed to make a quick draw.

"All right. Go ahead." Her words came out in a normal register.

"It would be best if I could come aboard your boat for this."

"Fat chance! How do I know you are who you say you are? You're not going anywhere until the Coasties show. You're going to stand right there where I can keep an eye on you and tell me where my people are."

"I promise I will," I said, working to keep my voice level. "But I need you to do something first. Kendra Ballard said you took the station's satellite phone when you went ashore."

"You spoke with Kendra? Where the hell is she? Why can't I raise her on the radio?"

If she could shrug off my questions, I could do the same with hers.

"I need you to use your sat phone to contact the Maine Department of Public Safety. A dispatcher will verify my identity. This will all be easier if you and I can get past this standoff."

What struck me about Maeve McLeary, above anything else, was the hardness of her expression. There was an intensity to her affect bordering on I didn't know what. Maybe it was madness.

"Someone's dead here," she said. "You wouldn't be talking in circles otherwise. Who is it? Kendra?"

"Doctor—"

"For fuck's sake, I'll get the damned phone."

I let my hands drop as she disappeared under the rain canopy. The Maine State Police would send a pair of homicide detectives out with the death scene examiner and an evidence response team. The primary investigator would loop in the attorney general's office, as well as the new Lincoln County sheriff, whom I had yet to meet.

Sheriff Pat Santum was a retired navy lieutenant commander who had recently won election to the post by running to the right of Attila the Hun. No one had predicted his scare campaign would work in one of Maine's most left-leaning counties. But Santum had eked out a win in a three-candidate race and was rebuilding the force in his own hard-nosed, hardheaded image.

McLeary was taking her sweet time.

I wondered how to get word to Stacey. She should have made the crossing to Ayers Island by now and had, hopefully, managed to get word to the mainland herself. Memories of the chuckleheads aboard the *Persuader* made me wish the nearest phones had been somewhere other than that village.

Questions were whirling around my skull not unlike the birds circling overhead.

*Should I tell the Coast Guard to look for Stacey if she hasn't already made contact?*

*What about putting out a marine APB for the missing skiff? Garrett Meadows might be aboard.*

*How would we search for forensic evidence of a homicide in a wildlife refuge that had been created to be disturbed as little as possible?*

McLeary was suddenly back.

"You checked out."

"That's a relief."

"No one can explain what you're doing on my rock, though. You weren't ordered here and didn't request permission."

"I can explain, but first I need to tell you about your staff." I steeled myself and made the statement in plain language, as police officers are trained to do. "I have very bad news for you. Kendra Ballard and Hillary Fitzgerald are both dead. There are signs they were attacked by an intruder. Garrett Meadows is missing. He might have taken your skiff, but I saw one of the oars floating off the west side of the island. The state police investigators need to do their work before I can say anything more. I'm deeply sorry for your loss."

She didn't react to this news with confusion or shock. She didn't fall in a heap on the deck. She seemed stricken but unsurprised, the way someone does who hears that a chronically ill friend has passed away. Certain deaths are foretold.

"I'm coming ashore," she said at last.

"That's not a good idea."

She continued pulling the dinghy close enough to the boat to board. "Excuse me? This is my fucking island."

"Actually, it's the state's fucking island."

"I'm coming ashore, Warden."

"No, ma'am. You're not. Baker Island is a crime scene, and I can't allow anyone—even you—to potentially contaminate it."

"Contaminate? Contaminate?"

She began readying her gray inflatable to cast off. She was going to force me to restrain her. I had no good idea how to do that.

I was saved by the sound of an engine.

There was no way a Coast Guard response boat could have traveled from Boothbay Harbor to Baker Island this fast, especially in a fog that concealed anchored and moving boats, as well as multiple other obstacles to navigation.

The boat powered down its dual outboards, and then a spotlight brighter than the one that blinded Saul of Tarsus cut a hole in the fog. The beam swung from the *Selkie* to McLeary in her dinghy to me standing on Plymouth Rock. I squeezed my eyelids shut, but too late.

An amplified voice boomed: "*Selkie, Selkie.* Maeve, are you all right?"

"No! This son of a bitch won't let me land."

"You on the shore, I need you to remain where you are until we can sort out this situation."

I could barely see through my dazzled pupils. "Spinney?"

"Mike? Is that you?"

It was my acquaintance from the Marine Patrol, the same man Hillary had mentioned bringing her doughnuts. I couldn't fathom how Specialist Rick Spinney had managed to beat the Coast Guard to Baker Island.

## 18

I'd first met Rick Spinney when I was a rookie warden patrolling the Midcoast. We'd run into each other at boat ramps and search-and-rescue missions. We had take-out lunches occasionally. Even though we worked for different departments with different missions, the Marine Patrol officer had taken me on as a part-time quasi-apprentice. I suspect he appreciated having a young person around, eager to learn and willing to listen to his oft-told tales of derring-do.

Back then, Spinney was a rising star with the Marine Patrol, a genuine hero in a service that got little press, although his department didn't like to put him in front of cameras. Physically, he was a lumpish man, big without being either fat or muscular, who moved with the grace of a golem. He had a square head with thinning ginger hair he would have been better off shaving. But his eyes were small and shrewd.

One night I'd accompanied him to a coastal creek in pursuit of elver poachers. Elvers are the larval stage of the American eel and are prized as a delicacy in Japan, selling for in excess of $2,000 a pound. Maine glass eels are worth more than their weight in gold.

The poachers were crafty and careful. They had managed to steal elvers out of legal seine nets for consecutive years while remaining only a rumor among the local fishermen. But Spinney had perceived a pattern in their seemingly random movements and accurately predicted which brook to stake out. Once we'd collared the criminals, they'd begged to hear how this seemingly oafish officer had seen through their subtle plans.

Rick just laughed in their faces.

He even refused to tell me how he'd done it. But that night on the elver stream taught me a valuable lesson: never reveal your methods to anyone who's not your superior or a prosecutor who needs to make charges stick. And even then, only tell them the bare minimum.

While Spinney and I hadn't seen each other in ages, I had heard through the grapevine that he was having problems even before Hillary Fitzgerald mentioned his impending divorce. By all accounts, Rick's self-confidence had turned to arrogance and his career was now hanging by a thread.

He held his boat in place off the rock while McLeary floated in her raft nearby. "I didn't expect to see you here, Mike."

"I didn't expect to be here."

The boat he was driving was one of the bureau's Protectors: a modified twenty-one-foot Boston Whaler with a center console, manned by a single officer. The last time Spinney and I had crossed paths, he'd been captaining the Marine Patrol's ship of the line, the forty-two-foot P/V *Endeavor*. It seemed further proof of his downward spiral to see him as a lowly patrol warden.

"Do you want to tell me what's going on?"

"It's bad. We need to get the state police Major Crimes Unit out here."

He looked past me, up the fog-wooled hillside. "Is Hillary OK?"

*Christ.*

I was trying to come up with a response that wasn't a rebuke to his lack of professionalism.

Fortunately, I was saved again by an engine, two of them this time.

We all turned seaward at the sound of the approaching motorboat. Whatever was heading our way was large and powerful.

Seconds later, a Coast Guard response boat came roaring up. It was an intimidating vessel: steel-gray hull with an orange gunwale, gun mounts fore and aft, ballistic plates around the cabin, dual engines capable of outrunning almost any boat common to Maine waters. It had been designed to give off an unmistakable "don't mess with us" aura.

Spinney held up a hand in greeting as the boat cut its engines. In his job, he must have known every Coastie from Kittery to Eastport.

There were five guardsmen on board—the captain in the cockpit, three young guys dressed in orange life vests over blue operational dress uniforms, and a lone female crew member in the front coxswain seat. All of them wore black gunbelts. At least they hadn't gotten out the automatic weapons.

The captain was actually a petty officer second class. He emerged from his bulletproof enclosure.

"Everything all right here, Spinney?"

"No, but I have it in hand."

The petty office reminded me of myself at twenty-four, not just in attitude but in his looks. We might have been blue-eyed cousins. "We got an emergency call about an intruder on the island. I was told to check with Dr. McLeary." He directed himself now at Maeve. "Are you all right, ma'am?"

"No, I'm not fucking all right. These two jackasses won't let me land on my own island."

Spinney had gone from her ally to my accomplice in the blink of an eye.

I held out my badge again, hoping the guardsmen would take it more seriously than McLeary had. "I'm an investigator with the Maine Warden Service. My name is Mike Bowditch. You can verify my identity with dispatch, but Specialist Spinney will also vouch for me, I hope."

Spinney nodded his big head. "He's who he says he is."

"I arrived at Baker Island just after dawn and found evidence of multiple felonies. I need to contact the Maine State Police. The island is under IF&W jurisdiction. Until the Major Crimes Unit arrives, it's my show."

"Are you talking about homicides?" asked my petty officer doppelgänger.

"How many?" said Spinney.

I was unsure how much detailed information to share with the guardsmen, especially within earshot of McLeary. But it didn't matter.

"Two are dead and one is missing," muttered McLeary. The shock had finally hit her.

"I know this isn't what you want to hear," I said, "but I can't say more until the state police arrive. And I can't let anyone ashore—that goes for you, too, Rick."

"We'll call dispatch," said the boat's commanding officer. He instructed his female crew member to contact the state authorities. His three male guardsmen looked restless. "Is there anything we can do?"

I considered sending them to find Stacey or to begin a search for the missing skiff, but those were not my directives to give. As the first officer at the scene of a homicide, my sole priority was to set up a perimeter.

"Just hang tight until the detectives arrive."

"It's all my fault," said Maeve mysteriously. She seemed to have aged a decade in the minutes since we'd met. For the first time since she'd sped past Stacey and me in the fog, I found myself feeling compassion for her.

"Dr. McLeary, I wonder if I can borrow your satellite phone."

She shuffled into the cabin, retrieved the thousand-dollar communications device, and threw it at me underhand, the way a softball pitcher might hurl a heater. She had excellent aim and arm strength. I was lucky to make the catch.

I keyed in Stacey's cell phone number, expecting to get her voice mail.

"Hello?" she said.

"You're there!"

"Mike? Where are you? Whose phone are you using?"

I turned my back to the cove and lowered my voice. "Maeve McLeary's. She showed up not long after you left. She was followed by Rick Spinney, the Marine Patrol officer Hillary mentioned. And now the Coast Guard is here, too."

"Did you find Garrett?"

"Not yet. But I'm pretty sure he took the skiff or tried to."

"Have you told Maeve about Kendra and Hillary?"

"Yeah, but I omitted the gory details. Where are you, Stace?"

"In Ayers Village. I'm warming up in the house of a very nice couple named Skip and Dorothea Ayers. I got a signal as I entered the passage between Ayers and Hatchet Island. The state police are on the way."

The thought that I might see them sooner rather than later was a relief.

"I hope you don't mind," she continued, "but I called Steve Klesko at home. I know he's your friend. He's getting himself assigned to the investigation."

"Steve's the best detective in the state since Soctomah got sick."

"I called my folks, too. They'd never forgive me if I didn't tell them about Kendra. Don't worry. I managed to talk my dad out of flying down here. You can imagine how difficult that was."

"How are you holding up, Stace?"

"I want so much to call Kendra's folks. They were really close, and it's going to be like the world ending for them. But I know I can't be the one to break the news. It has to be the police, right?"

"Steve will want to talk with them if Kendra mentioned anything about the island, anything that scared her. I know it sucks. But I can let you know after he's contacted them so you can reach out. Please send my condolences. Tell them I personally won't let this go."

"That's one of the reasons I love you," she said. "Is there any way you can persuade the colonel to make you part of the investigation?"

"I can try. Your voice sounds hoarse."

"I sobbed pretty hard while I was paddling. Being around strangers is making me hold myself together." She paused. "I've been thinking more about Garrett. As long as he's missing, the state police are going to treat him as the prime suspect."

"That makes sense," I said. "Under the circumstances."

"Plus, he happens to be Black."

"Come on, Stacey. You know Steve Klesko isn't a racist."

"There are going to be other cops working this case."

She'd brought Sheriff Santum back into my head. But I realized I was prejudging the man unfairly.

"I think you should stay there for the time being," I said.

"On Ayers, you mean?"

"You can't come back here. The island is off-limits to everyone until the detectives and the evidence response people complete their work. Better for you to rest and dry off."

"But Steve will want to interview me," she said. "He'll want to ask me about the conversation Kendra and I had while you were watching puffins in Garrett's blind."

"What did she tell you?"

"That Maeve was beginning to scare her. I didn't think she meant it literally. But now I'm not so certain."

McLeary wasn't acting like someone who had just committed two murders. Her shock and grief seemed so raw and genuine. And what possible reason would she have to kill her assistants since it would inevitably mean the end of her life's work? The Maine Seabird Initiative had already been on life support. Now there would be no saving it.

"I still think you should stay there," I said. "Steve and his partner will definitely want to interview Bear Goodale and his friend from the *Persuader*."

"They'll also want to talk with Justin Speer."

"Who?"

"The man we saw on the *Spindrift*. My hosts tell me that Justin and his wife Brenna are *artistes*. Skip is a lobsterman and his family has been on the island since before Maine was a state. He and Dorothea don't have much use for some of the young 'transplants' the Markhams brought over to live on Ayers."

"What did they say specifically about this Speer character?"

"That he is Clay Markham's photographic assistant and shares his same morbid sensibility. A dead whale washed up here last spring, and Justin spent days photographing the process of decomposition until Skip got so fed up, he towed the rotting carcass out to sea."

"Skip Ayers sounds like my kind of guy."

"You'd love him. Dorothea too. They remind me a little of my folks. Maybe it's because she's in a wheelchair now, recovering from double ankle surgery. She says she'll be up and walking in a few days, and I don't doubt her determination."

I could sense Stacey's sadness when she thought of her mother, who would never rise from her chair again. I decided to change the subject.

"What did you learn about Justin's wife, Brenna Speer?"

"The Speers have a newborn. It sounds like being a new mother is her full-time job. I've seen her pass by the house. She looks kind of meek and mousy, but Skip says she and her husband are 'cut out of the same piece of goods.'"

"I'd appreciate your giving the Speers a wide berth until I arrive."

"If it were up to me, I'd curl up in a corner here. But I don't have the luxury of falling to pieces now. Do I?"

"I'm sorry," I said. "I just don't like you being there without me."

"And I don't like you being on Baker without me. But those are the straws we've drawn."

A series of huge waves came crashing over the heap of granite that served as the cove's breakwater. The anchored boats began to rock from the unexplained swell. A big ship must have been passing far out to sea.

"This is our second vacation interrupted by a murder," she said.

"When was the first?"

"Was it five years ago? We'd just arrived at that cottage on Popham Beach when you were called away to look for those women missing on the Appalachian Trail in the Hundred-Mile Wilderness. And then I joined the search. As bad as that ended up being, this feels worse."

"Maybe we shouldn't go on vacation."

I'd meant it as a joke, but neither of us was in a mood to laugh.

## 19

M y next call was a conference with the commissioner of the Department of Inland Fisheries & Wildlife, the head of the wildlife division, and my commanding officer, warden colonel Jock DeFord.

"What a shit show," said the commissioner. He was a plump, bespectacled man who was a former state legislator turned lobbyist for a multinational electrical utility. He had been a major donor to the new governor and received the appointment, we all assumed, as a reward for his financial support. "How exposed is the department on this?"

"I wouldn't know, sir."

"I wasn't asking you, Bowditch. I was asking Jan. We have a memorandum of understanding with McLeary, correct?"

"That's right," said Jan Hunniwell, the head of the wildlife division. She had been a long-serving field biologist, a former colleague of Stacey's, known for her composure and good humor. "Baker Island is state land, but the seabird restoration project is McLeary's domain. Her nonprofit receives no taxpayer dollars."

"Thank heavens for that," said the commissioner. "So these girls who were killed—"

"I think we'll want to use the term *women* in our public statements," said Hunniwell.

"Yeah, yeah," sighed the commissioner. "Now these *women*, there's no way the press could categorize their safety as being our responsibility."

"We can't control how the media chooses to report this," said Colonel DeFord.

"But we have deniability. That's all I care about. What happened to them is horrible, of course. But it's vital the public recognizes that it was McLeary and her organization who left them alone out there undefended."

"Excuse me, sir," I said.

"What is it, Warden?"

"I would like to be assigned to this investigation. Whatever the arrangement is between the department and Maeve McLeary, the island is owned by the State of Maine and falls under the department's jurisdiction. I can be your eyes and ears here."

"I thought you said the administration was in the clear on this." The commissioner sounded peeved, but he always sounded peeved.

"I think the warden's right," said Hunniwell.

"Me, too," said DeFord. "I'll inform the state police that I've assigned you to the case, Mike."

The commissioner made a vague noise. "Are you sure you don't want to send one of your senior officers?"

"Warden Investigator Bowditch is already on the island," argued Hunniwell.

"His primary role will be as a liaison between the department and the homicide investigation," said DeFord. "But his secondary role will be to review McLeary's procedures and safety protocols and issue an evaluation of what she might have done differently. His place on the team will help insulate the governor from any political fallout."

It was a well-played gambit. I liked Colonel DeFord, but I had to remind myself that the man was a political animal.

"In that case, you have my permission," said the commissioner.

"Maeve has run a first-rate study for decades," said the head of the wildlife division. "I object to scapegoating her in advance."

The commissioner came back on the line. "You can be objective in your evaluation, can't you, Bowditch?"

"Yes, sir."

"Then there's no reason to be concerned about protecting McLeary's professional reputation. She was either negligent or not."

The head of the wildlife division went quiet. In the presence of the commissioner, seasoned bureaucrats in the department had a habit of pausing to weigh their words before they gave voice to them.

"Mike, you said Stacey isn't currently with you on Baker?" she said at last.

"She paddled to Ayers Island to call for help."

"In that case, I'd also ask that you act as the wildlife division's representative as well as the Warden Service's. Please remind the police that the island is a designated wildlife refuge and that a number of resident birds are on our endangered and threatened species list. They need to take care not to disturb them more than necessary."

"Aren't roseate terns on the federal list, too?" asked DeFord. But he already knew the answer. "The last thing those detectives will want is to have the U.S. Fish and Wildlife Service micromanaging their every move. That threat should keep Klesko and his team on their best behavior."

For better or worse, I was part of this now. I couldn't just paddle away in my kayak and go on with my life. I was in it till the end.

As the sun rose, the fog began burning off, just as it had the day before. The air already felt steamy. The guardsmen on board the response boat began rolling up the sleeves of their uniforms. Maeve McLeary reappeared from the cabin of the *Selkie,* having changed into her signature chambray shirt and jeans.

Realizing I wouldn't be paddling again, I removed my dry suit. Underneath, I wore a gray merino tee and charcoal soft-shell pants. I reattached my belt with my Beretta holstered and my badge clipped to it where others could see.

Across the water came the sound of yet another boat. I could tell that it was a big one from the overpowered engine and the crashing waves it left behind in its wake. A minute later, the bow burst through the haze, and I beheld the newest addition to the Marine Patrol's fleet and Spinney's former command, the P/V *Endeavor.*

The primary job of the Maine Marine Patrol is to police the state's commercial fishing industry, and the *Endeavor* was very much a lobsterboat, albeit a mammoth one, capable of hauling traps for inspection. As such, its deck had room for passengers. I tallied a total of twelve uniformed officers and jumpsuited evidence response technicians.

Since there was no room around the crowded mooring, it dropped anchor on the edge of the shelf that rimmed Baker Island.

The *Endeavor*'s crew launched a rigid inflatable boat, maybe fifteen feet long, and equipped with an outboard. It began ferrying passengers to Plymouth Rock where I stood waiting. My friend Detective Steven Klesko was in the first boat.

I stood ready to offer him a hand, but Steve was elbowed aside at the landing by Sheriff Pat Santum. He practically pulled me into the drink as I assisted him onto the rock.

In his campaign appearances, Santum had appeared every inch the clean-cut navy lieutenant commander. But since his election, he'd changed up his look. He now wore his hair shaved on the sides but parted on top and held in place with some sort of gel. He'd grown out a graying beard but kept it trimmed close to the jawline.

He was wearing his uniform and gun belt, which wasn't always the case with Maine sheriffs, in my experience. Santum had brought a detective whom I vaguely knew, as well as a uniformed deputy. They were all wearing pink breast cancer awareness pins on their chests.

Santum's nostrils flared. "My God! What is that noxious odor?"

"Guano?"

"There's something else, too."

"Leach's storm petrels."

"It smells like some thug's body spray."

He stepped past me without asking my name or introducing himself. I wondered who he thought I was. The island footman?

My gaze went to Maeve McLeary watching us with heronlike focus from the deck of the *Selkie*. It must have infuriated her not being allowed to set foot on the island she loved.

Now it was Klesko's turn to come up. He'd once been a star athlete at the University of Maine, but he had put on some pounds since his son's birth. His eyes were sunken from late-night feedings, and he hadn't gotten a haircut or trimmed his monobrow in ages. Even exhausted, he still projected the easy self-confidence, which, more than anything, accounted for his rise to a position of leadership in the department.

"Glad to see you here, Steve."

He wore a state police windbreaker over rumpled clothes he might have put on to run household errands. "Stacey was very persuasive in convincing me to take it. Rightfully, the case belonged to Finch. I had to call in a favor to get myself assigned."

"How are Kim and the baby?"

"Doing well." He turned to lend a hand to the person behind him. "Mike Bowditch, this is my new partner, Delphine Cruz."

Detective Delphine Cruz was the talk of state law enforcement circles. Historically, the Maine State Police had never hired detectives "from away." Bringing in an investigator from the Suffolk County District Attorney's Office who'd grown up in a Dominican neighborhood in Lawrence, Massachusetts, might have been tokenism. But gesture or not, the hiring would have been unthinkable three years before. Depending upon one's politics, Delphine Cruz represented the dawn of an age of enlightenment or the End of Days.

"Good to meet you," Cruz said. Her skin was richer than that of Garrett Meadows, but her irises were hazel with streaks of copper green. She was dressed in black jeans, a black safari jacket, and Doc Martens. Not the outfit I would have recommended for trekking around Baker Island. "I hear you're a game warden."

"A warden investigator," said Klesko.

"An officer from the fish and game division being assigned to a homicide investigation would be considered unusual where I come from," Cruz said.

She was new to Maine, I had to remind myself. The role the Massachusetts Environmental Police played in law enforcement differed from that of our Warden Service. In rural, sparsely populated states, agencies have to backstop each other when called upon to do so.

"The island is under the management of the Department of Inland Fisheries & Wildlife," I explained. "I've been assigned to be your liaison with the department. I'll be issuing my own independent investigative report for IF&W."

"Let's hope we're on the same page." She licked her lips, which were very chapped. "You were the one who found the bodies, right? So you're a material witness, too."

"My girlfriend, Stacey, and I were here yesterday," I said, choosing to overlook Cruz's abruptness. "We paddled out from East Boothbay."

"I thought no visitors were permitted on the island. Something about unexploded bombs."

"Stacey had been an intern here years ago and was friends with the project manager, Kendra Ballard, one of the victims. She asked us to come out because she was worried about Maeve McLeary's mental stability and some confrontations the staff had recently had with locals."

Klesko glanced out of the corners of his eyes at the *Selkie*. "Did you encounter McLeary yourself?"

"She never showed. As far as I know, she's been gone from the island for three nights and only returned an hour or so ago."

"If McLeary wasn't here, what exactly did you and Stacey do?"

Cruz produced a notebook and pen from a pocket. "What's Stacey's last name?"

"Stevens," I said. "Kendra Ballard gave us the details about McLeary's recent behavior and the stresses the island is under. Briefly, the project funding is drying up, the puffins aren't breeding, and some of the local fishermen are blaming the researchers for wanting to save right whales from extinction. We met the two interns: Hillary Fitzgerald and Garrett Meadows. He's the one who's missing. I did a hasty search of the island, but didn't come across him, alive or dead. The island skiff is gone. He may have managed to escape in it."

Cruz had a feline smile. "Good guess."

"Why do you say that?" I said.

"Because twenty minutes ago, a lobsterboat out of Christmas Cove found the missing rowboat adrift off Shooting Rock," said Klesko. "Garrett Meadows was alone on board, collapsed in the bottom and without any oars. He's suffering from shock and moderate hypothermia, but odds are, he's going to make it. The captain of the *Guttersnipe* is bringing Meadows to the public landing in Damariscotta for transport to LincolnHealth's Miles Campus."

"Has Garrett said anything about what happened?"

"Mostly he's been incoherent, the captain told me. He has a head wound and seems to be deeply traumatized by the events of last night. But there's one word he keeps repeating."

"What is it?"

"*Faceless,*" he said.

# 20

Delphine Cruz ran her tongue over her chapped lips and began ransacking the pockets of her safari jacket for some unknown object.

"You say you only met Meadows yesterday. What was your impression of him?"

"Do you mean, would I consider him a suspect? No way."

"That's not what I asked."

I paused to get my words right.

"My impression of Garrett Meadows is that he's a highly intelligent, affable young man who feels isolated here for a variety of reasons, chief of which would be his race."

"Meadows is Black?" asked Klesko.

Cruz raised a fashionably thick eyebrow. "And all his coworkers are, or were, white."

"Kendra and Hillary didn't seem to have a problem. And Maeve was the one who hired him. She should be able to fill you in on the group dynamics. That said, I personally observed Meadows being harassed by a couple of lobstermen from Ayers Island."

Cruz turned to her partner. "That's the big one we passed with all the trees?"

Klesko's sly grin revealed the gray tooth that was a souvenir of his days playing college hockey. "I guess you could describe Ayers that way. Tell us about these lobstermen, Mike."

"Their names are Bear—like the animal—Goodale and Chris Beckwith. Meadows suggested they come over regularly to harass him.

I got to see one of their performances while I was inside Meadows's observation blind. They blasted hip-hop and performed mocking dance moves. Their boat, the *Persuader,* was flying a Confederate flag."

"Did you interact personally with these brave sons of the South?" Cruz had finally located the tube of lip balm in her pocket.

"Damn right, I did. I identified myself as a law enforcement officer and told them to take down the flag."

Klesko made a sour face. "Legally, that might be problematic, Mike."

"Fuck it," I said. "It was obvious they were bullying Meadows. I don't care if the DA disagrees that it constituted criminal threatening. The sternman, Beckwith, gave me lip, but the captain, Goodale, came to his senses. They took down the flag, apologized, and left, but I thought Garrett seemed shaken, although he passed it off as no big deal."

"What did he say specifically?" Klesko asked.

"He didn't want to talk about it."

Cruz nodded as if Garrett's response confirmed my impression of his state of mind.

Behind the two detectives, I spotted Maine's longtime medical examiner Walter Kitteridge disembarking. He'd brought along one of his young female assistants. (Walt always seemed to have female assistants.) The ME was under fire for having given testimony a judge deemed not credible. Both death examiners wore windbreakers identifying their department but were dressed in civvies beneath the jackets.

I noticed that Spinney had been standing nearby, eavesdropping on my conversation with Klesko and Cruz.

As more investigators came ashore, spooked terns and laughing gulls took to the air. The birds were too intimidated by the crowd to dive on any of the newcomers, but that didn't stop them from giving voice to their grievances.

Now that the senior personnel had disembarked, leaving only the forensic specialists, Sheriff Santum had edged up the grassy bank with his two deputies. He kept one hand on the grip of his service weapon. I sensed—or probably just imagined—that he was eager to see the dead women.

Klesko told the captain of the Coast Guard boat that he and his crew of guardsmen were no longer needed. The P/V *Endeavor* would remain behind to transport members of the investigative team to the mainland, if needed.

He next addressed himself to the *Selkie*. "Dr. McLeary, I am sorry that we couldn't let you onto the island sooner. I realize it must have been difficult for you to wait."

"Difficult?" said McLeary. "More like fucking agonizing. I care more about this island than any human alive. I consider it my home."

"We're depending on your knowledge to guide us," said Klesko diplomatically.

"You should know I won't permit anyone to disturb my birds."

"That's going to be unavoidable," said Cruz. "Unfortunate, but unavoidable."

"I won't let you do it!"

Her hearing aids screeched from the feedback.

"Dr. McLeary," I said, "the Department of Inland Fisheries & Wildlife has charged me with protecting the birds while the investigation is ongoing. I'd suggest you brief the officers on the critical nesting areas as well as the parts of the island that might hide unexploded ordnance."

A ripple went through the crowd. Not everyone had heard about the bombs.

"I know for a fact the munitions were cleaned out years ago," pronounced Sheriff Santum as if he'd received a personal briefing on the subject from the Joint Chiefs. "The sign warning about unexploded ordnance is a phony prop to keep people from accessing public land. Baker should be open to taxpayers—after the birds migrate in the fall, of course."

"If you're so confident about the bombs, feel free to wander wherever you like, Sheriff." McLeary showed a ghoulish smile. "You have my permission."

"I don't need your permission."

"All right!" said Klesko, shouting more from frustration than to be heard above the relentless birds. "Warden Bowditch, I assume you were careful not to disturb anything that might have evidentiary value as you were making your initial search."

"I can point out the things Stacey and I touched. We avoided the trails between the structures. Instead, I blazed new paths through the bushes."

"You'd better not have stepped on my nests," said Maeve McLeary.

Klesko saved me from my big mouth.

"Dr. McLeary, as my partner said before, there's simply no way around the reality of the situation here. Our homicide investigation takes priority over everything else. Kendra Ballard and Hillary Fitzgerald are depending on us. We must do everything in our power to determine how they died and who killed them."

"Isn't it obvious it was Meadows?" Sheriff Santum said. "The man fled the scene, suggesting a guilty mind. Maybe listening to all these birds caused him to snap."

"That's nonsense," I said, looking to McCleary for support, but she was examining her boots.

It shocked me that she didn't rise to her intern's defense.

"On the contrary, *Warden*, it's the most straightforward explanation," said the sheriff. "I can assign one of my deputies to meet that lobsterboat when it docks in Damariscotta."

Klesko stared down Santum. "I've already arranged for troopers to accompany the ambulance to the hospital."

"So you agree he's the prime suspect?" the sheriff said.

"I haven't reached any conclusions."

"Bullshit."

"I don't conduct homicide investigations by throwing around unsubstantiated hypotheses," said Klesko, who rarely let his frustration come through in his tone. "I prefer to follow established protocols."

"What protocols would those be?" asked Santum.

"For one, I believe it's a good idea to start with actual evidence."
The sheriff snorted.

I have always found it a pleasure to watch someone work who's good at their job.

Steven Klesko was an extremely good detective.

He had me retrace my steps around the camp while a technician planted flags to mark my routes. He assigned Cruz to work with a contractor from a wireless network to install the cell signal booster the state police brought to remote crime scenes in Maine. He oversaw the Evidence Response Team as they unpacked their gear. He consulted with the death scene examiners. He kept Sheriff Santum and his deputies from wandering off. When Maeve McLeary announced she was returning to her tent, "to see what was disturbed," Klesko stopped her in her tracks, saying she would need to wait until he had an officer photograph the scene first.

McLeary carried herself with such toughness. I found it odd that she didn't want to see Kendra and Hillary now.

*Maybe she can't bring herself to face the reality that her protégées are dead? Maybe she's not as hard-bitten as she pretends to be?*

Biologists, in general, are rarely squeamish. And McLeary especially seemed too hard-boiled for that excuse.

With everything ready, I led the detectives, the sheriff, the death scene examiners, and an evidence tech up the hummock behind the cookhouse to Kendra's body. I felt a lump form in my throat as I caught sight of her waxen face. A kelp fly had alighted on her blue lips, as if it had designs on slipping inside her mouth, but it buzzed off when the shadow of the medical examiner fell across the corpse.

"I can't say that the blow to the head was the cause of death, but it would have been more than sufficient." Dr. Walt Kitteridge used a laser pointer to give us an anatomy lesson. "See how the temporal bone has been shattered with fragments driven into the brain? Minimal bleeding, under the circumstances, which suggests sudden death."

"So he beat her to death with the shotgun?" asked Sheriff Santum.

*He can't let it go,* I thought. *He's made up his mind it was Meadows.*

The man was so easy to despise. Unfortunately for my self-righteousness, I had remembered something about Santum from his campaign. His Korean-born wife had died young of breast cancer, leaving him with three children. Since he'd retired from the navy, Santum had been active in raising money for cancer research while he parented his school-age children as a single dad.

Hating is so much easier when we can pretend our enemy doesn't have redeeming qualities.

"It was definitely a blunt instrument," said the ME. "Beyond that, your guess is as good as mine. We'll have to match the butt of the gun to the wounds. One thing I can say for certain is that the lacerations and contusions on both of her arms were sustained premortem."

Cruz glanced up from her notebook. "Defensive wounds?"

"Presumably." Kitteridge took hold of Kendra's wrist with a gloved hand. "Rigor isn't fully involved. I'd estimate it's seven or eight hours along. How cold was it out here last night?"

I assumed the question had been intended for me. "There was rain, then fog. I'd guess the temperature dipped below sixty but not by much. The heaviest rain fell before midnight, which is why we're finding blood."

"In that case, time of death becomes harder to fix. Cold impedes the onset of rigor. I'll be able to pin down the TOD when I get her on the table."

I had watched several autopsies with dispassion, but my mouth went dry at the thought of Kendra's liver being lifted from her abdominal cavity and set on a bloody scale.

"Stacey and I heard the shotgun blast at 3:42."

Kitteridge peeked at his silver-and-gold Rolex. "That falls within the time frame. I need to see what's in her stomach. As I said, I'll be able to pin it down after I perform the autopsy."

"Why would he leave her posed like that?" asked Klesko. "As if she were holding the shotgun?"

I hadn't yet given the detectives my full statement, which meant they didn't know about the photographer who'd been stalking the researchers from the *Spindrift.*

"Signs of a struggle over here!"

Cruz had drifted away from the corpse and was pointing at a crushed swath of grass. Nothing about it immediately said *struggle* to me. I didn't spot the intruder's telltale boot prints. But then Cruz knelt and pointed with her ballpoint pen to what was unmistakably a blood spatter on a bayberry bush. And as she did so, the scene disclosed its secrets to my eyes. Suddenly, the edge of a boot print appeared in the mud beneath the lowest leaves. A shadow amid other shadows became a scrap of black nylon.

"From a woman's stocking?" Cruz waited for the photographer to get shots of the fabric, then lifted the cloth out with tweezers to drop it in an envelope provided by an attentive evidence tech. "I'm guessing these ladies didn't dress up a lot out here."

"*Faceless*," I said. "The intruder was wearing this over his head. Kendra tore it off him as she was fighting for her life."

"It's a possibility," said Cruz.

I had repressed Sheriff Santum's presence until he spoke. "Could be that the Meadows boy planned it, though. He had a story ready to go of an intruder wearing a stocking over his head. It doesn't necessarily exonerate him."

"That is correct," said Cruz. "It doesn't exonerate him."

Her agreement startled me until I realized she was merely following Klesko's example and not allowing herself to get ahead of the evidence.

I found that mindset harder to adopt.

To believe that the friendly, soft-spoken academic was a murderer meant accepting all kinds of far-fetched ideas. That he had obtained a pair of commercial fishing boots to disguise his prints. That he had hit himself in the head to appear to be a victim. That he had launched himself out to sea in an oarless boat, knowing he might capsize, contract hypothermia, or bleed out before he was found.

Never mind that there was no hint of a motive.

The suggestion was worse than ridiculous. It was offensive in its absurdity.

Klesko remained bent over the ground around Kendra's body. "I can't find any drag marks."

"Meaning she was likely killed there," said Cruz.

"He might've carried her to that spot from somewhere else," said Santum, refusing to relent.

Klesko straightened up. "Mike, how big a man is Garrett Meadows?"

"Five seven, one hundred and fifty pounds."

"About what Kendra Ballard weighs."

"He could've had an accomplice," said Santum, resting his hand on his gun again. "You all are assuming there was one killer, but Meadows might've had help."

"With respect, Sheriff," Cruz said, "the only one making assumptions here is you."

"Let's take a look at the other girl," said Santum.

Once again, I played the role of pathfinder, leading the investigative team to the outhouse where I'd found Hillary Fitzgerald's body. The sight of Hillary's underwear in the bushes brought the parade to a halt. I indicated where I had touched the wet, wooden door.

Cruz managed to swing it open without potentially smearing the killer's fingerprints. Not that the evidence technicians were likely to recover any trace.

"Same blunt force trauma to the temporal bone," said Kitteridge as sunlight fell upon the wan face of Hillary Fitzgerald. "Brain matter visible."

"Her tent and sleeping bag are covered in blood," I said. "And you saw the drag marks outside."

"That means she was asleep when he bludgeoned her with that rock," said the sheriff.

"Makes sense," said the ME. "She doesn't show the same lacerations and contusions as the other victim."

Cruz reached for the lip balm again. "We're going to need you to check for signs of sexual assault, Doc."

I hadn't wanted to entertain the thought that one or both had been raped.

"Both victims appear to have been posed postmortem," said Klesko. "Notable that the eyes of both are open."

The time had come to pull Steve Klesko aside and tell him everything I'd witnessed in the hours leading up to the slaughter.

# 21

First, though, Klesko and Cruz had to confer with the medical examiners.

Several of the troopers and techs who had gotten too far from the base camp already had wounds where the birds had pecked them. I took it upon myself to fetch Band-Aids from the first aid kit in my kayak. Kitteridge didn't have any, despite being a physician; his patients were all dead.

Upon my return, I noticed that Maeve McLeary was sitting with her legs crossed on the ground beside her tent, under the watchful eye of Rick Spinney, of all people. I wondered if Klesko had assigned him to babysit the ornithologist. Spinney kept glancing toward the grass outside the cookhouse, where the rest of the officers were being briefed. He looked like the loneliest man on earth.

"How are you, Rick?" I asked the Marine Patrol Officer.

"How do you think?" he said.

The aggressiveness of the question gave me pause. "I know you were friendly with the researchers."

"So what? Are you accusing me of something?"

"I just meant that it's always hard when you know the victims."

"Right." He rubbed his doughy face. "You ever play poker and find yourself getting dealt one lousy hand after another? I was supposed to be in court later. But that won't be happening."

Hillary had mentioned Spinney getting divorced. I had a hunch, from his bad temper, that his court appointment was not connected to his duties for the Marine Patrol.

"You mind if I talk to Dr. McLeary?"

"Why should I mind? I'm not guarding her, as far as I know. It's just like the staties to keep us out of the loop, isn't it?"

Maeve McLeary stared out to sea, but her eyes seemed unfocused. On a rock beside her was a large green bottle of Tanqueray gin. I wasn't sure if she'd brought it from the *Selkie* or implored the Marine Patrol officer to fetch it from inside her tent.

She took a pull from the half-gallon of liquor, wiped her mouth, then said to me without looking up, "Do you want a drink?"

"No."

"It's the good stuff."

"The detectives need you to have a clear head when they interview you."

"Well, they'd better get a wiggle on, because I intend to get pissed, as we used to say at St. Andrews. 'The Effect of Fish Processing Vessels on Pelagic Bird Populations and Diversity on the Grand Banks'—that was the title of my dissertation. It was a real page-turner, let me tell you."

"Is that why you hired Garrett?" I asked. "Because he was studying at your alma mater?"

"I hired him because I needed a body. And I thought he'd look good in my fundraising materials. Diversity, et cetera. It's probably not the first time a cynical marketing ploy blew up in the cynic's face."

Her silence when Santum had accused Garrett Meadows of being a killer continued to rankle me, even more since we'd discovered the black nylon swatch. And yet she undeniably knew more about her own intern than I did. Was my positive but brief interaction with the man clouding my vision?

"Where were you, Dr. McLeary? You've been gone a long time."

"Here and there. Asking people for money."

"They were worried about you. Not knowing where you were or when to expect you."

"Do you think I don't know that?" The anger passed as quickly as it arrived. "I'm sorry. That was uncalled for."

"You told your staff you were headed back to the island yesterday afternoon."

"You're Stacey's friend Mike," she said, looking at me for the first time with that intense, heron-like stare.

"I am."

"I heard from Rick Spinney that you and she were here yesterday. I'm sorry it took me all this time to make the connection. Where is she?"

"When we found the bodies, she paddled to Ayers to call for help."

"Of course she did," she said, smiling sadly. "That's my girl. Please tell her I'm sorry that I wasn't here yesterday. It would have been better if I'd stayed on the island—better for everyone."

I had no idea how to respond, but in these situations, I had found it was best to let a person keep talking.

"She must be devastated by what happened to Kendra," she said. "Those two were always so tight. I used to call Stacey the 'devil on Kendra's shoulder,' because she was always getting poor Ballard into trouble."

"She's grown up a lot since then."

Her gaze wandered out to sea again, and I realized she was watching the puffins and other seabirds in the water, but the sight no longer seemed to bring her joy. "I'm the last one to judge. I've always been hard on people, my interns especially. A hanging judge, that's what I've been. But now I've built my own gallows."

"How so?"

She raised her head, blinking as if to shake off a daydream, and I cursed myself for having interrupted what had been a confession. She smiled sadly again and shook her head and then took another swig from the gin bottle, signaling we were done. With luck, Klesko would let me sit in while he questioned her about her whereabouts and the multiple threats to the research station.

I turned to leave, but she had one last thing for me.

"Warden?"

"Yes?"

"Be good to her."

When I reached the top of the hill, Klesko buttonholed me. He was ready to take my statement. He suggested we sit at the same picnic table where I'd eaten lobster rolls the afternoon before.

Spruce Island was shining green in the sun. It seemed to have floated a mile closer in the light of day.

As we were taking our seats on the weathered planks, I said, "I expected you to bring along an assistant attorney general."

"She got held up in traffic, and the *Endeavor* needed to get going. She'll be here this afternoon, though. The U.S. Fish and Wildlife Service is also sending an agent and a biologist since roseate terns are federally protected. I guess they don't trust you to watch out for them."

They were right not to trust me, sad to say. I'd been so preoccupied with the murders I hadn't checked that the evidence technicians—not to mention Sheriff Santum and his deputies—weren't stepping on eggs.

"Won't Cruz be sitting in on this?" I asked.

"She has enough to do," he said. "And she trusts me to cover all the bases."

"She doesn't strike me as the trusting type."

Klesko had a dent in his nose from another hockey injury and tended to touch it when something amused him. "I can't blame her, considering the situation she walked into. We've been partners for four months, and she's only recently started speaking candidly around me. She had to see me in action to be sure I wasn't some Barney Fife."

"She certainly doesn't trust me," I said. "Being a mere game warden."

"That's not true. Cruz was impressed with how well you preserved the crime scene for us. And she was particularly won over by the connection you made between the nylon stocking and Garrett Meadows's spontaneous utterance about the faceless man."

"She seems smart."

"'Scary smart' is how my wife describes her." He removed a digital recorder from his windbreaker and placed it between us. "Let's get started. You know the drill."

He took notes in his pad and rarely interrupted me as I moved chronologically through the events of the previous days, starting with the message Stacey had gotten from Kendra, to our setting off from East Boothbay in our kayaks, to our landing on Baker Island and our interactions with the researchers, to the sighting of the unknown photographer aboard the *Spindrift*: the man Stacey had identified as Justin Speer of Ayers Island.

"I'm going to stop you there." Klesko had been a defenseman on the University of Maine hockey team. Even then, he'd been an enforcer. "As far as you know, has she spoken with this Speer yet?"

"Stacey knows better than that."

His expression was doubtful. So many people still thought of her as the reckless, insubordinate person she'd been when she worked as a state wildlife biologist. She had a lot of work to do, proving she had changed. I knew what that was like.

"Go on," he said.

I told him about my encounter with Bear Goodale and Chris Beckwith of the *Persuader* and how Garrett had reacted. I mentioned how I'd tried and failed to find a cell signal, adding that the researchers had one place where they got spotty coverage. (Reading Steve's writing upside down, I saw him underline the words: *where are their phones*?) I realized I had forgotten to bring up the short-tailed weasels and Kendra's assertion that someone with a grudge had released them to devastate the bird population, so I backtracked to include that information in the record.

"Wouldn't that argue for the secret landing place you mentioned?" he said.

"Not necessarily. The weasels could have been set loose over the winter. The Maine Seabird Initiative is only active from May through August. After that, a boat could anchor in the cove and send a dinghy over to Plymouth Rock."

"So you don't think there's another way onto the island?"

"Stacey looked for it when she was an intern—her thought was that it would be down near the abandoned lifesaving station, where there had once been a pier. But she came up empty. I'd love to have a look myself."

"Maybe when you and I are done here," suggested Klesko with a sly smile. "While you're reminding my people not to step on nests."

"Ha-ha."

"Sorry. Please continue."

Next I recounted my conversation with Hillary while we'd washed dishes. I told him how she'd received a call on the radio from Maeve after I'd left. Then, as I was about to discuss our last conversation with Kendra before we departed the island, he looked up from his notepad.

"I'm going to stop you there," he said. "This is great, Mike, very detailed and comprehensive. But was there anything odd you noticed? Maybe it didn't seem consequential at the time, but it left you feeling unsettled?"

I began stroking my chin. It was a habit I had picked up from Charley Stevens when the old pilot became pensive. I'd probably picked up a dozen habits from my mentor that I hadn't recognized.

"There's a photo in the cookhouse," I said at last. "There are a bunch of photos on the walls, almost all of them with McLeary front and center, but this one is unusual."

"Why?"

"Because it's of this young intern alone. And it's tacked up in a place of prominence. I remember thinking when I saw it, *This guy is dead*. It turns out I was right."

"Did you get his name?"

"Evan Levandowski. Kendra called him, 'Our dear Evan.'"

To my surprise, Klesko squeezed his eyes shut and hit his forehead with the heel of his hand.

"Dumb," he said. "Dumb, dumb, dumb."

"What?"

"When I got Stacey's call this morning about the homicides, I felt like I'd heard something about Baker Island not too long ago. It had come up in the news. I felt like I'd read it in the papers while I was on leave and then forgot about it because, you know, I've had a thousand other things to focus on."

"If it's any consolation, I didn't make the connection."

"You have an excuse at least," said Klesko. "I heard the whole story from a trooper who was at the scene. This guy got out of his Subaru halfway across the Penobscot Narrows Bridge. Vehicles stopped in both directions. A truck driver tried to grab him, but the guy was too fast. He didn't even hesitate, the trucker said."

"I've never understood why there isn't a suicide barrier along the bridge."

"Did you know it's one hundred and thirty-five feet from the road to the Penobscot River? Think how much time he had as he fell. You always figure people must have second thoughts. But all the witnesses said he was determined, and he couldn't have chosen a brutaler way to do it. The state police divers who fished his body out of the water, past Verona Island, where the currents had carried it, said it was like picking up a human rag doll. His body had turned to mush on impact."

## 22

A fat, fuzzy bumblebee landed on the tabletop and began to wander around in circles. It seemed very interested in the gull droppings. I planned on letting the insect alone. But Klesko flattened the bee with his fist.

"It wouldn't have stung us," I said.

"My dad always said, 'If you see a bee, kill it.'"

"Why?"

"He just always said it."

"I take it he wasn't in the honey business," I said. "But getting back to Levandowski . . ."

"His mom said he'd been having a rough time since he returned from Baker last year. He was a freshman at the Rhode Island School of Design studying photography. He was failing most of his courses. The school recommended he take a semester off, which he did." He massaged his forehead, still red from where he'd smacked it. "There's something else I'm forgetting."

We both waited for the memory to return, but it didn't.

"I'll make a call to Aaron Cyr," he said. "He handled the suicide investigation for us."

"You should also talk with McLeary about Evan Levandowski."

"I am planning on it."

"I mean there's something more I haven't told you. Kendra said Levandowski emailed McLeary the morning he killed himself, but she didn't know what the message said. Levandowski was supposed to come back to the island as a summer intern. McLeary had to scramble to find a replacement, and that's how she ended up hiring Garrett Meadows all the way from Scotland."

"This all feels peripheral." Klesko tapped his pen against the guano-splattered table. "I feel like we're wandering off track."

I couldn't see a connection between Levandowski's suicide and the murders, either, unless someone blamed the Maine Seabird Initiative for the young man's death and wanted revenge. That theory didn't even deserve to be called far-fetched.

"By the way," I said. "I stopped to talk with McLeary a few minutes ago. She's got a bottle of Tanqueray she's hitting pretty hard. You might want to interview her before she passes out."

"I guess we should speed this up, then. You said Stacey was worried about Kendra. Did she confide any specific fears or—"

"Not that I know of. But Stacey has this paranormal-level intuition. I told her to wait for you on Ayers, assuming you and Cruz will head over this afternoon."

"I hope it ends up being this afternoon and not this evening," he said. "So you and Stacey camped on Spruce, and at 3:42, you heard a gunshot from this direction."

"Correct."

"Just a single shot?"

"Correct."

"And that shot made you decide to paddle back to Baker in the morning—to check it out?"

"Correct again."

"But you said the researchers were shooting weasels that someone dropped here as a prank."

"Hardly a prank if it means hundreds of dead birds."

"Bad choice of words. What was it about the gunshot that made you suspicious enough to paddle back here?"

I'd been asking myself the same question for hours.

"There was so much tension between the researchers. The entire project was at risk of collapsing from lack of funds. I suppose it will collapse. Who's likely to donate a million dollars to a puffin project whose staff has been massacred?"

"Another reason for McLeary to be drowning herself in gin, not that she's short of reasons." Klesko clicked off the recorder. "Let's hear what she has to say for herself."

But a revelation had just come over me, and I remained seated while he slid his legs out from the picnic table.

"I can't believe I forgot this," I said. "There was someone else with us on Spruce last night, or more precisely, there was a motorboat anchored in the northwestern cove of the island. After we heard the gunshot, we crossed the island and hailed the boat from shore, asking if they could radio Baker for us."

Klesko crossed his arms. "What did the people on the boat say?"

"That's just it. They didn't say anything. They just took off. We heard the winch pulling up the anchor and then the outboard starting, and then they motored off. The fog was thick, and we couldn't see the boat from the beach, except for a red navigation light on the port bow."

"So the boat was definitely anchored off Spruce Island when you heard the gunshot?"

"Absolutely," I said. "But we can't assume the shot I heard was connected with the killings."

He scratched his dented nose. "Now you sound like me."

"No need to be insulting, Steve."

"The boat might or might not be relevant, in other words. And since you didn't get a good look at it, I doubt we'll have much luck making an identification. Let's go talk with Dr. McLeary, assuming she's still sober enough to string together sentences."

As I pushed myself to my feet, I felt a twinge in my thigh from the bullet wound I'd sustained six months before. The round had cut a shallow trench through my quadriceps. Most of the time, I forgot about the damage the muscle had sustained, but certain movements—like standing—brought it back.

Klesko reached into his pocket and removed two half-crushed granola bars. "You want one? Our conversation with McLeary might take a while."

"What I really need is coffee."

"You and me both, man. I was up half the night with our little guy. My father told me, 'Have kids while you're still young and have the energy to chase them around.' I can personally vouch for the wisdom of those words. How old are you, Mike—thirty-five?"

"Thirty-two."

"I thought you were older."

People always did.

As we neared McLeary's tent platform, we saw Spinney stalking off toward the landing. I called to him. He stopped but didn't return. Instead, he pointed his finger at a half dozen recreational boats that floated off the island. Murders and fatal fires always brought out curiosity seekers.

"Those fucking vultures!"

"I don't like it, either," Klesko called. "But they're not interfering. You can't just chase them off public waters."

"Watch me!"

I realized that McLeary had disappeared from her spot outside the tent. Both her backpack and her green bottle of Tanqueray were gone.

"Wait! Where's Maeve?"

"She had to take a piss, but because she can't use the outhouse, she was going in the bushes." He pointed to the shore path that curled around the base camp to the east. Then he trotted off toward his Boston Whaler.

There were no bushes on this side of the rise, but I remembered a field of bayberry and seaside goldenrod beyond.

"Do we wait?" Klesko asked.

"I think we should go after her."

"Why? It's an island."

"Because she took her backpack and her booze. And I don't think it's a good idea to let her out of our sight. I may be wrong, but my gut tells me she's the key to what happened here, or she can show us where the key is. The island's flat on the eastern side. We should be able to see her once we're on top."

"You're never going to take my advice about not making assumptions. But all right. I'll follow your lead."

When we crested the ridge, I spotted her immediately: a distant figure in blue, thirty yards from Hillary's observation blind. She was kneeling near a cairn-shaped pile of stones that was part of the island's natural wall. I had an excellent view of her silver ponytail, but I had no clue what she was doing.

Klesko cupped his hands around his mouth. "Dr. McLeary!"

Maeve barely glanced at us before she returned to whatever task or ritual she was performing.

"I don't like this."

I moved ahead of Klesko and began hurrying down the trail.

It would have been faster to make a dash through the bushes, but I worried about tripping on unseen rocks and stepping on nests, not to mention bombs. I remembered there was a sharp drop-off on the eastern side of Baker. I broke into a run. I dodged a tern that swooped down to harass me. I leaped over a granite boulder that would have fit comfortably in the sling of a medieval catapult.

I had closed to within thirty yards when she dropped the last grapefruit-size stone into her backpack. She got her arms under the shoulder straps, but she staggered under the weight. Her backside dislodged the Tanqueray bottle, balanced on a rock, and the glass smashed to the ground.

"Don't, Maeve!"

She managed to step onto the berm above the ocean.

Maeve McLeary gave me one final scowl and let herself fall backward, pulled by the weight of the stones, like a scuba diver going over a gunwale, into a surging sea.

# 23

The night before, I had studied Stacey's nautical chart. She'd embarrassed me with her comments about the old map I'd been using. Depths on the laminated chart were recorded in fathoms. One fathom equals six feet. Baker Island had once been a hillock on a plain before the last glaciers melted and the ocean flooded the coast. The sea bottom here was something like sixty fathoms deep.

I stood atop the granite block. Dragged down by ballast, McLeary had already disappeared into the blue-green depths. I tossed my Beretta on the grass and kicked off my kayaking shoes.

Klesko had lagged me on the trail. Now he called to me, imploring me not to do what I was about to do.

I dove into the surf, hoping my leap carried me far enough from any submerged boulders.

The sudden cold was immediate and all-encompassing. My skin seemed to tighten all over, and I had to squeeze my throat shut to suppress the reflexive gasp that is part of the shock response. My scrotum cramped around my testicles like a closed fist.

The salt water burned my eyes and blurred my vision. The density of plankton in the Gulf of Maine stops sunlight from penetrating more than a few yards beneath the surface. The water got dark fast.

Strong currents were already carrying me away from the island. The rising tide was sweeping me toward the mainland, but there were also invisible eddies that wanted to tumble me head over foot. In open-water swimming, it's usually three things that kill you: cold, exhaustion, and underestimating hydraulic forces.

Nor was I a practiced free diver. All I knew to do was hold my breath, while my heart rate quickened and the pressure built in my inner ears. I made a spear of my body, aimed ever downward.

From the start, I had to fight my body's natural buoyancy. When I scuba dived, the trick was easy enough: you empty the air from your lungs, only slowly refilling them from your tank as you reach your desired depth. But I didn't have a molecule of oxygen to spare.

I kicked and kicked, already feeling as if this unconsidered plunge would result in my own suicide.

As I descended, I refused to look up or retreat. My stinging eyes perceived the silvery movement of a ball of baitfish. The school parted so that I might pass through.

McLeary was dressed in blue, which might as well have been nautical camouflage, but her backpack was a fluorescent-yellow Sea to Summit dry bag. The weight of the stones inside meant she probably hadn't drifted as far as I had from the granite block.

Describing my thoughts and actions in these terms doesn't remotely describe the extent to which my subconscious guided me.

All I knew to do was kick hard and fight the increasing urge to seek air at the surface. I squinted through slitted eyelids, searching, searching. When I saw a yellow shape behind and beneath me, I felt that I might be falling prey to a hallucination.

But what else could I do but power toward it, using my arms to fight the currents pushing me away from the island?

McLeary had come to rest on a granite shelf. Her eyes were open, her lips were parted, her hair was unrestrained. The individual strands moved like the writhing of glass eels.

*Medusa.*

She'd lost one of her Bean boots. I managed to grab hold of her bony ankle and tried to pull. But she wouldn't rise with me. I could feel my lungs issuing stern demands on my central nervous system.

*Breathe in now,* they said.

Instead, I crawled my way down McLeary's weighted body until I'd reached her torso. She lay flat atop her backpack, which was held in place by the stones inside. Wasting precious oxygen, I tugged at one of the straps caught around her armpits before I realized that I needed to pull her arm free instead.

As soon as I did, her limp body twisted sideways, and the other arm slipped from under the pinioning strap. I thought she might rise, pulling me like a cork to the surface. But her lungs were empty of air, and she drifted like the lifeless thing she seemed to have become.

My left hand gripped her wrist so hard I might have cracked her radial bones. I planted my bare heels on the ledge, feeling the sharp barnacles like broken glass, then pushed off.

I hadn't looked up since I'd gone in the water. For a split second, I found myself disoriented by the darkness. I had expected that the sunlight would guide me back to the surface. Divers perish every year because, in the weightless dark, they confuse up with down. But I knew enough to trust my body's buoyancy. The climb couldn't have taken more than ten seconds, but they were the longest ten seconds of my life.

I was shocked when my head finally popped above the waves. I exhaled and inhaled, swallowing seawater in the process.

I was surrounded by frothing chop that made it impossible to get my bearings. Turning, I spotted human-shaped figures atop a wall of boulders, and I realized, to my horror, that I'd been carried many yards from the island.

I tried a sidestroke, towing McLeary behind me, but it was that nightmare sensation of not seeming to advance.

Then I caught sight of a man swimming toward me. Klesko kept his face down and only breathed every few strokes. I tried to meet him halfway, but my thighs and quads were sapped, and it was all I could do to tread water.

"You OK?" Steve asked, breathing hard.

"Yeah," I answered.

"Give her to me."

When I handed McCleary's limp form to him, I saw the recognition pass over his face. This was no longer a rescue.

"You sure you can make it?" he asked.

"Yeah."

He was off again, towing his burden back to the island.

I spent half a minute refilling my lungs, doing my best to tread water without drifting farther from land. Then I started back. My own strokes were sloppy. But I made slow and steady progress.

When I reached the boulder wall at last, I found two hands outstretched. They belonged to Sheriff Santum. He was very strong. For an instant, our faces were as close together as lovers. Then he let go of me.

Shivering, I staggered clear of the berm and flopped onto my back on the pebbled ground. I watched my rib cage rise and fall, and for some reason it made me think of my wolf back home. The seawater I'd swallowed found its way back up in a fit of coughing. Someone shouted that I needed a blanket. Finally, I felt recovered enough to sit up.

On the grass beyond the berm, Maine state medical examiner Walt Kitteridge knelt over Maeve McLeary, performing CPR. The chest compressions caused bloody froth bubbles to spill from the corners of her mouth. Kitteridge abandoned his lifesaving efforts quickly. But what would you expect of a physician who lived in a morgue?

Maeve McLeary was dead and headed for an appointment on the autopsy table.

# 24

W hy?"

It is the inevitable question that follows every suicide.

In this case, it was Delphine Cruz who spoke the word aloud. She'd hurried to the granite berm, along with most of the officers on the island.

I sat on a boulder with a space blanket around my shoulders, sipping from a thermos of coffee provided by someone I never thanked. I couldn't stop myself from checking the sea like it was some malevolent being that might try to kill me again. Puffins, guillemots, and eiders rose and fell on the waves.

"Why did she kill herself? Because her staff was just massacred, and she knew her project was finished," said Santum. "I don't think we need to look hard for an answer. Her own assistant said she was nuts."

Klesko twisted his index finger in his ear, trying to get the last salt water out.

"We'll search her tent and her boat," Klesko said. "Maybe we'll find some better answers there."

Santum rested his hand on his gun. "What else do you need—a piece of paper showing she had stage four cancer, too?"

A fuzzed voice came through the radio on Cruz's belt. It was Spinney calling from his patrol boat. A lobsterman was requesting permission to enter the no-go zone the Marine Patrol officer had set up around the island.

"That'll be my brother," said Santum. "I called him to take my men and me inshore. You state folks seemed to have matters well enough in hand, until you let McLeary sneak away to drown herself."

"Give it a rest, Sheriff," said Cruz.

"Excuse me?" He tightened his grip on his service weapon as if he'd forgotten how threatening a gesture it was.

Santum had come to his position without any law-enforcement experience. He'd commanded desks in the navy instead of frigates or aircraft squadrons. I wondered if he'd ever served in a war zone. Now he'd found himself in a job where he strapped on a semiautomatic pistol every morning. I recalled something Charley Stevens had said to me when we'd discussed the inevitability of bullies being drawn to careers as police.

"I worked with a few men in that category over my career, very few," he'd said. "They pray for the day they get to pull and fire their weapons. Usually, those types find a reason to do so."

"I take full responsibility for allowing Maeve McLeary to kill herself," said Klesko. "I'm the primary here, and her death is on me."

"Satisfied?" Cruz said to Santum.

The sheriff stroked his beard. I couldn't imagine him doing what Klesko had just done. He wasn't brave enough.

"My brother's boat is a Lowell 33," he said. "It has plenty of room for the death scene examiners and the three cadavers. Being out in the sun and heat can't be helping these corpses any. Am I right, Walt?"

Kitteridge's face showed his surprise at being addressed by his nickname by a man he hadn't met before that morning. "The sooner we get them on ice, the better, it's true."

"Sounds like a plan, then." Santum removed his own radio from his belt to speak with Spinney. As sheriff, he said he was giving special permission for his brother's boat to approach Baker. He didn't have that authority any more than Spinney did to label those waters as restricted.

Klesko and Cruz seemed disinclined to continue the conversation, and I could only imagine it was because the detectives were eager to be rid of the officious sheriff.

Kitteridge zipped up McLeary in a black body bag.

Steve finished lacing up his boots. "You know, Bowditch, I was about to say that was the dumbest thing you've ever done, but upon further reflection, I don't know if it even makes the top ten."

"Bowditch?" said Santum. His eyes opened as if with amazement. "You're Mike Bowditch?"

"Yes?"

He spun on his two officers, both of whom wore their hair like his. I hadn't heard either of them speak a word all day. I wondered if they were his new hires. "Why didn't one of you tell me who he was? I've heard of your exploits, Warden. I can't believe I spent half the day with you and didn't know who you were. I'd like to shake your hand, sir."

"OK?"

I had no clue what was behind this starstruck reaction. But I obliged him.

He then said something about getting together for coffee or lunch soon. I muttered a few noncommittal words in reply.

After he and his deputies had left, along with the others, to begin transporting the cadavers to the landing, I found Klesko grinning at me. Cruz looked bemused, to the extent I could locate an emotion behind her reliably wooden expression.

"What the hell was that about?" I asked.

"He knows you've killed people in the line of duty," said Klesko. "He admires you for being a gunslinger."

"I'm embarrassed by it!"

"You should be," said Cruz. "Police-involved shootings always represent a failure to achieve a nonlethal outcome."

Being praised by Pat Santum was not a mark in my favor. She'd probably concluded that I was one of those trigger-happy cops Charley had warned me about. Whatever points I'd earned with her previously, I'd just lost.

Klesko was too much of a professional to lose focus. "Have the ERTs located anything of interest while Mike and I were failing our lifeguard exams?"

"We're still scratching the surface," said Delphine Cruz. "This may be a small island, but it's a huge crime scene, especially when everyone's doing their best not to step on baby birds."

"How about the boot prints?" I said.

"We've found one set of impressions where he seems to have entered the camp from the south."

"That seems like it might be up your alley, Mike. If you feel up to doing some tracking."

"I'm happy to do whatever you need," I said. "But I want to make a suggestion first. I think it makes sense to track down McLeary's movements from the time she left the island until she returned this morning. Who did she go inshore to visit? Where did she tie up the boat? Where did she spend the night?"

"I already started making those calls," said Cruz, applying a fresh coat of sun-protectant lip balm.

I should have realized she had. It was yet another reminder that, despite my involvement in homicide investigations, I would never be "murder police."

Nor did I want to be. I had run into enough scrapes in my life as a game warden. And after having been unable to save McLeary from drowning, I welcomed the chance to do something I did well: track a human being across difficult terrain.

I made a stop at my kayak to put on dry clothes. The only ones I had were the dirty shirt and pants I'd worn the day before. I borrowed a handheld radio from one of the troopers acting as island quartermaster and had a forensic technician direct me to where they'd found the tracks entering the base camp.

It was the edge of a muddy puddle where the ridge trail emerged from the scrub. The intruder had been careful to avoid such places, but in the dark and the rain, he must have taken a wrong step. I judged the boot to be a size ten: larger than those worn by Garrett Meadows or any of the female researchers.

In most cases, it would have been easy enough to backtrack the intruder, but he'd been careful. He'd known to avoid the trail. I had to search for more subtle signs: creases in the foliage that looked recently made, broken and bent twigs, stones that had been kicked up, leaving pockmarks in the ground.

What started as a challenge soon became child's play. I crossed the island in minutes, following a one-man footpath that would've been invisible to me when I was a rookie warden but was as clear to my veteran eyes as if it had been marked with reflective paint.

I emerged from the waist-high bushes onto a field of pumpkin-size boulders. I hopped atop the biggest one and did a 360-degree turn.

Two hundred yards to the northeast was Garrett's former blind. A hundred yards to the east was the DANGER sign. Due south, across a wind-rippled field, was the lifesaving station, which had become more and more derelict-looking the closer I had gotten to it.

If there was a secret landing place, as there surely was, it had to be in the vicinity of the long-vanished pier that had served the long boats sent out from Baker Island to rescue sailors whose ships had been wrecked off the outer ledges.

The boot prints led the way.

I passed the old ruin. Its white paint was flaking away to reveal gray clapboard. The chimney had lost gouts of mortar. There was a black hollow where the door once was.

*Strange that the military didn't bomb this building during its many training missions.*

*Unless one of the goals was to practice precision bombing.*

Now I stood atop a jagged granite wall. The ocean is so powerful it can throw ten-ton blocks around. I'd seen breakwaters that had been plumb level a hundred years earlier that were uncrossable now by any animal that wasn't a mountain goat. Something like that had happened here.

I put on my polarized sunglasses to see better into the water and made out a couple of stumps at the water's edge that were all that was left of the old pilings. There was no pocket beach or obvious pullout or even a place to safely tie up a skiff. Below the berm on which I stood, the boulders tumbled into the deep blue water.

I did some math in my head. High tide had been at 11:30 p.m. That meant it had been mid-tide and ebbing when I'd heard the gunshot at 3:42 a.m. It was now 1:30 p.m. (approaching mid-tide again), which meant the view before me was a close facsimile of the situation the intruder had encountered.

Now I scanned the rocks, both those above and below the water-line. The few boulders that were emerging from the ocean as the tide receded were covered with ocher bladder wrack. The seaweed would be too slick to cross even if you wore crampons.

As I squinted, I noticed a black object suspended inches beneath the surface. It was obviously buoyant and about the size of a softball. But it was barely moving despite the waves.

The revelation came to me at once.

It was a secret mooring ball tied to a hidden anchor. The line connecting it to the weight was deliberately short. The concept was genius.

The black mooring ball was only visible for a brief window at mid-tide. No wonder people had missed seeing it.

When the sea was high, the restrained mooring ball would be pulled beneath the surface, held taut to the anchor below. Waves obviously crashed up and over the berm. A skiff that got too close would be pounded into splinters against the boulders.

When the sea was low, the camouflaged ball and loose line would have sat like flotsam amid the seaweed, waiting for the tide to return.

The scene told me three things about the intruder.

That they knew this part of the island extremely well.

That they had prepared the landing spot by cleverly rigging that secret mooring.

That they must have possessed significant upper-body strength to lift themselves up and over this wall.

As I was turning away, the sun sparkled off something in the Irish moss just below the berm. I peered closer. The rising sea had covered the object with six inches of water, and I had to wait for a wave to recede to get a better look. My breath caught in my throat.

I removed the radio from my belt and spoke into the mic.

"This is Bowditch. I'm down at the old lifesaving station. I've found where the perp came ashore and left the island. I've located something else, too. One of the women's phones. I'll bet the other missing cell is in the water here, too, dropped by the killer as he was leaving."

## 25

When I reached base camp, I found Delphine Cruz sitting cross-legged in McLeary's tent, going through the contents of the waterproof totes and dry bags in which the ornithologist had stored her clothing and other personal items. It's a truism in law enforcement that the dead are allowed no secrets.

"Congratulations," she said. "I heard you located the spot where our killer came ashore."

My back was slick with sweat from the hike down the island. "The missing cell phones, too."

"Keep this up, and I'm going to start worrying about my job security."

I couldn't help but smile. "How's it going here?"

"I found these." She showed me a collection of white bottles containing what looked like vitamins or supplements. Some bore an EarthMother label. I knew the founder of that company all too well. "MacuHealth. Lutein. Zeaxanthin. Omega-3 fish oil."

"She was worried about her eyes?"

"Good for you. Myself, I had to google what they did. These pills are more than just stuff you take to preserve your vision as you age. They're what ophthalmologists prescribe to ward off macular degeneration. The science on their effectiveness is shaky, and there's no proven treatment to stop the condition from worsening."

"So on top of everything else, Maeve McLeary was afraid of going blind, too? That's got to be especially brutal for someone who's spent their whole life watching birds."

"Sheriff Santum wasn't far off about her having a health condition on top of every other reason she had to off herself."

"He's gone, I hope."

She smiled without parting her lips. "You sound disappointed. He seems to be one of your most devoted fanboys. I didn't realize you were such a rock star."

"That prick doesn't know the first thing about me."

She nodded. I hoped the gesture was meant to signal her belief in what I said. "You missed his joke of the day. He had a bunch of the guys in stitches. 'Do you remember Wake Island in the Pacific?' he said. 'Well, we're going to have to start calling this place *Woke Island.*'"

"Classy," I said. "Did you find McLeary's phone?"

I had remembered the alleged email she'd gotten from Evan Levandowski the morning of his suicide.

"I think the good doctor took it with her down to Davy Jones's Locker."

"Where's Klesko?"

"He just finished calling the next of kin. I offered to do some, but he said it was only right that he be the one. That man carries too much weight. It's going to crush him someday. He left to go search the *Selkie*. That was the last I heard from him. Did you get lunch?"

"I had a granola bar."

"Damn, boy, you need to eat. You and Steve both think denying yourself will bring those women back. News flash: It won't."

"I lose my appetite when I'm working. But I'll make up for it later. I think I'll go check on Klesko."

She called after me as I ducked out of the tent, "At least grab a banana from the box!"

I hated being accused of having a martyr complex. My mother had raised me in the Catholic faith. I'd fallen away for years, partially because of the evil I'd seen in my job, but had returned on a whim for an Easter Mass—the cathedral had been thick with nostalgia and incense—and the service stirred up old emotions. I made a confession to a priest in Bangor and visited for coffee and conversation a few times before ghosting him. I couldn't have told you why.

The Warden Service chaplain asserted I would find my faith again. The yearning to believe was too strong in me, she said.

In the cove, I found the *Endeavor* anchored at the edge of the shelf and the *Selkie* moored to its chain. The seabirds had made my kayak look like a Jackson Pollock if he had painted in bird shit.

I didn't see Klesko, but the dinghy was tied up to McLeary's boat. I called across the water from Plymouth Rock.

He emerged from the cabin, looking miserable in his damp clothes. He must not have packed a change of outfits. Surely, he could have scavenged a spare jumpsuit from one of the evidence techs. But Cruz was right about her new partner: the man became an ascetic when he worked a homicide.

"I heard you spoke with the relatives," I said. "How did that go?"

"It's never easy, but this was as hard as it gets. Kendra and Hillary were both close to their parents, who all fell to pieces. McLeary's brother was as remote as can be, but he asked about her will. He lives in California. I had the feeling they were estranged. Tell me about the secret landing place you discovered."

I explained about the secret mooring the killer had used to tie up his boat.

"It's more evidence that exonerates Garrett Meadows. Santum seems intent on fingering the poor guy for this. I can't possibly understand why that might be."

Klesko refused to engage with my sarcasm.

"I heard you found the missing cell phones or what's left of them," he said. "I've torn up the *Selkie* looking for McLeary's personal phone, but so far, I've come up empty."

"Cruz hasn't found McLeary's cell in her tent, either. She thinks it might have been in her backpack when she went into the sea."

"Unless we get lucky, I'm beginning to think we won't find answers on Baker Island. Speaking of which, Spinney is taking you and me over to Ayers in an hour. Make sure you're ready to go at a moment's notice."

"Me?"

"Don't you want to see Stacey? Besides, I could use a sounding board, and Cruz needs to stay here until the evidence response team wraps up its work."

"Is Rick still chasing off looky-loos?"

"It seems to be how he works through his anger."

"I wish you'd known him back in the day. He was a hell of an officer once."

"I'll have to take your word on that," my friend said. "This job breaks a lot of good men."

"'And afterward many are strong at the broken places.'"

He raised his eyebrows.

"It's a line from a book," I explained. "You're going to need to get a statement from Spinney. I got the strong impression that his constant visits were creeping out Hillary and Kendra."

"I think I'll wait until after we're off his boat before I grill him as a murder suspect. How much do you know about marine engines? I was just about to start up the *Selkie*'s inboard."

"Why? Are you taking a joyride?"

"I happened to notice that McLeary has only ten gallons of fuel in the tank."

"That's barely enough to get back to the mainland!" I began stroking my chin again in imitation of that master of deduction, Charley Stevens. "I have an idea, but I don't think you're going to like it."

"Probably not."

"What if McLeary lied about being inshore? What if she went somewhere else yesterday—somewhere she couldn't refuel?"

"The *Selkie* doesn't have an automatic identification tracking transceiver, so there won't be a record of her whereabouts," he said. "It would be nice if we had her cell phone, but I can ask the attorney general to talk with her carrier."

"What about the satellite phone? It must have GPS, too."

His grin revealed his gray canine tooth. "That's inspired thinking. There's only one problem. The feds can issue a subpoena for a carrier to provide sat phone records, but the State of Maine doesn't have the same power. We're going to need to convince some highly intelligent and skeptical people that it's imperative we know where Maeve McLeary went the past few days."

"Because she's a suspect in a double homicide."

The frown returned. "Except we haven't named her as a suspect."

"There's no reason to tell that to the judge."

"You lie more easily than you did when we first met, Mike."

The statement felt accusatory, but at the same time, I knew in my heart it was an accurate assessment.

"My point is you need hard evidence of McLeary's whereabouts to rule her out as a suspect. Is that true or false?"

Klesko didn't respond. I could tell he was disappointed in my lack of ethics. He returned to the control panel inside the cabin. He started the blower to release any trapped fuel vapors from the engine compartment. He let the fan run a few minutes to be safe.

Two things happened when he turned the ignition key. The motor chugged to life, and a high-pitched whine issued from the *Selkie*.

"Wait!" I said.

He stepped out of the cabin but kept the motor running. Rather than trying to shout above the engine noise, he raised his hands, palms upward. *Yeah? What's going on?*

I cupped my hands to increase my volume. "That noise! What is it?"

"The boat's short on oil! There's a light flashing on the dash!"

"Turn it off!"

The motor sputtered until it died.

"You don't need to get her sat phone records," I called. "Not all of them, anyway."

"Why not?"

"Because I know where Maeve McLeary was last night. She was anchored off the back side of Spruce Island. It was her boat Stacey and I hailed in the fog."

"How sure are you?" he asked after he'd rowed back to the island.

"One hundred percent."

"I don't know, Mike. Is it possible you're saying you recognize the sound because you want it to be true?"

"The way I see it, Maeve being anchored off Spruce last night raises more questions than it answers."

"Care to name them?"

"One: Why would McLeary anchor off Spruce Island when Baker was just two miles away? Two: Assuming it was because of the rainstorm, why would she have left the mainland, or wherever she'd been, at all? Three: Why did she run off when Stacey and I called for help?"

His brow furrowed. "But you said the boat was anchored off Spruce when you heard the gunshot. That undermines your treating her as a potential suspect."

"Except we can't be sure the shot was Kendra firing at the intruder."

"I won't mislead the attorney general. That's a line I will never cross even if you're comfortable treating it like a jump rope."

Again, I found it hard to be insulted when he knew me so well.

"What I want to know is where she was *before* she landed at Spruce Island."

"How is that pertinent?"

"Because I'm stuck on the question of why the intruder chose last night to commit the murders. The storm would have made everything ten times more difficult. I refuse to believe the timing was random. He either acted because he believed McLeary was back on Baker or because he knew she wasn't."

Off the island a seal had raised his gray-spotted head from underwater and was watching us as if captivated by our ethical debate.

Klesko was not the kind of man to sigh, but he made the face of a person doing just that. "You read a lot of detective fiction as a kid. Didn't you, Mike?"

"You know I did."

"Then maybe you remember this quote: 'Imagination is a good servant and a bad master.'"

"I never pictured you as a reader of Agatha Christie, Steve."

"I wasn't. But Wayne Soctomah, who trained me, loved those books. Soctomah was the one who taught me not to come to conclusions too quickly when investigating a crime. Not unless time was of the essence."

"What makes you think time isn't of the essence here?"

He had no answer for that one.

"I'm going to call the AG and confer with him about getting her sat phone records," he said. "Kitteridge will be giving us time of death soon, and if the *Selkie* was at Spruce Island when the women were killed, it definitely rules her out as a suspect—unless someone else was using the boat."

After Klesko wandered off, I retrieved my cell where I'd plugged it into the power bank the police had brought along. Then I took advantage of their signal booster to call Stacey. I had been procrastinating for the past hour, telling myself I needed to prepare to tell her about McLeary. But really, I'd been summoning my courage.

"Stacey," I said. "Something's happened here."

"It's about Maeve, isn't it?"

I'd stopped bothering to ask how she sensed these things. It was enough to accept her powers.

"She killed herself, Stace."

There was a pause during which I thought I'd lost her.

Her voice came back as a monotone. "How did she do it?"

I told her the story, omitting nothing. I apologized for not having been able to save her mentor.

"It wouldn't have mattered. She would've found another way to kill herself. I'm just glad to hear that you didn't drown, too. Hillary warned you about the currents off Baker."

"I don't always think before I act."

She couldn't help but chuckle. "That's my line. If we ever have a kid, he's going to be the next Evel Knievel."

She mentioned the possibility so casually, the significance of her words almost didn't register. I recalled Klesko's advice about having children when you are young. I felt an overmastering need to change the subject.

"There's something else," I said.

"I heard about Garrett being found adrift. My hosts have a VHF radio in the kitchen, and the chatter among the fishermen has been Baker Island nonstop. Do you know how he's doing? All I'm hearing is slander and speculation."

I filled her in with the minimal information I possessed. When I'd exhausted the subject, I switched back to Maeve McLeary. I told Stacey how Klesko and I had deduced that the *Selkie* was the boat in the fog.

"Good work," she said.

I had expected her to be more surprised. Or at least, more generous with her praise.

"Steve is calling the attorney general. He's asking the AG to pressure the phone carrier to give us McLeary's GPS coordinates so we can track her movements, especially yesterday after she went speeding by us in the fog."

"There's no need," she said. "I can tell you exactly where Maeve was yesterday."

"How? Where?"

"Here on Ayers Island, visiting with the Markhams."

"What? Why?"

"Because Clay Markham was her anonymous donor."

"How did you figure that out?"

"I went for a walk and a little girl approached me, bold as anything. She was Bear Goodale's little sister Juniper. She asked if I'd really come from the puffin island. When I said I had, she told me she'd been to Baker Island with her family. Maeve even let her hold a baby puffin, she said. Not only that, but she claimed Clay Markham had taken a picture of her with the chick. I asked to see it, and sure enough, she came back with an amazing little portrait."

I scanned the murmuring cove and found that the harbor seal was still watching me with his black, soulful eyes.

"That doesn't prove Markham is 'Anonymous,'"

"Let me finish," she said. "Skip Ayers confirmed the *Selkie* was moored in the harbor all day while Maeve met with Clay and Alyce. I worked for a nonprofit, and you don't get that kind of access to the mega-rich if you don't already have a relationship."

The seal let out a snort and disappeared beneath the waves. He must have heard enough out of me.

"I'm sorry for doubting you, Stacey. Klesko will need more proof, though. He's been lecturing me about how intuitions and emotions aren't evidence."

"Emotions get a bad rap. More evil has been done by people denying their emotions than by people acknowledging what they truly feel. Self-deception is a soul killer."

"You sound like a transcendentalist."

"I was going more for Jedi knight."

We laughed together, and I remembered again how much I loved her.

# 26

Just after two o'clock, I was sitting on the deck of my beached kayak, eating a banana, when I heard and then saw a Marine Patrol vessel bucking the waves as it sped toward the island from the direction of Boothbay Harbor.

Rick Spinney had returned.

I had just been thinking about what I'd told Klesko about him. How Rick had changed for the worse since we'd met.

The Spinney I had met years earlier was one of the Marine Patrol's rising stars.

His first year on the job, he had saved an elderly couple whose sailboat was going down off North Haven. They'd had no business taking their sloop out in a gale, but the man had been a lifelong sailor and misjudged how age had diminished his capabilities. The wife, also, had early-stage Alzheimer's disease and was unable to follow her husband's directions. When their boat capsized, they should have died.

But Spinney rescued them single-handedly and at great risk to his own life.

Not only did he save the couple, but he rescued their dog, too.

It was that footnote to the story that earned Rick Spinney the attention of the national media: the fact he'd plunged into the icy water for their Maltese. Taking advantage of the good press, the legislature recognized Rick with a special proclamation honoring his heroism.

The next summer, Spinney made the news again when he was

first on the scene during an armed confrontation on Isle au Haut. One lobsterman shot and killed his cousin—they'd been unknowingly sleeping with the same woman—and he was preparing to put a bullet in his brain when Rick arrived. Somehow the Marine Patrol officer had persuaded the jealous shooter not to take his life.

The Spinney I had met was a jovial, self-effacing family man.

Until the stress of the job had eaten his soul from within.

People often lumped together the Marine Patrol and the Warden Service. It was true that our uniforms resembled one another's (except that their shirts were khaki instead of olive) and our patrol trucks had been the same shade of green before we had been given a new fleet of black Fords and GMCs.

But game wardens dealt almost entirely with citizens engaged in recreational pursuits (hunting, fishing, snowmobiling, canoeing). Most of our interactions with the public were neutral if not always friendly. We didn't stop lobstermen and scallop divers during their workdays with the implied rationale that they were violating commercial fishing laws or, worse, smuggling contraband in their holds.

The last time I'd heard Rick Spinney's name was in connection with a fistfight he'd gotten himself into with a foulmouthed lobsterman whose boat he had boarded. After the guy had called him some choice names, Spinney had pushed him over the transom. Like a shocking number of Maine lobstermen, this one had never learned to swim. The man almost drowned. Worse, the episode was caught on video by a person on a passing boat. Spinney ended up being suspended without pay and ordered to take anger management classes, which only made him more volatile, I'd heard.

The thought of Rick Spinney becoming a bully saddened me, even more than learning that his wife was divorcing him or hearing about his pathetic flirtation with twenty-year-old Hillary Fitzgerald.

"I've been ordered to take you and Klesko over to Ayers," he said as he expertly pulled his Boston Whaler alongside Plymouth Rock and manipulated his twin engines to hold it in place, inches from the stone. If he'd wanted to, he could have stepped onto the shore without getting his boots wet.

He was wearing heavy-duty sunglasses, and there was a white spot of zinc sunscreen in the nautilus of his ear.

"I'm ready whenever Klesko is."

"I heard about Maeve," he said without emotion. "What a sorry end for that woman."

"When you two were together outside her tent, did she give any indication that she might take her own life?"

Now he grew hot. "What are you suggesting? That I encouraged her?"

"Relax, Rick. All I meant is it caught us by surprise."

He studied me through his impenetrable sunglasses. Only the tightening of his mouth gave away his displeasure. I was aware again of what a hulking man he was. I would have hated being in a wrestling match with him.

"Can you tow my kayak?" I asked.

"Not at planing speed."

"Well, I need to get it to the mainland. I was hoping to paddle it back from Ayers when I'm done later."

"All right," he said, and reached for a bottle of water to take a swig. "I'll tow it for you. My reputation is already bad enough these days; I don't need you bad-mouthing me, too."

Klesko appeared, coming down the hill behind me. He had a nylon duffel over his shoulder bulging with the assorted gear homicide detectives carried. The hem of his still-soaked polo shirt had ridden up on that side, exposing his service weapon: a Heckler & Koch .45 Compact. Steve was a famously bad shot; every qualification test he took was a nail-biter.

"Grab anything you might need, Mike—an extra layer, boots, et cetera."

"Rick has agreed to tow my kayak."

Spinney grunted. "I've got to tie a floating line on it. Otherwise, it's going to want to dive underwater like a porpoise. I'd been hoping to make this a quick trip, but c'est la vie."

While the Marine Patrol officer rigged a line to my kayak, Klesko told me that Cruz would ride back to shore with the others aboard the *Endeavor*. She was currently arranging for a contractor to tow in the *Selkie* for a more thorough search.

Despite his protestations, it only took Spinney a few minutes to harness my kayak, and then we were off.

I immediately wished I'd put on my dry suit. Even on a hot summer day, it's always colder than you expect on the open ocean. Klesko must have been freezing in his wet clothes.

Spinney goaded me by increasing speed until my kayak started jumping around atop the wake his boat left behind. I knew better than to tell him to ease up. When the joke got old, he slowed down.

I had expected that we'd follow the route Stacey had taken, back along the cliffs, but Spinney decided to give us a scenic tour around the southern end of Ayers Island. We came around a spruce-capped headland to see a vast field of weeds and wildflowers. At the tip of the point rose the candy-striped tower of Ayers Light.

"I thought West Quoddy Head was the only red-and-white lighthouse in Maine," Klesko shouted over the outboards.

"It used to be all white, but Markham had it repainted," said Spinney. "Imagine choosing to waste your fortune on something that trivial. But it's his to deface as he pleases."

In the 1990s, Congress had authorized the Coast Guard to dispense with its Maine lighthouses. Human tenders had been replaced by automated beacons and foghorns, and more importantly, the towers themselves had been rendered superfluous by advances in radar and other aids to maritime navigation. Nonprofit organizations had bought up most of the lights, others were demolished, and some were purchased by fanciful millionaires like Clay Markham.

"He owns the entire island?" asked Klesko.

"Ayers and Hatchet, too. That's the next one over, across the channel. You wouldn't believe some of the stories I've heard about what goes on out here."

"Such as?" I asked.

"And get sued for slander? No, thank you. I'm already paying my lawyer enough."

"I was sorry to hear about your divorce, Rick," I said.

But it was as if he refused to hear me, or maybe the thought of Markham's millions had touched an exposed nerve.

"You wouldn't believe the wealth out here," he said. "These islands get listed for ridiculous sums, and they're on the market for two days. They cut down the trees and build self-glorifying mansions."

Spinney had worked himself into a state of agitation. In his anger, he began to push the throttle. The waves behind the boat —a V-shaped wake—grew higher and higher. A person could have surfed on those breakers. I worried my kayak would snap in two unless he eased off the gas.

"Would you mind slowing down, Rick?"

With a smirk, he throttled back the engines.

In the distance I could see westbound waves piling against the Brigands as the rising tide covered the ledges for the second time in twenty-four hours. If you didn't know about the submerged rocks and only saw the spray exploding in the air, you might have thought it was a humpback whale breaching.

The sea air felt bracing in my lungs.

As we came around Ayers Light, the sun caught the Fresnel lens atop the restored tower, and it seemed as if the ghost of the last keeper had ignited the beacon to guide us into the passage. A flock of seabirds—terns and gulls—circled the lighthouse. Their wings shone blindingly white. On any other day, under any other circumstances, in any other company, I would have found it an awesome spectacle.

# 27

I wasn't sure what made the boat catch my attention since it was no more than a speck against the horizon.

I shouted at Spinney above the roar of the dual Mercury outboards, "Can you stop for a second?"

"Why?"

"Just stop."

By then, I was rummaging through my backpack searching for my sea-watching binoculars. I adjusted the focus until the fuzzy boat shimmered into clarity.

"That's the *Persuader*!" I passed the Nikons to Klesko.

"The boat that was harassing Garrett Meadows?"

"We need to make a detour."

"Agreed."

"Bear Goodale is an idiot stoner," said Spinney. "The guy looks hard and acts tough, but he's a marshmallow. That whole family is wackadoodle. Who gives their kids names like Bear, Echo, Falcon, and Juniper? Imagine going through life with a name like Falcon. At my old school, the poor kid would've gotten his face shoved into a urinal every morning. Bear's not our guy."

"He's still a material witness," I said. "His sternman, too."

Spinney set an intercept course for the lobsterboat.

Even towing the kayak, we closed the mile distance in no time.

As we drew near the *Persuader*, Klesko leaned against the cockpit that shielded Spinney. "What are they doing?"

"They just seem to be drifting," I said.

It was Beckwith who heard us coming. He dropped the line he was coiling and shouted into the cabin.

The scar-faced man was shirtless again; it was an ill-advised choice on a working boat equipped with whiplash lines and finger-severing winches. Except for his Malibu-ready board shorts and white fishing boots, his attire consisted of mirrored sunglasses and a sailor's rope bracelet around one sun-bronzed wrist. A little cigar was tucked in the corner of his mouth. A cigarillo.

Spinney turned the wheel sharply as he cut his speed, causing our wake to send the *Persuader* rocking ferociously. Beckwith swayed with the boat so that his upper half remained perfectly vertical, almost motionless. His sea legs couldn't have been better.

"Hey, Officer Spinney," he said. "You want to check our catch?"

"Where's your captain?"

"Down below. Hey, Bear, wake up! The clam cop wants a word with you."

Spinney must've been close to biting his tongue in half. He dropped the bumpers to cushion the boats as we rafted up together. He scowled at Beckwith as he took the line to make us fast.

Bear Goodale dragged himself out into the sunlight. He was dressed in the same Grundéns pants he'd worn the day before, but today he was wearing an unbuttoned Hawaiian shirt that revealed his shark's tooth necklace against his pale belly. His eyes were puffy and inflamed.

"Bear Goodale, this is Detective Klesko with the Maine State Police," said Spinney. "He has some questions for you, and I strongly suggest you answer them without any lip. You, too, Blondie."

"Blondie!" said Beckwith, amused.

"I heard Kendra and Hillary were killed," Bear said, blinking. "It's been all over the radio."

"You're forgetting about Garrett Meadows," I said.

"Did they murder him, too?" Goodale sounded genuinely surprised. Alarmed even.

"Garrett managed to escape," I said. "But he was badly injured in the attack. You said 'they' just now. What makes you think more than one person was involved?"

"I meant *they* in the gender-neutral sense."

Spinney shook with laughter at this answer. "*Gender-neutral!* Listen to this guy."

"My sisters get on me about my pronouns." Goodale drowsily scratched his cleft chin. He was unshaven, and there was red and blond amid the brown stubble. In the sun his chest hair was equally vibrant. "You want to come aboard to ask your questions? Or do you want us to come over to you?"

"Where we are is fine," said Klesko.

Spinney was right about Bear Goodale being a piece of work. The same man who saw no harm in flying a Confederate flag endeavored to be politically correct in his speech. He was immune from cognitive dissonance. Was it possible he truly didn't see the offense he'd caused Garrett?

The breeze blew the smoke from Beckwith's mouth into my face. The tobacco must have been flavored. It carried a sickening sweetness.

The sun shone down on him, revealing raised red lines across his chin, cheekbones, and nose. I tried to think of what could have disfigured him in that way, from the eyes down. Some strange accident involving shards of glass? A knife fight that ended with the victor carving up his face?

"At this stage," said Klesko, "we're talking to everyone who was on or around Baker Island yesterday, trying to get an overview."

"That makes things simple, then," said Goodale. More and more, I was coming to think he was as thoroughly baked as grandma's fruitcake. "After our conversation with the warden, we motored back home. I worked on a stone wall I'm building around the old cemetery, had supper with my folks, then took the boat inshore to spend the night with a friend of mine. She'll tell you we were together. Her name's Brandi Waite; she lives in South Bristol."

"Did you see any boats lurking around Baker Island yesterday?"

"My territory is south and east of Ayers and out past the Brigands. I don't have any traps around Baker. I just go over there to see the girls."

I knew this to be a lie. Stacey and I had seen his orange buoys west of the seabird colony. But this was Klesko's interview, and I kept my mouth shut.

Goodale squeezed his nostrils between forefinger and thumb. "I keep thinking they're alive, you know. They were such cool chicks."

Spinney crossed his arms. "Good-looking, too."

Bear gave him a blank look. He seemed unsure how to read the remark. As an accusation?

"I had no cause to hurt those girls," he rasped. "I had nothing to do with their murders."

"What about you?" I asked Beckwith. "Where were you last night?"

"None of your business."

"What are you hiding, Blondie?" asked Spinney.

"Besides a ten-inch dick? Nothing."

"Knock it off, Chris," Bear snarled. "I've already told you I'm in no mood for your negativity today."

The sternman flicked his cigarillo away and reached into his back pocket for his smokes. They were Swisher Sweets. It was a brand I associated with thirteen-year-old boys who'd shoplifted them from variety stores.

"All right," Beckwith said. "I was in my apartment, alone, listening to some tunes and enjoying an adult beverage until I passed out. No one saw me, because no one was outside. It was fucking pouring, if you remember."

Klesko removed his own sunglasses to make eye contact with the lobstermen. The gesture seemed more a friendly courtesy than an invitation to a staredown. "Warden Bowditch told me about the show you put on for Garrett Meadows yesterday. It sounded deliberately offensive, playing that music, flying that flag. Do you have a personal problem with him or is it something else?"

Goodale shook his head with surprising violence. "You guys have got the wrong idea. Garrett needles us, and we needle him."

Beckwith chimed in. "He calls us 'Chowder Crackers.' How is that not racist?"

"It was all in good fun," said Bear, ignoring the leaner, meaner man.

"You think racial harassment is fun?"

The change in Spinney's demeanor puzzled me. He'd previously dismissed the possibility of softhearted Bear Goodale being involved in the murders. Now he was going out of his way to provoke the lobsterman.

Like his namesake, Bear wasn't easily provoked, but he seemed to be shaking off his stupor. "What about sexual harassment, Spinney? Rumors are you were hitting on that redheaded hottie. Don't pretend it's a lie, dude."

"Shut up."

"You should be ashamed, a man your age embarrassing himself that way."

I heard the squeaking of the fenders between the two boats, the sloshing of water out the scupper of the *Persuader,* and the thin cries of terns overhead.

A moment later, Rick Spinney vaulted over the adjacent gunwales and threw himself without warning on Bear Goodale.

Klesko and I were caught off guard. Spinney had surprised us with his quickness. We had to scramble over the bumping hulls. By the time we'd set foot on the *Persuader,* the two big men were engaged in a standing wrestling match that reminded me of an image you might see on a Grecian urn.

Spinney had managed to duck behind Bear and get him by his fat midsection, but the lobsterman wouldn't go down. He tried throwing a punch over his shoulder in the direction of his opponent's face but missed by inches. The Marine Patrol officer responded by snaking his right biceps around Goodale's thick neck. Spinney was trying to use a carotid hold that would cause near-instant unconsciousness. Like police elsewhere, Maine law enforcement officers had been prohibited from using choke holds.

"Break it up!" Klesko made it sound like it was a schoolyard scuffle.

But Spinney's sunglasses had come off, and there was murder in his too-small eyes.

I had assigned myself the job of watching Beckwith. He probably wasn't concealing a gun in those shorts. But a knife, maybe. And there was a shotgun inside the cabin. I'd glimpsed it the day before:

a Mossberg 590 Mariner with a pistol grip and a shining, corrosion-resistant barrel.

To my surprise, the sternman began howling with laughter.

Despite his lumbering slowness, Bear Goodale turned out to be a hell of a wrestler. With Spinney wrapped around his back, he managed to get his legs braced and his weight balanced. Then he fell forward, swinging the Marine Patrol officer around his torso like a sling bag and slamming him onto the deck with such force I was surprised Spinney's lungs didn't burst like balloons.

The lobsterman huffed. "Had enough? Had enough?"

Spinney's right hand moved in the direction of the sidearm on his belt. Before he could pull the pistol from the holster, Klesko stepped on his wrist.

"No, Rick."

"Get off me!"

"No, Rick. Not until you stop."

Spinney grabbed Klesko's ankle but couldn't move it. "What are you doing? Get off me!"

Bear Goodale was sitting in a puddle of salt water on the deck, breathing hard. He touched the corner of his eye where it had been gouged. His fingertip came away bloody.

Beckwith smoked quietly.

"It's over, understand?" said Klesko.

"I understand! But tell me you're going to arrest the motherfucker. Tell me that at least."

Slowly, the detective lifted his foot. "We're not arresting anyone, Rick. Not him. And not you."

Spinney rose to his knees, clutching his injured wrist with his uninjured hand. His collar had lost a button. And his ballcap lay in the same puddle in which his opponent was soaking. "He attacked me. You both saw it."

"That's not true, Rick," I said.

"He came after me!" said Bear. "Chris is my witness."

Klesko stepped between the two collapsed wrestlers, looking every inch the badass hockey player he'd been in college. "Bear, I need you to back off. And Rick, I want you to return to your boat. We're done here."

Spinney kept opening and closing his mouth, he was in such a state of disbelief. He clutched his wrist. "He assaulted a law enforcement officer."

"No, he didn't," I said.

He glared at me like I was a traitor to my country.

Klesko helped the unsteady lobsterman to his feet. "If I ask you to be at the Ayers Island wharf later—five o'clock sharp—you're not going to make a fool of me, right? I won't need to chase you?"

"Is fatso going to be there?" asked Goodale.

"Fucking right, I will be," said Spinney, snatching up his wet cap.

"We're not going to have a repeat of this," said Klesko firmly. "You have my word on that."

Beckwith was leaning against the cabin with his hands dug deep in the pockets of his shorts and a lopsided, mocking grin.

When we'd cast off and the waves were shoving us away from the *Persuader,* Klesko put his sunglasses on and leaned close to Spinney. "You're lucky I don't report you. I hope you appreciate what a violation that is of my personal code of ethics."

But Rick's glare was burning a hole in me. "I won't forget this."

He started the engines.

# 28

Spinney kept massaging his sore wrist while he steered the boat toward the islands.

"What you guys did, I would never have done to a fellow officer."

"I wasn't going to let you shoot him, Rick," said Klesko in a clear, penetrating voice.

"Don't use my first name. We're not friends, especially after today. I'll taxi you around because I was ordered to, but if we ever see each other off duty—"

"Do not finish that sentence, Rick," I said.

"Fuck you, Bowditch. Throwing me under the bus like that. You realize I'm going to be out here tomorrow and every day, and you won't be around the next time I stop the *Persuader* and decide that Bear Goodale needs to lose his license and a few teeth."

"There's another sentence you shouldn't have finished," I said, steadying myself against the Whaler's speed across the choppy water. "What's gotten into you, Rick? You're better than this shit."

"Am I?"

Between Ayers Island and its smaller neighbor, Hatchet Island, there was a sheltered channel, perhaps fifty yards wide, that served the residents as a harbor. A sailing yacht, the *Fūjin*, all gleaming mahogany and polished brass, was moored in the center of the passage. Nearby floated a gleaming Hinckley picnic boat, the *Solitude*, that must have cost a mint to commission.

The only other vessel in the "harbor" was a lobsterboat pulled alongside a half-submerged "lobster car," into which a fisherman was dumping his day's catch for safekeeping. He was a great ruddy man with a white goatee and scrolls of white hair falling down his sunburned neck. I felt certain this old salt was the person Stacey had mentioned: Skip Ayers, whose family had settled the island before the arrival of the granite magnates and celebrity photographers. The name of his boat was the *Frost Flower*.

"They pretend this is a working waterfront," said Spinney, "as if two lobsterboats make a fleet."

I was eager to be away from the man and his anger at a life that hadn't turned out the way he'd planned. Whose life ever does?

As we maneuvered past the yachts, I spotted Stacey's kayak tied to the backside of the wharf, bow to stern with the *Spindrift*. I'd wondered where that launch was hiding.

On the green hillside above the public landing was a cluster of houses, barns, and outbuildings, perhaps as many as twenty receding into the spruce forest that seemed, from the water, to cover most of the island. There were roads of a sort running between the buildings and down to the wharf, but they were not paved, and close-cut grass grew between the tire ruts. Each of the homesteads had bright, blooming gardens of daylilies—mostly orange and yellow—globe thistle, and coneflowers. Apple trees that must have been planted within the same year, being all the same height, but were not yet mature enough to yield decent fruit, grew along stone walls that were square and true; unlike most of the tumbled boundaries you find in the Maine woods, where farms and pastures are only memories of a long-vanished era.

The houses were boxy Colonials of the kind you see in northern New England fishing villages. They all had granite chimneys and were shingled with cedar shakes or clad in clapboards. Among the homes were a few smaller crofts constructed entirely of quarry stones. With sod roofs, these crude structures looked like they belonged on the coast of Scotland and not Maine.

It was one of the prettiest places I'd seen, and it was fake from start to finish: a Potemkin village.

A real lobstering town would have had stinking traps stacked in the yards to be repaired, coils of multicolor ropes, and buoys strung up on lines for repainting. There would have been busted appliances dragged out into the weather to rust and also lawn mowers abandoned in mid-mow while the homeowner took a coffee break, got drunk, or decided the job could wait.

Moreover, the place would have smelled—not unpleasantly, except near the traps. Diesel exhaust, baking bread, hot tar, paint, freshly laundered sheets flapping on lines: odors that carry the message, "This place is inhabited by human beings living their curious, wayward lives." But all my nose could detect from the shore were the blossoming flowers and the resinous evergreens on the hill above the town.

"This place looks like a movie set," said Klesko, as if reading my mind.

"Here come a few of the extras now," said Spinney.

The sound of his engine had lured a handful of souls from their houses. I wouldn't have been surprised to see them in nineteenth-century costumes, but they wore the same blue jeans, tees, and coveralls you'd see inside any Walmart.

Where was Stacey?

One young guy was wearing a short-sleeve neoprene wetsuit, the kind favored by long-distance swimmers, and drying his blond hair with a towel.

"*Hola!*" he said, giving himself away as a nonnative Spanish speaker in one word.

Spinney said, "You still swimming around the islands, Heath?"

The man kept drying his locks. He had a too-white smile. "Every day. Got to be ready for the qualifier."

"You must have heard there are great white sharks off the Maine coast."

"We have them back in San Diego, too."

"In that wetsuit, you couldn't look more like a gray seal if you tried. Those are their favorite snacks."

"If a shark bites me, a shark bites me. Life happens. No point thinking too hard."

This Heath character was the only one who seemed jovial. The other islanders carried their sadness like a weight.

In all, seven people met us at the wharf.

The man who caught Spinney's bowline and tied it off looked to be pushing sixty with a belly that reminded me of Bear Goodale's. He wore his receding hair in a ponytail, and his face was heavily stubbled. His outfit consisted of boat shoes with holes in the toes, a loose cotton shirt unbuttoned to the sternum, and bell-bottomed jeans fraying at the hems.

"We've been expecting you, Rick," he said in a perfect imitation of Bear's voice.

"What's that supposed to mean?"

"We heard the detectives were coming over from Baker. And it made sense that a Marine Patrol boat would bring them. You're the local patrol officer so it stands to reason . . ."

Spinney spat into the harbor.

Klesko and I introduced ourselves, and the man gave his name as Jonathan Goodale as he extended a calloused hand.

"And this is my wife, Lisa," he said.

Bear's mother was a tall woman, six feet at least. Her hair was brown, streaked with gray, and cut shorter than her husband's, but she was dressed in similarly worn jeans and a sleeveless top that revealed a lifetime of sun damage below her neck and on muscled brown arms.

"We heard what happened," she said. "I have always been afraid for those researchers, being so young and isolated."

"Maeve is *old*," said a little Goodale girl. She had to be the one Stacey had spoken with: Juniper.

I wondered exactly what the islanders knew of the killings. Little Juniper, at least, didn't seem to know that McLeary was dead. I had a hunch, from their blank expressions when Maeve's name was invoked, that the adults hadn't heard about her suicide, either.

"If there's anything we can do to help," said Lisa Goodale.

Klesko nodded kindly. "We appreciate your cooperation."

"Do you know why he killed them?"

The voice had come from the back of the wharf.

"*He?*" Klesko said.

"Garrett Meadows."

I recognized the speaker immediately, although I'd only glimpsed the captain of the *Spindrift* from a distance. Stacey had identified him as Justin Speer. He was of medium height but so long in the torso it gave him the illusion of being tall. The plastic brim of his swordfishing cap was cocked above a smug face that narrowed to a pointed chin.

"We heard some lobsterman found him adrift," Speer said. "Did he have some sort of psychotic break like the kid did last summer?"

*The kid? Does he mean Evan Levandowski?*

"I wouldn't put stock in what you're hearing over your radios," said Klesko. "We haven't named any suspects."

Justin snorted in disbelief. "Oh, I'm sure it's a coincidence that Meadows survived."

Lisa Goodale scowled at Speer. "Who's to say that young man wasn't also a victim? Is it because of the color of his skin, Justin, that you assume he had to be the one who murdered those girls?"

"I hope you're not accusing my husband of being a racist, Lisa," said a young woman with brown bangs and a tiny bundle in her arms. Brenna Speer wore blue overalls and leather sandals.

"I'm trying to explain why the police might be reluctant to immediately name a Black man as a suspect."

Listening to the islanders debate, I formed the idea that these were mostly educated people. Nor did they have a trace of the Maine accent I would've heard on any of the state's working waterfronts.

Klesko stepped forward, assuming an attitude of command that even I found intimidating.

"Folks, I know you're upset by what you've heard, much of which I guarantee isn't true. Please keep in mind that it's early in our investigation. We have forensic technicians on Baker Island collecting evidence that will be carefully examined. We'll also be conducting interviews to get a fuller picture of the situation at the refuge prior to the attacks. That's why Warden Bowditch and I are here—to speak with you."

"I can't imagine what we'd be able to contribute," said big-bellied Jonathan Goodale. There was something of the Key West barfly about the sloppy, sunburned man. He had the squint of someone who'd spent years at sea, and his leathery skin would have given a dermatologist nightmares.

"You didn't know any of the staff there?" I asked.

No one spoke at first. I noticed Jonathan take and squeeze Juniper's hand.

"Maeve McLeary has visited Ayers over the years," Lisa Goodale said carefully. "But the other researchers . . ."

*"Over the years,"* I thought. *Not "yesterday." Why would they play dumb about Maeve just having been here?*

Lies are like mice, I have found. Where there's one, there are always many.

Spinney had remained standing beside his boat with his thick arms crossed the whole time. I'd almost forgotten about him until he said, "They haven't had time to get the official story straight."

"What is that supposed to mean?" asked Justin Speer.

"Your lord and lady haven't told you what you're supposed to say."

The islanders fell silent again.

Heath, the worry-free swimmer, laughed and threw his towel over his shoulder and began striding up the grassy hill as if none of this concerned him. I felt an impulse to call the man to task. But I had no authority to do so.

"We're not Clay Markham's serfs," said Jonathan Goodale. "Whatever people might say about us on the mainland."

His wife jumped in. "And as someone who's been here as much as you have, Rick Spinney, it's shameful for you to be repeating that kind of slander."

"Officer," he said. "Officer Spinney."

"Oh, please," said Justin Speer. "Get over yourself."

Spinney pointed his index finger at Speer. "Don't."

"Or what? You'll arrest me?"

"I'm only telling you once."

"Hey, Justin, be cool," said Jonathan Goodale. "The officers are just doing their jobs. Don't take it personally."

"I have a question," I said, hoping a change of subject would restore order. "The woman who paddled here for help, Stacey Stevens. Where is she? I see her kayak tied up to the dock. I believe she was waiting for us at the Ayers's house."

"Oh, she's up at the manse now," said Brenna Speer. "When Clay heard a woman had come here from Baker, he sent a cart for her."

And Stacey, being Stacey, had jumped at the chance to meet the legendary photographer.

"Mr. Speer, we'd like to speak with you first," said Klesko, removing his windbreaker and folding it over his arm so that the gun on his belt was in plain view. "I have a feeling you know why that is. Somewhere private would be best."

"That's my place right there." He indicated the second house up from the water. It had a magnificent flower garden. "We can talk in my studio. It's a little cramped. *Officer* Spinney will have to wait outside."

# 29

Justin Speer's photography studio was in one of the Neolithic-looking buildings I'd spotted from the channel. It had four stone walls and a turf roof. He wasn't lying about the quarters being tight.

Fortunately for everyone, Spinney had no interest in sitting in on the interview, maybe because he'd concluded there was nothing new to be learned. Instead, he'd asked, in a tone that sounded more like a demand, that Jonathan Goodale show him around the new Hinckley in the harbor. The elder Goodale, I gathered, captained both the sailing yacht and the picnic boat for Clay Markham.

To say the studio consisted of a single room would be both true and false, for in one corner was a darkroom partition, created by suspending heavy black curtains from the timbers overhead. It was cool in the stone house, although a pungent metallic odor threatened to choke us until Speer opened a window.

"You develop your own film," I said, between coughs.

Speer grabbed the only stool in the room, leaving Klesko and me to stand. "I wouldn't be a real photographer if I didn't."

"Not a fan of digital?" said the detective.

He had leaned against the door as if to indicate that no one would be going out or coming in until we'd finished our discussion. His expression remained friendly, relaxed. There was nothing threatening in his affect, but the message was unmistakable. He was in charge.

Speer removed his long-brimmed cap, a tuft of greasy hair standing upright on his head. He was oblivious to the comic display he made. His stained T-shirt fit tightly around his elongated torso. I realized now what he reminded me of: a weasel.

"Everyone thinks they're a photographer these days," said Justin Speer as if returning to a former conversation we'd never had. "Fucking smartphones."

"You sound like a man with a grudge," I said.

"Computers are incapable of reflecting the real world," he said bitterly. "I don't know how much you know about the history of photography, but the first modern cameras—created by Louis Daguerre—literally captured light on silver-treated plates. There was no intermediating device. Digital cameras translate reality into ones and zeros and then re-create it as an essentially false image."

Klesko brandished his smartphone. "The pictures I take on this look true enough to me."

"You're talking about facsimiles of truth rather than objective truth. With digital cameras, the computer has already manipulated the image, because it has, by definition, *created* the image, even before you see it."

Through the open window came the unexpected sound of a goat bleating. I hadn't noticed livestock before, but it explained how the islanders kept the grass short.

"You sound like a philosopher," I said.

He sighed and waved a long hand in the air. "I get it—you're indulging me with these questions. Because you know I was taking pictures of the researchers at Baker Island, and that inevitably makes me suspicious if not a suspect. They probably called me a stalker. I know you were the one who hailed me on the radio yesterday, Warden."

"Why didn't you respond?"

His laugh echoed off the hard walls. "And say what? You knew perfectly well that my boat wasn't in distress. You wanted to scare me off, but I was already done shooting for the day. I indulged you by leaving."

"Why were you taking pictures of the researchers?"

"Because I'm a pervert, naturally." He let the silence stretch as if it were elastic; I waited for the inevitable snap.

"Is that a confession?" I asked.

"Hardly!" Then he said mysteriously, "Who watches the watchers?"

"Is that a line from a movie I should have seen?" asked Klesko.

"My professional interest is in the experience of the uncanny," Speer said, growing animated. "You've heard the word before, right? You probably think *uncanny* just means *strange,* but it's more than that. The term describes the psychological discomfort of encountering a seemingly familiar person or object in a confusing context. Like seeing a mannequin that looks a little too lifelike. Or a person with a glass eye that doesn't move in concert with the natural one. 'That creeps me out,' a person will say, but they can't explain why the experience creeps them out."

"Mr. Speer, you have an unusual way of not answering simple questions," said the detective. "Our time is limited, you understand."

"Justin is getting to his point," I said. "He needs us to understand some things first."

Speer looked at me with a quizzical expression, unsure whether I followed his zigzagging line of conversation or was merely mocking him.

"When a person says someone is creepy," he explained, "it's because they're struggling with an ambiguous situation that might or might not be dangerous. It's a survival instinct that doesn't have much use in the modern world. Psychologists have done studies. For instance, one of the things that most unnerves us is a person silently watching."

"I don't need a psychologist to tell me that," said Klesko.

Speer struck me as someone used to giving monologues and was exasperated by these interruptions. "But it's not just the strange man on the street staring at you. It's any kind of silent watching. Psychologists have found that even a harmless hobby like bird-watching creeps out a lot of people. It provokes the experience of the uncanny valley, where we feel threatened without knowing why. Here, these will explain what I mean."

He reached for a leather portfolio and unzipped it and removed a series of black-and-white photographs. He handed the top one to me.

The picture showed Kendra Ballard outlined atop a hummock on the island, as if she had paused while crossing the ridge. She was staring into Speer's camera with her binoculars half-raised, about to train the lenses on the photographer. Her brow was knitted, her mouth was drawn taut.

I passed the first photo to Klesko while I examined the second. This one had caught Garrett Meadows unaware, studying a laughing gull posed on a rock. The gull was looking out to sea.

I began to understand something of what Speer was saying. The photographer was watching the birder who was watching the bird, which was watching God only knew what. The image was a meditation on the act of observation.

The third photo was of Hillary Fitzgerald and Kendra Ballard hanging laundry on a line in a brisk wind. The two women had stopped to gaze directly at Speer's unblinking camera. There was nothing remotely lurid about the image, but it sent chills up my spine.

"Memento mori," I said.

"But not intentionally so! I didn't know they were going to be killed. I was merely trying to provoke a response."

"In them or us?" asked Klesko. "Because it certainly weirds me out."

"You know they were murdered, but I believe you would have had a similar response even if you didn't possess that knowledge."

"Who watches the watchers?" I said.

"Exactly!"

I knew Justin Speer would appreciate being quoted.

Klesko passed back the photograph in his hand. I was struck again by how weary my friend, the new father, looked. "Let me get this straight. You were going over there and taking pictures as part of some sort of art project?"

"It was paramount that I not speak to them. They couldn't know why I was there or what I was doing, or they wouldn't react honestly."

I could see Klesko's growing frustration; he had passed the point where he might have endured an elliptical conversation.

"Where were you last night, Justin?"

"Home with Brenna and the baby."

"What size shoes do you wear?" the detective asked next.

Speer couldn't help but glance at his sandals. "Tens. Sometimes ten and a halfs. Sometimes even elevens. Why?"

"We found prints on the island that didn't belong to any of the researchers."

"Garrett Meadows told me he saw you rowing away from the island one morning at dawn," I added. "He believed you were looking to come ashore or maybe already had."

"What? I had no reason to land on the island. It was imperative that I not communicate with them."

"So you say," said Klesko.

"I have never set foot on Baker Island, not once in my life," he said. "And Brenna will tell you I was home all night. Both of us were up at times with the baby. I'm a photographer. It was raining! Why would I have gone there in a storm? Hook me up to a polygraph if you doubt I'm telling the truth."

The man was so arrogant I couldn't resist needling him. "I thought you didn't trust machines to tell the truth. Or does that only apply to cameras?"

Speer slid off the stool, causing it to wobble, and advanced on Klesko.

"My boots are in the house. You're welcome to take them to examine. You can take my fingerprints and a DNA sample while you're at it. I won't hide behind a lawyer because I have nothing to hide."

"We'll take you up on the offer," said Klesko. "I'll tell a member of our Evidence Response Team to pay you a visit. There's one last thing, though."

"Yes?"

"What do you do here when you're not taking pictures of strangers without their consent?"

The remark brought color to Speer's pointed face. "I'm Clay Markham's chief photographic assistant. Seven years ago, he saw an exhibit of my work at the Center for Maine Contemporary Art and invited Brenna and me to come live on the island. He was a terrific teacher at first. Less so recently. I've outgrown him, you see. Now I assume you'll want to check my quote-unquote alibi for last night. I'll take you to Brenna, who will verify everything I've told you."

Klesko opened the door. "We appreciate your cooperation."

# 30

Brenna Speer vouched for her husband's whereabouts the night before. She knew every hour he'd arisen to pick up their crying baby. Their practice was to take turns, she said.

Klesko and I spoke to her in their tidy kitchen. Her husband, knowing he wasn't invited to sit in on our interview, had wandered off on some unspecified errand. She made us coffee—never have I welcomed a cup more—and sat across an antique dining room table from us, openly nursing her baby, a little boy. I found the sight of her bare breast and the sound of the infant sucking away discomfiting. I hadn't imagined I would be squeamish about something so natural.

Being a new father himself, Klesko took it in stride. "What's his name?"

In the dim kitchen, with only natural light from the windows, dark circles had appeared beneath the new mother's eyes. She hadn't washed her hair in days.

"Leo. Justin wanted to go all the way with Leonardo, after his hero—the artist, not the actor—but I put my foot down. Repeatedly. He can be very persistent, as I'm sure you have discovered."

"Where did you two meet?" Klesko often peppered his interrogations with friendly inquiries to keep the subject off-balance.

"The Rhode Island School of Design. He was studying photography. I was studying painting."

It was the same college Levandowski had attended—although the Speers were a decade older than Evan had been when he died.

I had noticed some small watercolors on the wall. "Are those yours?"

"No, I stopped painting years ago when I realized that I didn't have the gift. When I was young, my parents had friends whose daughter wanted to be an opera singer. They sent her to all the best schools in Europe and paid for her living expenses in Milan and Naples. But as good as she was, she lacked that special something. And sadly, she couldn't bring herself to admit the truth. Maybe her parents couldn't, either. I decided I never wanted to be a mediocre opera singer, never wanted to be that woman. Justin is the one with the special talent, and I am content being his helpmate."

I leaned my elbows on the creaking table. "What do you think of his series of photographs of the Baker Island scientists?"

"They're genius. And it's a shame he'll never be able to show them now."

"What do you mean?" asked Klesko.

"No respectable gallery would put on an exhibit of pictures of people who'd been murdered. Clay was pilloried for *Children in Their Caskets,* and his models were only pretending to be dead."

"The pillorying couldn't have hurt too much," I said. "Wasn't there a bestselling book published of those photos?"

"Sometimes books sell because the media is obsessed with a scandal and everyone is talking about it. Mapplethorpe, back in the 1980s, for instance. Jesse Helms should have gotten a cut of the profits from the sales of Mapplethorpe's portraits."

"I'm sorry," interrupted Klesko, "but I'm not up on contemporary art. What is *Children in Their Caskets*?"

When she laughed, I saw she had a fetching gap between her front teeth. "I can imagine how the name of that series must sound out of context."

Brenna then gave us a quick description of the exhibit and the ensuing firestorm that put Clay Markham back on the cover of *Time* magazine, after decades.

"The series he's doing now is titled *My Atrocities,*" she said. "I haven't seen any of the images, and Justin won't tell me the details. Clay made him sign a new nondisclosure agreement, in addition to the others we've both previously signed. Justin will only say that the new photographs make *Children* look like Norman Rockwell images."

"Do you have a copy of Markham's book from that coffin exhibition?" Klesko glanced around as if it might be sitting on a countertop or the flour-dusted sideboard.

"God, no!" Then, seeing that her answer puzzled us, she added, "Justin was Clay's primary assistant on those shoots. That project dominated every aspect of our life, our first year here. I did the makeup on the kids. It was fun at the time. We all laughed like it was some parlor game. Then I saw the photos Clay took, and I've never been more terrified in my life. It was like a fortune-teller had foreseen the hour of my death. I never, ever need to see Echo Goodale playing dead again in a coffin."

Klesko's phone rang. He excused himself to take the call, which, I had a feeling, was either from his wife or the attorney general, or maybe the medical examiner, since there was no one else whom he would've allowed to interrupt an interrogation.

I am usually fine at making small talk, not great but fine. But while Brenna and I were alone, I found myself at a loss for words. She watched me with such intense concentration.

"So you and Stacey are a couple?" she said after a spell.

"Why do you say that?"

"Justin saw you and she together on Baker. When I saw her come ashore here, I was thinking we must be close to the same age. Ayers Island is a lonely place to be a young woman. Skip and Dorothea Ayers are so ancient and not what you would call intellectuals. The Goodales are free-spirited, theatrical people. Even if one of the girls was older, I doubt we'd connect. That leaves Clay and his wife, Alyce. The Markhams had fascinating lives and tell great stories, but they're not the kind of people you invite over for burgers and beers. As for Clay's personal assistants, the less said the better."

With Klesko gone, she'd let her guard down. I decided to capitalize on the opportunity. "Is that guy Heath one of Markham's assistants?"

"He works up at the manse, yes."

A goat bleated outside the window. It sounded like a lamb that had lost sight of its mother.

"It must be weird for you," Brenna said.

"What must be weird?"

"Being a game warden caught up in this. You must be used to working in the North Woods. You must feel out of your element here, on an incestuous offshore island like Ayers."

"I've worked on an offshore island before. And there are plenty of incestuous villages in the North Woods, too."

Brenna showed me her fetching smile again. "Ayers isn't as uniquely peculiar as I'd thought, then."

"It's not like anyplace else I've been in Maine. I'll say that for it. But I'm interested in hearing why you describe the island as incestuous."

Without breaking eye contact, she detached her infant from her breast. "I've already said too much. I'll be stoned to death if I share any of my neighbors' actual secrets with you. There may only be a dozen or so people living on this rock, but we're a diverse cast of characters, I'll say that much for us."

"Who'd throw the first stone?"

"Nice try."

"How about this, then. Did you speak with Maeve McLeary when she was here yesterday?"

The question caught her off guard. She pursed her lips and turned her attention to the baby. I could sense her thoughts quickening.

"She only ever comes here to speak with Clay and Alyce. The rest of us don't interest her, not being rich enough to support her puffin research. I saw her walk past the house on her way up the hill, but that was all."

"Did you see her again when she left?"

"No."

"Did you mark the time you heard her boat leave the harbor?"

"Why would I have done that?"

Now I felt guilty to be grilling Brenna in Klesko's absence. The chance had presented itself, I would tell him in my defense. What was I to do?

"Speaking of boats," I said, "does the *Spindrift* belong to you and Justin, or has he been borrowing it from someone else?"

Another careful pause as, like a chess player, her mind explored every possible move and countermove.

"It's Alyce Markham's boat," she said at last. "Her personal runabout. But she lets anyone use it who wants to—almost anyone— since she rarely takes it out anymore. The keys are in a lockbox down at the wharf. But everyone knows the combination."

"Who else has been using it lately, aside from your husband?"

"I'm not sure I would know."

*Interesting turn of phrase.*

"You haven't seen anyone other than Justin driving the *Spindrift* in the last week?"

"If I did, I can't remember."

Klesko appeared in the doorway, the phone still pressed to his ear, and beckoned to me. Clearly something pressing had come up. More pressing than our interview.

"Thank you for your time, Brenna," I said. "Detective Klesko and his partner might have more questions for you and Justin. But I imagine you don't have plans to leave the island."

She put the infant against her shoulder. "We were just discussing that subject this morning. But no, we're not going anywhere—not today at least."

"I would plan on sticking around the island until the detectives conduct all of their interviews. It'll be easier if they don't need to chase after you and Justin with any additional questions they might have."

"Speaking of plans," she said, patting the infant's back.

"Yes?"

"I don't know who you and the detective are planning on interrogating next. But I would recommend you hike up to the manse, and not just because your girlfriend's there. The Markhams think they know everything that goes on among us 'cottagers,' but they don't, not by a long shot. That said, you're never going to begin to understand our little hamlet until you speak with the lord and lady of Ayers Island, as your friend Spinney called them."

# 31

When we were outside and clear of the house, Klesko told me about his phone call with the new attorney general.

"She said that Santum just talked to a TV reporter outside Lincoln-Health in Damariscotta—that's the old Miles Hospital. It's where Garrett Meadows is being treated. He's going to be fine, but the docs have him sedated, so he won't be giving a statement anytime soon."

A great swarm of honeybees buzzed about us as if we'd been standing too close to a hive. They seemed especially drawn to the hollyhocks that spired over our heads. The bleating goats had drifted up the hill.

"What did the sheriff say?"

Klesko waved his big hands in the air angrily. The sudden cloud of bees seemed the manifestation of his annoyance.

"That the police had a suspect in the homicides, currently under guard by one of his deputies, but there was no cause for concern among Lincoln County residents."

"He can't do that."

"Obviously, he still thinks Meadows is the perp, evidence be damned, and wants to claim the credit for his apprehension," Klesko said. "He's screwed us in ways I wouldn't have thought anatomically possible. The attorney general is livid. She's been forced to call a news conference in Augusta with the command staff, your colonel, and the Lincoln County DA to clarify the the sheriff's limited role in our investigation. She wanted me there, too, but I talked her down. What a fucking shit show."

"Santum's going to find his department isolated after this. The next time Lincoln County calls for mutual aid—"

"All he cares about is getting on camera as the face of law and order. Santum is defining himself as David against the Goliath of the new administration. He'll be running for governor in three years. Just wait and see."

It felt surreal to know about all the frantic phone calls flying around the state capital, while on Ayers Island, the day couldn't have been more idyllic. The sky empty of clouds, the air hot but with just enough of a sea breeze to make it comfortable, green, growing things everywhere, and the high-pitched shouts of the youngest Goodale children jumping from the wharf into the shiver-inducing sea.

My friend was worried that he would be blamed for Santum's misdeeds—and rightly so since the AG would claim he should have warned her the sheriff might go rogue. I felt blessed not to have Steve Klesko's personal ambition. All I cared about was finding the person who had murdered Kendra and Hillary, nearly killed Garrett, and precipitated Maeve's suicide.

"Maybe we should go over what we learned from the Speers," I offered.

He rubbed sweat from the back of his neck. "What did we learn?"

"That the evidence doesn't just point in Justin's direction," I said. "It completely incriminates him. He assisted Markham with that series of photos taken of kids pretending to be dead. He's been stalking the researchers on Baker, getting to know their routines. Killing Kendra and Hillary and taking pictures of their corpses seems like the inevitable next step in his ghoulish career."

Klesko was recovering his composure. "Speer seems smart enough to know we'd focus on him."

"That's what I mean. It's one thing to pose the bodies. It's another thing to leave them positioned that way when you're done snapping pictures."

"So you're saying he did everything he could to incriminate himself, because he trusted we'd never believe anyone would be that

stupid? That's putting a lot of faith in our intelligence as police investigators."

"Justin strikes me as the type of guy who overthinks everything."

He touched his dented nose in amusement. "I couldn't tell if he
was legitimately smart or just full of shit. Did you understand what
he meant by digital mediation and the uncanny valley?"

"Not really."

"Bullshit," he said, showing a hint of a smile at last. "You want
everyone you work with to forget you graduated with honors from
Colby. I'm glad to have a partner who's smarter than me."

His use of the word *partner* touched me. Despite our friendship,
I had worried he viewed me as someone he'd been stuck with. I was
the Department of Inland Fisheries & Wildlife's unwelcome proxy.

"I'm talking about Delphine Cruz," he added.

"Oh."

He smiled even more widely, giving me a view of his gray tooth.
"Sorry, Mike, but I couldn't resist."

"Now I feel like I have to prove myself. If Speer committed those
murders, he had one hell of an accomplice. Brenna only slipped
once while I was interviewing her. After you'd left the house, I got
her to admit Maeve McLeary visited the island yesterday, in case
we need additional confirmation. I should have waited until you
returned, but I saw an opening and went for it."

"Tell me at least you got her on tape."

"I thought she'd be more carefree if we seemed to be chatting," I
said sheepishly. "But she won't deny having said it."

"How can you say that with certainty?"

"Because she's smarter than her husband, and she knows that
we'll find others who will confirm McLeary was here. Brenna said
our next interview should be with Clay and Alyce Markham, and I
agree. I am one hundred percent positive Maeve came here to solicit
funds from them."

"That's another unproven assumption, buddy."

"Hear me out. Hours after McLeary leaves Ayers Island, someone
attacks and/or kills her staff. What if our assailant went to Baker
looking for McLeary?"

"He would have noticed her boat wasn't at the mooring."

"Not if he anchored off the south end and tied up to that secret mooring ball."

He shook his head with sadness that might or might not have been feigned. "You're incorrigible, Mike. You are utterly unable or unwilling to rein in your imagination."

"Maybe, but you have to agree that McLeary's relationship with the Markhams is something we can't ignore."

"I don't intend to ignore it. But unlike you, I am doing my best to keep an open mind."

I didn't disdain his methods or fail to see the wisdom behind them. But I was used to bouncing suppositions off my warden friends—and now, Stacey—and I had achieved good results in my career. Why should I apologize for doing things the Mike Bowditch way?

"Hasn't it bothered you that, aside from Speer's fascination with haunting photos, we haven't come close to finding a motive?"

"Locate means and opportunity first. Motive after. That was what Soctomah taught me."

"My mind isn't that orderly."

"You're telling me. But yeah, it makes sense to interview the Markhams next, given that this is their island. Is it a coincidence that you want to make a beeline for the place where Stacey is waiting for us?"

"I need to see her, Steve."

He put his strong hand on my shoulder. "That's the most honest thing you've said all day, partner."

We followed a grass road that led up the hill through a field of faded lupines that the goats were eating their way through. I'd read that lupines are poisonous to sheep but the toxins have no effect on the cast-iron stomachs of goats. We paused at a curve and looked down at the village. The channel was sparkling like a broken blue bottle in the sun. I noticed my kayak tied to the wharf behind Stacey's, but the Marine Patrol boat was nowhere to be seen.

"Where did Spinney go?"

"He texted to say he was going to swing around the islands and check some lobsterboats. If it helps him blow off steam, I'll be glad. But I don't envy the fishermen he stops this afternoon."

"He used to be a good officer." I realized I kept making excuses for a man I no longer recognized.

"The job takes a toll on even the best of us, and if it doesn't, it probably means you're not taking it seriously enough. What's this I hear about Rick losing his family?"

The word *family* brought me up short.

"Can you hang on a second?" I said. "I just realized I need to make a call."

Klesko glanced around for a place to sit and located a storm-toppled balsam in the cool shadows along the tree line. I was going to warn him to watch out for pitch, but I was too late. When he pressed his hand carelessly against the trunk, it stuck to the bark. His palm came away black when he succeeded in pulling it loose.

The call I made was a video chat with Logan Cronk, the boy who tended to Shadow while I was away.

Logan was eleven, and his greatest wish was that the wolf hybrid would accept him as a friend. I alone could touch Shadow without fear. He welcomed me scratching him under the chin and between the ears, but I never forgot he was no domestic dog.

I reached Logan at my house. Whenever I went away and put him in charge of Shadow's care and feeding, he would pitch a tent outside the fenced enclosure in which the animal lived. I'd begun bringing the wolf into the house on select occasions, having built a kennel run between the pen and my back door for that purpose. But I forbade Logan Cronk from entering the enclosure.

"Hi, Uncle Mike!"

Logan was a big blond boy with eyelashes so pale he seemed not to possess them. He'd recently been afflicted with acne. I felt sympathetic pain to see his red, pimpled face looming in close-up on my phone.

"How's he doing, Logan?"

"He misses you."

"How do you know that?"

"I can *sense* it."

The boy had begun to imagine that he was establishing a psychic bond with the wolf. I was trying to disabuse him of these fantasies, but what could I do? Logan was eleven years old. Wild animals, I'd explained, were unknowable, which is why we couldn't domesticate them.

"Yeah, but cavemen tamed wolves back in the Ice Age," he'd argued. "That's how they became dogs."

"There's a difference between domesticated and tame. The process took generations upon generations, Logan, and even today, there are domestic dogs that behave unpredictably and aggressively."

"But Shadow lets you touch him now. Maybe he's domesticating superfast."

As I said, he was eleven, and there was no combatting his wishful thinking.

"Can I see him?" I said.

"Sure!"

Logan held the camera up to the wire and started calling for Shadow, who, I could see, was lying beneath a leafy birch inside the pen.

"Hey, bud," I said, trying to make myself heard through the speaker. "How's it going?"

The wolf swiveled his ears. Then he put his chin back down on his paws.

"You're pissed at me for going away and not being allowed inside the house. I get it."

Shadow turned his head and focused his yellow eyes at the screen Logan was pressing against the fence. Suddenly, the wolf arose and padded toward the phone. I heard Logan gulp down an excited breath.

I continued to speak conversationally: "I should be home tonight, very late, I'm guessing."

Some biologists have claimed that domestic dogs can learn or recognize upward of 250 words, and wolves are generally more intelligent than other canines. I didn't want to flatter myself into believing he understood me. I tried to keep a clinical detachment from my own wishes.

Shadow drew closer to the fence. For an instant, I thought he might lick the wire with his obscenely long tongue.

"I know I've stood you up before, but this time, I promise to come home," I said.

He twitched his black nose. He stared into the camera with that wild wolfish intensity I'd gotten to know so well.

And then he squatted down to take a dump.

"Gross!" Logan staggered back from the fence.

Meanwhile, a voice in my head was saying, *Shadow knew every goddamned thing you said to him.*

I thanked Logan again for being such a truly excellent caretaker and signed off, promising to text or call again later. Then I recounted what the wolf had just done to Klesko, who was having no success rubbing the sap from his hands. Immediately, his frustrated face lightened, and he burst into laughter.

"I guess he showed you."

"I can't afford to think that way. I always have to remember how dangerous he is."

"Why?"

"Because he might hurt me or someone else."

"You have a special bond with that animal, Mike. He trusts you. Maybe you should do the same."

"You sound like Stacey."

"Are you ready to face the Markhams?"

"Ready as I'll ever be."

After our brief rest and the diversion of the wolf, it was unreal how fast the grim reality returned.

Someone had bludgeoned Kendra Ballard and Hillary Fitzgerald to death and came close to murdering Garrett Meadows, too, and there were good reasons to suspect that person was on the island at this very moment.

As it climbed, the road ran in a straight line between parallel rows of cellar holes. These rectangular depressions in the earth were the cracked and sometimes fire-blackened foundations of vanished buildings, and they were now overgrown with raspberries, ragweed, and multiflora rose—plants that recovered quickly from the goats' predations.

Most of the ruins were small and square, clearly single-family homes, but a few were long enough to have been a church or a schoolhouse. Looking closely, I perceived amid the vegetation the rusted remnants of church pews and child-size desks left to decay. Grassy avenues, lined with yet more dugouts, ran off from the main road where there had once been actual streets. Without intention, we had wandered into a ghost town.

"It looks like there was quite a settlement here once," said Klesko, who knew even less than I did about the island apparently.

I found myself speaking softly, out of respect for ghosts in which I did not believe. "It was called Ayerstown. I guess this is where the miners lived who worked in the quarry across the channel."

My gaze wandered in the direction of Hatchet Island. I could not see a single building there, just a dark forest and granite cliffs rising to a bare summit. Spruces grew wherever there was a toehold for them to take root, and many of the boughs were strung with old-man's beard lichen.

The quarry must have been on the far side of the island, I realized. Hatchet Island appeared to be a fog-soaked place where trees toppled in storms and rocks fell unpredictably from the heights. It didn't surprise me that the original miners had chosen Ayers to make their village.

"How did the workers get across?" Klesko asked.

"I assume there was a ferry on a rope line."

"Weird they didn't build the town there."

"Does it look like a place you'd want to raise your family?"

"Good point."

"The Brooklyn Bridge contains Hatchet Island granite."

"It's nice to know a Colby history degree comes in handy for something."

"Actually, it was Stacey who told me this last night at supper," I said. "What did you major in at the University of Maine? You've never told me."

"Hockey. But I must have taken some actual courses because they gave me a piece of paper with a gold seal."

Past the vanished village, we glimpsed the old graveyard of Ayerstown. It was clearly a workers' cemetery, since there were no great monuments to rich and powerful men, just granite stones crusted with lichen. The elements had blurred if not erased the names of the dead from most of them. But I could easily imagine the buried bones of quarrymen crushed beneath ten-ton blocks or blown up in explosions; the remains of their wives who'd perished in childbirth; and the skeletons of their children, dead from disease.

"Children in their caskets."

Klesko paused. "What did you say?"

"I wonder if Clay Markham got the idea for his photo series from wandering among these graves."

Three goats wandered blithely past to finish their lawn mowing. We moved up the hill.

Soon the spruce forest closed in again on the road, the air became cool and fragrant with the sweetness of budding evergreens. In the distance a cock pheasant squawked. The Markhams must have brought the gamebirds over to hunt.

Pollen-dusted sunlight shimmered between the trunks of the trees ahead. And we emerged onto a vast lawn from which rose a clapboard mansion. In design, it resembled the homes in the village taken to extreme proportions. It stood three stories tall, with two small windmills, solar panels, and another rooftop array consisting of what looked like rows of pipes.

"That's a solar water heater," Klesko explained, before I could ask the question. "It was engineering, by the way. My degree from the University of Maine."

The mansion was part of a compound of buildings designed seemingly by the same architect: a four-bay car garage, a barn big enough to host a square dance, a stable, guest cottages larger than my house, assorted faux historic structures.

Two blond men were tending to the landscaping. Heath was whacking weeds along a stone wall. The other, whom I hadn't met, was heading toward an apple orchard with a limb pruner over his shoulder. Both were young, slim, tanned, and dressed in an informal uniform of navy polos and shorts.

"Does Markham only hire blonds?" I asked.

"How much do you know about the sexual assault accusation against him?"

"Only that the guy who made it conveniently died of an overdose before he could be deposed or sell his story to the tabloids."

"It wasn't convenient for the man who died."

"You know what I mean, Steve."

"Menario was assigned the case, before it fell apart, and said it was true, but he always believed that about crimes where the alleged perpetrators were gay or bisexual. You have to figure that a man like Markham, who is already so notorious, would be an easy mark for wannabe blackmailers and extortionists."

Someone must have been spying on us from the house because the double doors opened, and Stacey came running out.

She had showered and changed into a fresh outfit. It seemed to be a version of the uniform worn by Markham's houseboys: navy polo and shorts. Only the frayed Chuck Taylors were hers.

"I thought you'd never get here!"

"We stopped at the pub for a couple of pints."

"You mock," she said, slowing to a walk, "but the Markhams

brought an actual brewer to live on the island. He moved off last winter, but he left barrels behind of a damned good IPA."

I opened my arms, and she stepped into them. Her hair smelled of an unfamiliar, honey-scented shampoo. As she pressed herself into me, I felt her shiver, and I knew it was because she was struggling to hide her grief.

"What is this place?" I whispered.

"A garden of earthly delights," she said softly. "So beautiful and so horrible."

Her answer made me want to see her face. She was straining hard to smile.

*She's acting because she knows we're being watched.*

I leaned over her again. "Are you all right?"

"I've thrown up three times. I can't seem to keep anything down. Why did she do it, Mike? Why did Maeve kill herself?"

"She said it was all her fault."

"Because it was her research project and they never would've been on the island otherwise?"

"I think she meant something more specific. The vandalism started after people learned she supported the closure of those offshore lobstering grounds. Or it might have been another reason altogether."

"Hello, Stacey," said Klesko, who had waited patiently for us to have our reunion. "I'm sorry to be seeing you again under these circumstances. I know Kendra was your friend."

She wiped one eye, then stood on her toes to give the detective a surprise kiss on the cheek.

"That means a lot, Steve. Thank you. Congratulations on the new baby. Please give Kim my best wishes. I can't imagine how your life must have changed."

"We've learned why sleep deprivation is considered a form of torture."

She glanced sideways at the house, then lowered her voice again, including both of us this time. "Did you ever find Kendra's shillelagh?"

"Her what?" Klesko asked.

"Shit, I forgot all about it," I said. "It's a heavy blackthorn walking stick from Ireland that McLeary gave her. Did your people find it in her tent?"

"No," he said. "We didn't find anything resembling a walking stick. But we haven't searched the whole island."

"It means something that it's missing," said Stacey.

"I can see another thing you two have in common," said Klesko with a smile that could have been read as amused or patronizing. "You're both prone to making unfounded deductions."

The silhouette of a man appeared in the open door of the manse. Stacey put on a phony smile and said loudly, "And for what it's worth, guys, you both smell *really* bad."

"We took an unexpected dip in the ocean," I said.

"That explains the faint fishiness on top of the BO."

Klesko was determined not to be distracted by jokes again. "Stacey, I'm going to need to interview you, and it makes sense that we take care of that before Mike and I speak with the Markhams."

"Clay and Alyce aren't the kinds of people you keep waiting."

"Just watch me."

Without warning or seemingly cause, Steve Klesko slapped the side of his own face fast and hard.

"Son of a bitch!"

"Did something sting you?" asked Stacey.

He opened his palm, revealing a dead honeybee. Its lower abdomen was a pus-colored smear. He shook the crushed insect off his pitch-stained hand.

On his red cheek, the embedded barb was clearly visible. The detached stinger continued to pulse disgustingly, pumping venom into the wound. He scratched it out with the nail of his index finger. A welt was already rising around the bloody pinpoint.

The bee would have died anyway, even if Steve hadn't flattened it. Bees, unlike wasps and hornets, have barbed stingers, meaning that they tear themselves in two when they use them, since they are unable to detach themselves from whatever they've stung.

"Motherfucker," he said. "That fucking hurt. It still fucking hurts."

"You're lucky it didn't get you on the nose," I said cheerily. "I was in a cedar swamp last year and stepped on a rotten log full of yellow jackets. They chased me half a mile back to that Jeep I used to drive."

Instead of laughing along, Stacey was studying my friend's face with increasing worry.

"I counted thirty-something stings," I went on. "I looked like a wino, my nose was so swollen."

"Do you know if you're allergic to bee stings?" Stacey asked Klesko.

He coughed into his closed fist, then tried to clear his throat. "I can't ever remember being stung." He coughed again. "No, I don't think so."

He touched the hollow beneath his Adam's apple. Except for the red welt and the scratch across his cheek, his face was steadily losing color.

"Steve," she said, "you seem to be having a severe allergic reaction."

He whipped off his sunglasses and let them drop. He was blinking hard, almost in time with his coughs to clear his throat. He made eye contact with Stacey.

She saw something terrible there. "Do you have an EpiPen?"

"No," he sputtered. "Never thought . . ."

"Steve, you need to lie down, right here."

He didn't resist as we helped him onto the grass. Stacey grabbed his duffel, then tore my pack from my shoulders with such force I couldn't have held on if I'd tried. She wedged the bags beneath Steve's legs to elevate them. She looked up at me from her knees.

"Do you have antihistamines in your first aid kit?"

"I should. It's the red pouch inside the pack."

She reached under Klesko's legs to unzip my pack. She found my first aid kit and shook out the random meds in sealed packets. Tylenol. Imodium, Pepto Bismol.

And Benadryl.

"Fuck," she said. "It's only twenty-five milligrams."

She bit the packet open and shook out a single tab onto her palm, then gave Steve water from my Nalgene bottle to help swallow the pill. He was coughing so hard, he barely got the medicine down.

Stacey eased his head back and then sprang to her feet.

"Call 9-1-1 and get a LifeFlight helicopter here fast. Tell them there's a Maine State Police detective going into anaphylactic shock. Then go to the house. Ask Ridge if they have an EpiPen. It's unlikely, but you never know. You need to cut his pant leg and inject the epinephrine into the upper thigh. Got it?"

"Where are you going?"

"To get my EMT bag!"

Before I could utter a syllable, she was sprinting down the hill toward the fishing village below.

# 33

I told the dispatcher that I was a game warden and there was a medical emergency on Ayers Island, south of East Boothbay. A Maine State Police detective had been stung by a bee and was going into anaphylactic shock. He required a LifeFlight helicopter. She said it would take twenty minutes for the chopper to arrive. She asked if I wanted to stay on the phone with her or speak with a paramedic. I answered that I was all set: a trained EMT was on the scene.

Steve was conscious for this conversation. It was the first time I had seen my friend afraid.

Despite Stacey's command that I should go to the house to ask if they had an EpiPen, I found myself unwilling to leave his side. He looked so frightened and was having so much trouble breathing.

*What if he goes into cardiac arrest?*

Finally, I willed myself to move. I made a dash toward the double doors of the house, running hard.

Just before I reached the wide stone steps, the man who had been standing in the doors stepped forward. He was barrel-chested with a black beard and a shaved head half hidden beneath a newsboy cap. He wore a crisp white shirt tucked into houndstooth trousers held up by blue suspenders. Saddle shoes completed the hipster ensemble.

"Are you Ridge?"

"What's happening to the detective?" he asked.

I didn't bother asking how he knew Klesko's job. Heath had probably told him.

"He was stung by a bee and is allergic. He's going into anaphylactic shock and might die. Do you have epinephrine in the house?"

"I don't know what that is."

"It's adrenaline."

"Heavens no." He followed these words with a tittering noise.

"Is something funny?"

"I laugh when I'm nervous. I always have. Please don't take it personally. I meant no offense."

I glanced back at Steve, motionless on the ground. Then I threw imploring looks at Markham's blond servants, who were watching but had made no move to assist us. The airheads didn't have a clue.

"Come with me, please. I need your help."

"Of course! Heh-heh."

Klesko had closed his eyes. His lips had swollen grotesquely. Each breath he took came as a whistle. I felt his wrist for a pulse and was horrified not to find one, then I realized it was because his heartbeat was so weak.

"Steve? Steve? Can you hear me?"

No response.

The whistling coming from his throat stopped. His trachea must have contracted, and he could no longer breathe.

I grabbed my bag from under Klesko's legs and unzipped the outer pocket until I found one of the ballpoint pens issued to me by the Warden Service. I unscrewed it, shook out the cartridge, and looked through the upper piece to be certain the tube was clear

Then I reached into my pocket and removed my knife. It was a heavy Gerber 06 automatic: made for combat, not field surgery. But I made a practice—call it a ritual—of honing the point to razor-sharpness.

"I've never seen a tracheotomy performed before." Ridge punctuated the sentence with a nervous laugh.

I pulled on a pair of nitrile gloves from my first aid kit. "Well, I've never performed a tracheotomy before, so it'll be an adventure for both of us."

My limited knowledge of the procedure told me to feel for an indentation below the Adam's apple, but I wasn't certain how far below. Nor did I know whether to make a vertical or horizontal incision. Was there an important blood vessel I risked severing if I was off by several centimeters?

I squeezed the big knife between my thumb and index finger and sliced into and through the skin. At first, no blood ran from the incision. Then a few red spots appeared. The wound began to flow. I peeled the opening apart with my left hand and saw the ringed cartilage of his windpipe. Presumably, I needed to cut a hole between the rings. That was what I did.

I slid the pen into the bloody opening.

"I believe you're supposed to blow into it," said Ridge, squinting through his readers at the wound. "To clear the airway of any blockages."

He sounded so confident I found myself doing what he told me. I leaned over, pinched the tube carefully in place, and blew several short breaths into it. Air rushed out when I stopped. Then I heard wheezing as his unconscious body began sucking oxygen through the hollow pen.

"You need to bandage the tube in place now," said my surgical assistant.

"Can you hold it in place while I cut some tape?"

My hands were red to the wrists, and I got blood everywhere, including on the outside of the makeshift bandage. I was inspecting my work when, out of the corner of my eye, I saw Stacey running toward us. Her face and throat were ruddy and slick with perspiration. But she had her EMT bag slung over her shoulders, and in her hand was an EpiPen.

"He stopped breathing?"

"Yeah. But he's started again through the tube."

"You gave him a tracheotomy? Wow, Mike, good work." She dropped beside me and gestured to the knife lying on the grass. Bits of cut grass clung to the sticky blade. "Now you need to cut a long hole in his pants all the way down his thigh."

I obliged.

Even before I finished, she'd plunged the tip of the pen into his muscular quadriceps, and a hidden syringe forced adrenaline into his bloodstream. His body convulsed, his head went back, and he arched his spine when the drug reached his heart. Stacey had to clutch the tube in his throat to keep it from being dislodged by his spasm.

I could hear his breaths now, coming strongly through the narrow opening of my former ballpoint.

I looked at her in wonder. "You did it."

Her face showed none of the hopefulness I was feeling. "Maybe, but it might have been too late."

# 34

Clay and Alyce Markham made their appearance, walking hand in hand from the direction of the horse stable.

I had expected the notorious photographer to be outfitted in some bizarre costume that matched his macabre reputation: done up like a bullfighting aficionado in a Basque beret and white homespun or dressed as laird of the glen in a quilted waistcoat and tweed hunting breeches.

Instead, Markham was attired in a white T-shirt, blue jeans, and much-scuffed cowboy boots: his lone affectation.

He stood about six feet tall and was still broad-shouldered and muscled in a rawboned way despite his advanced years. His mostly gray hair still had some black in it. His nose and ears were large, as sometimes happens with elderly men for whom those appendages never stop growing. These exaggerated features made him ruggedly handsome. He had the face of a Founding Father, minus the powdered wig.

"I'm Markham," he said in a drawl. "This is my wife, Alyce."

She was a foot shorter than he was but broadly built. No amount of diet or exercise could compensate for those big bones. She wore red-framed glasses, and her hair had been cut in silver bangs. She was dressed for gardening—rubber shoes, camp pants, and cotton smock—and the outfit was convincingly green at the knees. A pair of pruning shears projected from her back pocket.

"How is the poor man?" She had no trace of her husband's Southern accent. "Will he be all right?"

I knelt beside Klesko, clenching my friend's hand, while hives spread up his arms like a fast-moving plague. His pulse was weak and thready. Beneath his fluttering eyelids, his pupils had grown enormous, all but consuming his irises.

"He's in serious condition," said Stacey. "We need to have him ready for LifeFlight."

"I've told the boys to bring the UTV," the photographer said in his slow, syrupy voice. "What do you think, Ridge? We should be able to fit him in the bed, wouldn't you say?"

The nervous, bearded man chuckled. "His feet will hang off the end, but I don't see a better option."

His nervous tic was getting under my skin. I didn't care if he couldn't stop it.

"It's a heck of a thing to be allergic to bees and not know it," said Markham, shaking his head.

"People are, dear," said his wife.

"You'd think the police would test their officers for such things." His skin was the splotchy bronze of a professional safari guide or a lifelong yachtsman. "It's a heck of a thing."

I heard an engine. The two "boys"—Heath and the other blond man—had returned with the estate's utility terrain vehicle. It was a six-wheeled John Deere with a cargo box that resembled a miniature truck bed. They had become common on certain islands as alternatives to gas-guzzling pickups.

Markham, as the head of the household, assumed command. I wagered he always assumed command.

"Finn, take his legs. Heath, you get his arms. Be careful of his head, boys."

Steve was sweating heavily. I let go of his hand. Stacey hopped in beside him in the cargo box. Finn made way for Markham to take the wheel. The green-and-yellow UTV shot away across the lawn with Finn trotting behind like a golden retriever and Ridge doing the best he could do to keep up.

I found myself alone with Alyce Markham. She removed a red kerchief she'd worn knotted around her throat and shook it out.

I pointed to the bloodstained nitrile gloves on the ground. "You wouldn't have a trash bag where I can get rid of these?"

"You can leave them there."

"They're contaminated."

"I know all about medical waste," she said. "I'll make sure they are disposed of appropriately. Please don't argue with me, Warden. I know you must be eager to be there when the helicopter arrives."

I thanked her, grabbed Klesko's murder bag, and began trotting along in the grooved tracks left by the UTV. It had circled behind the buildings, past an ice pond that was tucked into an alcove of the forest, and across another lawn on the south side of the hilltop. There I was greeted by one of the most spectacular vistas I'd encountered in Maine.

The hill fell off so abruptly it might have been a green cliff. I gazed over the tops of tall spruces growing down the steep hillside. The beacon of Ayers Light rose on its grassy headland. Beyond the red-and-white tower was a stretch of relatively flat water, protected from the larger waves by two tidal ledges. These were named Boar and Sow, if I remembered right. White surf exploded along these emergent rock walls, making a sound like thunder from a storm that will pass you by. In the hazy distance, the ocean stretched unbroken to the luminous horizon.

The UTV had come to a halt at the edge of the lawn. Klesko remained in the vehicle while Stacey held his hand and Markham ordered one of his servants to bring a "cold compress": a term I hadn't heard in years and not a treatment for anaphylactic shock, as far as I knew. The photographer carried himself as a man of action. Ridge glanced back and forth at the western sky. The LifeFlight helicopter would be coming from the inland city of Lewiston, along the Androscoggin River.

"How is he?" I asked Stacey, who was cleaning up the tracheotomy with antiseptic, fresh gauze, and tape.

"Not good. I wish we'd been able to administer the epinephrine sooner."

"Hang in there, buddy." I touched my friend's swollen hand.

Klesko tried to speak, but the pen in his throat made it impossible.

"I'll call Kim for you," I said, thinking this would have been the natural thing he'd want to ask of us. "I'll see if I can arrange for a state police plane to fly her to Lewiston."

He tried to speak again, with even less success.

"Young man," Markham said, leaning over Klesko and addressing him with patriarchal self-confidence, "I forbid people dying on my property. I simply won't have it. Understand?"

Over my shoulder, I became aware of the sound of a descending helicopter. Most people think they're hearing the thwacking rotors when it's the engine or engines drowning out the fainter noises made by the blades. The LifeFlight fleet included three AW109s. These birds possessed twin turbo engines capable of speeds topping 165 miles per hour.

The rotors whipped up a green whirlwind of newly cut grass.

The copter touched down, but the blades continued to spin.

Knowing that these aircraft had no room for passengers, I said my goodbyes to my friend. In some places, his skin was the color of curdled milk. Where the hives had risen on his arms, it looked like someone had taken off the top layer with a belt sander.

"Hey, man, you've got to hang in there!" I shouted to be heard as the airborne paramedics exited the chopper. "You've got a beautiful wife and son at home!"

He tried to speak again. I didn't know why, but I had the sense he wanted to tell me something about the case, of all things. He was confused. Whatever it was must have been meaningless. But that didn't quiet the voice in my head.

A moment later, I was asked to step aside by a woman in a green jumpsuit, who began readying the patient for transport. Stacey was briefing another crewman while the pilot remained at the controls; their goal was to be airborne again in minutes. I handed the crewman the duffel with Steve's personal effects.

Having participated in countless rescues, I had learned that if you're not part of the medevac team, the most helpful thing you can do is stay out of their way. Markham, however, remained in place, craning his head to overhear Stacey's conversation with the female flight medic.

"We should give them room to work!" I shouted at the photographer, being so bold as to put my hand on his upper arm.

His expression told me he didn't appreciate being touched, but he nodded his long head and backed off.

We retreated to a safe distance to watch the flight medic and the crewman secure Klesko onto a litter. They wheeled him to the side door and slid the contraption inside—the wheels folded beneath the stretcher—with the efficiency of a team that had practiced this drill blindfolded.

As the rotors began to accelerate, I raised a hand to protect my eyes against wind-whipped projectiles.

"Godspeed," I heard Markham say. "Godspeed."

The chopper was airborne again. Tail raised, it moved out over Ayers Island Light before banking sharply to the west. It passed across the blinding nimbus around the sun. As the sound of the engines diminished, I became aware that the loudness of the machine had filled my head with a noise not unlike the buzzing of bees.

Stacey crossed the lawn and wrapped an arm around my waist and leaned into my embrace.

"I take it you've had medical training," Markham said in the most Southern way possible. "What do you suppose his chances are? Be honest."

"I don't know. It was such a long time between when he was stung and when I injected the adrenaline." Her voice broke as she raised her face to mine. "I can't lose another friend today, Mike. It'll break me if Steve doesn't make it."

"Let's think positively."

"Hear, hear," said Markham, who hadn't seemed to consider that Stacey and I might want privacy at this moment. "We haven't been formally introduced. I'm Clay Markham. This is my spread."

I thought he might shake my hand, and he almost did but stopped himself.

"This is my friend Mike Bowditch," said Stacey.

"I gathered as much. Warden, my wife and I are at your disposal, along with our entire staff."

"Thank you, Mr. Markham. Can you give Stacey and me a minute?"

"Heck," he said. "Take as long as you need."

We watched him stride across the lawn toward Ridge, who was waiting with a cigarette pinched between his fingers. Finn had returned with a white facecloth that must have been the cold compress.

"Nice of him to grant us a moment alone."

She rubbed her wet eyes with the back of her hand. "Now what?"

"I've got to call Kim," I said, "then Steve's superiors at the state police, and mine, too. The AG will want to speak with me, I'm sure. Bureaucrats think of freak occurrences as failures. The idea that a high-profile investigation could be derailed by a honeybee exceeds the limits of their imaginations."

"You're forgetting I used to be a state employee. I know about bureaucrats and their limited imaginations."

Her mention of having worked for the State of Maine ushered an unlikely question into my mind. "You didn't happen to see Spinney down at the dock?"

"I don't think so. Why?"

"I would've expected to get a call from him when the LifeFlight alert went out. He would have gotten a notification. He was also our ride back to shore. I guess he still is, except . . ."

"What?"

I gazed out at the lighthouse. The eastern side of the tower was in shadow, but the sun reflecting off the Fresnel lens in the turret was as blinding as if the electric lamp were illuminated.

"Now that Steve's gone, I'm worried what will happen if we leave," I said. "There's a strong chance I'll be sidelined. The justification for my involvement always had to do with being the department's representative on the scene at Baker Island."

"Are you looking for an excuse to stay, Mike?"

She knew me too well. "Spinney said something I can't stop thinking about. The islanders 'haven't had time to get the official story straight.' I feel like he's right about that. These people can't all be trusted. For Steve's sake, and the sake of the victims, I can't waste valuable time."

She straightened her spine to affect an attitude of authority. "In my professional opinion as a Registered Maine Sea Kayaking Guide, I think it would be inadvisable for us to paddle back tonight."

"Really?"

"Night kayaking is always more dangerous, and in this case, we'd have to cross the Fish Island passage. There can be a lot of fast-moving traffic through that channel this time of year. The risk of a collision in the dark is too high."

I smiled with relief. "That settles it, then. We're staying."

"Glad to help."

# 35

Klesko's wife, Kim, was my first call, and I was surprised by the evenness in her voice as she received the news.

"Before we got married," she explained, "Steve told me I might get this phone call someday. He wanted me to know what I was getting into because so many couples in the law enforcement community avoid the conversation. 'I might be in a car crash,' he said, 'or I might be shot or stabbed.' Never in my wildest dreams did I imagine the call would be about a bee sting."

"Me neither."

"You and Stacey should have that conversation, Mike."

I didn't tell her we had no need.

Stacey had grown up as the daughter of the chief warden pilot, known police all her life, attended their funerals. More importantly, she'd been at my side during a few near-death experiences. She could identify every scar on my body and tell you where and when I'd received it. There were precious few secrets I had not shared with her. It raised a lump in my throat to realize how well she knew me, despite my best efforts to remain aloof.

"Kim, I'm going to ask the state police colonel to arrange for one of their planes to fly you to Lewiston."

"Thank you, Mike. You're a good friend. And I've met enough police now to know that you're suffering with this, too. Don't try to tough it out."

She might have been describing the state police colonel. He was my next call and had already gotten the news. He received the additional details I provided with such stoicism, it came across as indifference.

I risked the question. "What do you expect will happen with the investigation now, Colonel?"

"Detective Cruz is taking over and will want a briefing from you. I'd expect a call soon. Thank you for everything you did for my trooper, Bowditch."

He didn't need to speak the words: I was excluded from the case.

I might or might not be able to persuade my own colonel, Jock DeFord, to go to bat for me. But I doubted he would want to pressure the Major Crimes Unit now that the homicide investigation had entered a new stage. I had just been a warden along for a ride that had now ended.

While I was making my calls, Stacey had gotten out her camera and was wandering around the ice pond, taking pictures of the twilight reflecting in the water and the blossoming lilies that grew in the shallows along the edge.

I was preparing myself to call Delphine Cruz when the phone rang, and it was she who was calling.

"I've seen some bizarre things in my fifteen years on the job, but this ranks right up there," she said. "How did he look?"

"Not good."

"Shit."

"I just got off the phone with your colonel, and he never even asked me that question."

"Par for the course. He called me a few minutes ago to tell me I was taking over as primary. The conversation lasted two minutes. Klesko and I only worked together a few months, but he *was* my partner."

"Steve's a good detective," I said.

She wouldn't go that far, not yet. "He puts a lot of trust in you. That much is obvious. How about you bring me up to speed on what you did and who you spoke to out there?"

I obliged her with my tale.

When I'd concluded my account of the afternoon, she asked, "So what's your take on Speer? Do you like him for the murders?"

I had never heard a Maine cop use that phrase; I'd only ever encountered it in movie dialogue.

"Do you mean, did he commit murder for the sake of his art?" I said. "It's unlikely, but stranger things have happened, and I'd say he was a little too eager to show us his creepy photos. But if Speer killed the women, his wife was in on it, too. She's smarter than he is. She might even have told him to pose the bodies to throw suspicion on himself. That way it would look like a bad setup, and he'd have an alibi ready since Brenna claims he was home."

"That explanation presumes premeditation. What if he was regularly trespassing over on Baker and got caught and panicked?"

"Klesko would hate to hear us speculating like this."

"Yeah, he would."

I had no idea how Delphine Cruz would receive this next statement, but I took a chance. "I'm spending the night here and can meet you at the wharf in the morning."

"I hadn't heard there was a bed-and-breakfast on Ayers Island."

"Stacey and I will probably find somewhere to camp. She says it's too risky paddling back in the dark."

She made a vague noise that gave me no indication of how she felt about any of this. "I plan to be there at 0500."

"I'll be at the wharf, waiting."

The east side of the lighthouse was wrapped entirely in shadow. I listened to the waves pounding the rocks below, as relentless as quarrymen, and watched the dark silhouettes in the sky of the herring gulls streaming toward their roosts. Then I went for Stacey, who'd disappeared from view while I'd been on the phone with Cruz.

Instead, I came upon the lumbering form of Rick Spinney trudging up the hill.

"Well?" he shouted.

"Well what?"

"Were you ever going to call me back?"

"What do you mean?"

His face was sweaty and red from the climb. "Check your messages!"

Sure enough, Spinney had left a voice mail when he'd gotten word that LifeFlight had been summoned. I had never turned off my do-not-disturb setting after we'd finished interviewing the Speers. I had many messages in my in-box.

"I'm sorry." My excuse sounded even lamer out loud than it had in my head. "Everything was so frantic."

"It was nice getting the news over the VHF that a detective was being medevaced from the island. I watched the chopper land and leave from my boat. I had to call dispatch to find out what was happening and they wouldn't tell me the details."

"I said I'm sorry, Rick."

"I only know Klesko got stung by a bee because they're all talking about it at the wharf. Everything about this fucking island sickens me."

The first-floor windows were all alight now. "Keep your voice down."

"That's what you have to say to me?"

"I already apologized. What more do you want? I had to give Steve Klesko a tracheotomy because he'd stopped breathing. And then I had to call his wife to tell her he might not make it. So why don't you knock off the self-pity?"

"Fuck you. Do you need a ride back to shore or not?"

"Stacey's here, too. She paddled over. Remember?"

"I can't tow both of your kayaks without getting them tangled."

"In that case, I guess we're spending the night here," I said as if we hadn't already made our decision.

We had our tent and camping gear in our kayaks and, in extremis, could probably find a sheltered place on the backside of Hatchet.

"Where are you going to stay? With that pervert Markham?"

"Keep your voice down."

"I have a right to be pissed. You and Klesko treated me like a suspect, for fuck's sake. And then you humiliated me in front of Goodale and Blondie."

"I know things have been rough lately."

"Is that so? You are so fucking arrogant, Bowditch. Do you know how many of your fellow wardens hate your guts?"

"I don't have a specific number, but I suspect it's in the double digits."

"The high double digits."

"Come on, Rick. You've made your point."

"Hillary is in the morgue on an autopsy table. Kendra, too. You don't seem as troubled by the image of them being sliced open as I am. You must be one hell of a tough guy, Bowditch." He spun around and waved his hand dismissively as he descended into shadow. "Enjoy your romantic evening."

# 36

Carrying my backpack, as well as Stacey's, I felt like a weary traveler arriving at an inn. Ridge opened the door mere seconds after I rang. He peered past me into the twilight.

"I thought I heard voices."

"I was speaking with a Marine Patrol officer. He just left."

"Wasn't he your ride? I was under the impression that you and Stacey were going back to shore with him."

It passed through my mind to ask why our plans were any of his business.

"We have our kayaks to deal with."

"If you're willing to leave them for now, I don't mind taking you back on the *Spindrift*—with Alyce's permission, of course."

Ridge had waxed and curled the tips of his mustache. His beard looked to have been dyed to hide the gray. He struck me as too old to dress like a hipster. And wasn't that trend over even in Brooklyn or wherever?

"We're still discussing our options," I said. "I didn't get a chance to introduce myself before. I'm Mike Bowditch with the Maine Warden Service."

"Yes, I know."

"I didn't get your last name."

"Ridge is my last name. You didn't get my first name because no one ever uses it. But it's Derrick—like the oil rig."

"You wouldn't have happened to see my girlfriend, Derrick?"

I might have imagined it, but Ridge seemed uncomfortable being addressed by his given name.

"Stacey's in the great room with the Markhams. I saw her wandering around outside with her camera, looking a little lost, and thought she might want to clean up after the incident with the bee."

*The incident with the bee?* He made it sound like a Tintin adventure.

"May I come inside, Derrick?"

"My apologies!" Ridge stepped backward, the movement almost waltz-like, and opened the door wide. "Come right in, please."

The entryway was illuminated by a wrought iron chandelier. The floor was of granite, gray with specks of pink and blue that sparkled beneath the brightness of the bulbs. I assumed the stones must have been quarried over at Hatchet Island. I understood now why those blocks had been so highly prized by the enterprising builders of the nineteenth century.

A framed photograph hung beside the door. I felt a funereal chill descend without warning.

"You recognize *Shipbreaker,* I see!" said Ridge.

"We had a print in my house growing up. I've seen it in waiting rooms and college dorms. That picture seems to be everywhere."

He leaned forward conspiratorially. He'd brushed his teeth since smoking his last cigarette, too. An exotic-smelling cologne emanated from his skin. His mustache wax had its own odor. He was one of those highly fragrant men. "Don't let Alyce hear you using that word about one of Clay's images."

"Which word?"

"*Picture.*"

"Do you mind if I take a *photo* of this?"

He leaned close again. "Clay frowns on people doing that. He hates that Alyce even hung the photograph here. He'd prefer his more recent works be displayed."

"You mean the dead children?"

Ridge chuckled as only a barrel-chested man can. "They're not *really* dead. Have you seen the photos?"

"No, and I don't care to. I am going to take Alyce's side in the choice of wall art."

"She's always been his best publicist. She recognizes the importance of an artist cultivating a certain mystique. She hung *Shipbreaker* there for certain visitors to the house—gallerists and art writers—because it announces they are entering the home of a genius." When he grinned, the effect was heightened by the curled tips of his mustache. "Go ahead and take a photo. It'll be our little secret."

While I was lining up the shot, getting the focus right, I asked, "I've always wondered. Did the fishermen onboard the boat survive? It seems impossible they could've lived."

"But you don't know for sure!" he said. "The uncertainty is central to the work's greatness. Did they survive or didn't they survive? What answer would you secretly prefer?"

"Why *secretly*?"

"Because we all have desires we won't admit, even to ourselves."

I felt like I was back in Justin Speer's studio listening to him drone on about the uncanny valley. To say I didn't have the patience for another conversation about aesthetics would be the understatement of this miserable day.

"I have no secret desires. As someone who's devoted his life to rescuing people, I hope the fishermen made it."

Ridge must have been the house docent, in addition to his other vague duties, because he seemed to have given this lecture before. "Why does it matter? People die every day. And this photograph was taken before you and I were born. Clay would argue that your desire for a yes-or-no answer is an excuse to avoid facing your emotional response to the image."

"What would I argue?" The drawling voice echoed off all that stone as it might have down a mine shaft.

Clay Markham stood in shadow, at the end of a hall.

"The warden and I were just discussing *Shipbreaker*."

"I told Alyce to take that monstrosity down." The photographer advanced into the pooling light of the chandelier. His cowboy boots echoed off the granite. "I would have thought you'd be talking about that poor detective. Have you gotten word about his condition, Warden Bowditch?"

"I haven't, Mr. Markham."

"In my house, everyone calls me Clay—unless they're here to sell me something or ask for a donation. It's the curse of wealth and fame, Warden. There's always another beggar with a tin cup."

His wife appeared behind him. The silver color of her hair, seen in this icy light, seemed intensely metallic. She had put on a red cardigan meant to complement her red-framed glasses. She had also removed her gardening shoes. I found it surprising she went barefoot on the cold flagstones.

"Officer Spinney has left the island," said Ridge, "and Mike and Stacey don't have a ride back to shore. Alyce, would it be all right with you if I took them in on the *Spindrift*?"

"They're staying with us," pronounced Alyce Markham.

I couldn't stop myself. "We are?"

"God knows we have room for guests. Unless you need to be home tonight . . ."

I thought of Shadow. One night away, and I missed the big guy. But Logan Cronk would happily keep an eye on the wolf. The brute would punish me for my absence, however; of that I was certain.

"It seems bad form to pressure them." Derrick Ridge was doing his utmost to convey that he wanted to be rid of us.

"Stop being a nincompoop, Ridge," said Alyce. "We're not holding these people captive. We're merely offering them a room."

"Thank you," I said. "But Stacey and I don't want to put you out. We thought we might camp over on Hatchet—"

"Out of the question," said Clay with such force that his words echoed down the mineshaft and into darkened chambers beyond. He forced himself to take a calming breath. "What I meant to say is we take pride in how we treat our guests on Ayers. Forcing you to sleep outside defies every tenet of Southern hospitality. It's one of the last traditions I observe from my upbringing."

Now it was Stacey's turn to make her entrance onstage.

"We don't want to impose," she said.

"If you were imposing, you'd already have felt my boots on your behinds," said Clay Markham.

"Don't believe him," said Alyce. "Clay plays the rough character, but he's the softest touch I know. I've spent our entire marriage standing between the man and those who would exploit him. He'd offer you our own bed if I weren't here to curb his overgenerous impulses."

My head hurt, my muscles were sore, and I didn't know if I had it in me to continue bantering with these people.

"There's an ethical issue involved," I said. "In my position as a law enforcement officer investigating multiple crimes, accepting a gift from you might be seen—would be seen—as a conflict of interest."

"That would only be true if you consider us suspects," said Alyce perceptively. "Are we suspects?"

Markham raised his big hands. "You've got me, Warden. I confess."

"Shut up, Clay," said Alyce with sudden sharpness. "This is a legitimate question."

"A man can't make a joke." The photographer shook his handsome head with exaggerated world-weariness. "Best to tell my wife the truth, Warden. The woman has a lie detector where her heart should be."

Stacey locked gazes with me, both of us thinking the same thought. *Charming couple.*

"First, I should say that I'm not an investigating detective," I said. "But you should understand that I'm working closely with the state police and will be obliged to tell the new primary anything you might disclose to me about Baker Island."

"What is a primary?" said Markham.

You don't become a world-famous photographer without being curious to a fault, I thought.

Alyce answered his question for me. "It's the new lead detective taking over for the other one. What is his name? Do you know yet?"

"*Her* name is Detective Delphine Cruz."

"That's quite a moniker!" said Markham. "And she's a homicide detective, you say?"

"There are female detectives now, dear," Alyce said. "There have been for a very long time. I'll never understand how you've lived three-quarters of a century and managed to remain such a naif."

For a moment, I wasn't sure how Markham would receive this

judgment on his character. Then he let out a laugh that would have shamed a donkey.

"Mr. Shakespeare has an answer for that. 'The fool doth think he is wise, but the wise man knows himself to be a fool.' I've always known what I am, my dear. Pity I can't remember the play."

"*As You Like It*!" said Ridge with the eagerness of the first student in class to raise his hand.

The Markhams ignored him.

"May I make a suggestion?" Alyce Markham included both Stacey and me in her address. "Would you join us for drinks and dinner before you make a decision about staying? I'm not Southern—as you've no doubt noticed—but I try to hold myself to my husband's standard of courtesy. I think we should be able to get through a meal without Clay confessing to the Gardner Museum heist."

"I was in New Guinea for that art robbery," said Markham mischievously. "Please do indulge us. You must be famished from the day you've had."

"It's been ages since we entertained visitors," said Alyce. "We promise not to interrogate you about what happened on the puffin island."

"Who promises?" Clay gave Stacey a wink. "I never promised."

"I am hungry," I admitted. "How about you, Stace?"

Before she could answer, Alyce Markham instructed Ridge that we would be having the cioppino she'd made the night before.

"You two are in for a treat." Clay all but licked his lips. "My wife is one heck of a cook. And a better mixologist. This way to the saloon."

He led us down four steps into a spacious room that turned out, when he hit the light switch, to be even more cavernous than the entryway. Decorated in the Maine cottage style, wood-paneled, and with a surfeit of couches and rocking chairs, it resembled the lobby of some grand hotel. A wall of plate glass windows offered a view of the lighthouse. The beacon had finally been ignited and was turning in thirty-second rotations against a sky deepening to indigo.

Stacey and I sat facing Clay Markham across a coffee table the size of a barn door.

On the tabletop was a creased and coffee-spotted landscaper's map documenting all the construction Alyce Markham had overseen in bringing her vision for Ayers Island into being. The new houses were overlaid atop the ghost roads and buildings of the long-abandoned mining town.

Meanwhile, Alyce slipped behind a zinc bar long enough to fit five stools. A horizontal mirror mounted on the wall showed the back of her silvery head.

"What'll you have?" she asked.

"The usual," said Clay.

"I know what you'll have. I'm speaking to our guests."

"A beer?" said Stacey.

"You need to be more specific. Do you want a lager, a pale ale, a stout? We have multiple choices."

"You decide for me."

This nonanswer seemed to displease Alyce. "What about you, Warden? Let me guess. Club soda because you're working? Believe it or not, this isn't the first time we have entertained the police in this room, although the less said about that travesty of justice, the better."

Her husband frowned. His eyes began to shift around the room as if following a flying insect. I followed his gaze to a gun case against the far wall. The glass-fronted cabinet contained half a dozen double-barreled shotguns.

Stacey attempted to break the mood. "Where and when did you two meet?"

"That's a blunt question!" Alyce said, pouring a double Laphroaig into a tumbler.

"I've never been good with small talk," Stacey admitted, flushing.

"That makes two of us," said Markham kindly. "I was never much for sweet talk. I stole Alyce away from her studies with my brooding good looks. This was back in the city, how many years ago?"

"Fifty-two. I was a premed at Columbia with dreams of being the next Dr. Schweitzer, trekking into the jungle to bring modern medicine to the natives. Then along came this swashbuckling photographer with his Southern drawl, and he said, 'Heck, I can take you to Kenya tomorrow if you're hot to go on safari.' Remember the flamingos, Clay? There must have been a million of them at Lake Bogoria.'"

The nostalgic memory prompted the long-married couple to gaze at each other with affection.

"I'd so love to see East Africa," said Stacey.

"It's gotten dirtier since we first visited." Alyce returned to her bartending. "But Kenya is where I first fell in love with birds. I suppose you already know, Warden, how much money we've given the Maine Seabird Initiative over the years."

"I imagine quite a lot."

Clay peered directly into my eyes. "The short answer is, 'Too much.'"

"Were you aware of the difficulties—financial and otherwise—the Seabird Initiative is facing?" I asked.

"Of course we were aware," said Alyce as if the question had insulted her.

"Maeve McLeary told you?" Stacey blurted out.

As far as I knew, the Markhams were unaware of Maeve's suicide, unless Ridge had picked up the news in the village along with the other gossip. I felt it best not to break it to them. I was concerned the revelation might shut them up.

Markham cast a questioning glance at his wife, as if seeking her permission. When she didn't respond, he remained quiet, too.

"How would you describe your relationship with Dr. McLeary?" I asked.

"Is this conversation turning into an interrogation?" Alyce said.

"I wouldn't use that term." I tried to keep my tone light. "But since you volunteered that you've had a longstanding connection with Baker Island—"

"You decided to get out the thumbscrews."

"It'll be painless, I promise."

"Said the proctologist to the man on the table," said Markham.

Alyce came over with a silver tray on which she'd set four glasses. Club soda for me. A pint of the local IPA for Stacey. The double scotch for her husband. And a fizzing gin and tonic for herself. I'd watched her in the mirror while she poured the Tanqueray.

# 37

"How would you describe the nature of your relationship with Dr. McLeary?" I asked again.

Clay settled back on the creaking leather couch, cupping the glass of scotch with both hands. "I believe my wife just admitted that we have enthusiastically supported Maeve's work, as star-crossed as it might be."

"May I ask why you chose to remain anonymous?" Stacey said, unable to help herself.

Alyce bent her knees beneath her as she settled in beside her husband on the sofa. "You don't hold back your opinions. Do you, Stacey?"

"My parents raised me to speak my mind. It's a blessing and a curse, frankly."

Markham tugged on one of his earlobes. "I support every cause I donate to anonymously to discourage those beggars I mentioned."

"But you were a major donor to the Maine Seabird Initiative," I said.

"Yes, *we* were," said Alyce.

"Is that why Dr. McLeary came to Ayers Island yesterday, to speak with you about upping your annual gift?"

Clay Markham leaned across the table, grinning an impish grin. "Now how did you know Maeve was here yesterday? Which of the cottagers told you? It was that troublemaker Speer, wasn't it?"

A bead of perspiration rolled down the side of my glass and dropped onto my knee. "Why do you say that?"

"He's always up to some mischief. You know the tale of the

sorcerer's apprentice? That's Justin Speer. Mickey Mouse facing an army of brooms."

Alyce cleared her throat.

"Justin knows what I think of him," said Markham.

"Which is what?" I asked.

"That I admire his ambition more than his talent."

"Maeve was here briefly," said Alyce now with something like boredom. "She arrived just after Clay and I had returned from a morning sail around Monhegan. We invited her on board the *Fūjin*—"

"That's the name of your schooner?"

She barely nodded. "We invited her on board the *Fūjin* to speak privately. From the start, I could see she was agitated even beyond her usual frenetic presence. She'd come here to ask for the moon."

"You didn't come up to the house for this conversation?" I said.

"No," said Clay, looking me straight in the eyes again. "We sat on the sailboat and drank iced tea and listened while she made her ask."

*"I saw her walk past the house on her way up the hill,"* Brenna Speer had said.

Stacey had no patience for the gamesmanship of interviewing. "Did she say why she needed the money?"

Alyce rattled the ice around her glass. "She respects our intelligence enough to be frank and not attempt to mislead us. She said another of her major donors had recently died, and the heirs had no interest in environmentalism. In turn, we informed her that we'd already decided to decrease our donation. Maeve has been required to disclose in her annual reports that the puffins aren't reproducing the way they once did, and there comes a point where even we Markhams won't throw good money after bad."

Behind them the sky had grown so dark that, except for the occasional sweeping flashes from the lighthouse, the windows had become mirrors, reflecting the room.

"Don't suppose for one minute it was easy for us," Markham said. "Maeve's always been so passionate about the birds, and we could see she was at her wit's end. The puffins are her whole life."

"She made it worse, I have to say, by refusing to take no for an answer," added Alyce dryly. "Persistence isn't a virtue when it becomes bullheadedness."

"We were heartbroken for her," said Markham. "Genuinely heartbroken."

Clay Markham had wanted to give Maeve McLeary the money. It had been Alyce who had refused. And from what I had learned about Mrs. Markham tonight, she hadn't wasted time doing it.

"It sounds like a short conversation," I said.

"I wouldn't call an hour *short*," said Alyce. "We let her make her arguments and counterarguments. We owed her that much. But at a certain point, you need to come out with a firm no. We wished her luck and said our goodbyes, and then Clay and I came up to the house. That was the last we saw of her. Isn't that right, dear?"

Markham spoke definitively. "It is."

"You didn't think it was strange that she stuck around the island all day after having her plea refused?" Stacey said.

This time I didn't mind her showing our ace in the hole. The time was right to challenge them.

"I am not following you," said Markham.

"The front of the house has a view of the channel," I said. "You must have noticed the *Selkie* anchored there. You didn't wonder why she didn't immediately depart for Baker Island?"

Alyce's mouth tightened until her lips disappeared. She set her drink down on a cork coaster. Only then did she speak. "You knew she was here all day, and you let us talk ourselves into a net. So much for hospitality being rewarded."

"I'm disappointed in you, young lady," said Markham, as if he was accustomed to law enforcement officers being dissemblers.

"There's something else they've been hiding from you," said Ridge's voice from the hallway. Somehow he'd crept up on the room without making a sound. He'd even known where to stand so his reflection wouldn't show in the plate windows. "Maeve McLeary killed herself this afternoon."

"Maeve? Dead?" Clay Markham sloshed his drink over his pants as he stood up.

"Is this true?" said Alyce. "You've been concealing her death from us since you arrived?"

I saw no advantage in denying it. "How did you find out, Derrick?"

Ridge stepped forward. "Does it matter?"

Markham flushed with outrage. "She was our friend!"

"Mine, too," said Stacey. But her words might as well have been uttered into a void.

"I wasn't trying to mislead you about her," I said, slipping into another easy lie. "But we're not allowed to talk about suicides before the next of kin has been notified."

"Oh, please," said Alyce.

Clay Markham had finally noticed the scotch on his pants and was trying ineffectually to brush off the stains. "How did she do it? Can you at least tell us that?"

"She weighed her backpack down with stones and drowned herself," said Ridge, revealing that his source was well-placed indeed. "Warden Bowditch himself tried to save her, but it was too late."

Markham sent daggers flying at me, one after the next. "Is that true?"

"Yes, sir. It is. Sergeant Klesko assisted me, but as Derrick said, we were unable to resuscitate Dr. McLeary. I'm sorry for the loss of your friend."

Alyce Markham hadn't budged from the couch. "Drowning herself with stones—I always said Maeve had a flair for the melodramatic."

"You didn't like her." Stacey made no attempt to hide her disdain.

"I wouldn't go that far," said Alyce. "She was a strong, intelligent woman with a fantastic sense of humor. That said, she also effectively bilked us out of hundreds of thousands of dollars."

As eulogies went, this one seemed short of warmth. *Icy* seemed the apt word.

"Bilked?" said Markham, his voice rising. "We gave her that money of our own accord."

"Would you like me to fetch you a change of trousers, Clay?" said Derrick Ridge.

"I can change my own damned pants!" He made another half-hearted brushing motion over his wet crotch. "Alyce, I want you to be kind to this girl while I'm upstairs. She suffered a grievous blow today. And however disrespectfully he's treated us, it sounds like the warden behaved heroically, trying to save Maeve's life. Let's treat our guests with courtesy even if they don't deserve it."

"When have I ever been less than courteous to a guest?"

"I can think of a recent occasion!"

*He means yesterday onboard their schooner,* I thought.

Ridge trailed behind his master.

Alyce returned to the bar to mix herself another gin and tonic. "I suppose you were also lying about us not being suspects."

"I haven't lied to you, Mrs. Markham. I withheld information. And in my capacity as a warden investigator, my job isn't to keep a list of suspects."

"You've lied by omission. My husband refuses to learn life lessons, but I should have known better. As I said earlier, you're not the first police officer to sit in that seat." She set down the green bottle of gin. "I gather you believe that one or more of our island's residents murdered those researchers. Am I correct?"

"The detectives haven't ruled anyone out."

"Including my husband and myself? So they do consider us to be suspects. May I at least request, *Warden*, that you inform the real detectives of our diminished physical capacity? Clay has had open-heart surgery and received a pacemaker, and I'm overdue for a hip replacement, if you haven't noticed my graceful gait."

The room became quiet enough that I could hear the sea through the windows.

Alyce finished her second drink in several long gulps. She dumped the ice cubes into the sink and ran water to rinse the glass. She started to reach below the zinc countertop, then caught herself and set the glass upside down on a green towel for drying.

I was waiting for her to tell us to leave her home.

Visibly uncomfortable, Stacey stared intently at the landscaper's map of Ayers Island on the coffee table. She wasn't just distracting herself. I could tell she was seeing something new in the old chart.

"If you're so interested in history," said Alyce with no particular kindness, "we have a room down the hall with antique photographs, town records, and artifacts from the Hatchet Island Granite Company."

Stacey looked up from the map, eyes widening. "You and Maeve McLeary were the same."

Alyce Markham blinked as if she'd been slapped. "Excuse me?"

"You both wanted to restore an island to its former self."

"That's absurd! I'm not some silly dreamer. I didn't kidnap puffins from Labrador!"

"You both had grand visions," Stacey said. "You had more in common than you realize."

"Is that so?" Alyce hobbled out from behind the bar. "The fact that I personally paid for the work we've had done doesn't count? It doesn't matter that I nevered duped wealthy donors into thinking I was an environmental visionary?"

"Maeve McLeary was my mentor, Alyce," said Stacey. "To me, she will always be a visionary. I don't fully understand what your dream is for Ayers Island, Alyce, but I respect that it's based on a heartfelt sense of purpose."

"Please address me as Mrs. Markham. Clay may be fine with phony casualness, but I am not." She stalked on her bad hip toward the hall. "I'm going to leave you charming people alone while I check on dinner."

The beam from the lighthouse swept the windows again.

"That could have gone better," Stacey said.

I couldn't help but smile. "I found it revealing."

"My mouth always gets me into trouble. Next time, you should put a gag on me."

"Never," I said. "You might not know it, but you got them to reveal things I never could have."

"Like what?"

"Clay Markham is one hell of an actor."

# 38

I couldn't blame Stacey for helping herself to another beer. She slid behind the bar and pulled the tap with the expertise of an Irish publican, filling the glass while keeping the foam from overflowing.

"Care to explain what you mean about Clay?" she said.

"Not quite yet," I said. "While you're there, do me a favor and check the dishwasher."

She peeked beneath the bar. "How did you know there's a dishwasher?"

"Anything inside?"

"Two highball glasses. Why?"

"I just had a hunch. For all the umbrage they took at us for not being candid, the Markhams haven't been telling us the whole truth either. What is it about Ayers Island that the people here can't help themselves from behaving suspiciously?"

She plopped down beside me on the couch again. "They're not all shifty. Skip and Dorothea Ayers—you haven't met them—are sweet old Mainers. And the Goodales are a colorful clan, if nothing else. They were basically sea nomads before they washed up in Maine, sailing from port to port, homeschooling their kids. Jonathan seems like the ideal skipper for Clay, outwardly laid-back but quietly competent."

"You didn't meet their son Bear."

"True."

I realized I'd forgotten to tell her about our tense encounter with the *Persuader* on our ride over. I remedied the lapse now.

"Bear seemed devastated," I said. "I don't know what to make of that. It could have been guilt or it could have been genuine grief. Maybe he was as infatuated with Hillary Fitzgerald as every other man in a hundred-mile radius seems to have been."

"Your friend Spinney, for instance."

I blanched at her referring to him as my friend in light of his recent behavior.

"I've decided to stop making excuses for Rick based on who he used to be. The man's become a total asshole."

"Or worse," she said. "He did show up at Baker Island suspiciously early this morning. It was definitely before you made your 9-1-1 call. It might even have been before I made mine. So what was he doing there?"

"Delivering doughnuts?"

"That's not funny."

"You're right that the timing of his arrival is suspicious. I'm upset at myself for not having had that insight myself. But whatever else he might be, I can't see Rick Spinney as a cold-blooded killer."

"Might he be a hot-blooded one, though? You just admitted you've stopped making excuses for his conduct. Maybe you should talk with his supervisor about what you witnessed on board the *Persuader*."

"And be responsible for getting him suspended or worse?"

"He shouldn't be in the field, Mike. His fellow officers don't deserve him out there representing them."

When faced with these decisions, I often asked myself, *What would Charley Stevens do?* Stacey's father wasn't perfect. He had his share of flaws. But I could do worse choosing an ethical lodestar.

Deciding what to do about Spinney could wait, however. A murderer was on the loose. Maybe more than one murderer.

"What did you make of the Speers?" Stacey asked, reading my mind again. "I'll tell you that Skip and Dorothea don't have much use for them."

"Justin is a pseudo-intellectual. Brenna is the brains in the family. She seemed lonely to me, though."

"Don't fall for that act."

"What do you mean?"

"When I got here and saw this pretend village, I felt sorry for these people, too. It seemed like they were all Clay and Alyce's playthings. It was like I'd landed on the Island of Misfit Toys. But Brenna Speer knows the score. Same with the Goodales. As long as the Markhams lavish them with freebies, they'll happily assume the role of serfs."

Again, Stacey had come to a revelation I had failed to grasp. Apart from the Goodale children, the islanders were all here by choice, not necessity. They were not modern versions of the immigrants who had died in the quarries and the birthing beds and were buried now beneath nameless headstones.

"I'd like to have a peek at those historic artifacts Alyce mentioned." I gestured toward the next room. "Care to join me?"

"Do you think they might have something to do with the murders?"

I shrugged. "Probably not, but you know how much I love history."

We drifted down the hall and found the little museum behind a glass door. The room was small and lacked windows and had been designed to serve as a climate-controlled archive. Display cases held stone-cutting tools, mauls and spikes and wedges; a bound volume with the name *Shakespeare* embossed in gold across the front; multicolored bottles that once contained tinctures and patent medicines; blue china plates carried to Maine by windjammers from the Far East.

The eggshell walls had been chosen to show off the period photos of Ayerstown. It was an amazing exhibit of images: half a hundred foreign-looking children standing outside their schoolhouse; a young man herding sheep through the village; schooners pulled up to a wharf, being loaded and unloaded by longshoremen.

Other photographs showed the quarrying operation on Hatchet Island: the vast excavation in the cliffside with fractal lines where blocks had been removed; barges riding low in the water from the weight of heavy slabs; quarrymen posed at the bottom of the deep pit, looking as small as Lilliputians.

"Clay has his studio over on Hatchet Island," said Stacey off-handedly. "The pit is filled with water now. Someone brought over brown trout a long time ago. He says there are trophy-size fish in the pond because he forbids fishing."

"Does he row himself back and forth?"

"Most of the time he just walks."

"Across the water?"

She laughed at the Galilean image I'd evoked. "There's a sandbar across the channel at low tide. Didn't you wonder why all the boats are moored at the north approach of the passage? It's because the water's too shallow for them at the south end—at least for most of the day."

"The islands are conjoined." I felt again like an idiot. "My old map didn't show the bar."

"I told you to get a real nautical chart!"

"I never imagined we'd be visiting this place, given its unwelcoming reputation."

She shivered. The recirculating cold air made it feel like we were trapped inside a refrigerator.

"Dorothea told me the Markhams used to welcome visitors," Stacey said. "That was before the state opened an investigation into Clay's treatment of that young employee. The one who overdosed before the district attorney could bring charges of sexual assault."

"Conveniently overdosed."

"I already told you not every death is a murder."

"Yeah, but that was before we set foot on Ayers Island. The scandal may have made Markham less welcoming, but it hasn't changed his hiring preferences. Those two blond dudes really stand out among the islanders."

"You mean Heath and Finn?" Stacey said. "At least, they're adults. If Markham wants to have a couple of pretty boys around, and everyone's cool with the situation, it's none of my business."

"I heard Markham sent one of them in a golf cart to pick you up when he heard you were on the island."

"He didn't send the cart. Alyce did."

"Interesting."

"She tried to pry information out of me about what happened on Baker last night. But when she realized I wasn't going to satisfy her curiosity, she let up." She leaned into me, shivering again. "Oh, Mike, I'm barely holding it together. I've tried to distract myself, but when I remember how Kendra was beaten and laid out like a mannequin, it makes me want to kill whoever did it."

"I feel the same way."

"The difference is you wouldn't actually murder someone out of revenge."

*Wouldn't I?*

"You wouldn't, either, Stace. You're tempted by the idea. But it's different when the person is in front of you, and you realize they're a human being, whatever monstrous thing they did."

She touched the side of my unshaven face. "No one has ever trusted me the way you do, not even my folks."

"A wise man named Steve Klesko once said, 'Don't judge a person until all the evidence is in.'"

"In my case, I would think you have more than enough evidence." She wiped the corners of her eyes with her polo shirt hem. "Speaking of Steve, I hope he's doing OK."

I checked my phone, which I'd again put into airplane mode for our conversation with the Markhams. When I connected again to the island cell tower, I found a text waiting.

"It's from Kim," I said. "Steve is conscious and stable!"

"Thank God." Stacey wrapped her arms around me and pressed her head against my shoulder. She started to shake, not just from the cold. "What a day, huh?"

"Yeah," I said. "What a day."

The door behind me opened with a click, and I felt the air change. It was Derrick Ridge telling us dinner was ready.

# 39

The black-bearded hipster led us into a spacious kitchen that combined modern appliances with white wainscoting and hooked rugs. Two dinner settings had been set across from each other on a breakfast island. Our bowls were filled with fragrant cioppino, and there was a basket of steaming bread and a carafe of ice water.

Neither of the Markhams was present. Evidently, we would be dining alone.

Ridge made a big fuss about our having everything we needed, laughing nervously the whole time. "Anything else before I leave you two alone?"

"You can tell us if you were on the boat with the Markhams when Maeve McLeary asked them for more money."

His face hardened. "I meant do you need wine? I'll take it you're fine with water."

Then he was gone.

Stacey and I stood beside the island looking at each other.

"I shouldn't have spoken to him like that," I said. "But something about that man rubs me the wrong way. I have the sneaking feeling he was googling me while we were having drinks with his employers."

She pulled out a chair-backed stool from the counter. "You're not the only one with bad manners. I must have really insulted Alyce when I compared her with Maeve. Should we even eat this or do you think it's been poisoned?"

"We'd better take the risk," I said. "We might not have a chance again tonight."

"It'll be the first thing I've had all day."

"All the more reason," I said.

"I hope I can keep it down." She settled herself on the stool.

I remained standing as I reached for a slice of bread. "I need to make a call."

"You just said we should eat!"

I took a bite and said with my mouthful, "I am eating. I'd just like to talk with Kim Klesko."

Stacey let her soupspoon hover over the bowl. "If I die eating this, just know that I will haunt you for eternity, Mike Bowditch."

I passed through a well-stocked pantry and then a mudroom before I found a door to the outside.

For a split second, I saw Jupiter and Saturn bright in the cloudless night sky. Then motion-sensitive lights snapped on as I moved clear of the house, and I lost my view of the planets.

My call to Kim went to voice mail.

Delphine Cruz had left me a text.

Call me when you can.

She answered on the second ring.

"I just interviewed Garrett Meadows," she said before I could speak.

"What?"

"He's still in a state of extreme agitation, but the docs don't want to give him benzos because of the concussion. They said he was cogent enough to answer questions."

"You don't think you should have waited?"

"Why?"

A lawyer could make a strong case that Garrett, even without drugs in his system, hadn't been able to give consent due to the nature of his injuries.

"You're thinking I might have fucked up the case," Cruz said before I could frame my objection politely. "But I made sure to record him waiving his rights. He trusted me the moment I walked in the room. It helps that we share a similar complexion. The poor guy said he hasn't seen a black face since he got off the plane in Boston."

"What else did you learn?"

"Don't get all touchy with me, Warden. Garrett Meadows is a victim, not a suspect. And that's how I treated him."

"What does he remember?"

"He only woke up when he heard the shotgun blast. Which means he was asleep when Fitzgerald was killed. He didn't know what was happening, but when he heard Ballard scream, he took off running in his underwear. He can't see five feet without his glasses, but somehow, he made it to the landing. He was trying to get up the nerve to go for the rowboat when a shadow came toward him out of the rain."

"How did he see a shadow if it was dark and he's half-blind?"

"Because the man had turned on a flashlight, like he didn't care about being spotted anymore. Garrett couldn't see much, but it looked to him like the man had a black hole where his face should have been. He was so terrified, he jumped into the ocean and swam out to the skiff. When he pulled the rope, the rowboat crashed into his head. Somehow, he pulled himself up over the side. He had no clothes, no oars, and was bleeding from his head. Plus, he was expecting the killer to pull him in since the boat was still tied to that rock."

"He doesn't remember cutting the rope?"

"He claims he didn't have a knife."

"I saw that rope, Cruz, and it was definitely cut. Garrett must have had a knife with him. There's no other . . ."

"Keep going."

"Unless the murderer cut the rope. But why would he do that? Why let a witness escape?"

"Maybe he figured Garrett would die at sea. And it would be better having the authorities chasing around a missing boat. Because the women were killed with 'found' weapons, we would assume Meadows had murdered them."

It was such a convincing theory, but even I knew Steve Klesko would hate it.

"Anything else?"

"Garrett said he recognized the sound of the boat engine."

"What boat engine?"

"While he was adrift, he heard a boat come around the island. He thinks the killer was checking to see if he was dead. He swears it was Speer's boat, the *Spindrift*."

I explained to her that the *Spindrift* was, in fact, Alyce Markham's boat and that she let most of the islanders use it. I told her about the box where she kept the keys.

"Everyone knows the combination, I was told."

"Told by who?"

"Brenna Speer." I paused, catching myself. "I guess I might want to double-check if that's true."

"I guess you might."

"Did Garrett ever see the boat?"

"Nope."

I thought again of the word he'd muttered to the lobsterman who'd rescued him: *faceless*. It briefly occurred to me that I hadn't yet met anyone on Ayers Island whom I could imagine in black pantyhose. Except maybe Ridge, I thought, smiling at the comical image that came into my head.

# 40

When I returned to the kitchen, I found that Stacey had finished her bowl of cioppino and was halfway through mine.

"You snooze, you lose," she said.

It cheered me that she'd gotten her appetite back. Also her sense of humor.

"This stew is pretty damned scrumptious," she said. "Did you speak with Kim?"

I reached for the last piece of bread. "I got her voice mail. I left a message telling her that I'd check in again in the morning, and that I hoped Steve would forgive me for literally cutting his throat."

"What kept you, then? Stargazing?"

"Delphine Cruz wanted to speak with me. She's in Damariscotta, having talked her way into Garrett's hospital room. He's going to pull through, but Cruz says he had quite an ordeal."

Stacey placed her spoon down carefully and steadied herself. "What did he say happened?"

I mouthed the words, *Not here.*

She scanned the room, realizing that just because we were alone didn't mean we weren't being listened to or watched. Ridge struck me as a tech nerd. I had no doubt the motion-sensing lights outside were his idea. He might have talked the Markhams into installing a home monitoring system that included eavesdropping capabilities.

"I wish there was news, but Garrett doesn't remember anything," I said, lying for any secret listener.

"That's too bad," Stacey said. "I was hoping he could make an identification."

"We're not catching a lot of breaks on this case, I'm afraid."

Stacey excused herself to use the bathroom.

I picked up her spoon and dipped it into what was left of my fish stew. The cioppino was lukewarm, but she hadn't been exaggerating its deliciousness. Lots of garlic and not too much fennel.

I heard soft footsteps coming down the stony hall behind me.

"This is excellent, Mrs. Markham," I said.

"You recognized me by the sound of my feet!"

"You're the only one in the house who goes barefoot around here."

"You enjoy showing off your skills as a woodsman," she said.

"I suppose I do."

"Where's Stacey?"

"The bathroom."

"I see you enjoyed the cioppino. I took a monthlong cooking class in Tuscany when I was your age. They have their own version of the dish called *cacciucco*. Clay was off photographing headhunters in New Guinea and nearly ended up on a menu himself. He hoped the tribesmen's cannibalism would manifest in their portraits, but they looked like ordinary people, he said. We've lived a strange life, Clay and I: an unimaginable life, when I think back to the sheltered girl I was when we met."

She had talked herself into an unintended reverie. Now she snapped out of it.

"You'll be staying in one of the guest cottages. We keep it made up, so you shouldn't need anything. Ridge will show you the way and give you the key. There's stuff for breakfast in the refrigerator and cupboards. You don't need to check in here before you go. I assume you'll be making an early start for home."

"I'm afraid not. The state police will be sending out two more detectives to continue interviewing the islanders. Detective Cruz has taken over the case, as I'd expected, and she wants to sit down with you and Clay in light of what I told her about Maeve's visit."

Alyce Markham touched her silver hair, the way someone does

who has recently had it cut after wearing it in a different style. "We're eager to put this past us, but you can tell Delphine that we're at her beck and call."

She had fixed her dark eyes on mine, perhaps hoping that I would respond to the gratuitous use of Cruz's first name, but when I refused to rise to the bait, she tried another approach.

"I just realized I saw you yesterday," she said.

"Really?"

"I go for a walk every morning around the island. I was over on the west side and saw a man and a woman in kayaks headed toward Baker. I realized when I was upstairs that it had been you and Stacey."

Alyce Markham had been the figure in gray standing atop the cliff: the driftwood-colored shape I wasn't sure was human. Something Justin Speer had said came into my mind: about the experience of the uncanny and why silent watchers can be so disturbing.

"You didn't wave back when I waved at you," I said.

"I didn't want to give you the idea you were welcome to land on our island. And yet here you are."

"Hello, Mrs. Markham," said Stacey, appearing in the pantry door.

"Ridge will show you to the guest cottage," she repeated, pointedly ignoring Stacey.

She turned on her heel and padded off down the hall.

"She's still mad at me for comparing her to Maeve," whispered Stacey. "What did she have to say?"

"She said that she and Clay have lived a very strange life."

"That's for damn sure."

I heard quick, unfamiliar footsteps. Instead of Ridge, it was the smaller of Markham's personal assistants, the welterweight named Finn, who'd been sent to guide us to our room. His features were perfectly symmetrical and therefore photogenic. He was even tanner than his colleague, Heath.

"You can follow me to the cottage," he said with a big grin.

"We were expecting Ridge," I said.

He laughed as if I had made a joke. "You guys must have luggage. You want me to fetch it?"

"We'll carry our own bags, thanks."

The stone path had sensors that triggered lights. Our way seemed to appear magically before us, then disappeared after we'd passed.

"Is Finn your first or last name?" Stacey asked, hitching her thumb under the strap of her pack.

"First!"

He didn't share his surname. It didn't seem to be an act of insolence. His neurons simply didn't make the connection.

"How long have you worked for the Markhams?" Stacey asked.

"A couple of summers."

"You don't live on the island year-round?"

"God, no."

"Where are you from originally?"

"Not Maine!"

He wasn't trying to be insolent. I had the impression that maybe he was stoned.

"What do you do here exactly?" I asked.

The question stopped him in his tracks. "Heath and I do whatever Clay asks us to do. We don't have, like, job descriptions or titles or anything. The Markhams aren't uptight people. Ridge is, though. He's got a stick so far up his ass it ought to be coming out his mouth."

Then he started forward again.

Ayers Island Light swept the hilltop with its beam every thirty seconds.

"This is it," said Finn. "The honeymoon suite."

The guest "cottage" was the size of my house. Coach lantern lights mounted on opposite sides of the door were attracting moths of different colors, shapes, and sizes. The lamps illuminated a semicircle of lawn. The greenness of the grass seemed artificial in the LED glow.

In the harsh light, I registered that Stacey and Finn were wearing identical polos and shorts.

The revelation made me gasp out loud.

I'd seen the uniform before we'd come to Ayers.

Finn opened the door and flicked on the light. His eyes twinkled as he handed me the key. Without showing us around, he went whistling back down the magic path.

I caught Stacey's arm before she could step over the threshold.

"What?" she asked. "What's going on?"

I pulled her into the shadows, so that anyone who might be watching would think I was stealing a kiss. "I know why Maeve stayed here all day and why she came to the house later. If I'm right, it explains why Kendra and Hillary were murdered. It also explains why McLeary felt she had no choice but to kill herself."

# 41

I hated to make Stacey wait, but there was one crucial piece of information I needed to validate my deduction. I told her to go inside while I wandered off into the night to call the Bucksport Police Department.

The assistant chief was on duty and gave me the number I requested after I had identified myself. The next call was difficult, painful even, because I couldn't explain to the woman on the other end why I was asking my cruel, seemingly senseless questions.

Stacey stood in the foyer, beside our packs, with her arms crossed as if the room were freezing. In fact, the sea breeze rippling the curtains was warm, almost subtropical.

I took her by the shoulder and kissed her hard. "Come with me."

"Mike? What is this?"

I led her to the master bedroom and then into the attached bath. I closed the door and started the shower. The sound of the jets would hide our conversation from any electronic ears.

Stacey smiled when she realized my game.

"This place probably isn't bugged, but we can't be too careful," I said. "I just spoke to Evan Levandowski's mom. The Bucksport PD gave me the number. She confirmed what I had suspected. After Evan finished his internship on Baker, Maeve got him a two-week photography class with Clay Markham."

"But Clay told me he doesn't teach classes. I asked if I could study with him sometime."

"Mrs. Levandowski doesn't know that, and Evan didn't, either.

His greatest wish in life was to become a professional photographer, and here's his new mentor, Maeve McLeary, offering him an apprenticeship with a living legend. As far as Evan was concerned, he'd won the golden ticket."

"Maeve would never—she would *never* have pimped a child to Markham."

"He was eighteen."

"It doesn't matter. She would never have done it."

I took her gently by the shoulders. "It sounds like Clay Markham behaved himself after his accuser overdosed. Maeve might've thought to herself, *Clay will enjoy having a beautiful boy around for a couple of weeks. Evan will learn about photography, and the next time I ask for a donation, the Markhams will owe me.*"

Stacey shook me off. "You're saying that Clay Markham raped Evan."

"Held him down and did it?" I rubbed my forehead, which was becoming sweaty from the steaming shower. "Markham strikes me more as a seducer. He plies Evan with booze or drugs and says he wants to take his portrait. Off comes the shirt, and then . . ."

The mirrors had fully clouded. Stacey fell silent.

"It would explain why the poor kid fell apart last year," I said. "It would explain his suicide. Especially if he associated returning to Baker with a return trip to Markham's studio."

The room had become as close as a greenhouse. Stacey, always smarter than I, switched on the fan, then reached into the shower to turn the water to cold.

"There's one problem with your theory," she said. "Kendra would have known that Maeve had arranged for Evan to come here."

"Not if Maeve swore Evan to secrecy."

"But why would she, if she didn't expect anything bad to happen?"

"That's a question only Maeve could answer."

"She had a conscience, Mike. After Evan jumped off that bridge, I can't believe Maeve wouldn't have gone to the police if she knew anything about Markham having been the cause."

Stacey was fighting valiantly for her mentor. I admired her loyalty. But I needed her acceptance.

"Levandowski was legally an adult," I said. "I'm guessing he was forced to have sex without his consent, but you know how hard it is to prove sexual assault when the victim was impaired. Evan didn't leave a suicide note. But Kendra told you he emailed McLeary the morning he jumped off the bridge. I think he told her what happened with Markham, if he hadn't already done so. Maybe he even blamed her."

Her expression showed shock, fear, disbelief. It pained me to have prompted this reaction. But I could sense that I had broken through the cardboard defenses she'd erected to protect McLeary's memory.

"How did you know Evan came to Ayers Island? Did someone mention seeing him? What made you think to call his mother?"

The mirrors were clearing again as the fan sucked the humidity from the confined space.

"It was the outfit he was wearing in that photograph back at the cookhouse on Baker. He was dressed in the same clothes you're wearing now. The picture had been taken against a backdrop of spruce trees."

"And there are no trees on Baker Island."

"But Ayers and Hatchet are covered with them. Hillary thought that Maeve had taken the photo. She forbade her interns from moving it. That photograph wasn't just a memorial, it was a mortification."

Stacey yanked the polo over her head, revealing her sports bra. She stepped out of the navy shorts without removing her sneakers. She stood there in her sports bra and underwear.

"I can't wear this," she said. "It makes me feel gross. Even being in this house makes my skin crawl."

"I don't feel like we're under any obligation to stay."

"Damn right, we're not staying!"

She threw open the door and made for her backpack in the foyer. I turned off the shower. I found her in the entryway, pulling out clothes at random, dumping them on the stone tiles.

She began buttoning up her sweat-stained hiking shirt. "How could Maeve have been so naive?"

"Maybe she thought she was doing Evan a favor. She might have assumed Markham would behave himself. One of the last comments she made was about cynicism blowing up in a cynic's face."

We were out in the open now, with no background noise to obscure our dialogue, and if Ridge was watching or listening, there was nothing to be done.

"Maybe, maybe, maybe." Stacey knelt to retie her sneakers. "You still haven't explained how you know Maeve came to the manse yesterday."

"The Markhams say she never left the waterfront, but Brenna claims to have seen her passing up the hill."

"You're putting a lot of trust in Brenna Speer."

"There's something else," I said. "We know from Maeve's sat phone GPS that the *Selkie* didn't leave the harbor yesterday until late. I think she stuck around, probably debating with herself how far she was willing to go to save Baker Island, whether she was capable of blackmail."

"And eventually she made the decision to go to the house and confront Alyce Markham," Stacey said.

"I don't think it's a coincidence Alyce was drinking Maeve's gin of choice tonight. Or that there were two highball glasses in the dishwasher."

She was keeping pace with me now. "That's why you had me look."

"Maeve McLeary threatened Alyce Markham. She might have claimed she had an incriminating note from Evan, laying out what Clay had done to him. Either the Markhams ponied up the funds to save the Maine Seabird Initiative, or she would go to the police and/ or the press."

"And Alyce sent Ridge to kill her on Baker Island?"

"Not Ridge. He seems too tightly wound for cold-blooded butchery."

"The nervousness could be an act."

"True," I said. "Heath and Finn are possibilities. The point is that Alyce sent *someone* to Baker to kill Maeve."

Stacey's lips parted. "Only Maeve wasn't there! She was anchored off Spruce Island because she'd been caught in the rainstorm."

"Spruce is closer with easy anchorage."

"Then Kendra, Hillary, and Garrett were never the targets."

"They were collateral damage," I said.

Just then, we heard the growl of an engine, growing louder as it passed the cottage.

"That's an ATV," said Stacey.

She threw open the front door. Two bobbing headlights came around the manse. The four-wheeler triggered the motion-sensitive lights, and I glimpsed the regal man behind the handlebars.

"It's Clay Markham," I said. "Where the hell can he be going?"

"To his studio on Hatchet Island. When we were talking photography, he told me he likes to develop film there at night. The tide is falling, and the bar across the thoroughfare must be above water."

I stepped around her and closed the door.

"What did you do that for?" she asked.

"We need to follow him. But we can't let Alyce or Ridge know we've left the cottage, presuming I haven't just told them."

"We should confront her! We should tell her what you know."

"She'd only deny it. And I don't have any actual proof. I'm just hoping that Delphine Cruz listens to what I have to say. It would help if I had a confession, and I think I have a chance of getting one from Clay, at least."

"He's a fucking rapist! Why should we believe anything Clay Markham says about himself? You seem to be assuming he wasn't part of the decision to kill Maeve."

"We need to follow him, Stace. I need you to trust me that getting him alone is the key."

She could see I was determined to pursue the four-wheeler.

She picked up her pack from the floor and looped the straps over her shoulders. I slung mine across my body so it wouldn't interfere if I needed to draw my Beretta from its holster.

"What's our escape plan?" she asked.

# 42

It was selfish, reckless, and risky, but I wanted to be the one to get a confession out of Clay Markham. To the state police colonel, I was a mere game warden who had no business being attached to a homicide investigation. I wanted to validate Klesko's faith in me.

I hadn't spotted security cameras around the property, but that only meant they'd been installed by a professional. Knowing the value of Clay Markham's images, along with the couple's other belongings—those handcrafted European shotguns!—I had to believe the compound was being actively watched. An image of Derrick Ridge sitting before a bank of monitors flashed through my head.

I guided Stacey through a side window that opened onto a pale carpet of newly mowed lawn. Fireflies floated like flickering fairy lights, lost and aimless above the grass. Beyond, the spruce forest made a jagged black edge against a sky bright with stars. The moon would be up above the trees soon. I wasn't sure if that would be a help or a hindrance.

We timed our sprint for the thirty seconds of darkness between the rotations of the lighthouse. As soon as the beam passed, we raced across the lawn to the woods. An odor of moldering needles and rotting logs rose from the damp forest floor. Neither of us dared to put on our headlamps while we might be visible from the house.

"Now where?" asked Stacey.

"I think we should blaze a trail parallel to the edge of the field until we're below the compound. Then we can follow the grass road down through the remains of the old town to the village."

"Or we can follow Markham's private ATV path." Although her face was hidden in the darkness, I could tell she was grinning.

"What private ATV path?"

"Honestly, Bowditch, I'm not sure how you've survived this long without me. You didn't notice that Clay turned his four-wheeler into the woods after starting down the hill? Here, I'll show you."

I let her lead the way, and sure enough, she found a narrow trail branching off the road. The starlight revealed fresh tire treads stamped into the mud.

"It makes sense for Markham to have a direct route to the sand-bar and his studio," I said. "That way, the busybodies in town can't keep a log of his comings and goings."

"Now you're thinking like a woodsman."

I would've preferred to descend the hill under the cover of dark-ness. But the trail through the forest was crisscrossed with exposed roots and hidden holes where it would be easy to twist an ankle.

We fastened the straps of our headlamps atop our caps so that the beams shimmered over the brims. Then we started off down the slick and slippery hill.

Stacey immediately grabbed at a sapling to stop her feet from sliding out from under her.

"These sneakers weren't made for hiking," she said.

"Neither were these kayaking shoes."

Markham's trail skirted the back of the ice pond. The green frogs had begun a discordant chorus, and the blossoming water lilies—Charley called the flowers *beaver roots*—brought a passing sweet-ness to the air.

As we picked our way from tree to tree, I caught glimpses of the houses in Ayers Village. A deep cellar hole choked with barberry opened up beside the path. The spinning ATV tires had caused the earth to erode dangerously above the pit.

A moment later we heard a rustle beyond the bushes and an in-take of breath.

"Who's there?" said Stacey.

A goat bleated in reply. What could we do but smile?

A faint scent of hollyhocks and foxgloves told me we had come near the bright gardens outside Brenna Speer's door. It seemed odd not to hear the buzzing of bees, but the insects were asleep in their hives. Night belonged to the mosquitoes, which were out in force.

Suddenly, I stopped short and swung an arm across her chest.

"Watch your step!"

The trail made a hairpin turn where it emerged from the woods above the channel. I had been watching Markham's tracks and noticed that he'd hit his brakes hard. If we hadn't stopped, we might have fallen twenty feet onto the leg-breaking ledge below. Winter storms had excavated the undercut, washing away the soil and exposing the roots of the leaning trees.

The old photographer was more of a daredevil than I gave him credit for being. I had to remember this was the same man who'd journeyed to New Guinea to photograph hill people who might well have eaten him.

We followed tire treads down to the waterline. I tasted brine on my lips and heard, far away, a bell buoy being knocked around by the moonlit waves. As the surf hit the shore, it made a rustling, rumbling noise.

"The bar can't be far now."

At the bottom we came upon a field of dinosaur eggs. These were sea-smoothed stones, some palm-size, others bigger than my fist, all made of speckled granite. Round as they were, they rolled easily in the wash. The water was so clear in my headlamp I could see crabs scrambling for cover, whelks creeping in search of mussels.

"This island is so amazing," Stacey said, speaking as softly as if we had entered a place of worship. "Markham captured the darkness of Maine in his seascapes, but he missed the beauty here."

"He's blind to it because he's obsessed with death. Maybe you should come back with your camera."

"No," she said, "it's ruined for me now."

I felt the same. After the case was done, I would never return willingly to these islands. It hadn't occurred to me yet that I might not be leaving them alive.

"There's the sandbar, and those are his tracks," said Stacey. "He couldn't have made it easier to follow him if he'd tried."

When she had told me of the sandbar between Ayers and Hatchet Islands, I had wondered why the old granite company hadn't dredged the channel to open a permanent passage for its ships.

I literally stumbled upon the answer when I stubbed my toe on a stone outcropping. The bar consisted of a wide ridge of solid granite with just enough sand and rockweed to conceal its lurking presence. The quarry owners must have calculated that blowing the natural bridge to pieces wasn't worth the cost of dynamite, especially when the ocean could always undo their work in a single winter.

The powerful arc lights that illuminated the Ayers wharf revealed our shadows on the surface of the water. We thought it best to turn off our headlamps to make the crossing. If someone happened to be night fishing for cunner from the dock, we might be spotted.

It takes as long as half an hour for the human eye to adjust to darkness. We didn't have the luxury of waiting. When I could make out the constellations of Cassiopeia and Perseus overhead, I deemed it time to go.

From years of traveling back and forth to Hatchet Island, Clay Markham knew where the ledge posed a danger to his tires. We had only to walk in his tracks to keep our footing. Mostly, we felt flat granite beneath our soles, only occasionally sliding off into the sand.

The tide had been high at six o'clock, which meant the bar would continue widening into the night. Unless we got held up for six hours—in which case, we would be facing far worse problems—we were in no danger of being stranded on Hatchet.

As we neared the end, I saw what I thought were two strange bushes ahead. The trail seemed to pass between the ragged balls. They were tangles of rusted razor wire the size of hay bales. Dead leaves had impaled themselves on the steel thorns, and gull feathers were caught in the concertina. Someone (maybe one of the younger Goodales) had hung crab shells, twine, and the black egg cases of skates from the barbs, too. The effect of these decorations was less whimsical than foreboding.

A NO TRESPASSING sign was hammered into the sandy earth beyond the wire. It included an addendum written in such large letters I had no trouble reading it by moonlight.

"'Violators will be shot,'" I said.

"As if the name isn't ominous enough," added Stacey. "Hatchet Island. Who named this place? Nancy Drew?"

I reached for the grip of my Beretta, raised the gun in the holster to be sure it would come out smoothly if needed, then pushed it down until I heard a satisfying click from the thumb release.

I felt Stacey at my shoulder. "Why don't you take the lead."

"Thanks."

"You know I'll always have your back, Bowditch. Literally!"

We had pursued Markham's ATV with almost careless enthusiasm, but that excitement had dissipated. We were bantering, I realized, because the wire bales and the sign felt genuinely threatening. I wasn't scared of Clay Markham, armed or not. But for the first time, a premonition had come over me that unknown dangers lay ahead.

I reached into my pocket for my Fenix tactical light. It was only five inches long with an adjustable illumination output. I switched the beam to the lowest setting of fifteen lumens, keeping the bulb pointed at the ground. I would want a light ready if I was forced to draw my weapon.

"Do you think that's a good idea?" she asked.

"Better than stepping into a bear trap."

"My dad did that once."

"He told me the story. I think we should keep quiet from here. Just to be on the safe side."

We passed between the gap in the wire and found ourselves almost immediately at a crossroads. One trail, wide as a road, followed the shoreline to the north. A second path plunged straight ahead into the forest, ascending to the bare ledges on Hatchet Island's central hill, if my internal compass was to be believed. The third trail, also broad, headed south along the channel. It must once have led to the ferry that carried miners back and forth to Ayerstown when the tide was too high to wade.

For us, the decision was predetermined. The ATV tracks followed the first trail. We continued along the northern shore.

We came first to a field overgrown with bush honeysuckle, raspberry, and poison ivy. Rising from amid the bushes was a gigantic metal artifact crusted with rust and lichen. It was some great engine from the quarries abandoned here after the last barge had carried away the last blocks of granite.

Out of curiosity, I let the flashlight roam over the industrial fossil until I heard Stacey clear her throat. This was the wrong time for a historic walking tour of Hatchet Island. I took several steps forward, following the thin pale beam, which I held centered on the tracks of the four-wheeler.

That was when I saw the boot prints.

They joined the trail via a narrow footpath that was more like a vee in the bushes, something a stag might have made. A man had recently come this way—within the hour, I judged. I recognized the tracks because they appeared identical to the ones I'd found on Baker Island.

I crouched and drew Stacey's attention to the prints.

Whoever he was, he seemed to be following Markham toward his studio on the east side of the island, near the old quarry. From the relative shallowness of the prints, I could determine the man was not particularly heavy. From the striding distance between them, I could tell he was moving fast.

Stacey pressed her lips to my ear. "Do you think Clay is in danger?"

"If he's not, we are."

I drew my Beretta.

There was enough of a glow from the moon that I could make out the ATV tracks with my naked eye, but I needed better illumination to see the boot prints. There was no sign of the mysterious man having returned, which meant he might be ahead of us.

I decided to risk the flashlight.

The trail widened the farther we got from the wire bales. As I had guessed, it had once been the chief road used by the quarrymen. I could almost perceive the ghosts of those long-dead miners streaming past us to their spectral homes across the channel.

Near the harbor, the dominant cover had been leafy birches and upstart oaks. Now the road passed through a tunnel formed of interlacing spruce and fir boughs. The temperature under the evergreens felt much cooler than it had in the open. The lowest branches were hung with old-man's beard. Everywhere among the scaly trunks were discarded granite blocks. Some were pale enough to see in the darkness; others were blanketed by the green pincushion moss that seemed intent on overspreading the island.

As we climbed toward what I suspected was the lip of the old quarry, I let my flashlight beam wander off-trail. The light found a sodden cigarette filter in the mud. It had been there awhile—days, maybe weeks. My younger self wouldn't have given the piece of litter a second thought. It had taken years and many hard lessons for me to learn that noticing details was the essence of my craft.

I knelt for a closer look and saw that it wasn't a cigarette filter at all but the discarded end of a cigarillo. There were others, too, as if the smoker was accustomed to flicking away his butts before he approached the quarry. My nose conjured the smell from memory: a cloying sweetness atop the harsh reek of low-grade tobacco.

As I rose to my feet, I clicked off my light and dropped my pack to the ground. I extended the pistol ahead of me so that I was looking at the path through the red tritium sights.

Behind me, Stacey drew a breath.

What was Chris Beckwith doing on Hatchet Island?

# 43

M y mouth brushed Stacey's hair as I drew her close.

"I know who we've been following. It's Bear Goodale's sternman, Chris Beckwith. These butts are Swisher Sweets. Beckwith chain-smokes them."

Now it was her turn to press her lips to my ear. "Are you sure?"

"Not until I see him. But I know he wears boots that match these tracks. He's been here often from the looks of things. And I think he is here now."

"Are you saying this Beckwith guy . . . ?"

"Is the one who killed Kendra and Hillary? He's been around Baker Island a thousand times and probably knows the location of that secret landing, if he didn't rig that camouflaged mooring ball himself. He's strong enough to have wrestled the shotgun away from Kendra."

"But why? He has no connection to the Markhams."

"No connection we know about yet."

I reached into my front pocket. "Here, I want you to take this."

My gift was my Gerber 06 automatic knife. She pushed the button, and the razor-edged blade swung out of the handle. Unlike other knives that have benign uses, the 06 had been designed as a man-killing weapon of war.

"I wish you were giving me a gun."

"Me, too," I said. "I need to ask you an important question now. Do you think Clay Markham's life is in danger?"

"No."

I had expected her to say yes.

"I asked the question because, if I end up having to shoot Beck-with, the attorney general will want to verify that I acted either in self-defense or to protect the life of a vulnerable person."

"In that case, yes, I think his life is in danger," she said. "But so is Beckwith's. You see Clay as an old man with heart trouble. But he has a lot of muscle mass for someone his age. I wouldn't underesti-mate Markham."

"I guess we'll have to find out for ourselves, then."

"Find out what?"

"Which of them is the more dangerous."

The moonglow caught the sharp edge of the knife in her hand. "You'd better not tell me to wait here."

"I wouldn't dream of it," I said honestly. "Just stay a few steps behind me."

We hunched over as we neared the lip of the quarry and went down on our hands and knees. A yellow light was rising from the flooded pit as if the water itself were generating the sickly lumines-cence.

On the mainland, there were quarry ponds so deep, with such polluted bottoms, that their lowest reaches were anoxic. Fish could not survive in those depths because the water contained no dissolved oxygen. Nor did man-made objects decay the way they did where bacteria could go about their business. At the bottom of one abyss in Rockland, a diver had discovered a near-perfectly preserved ma-hogany captain's desk from the golden age of sail. It sold at auction for ten grand.

Somewhere in the dark spruces, a bird sang a few notes, then went silent. I recognized the tune. It was a parula, a warbler that had no business being awake before dawn.

"Maybe it had a nightmare," Stacey whispered.

"Can you blame him, living here?"

Flat on our stomachs, we peered over the edge.

The source of the sulfurous glow revealed itself as an ungainly building at the edge of the pond. It seemed to consist of several mis-matched structures, hammered together to make one. Some of the sides were newly shingled, others had clapboards that were decades old. Solar panels on the roof powered the machines inside. There were also two propane tanks for days when the fog refused to lift.

High-tech and no-tech, new and old, straight in places and off-kilter in others—Clay Markham's studio was Frankenstein's monster as a work of architecture.

Incandescent light streamed out a back window onto a stubby dock facing the mercury-colored water. Other windows faced the land. But Markham had drawn the blinds, and so they appeared to us as orange rectangles. A mud-spattered ATV was parked outside the main door.

I decided to approach the studio from one of its windowless sides. I slipped over the rise and then, with my back bent, jogged down a weedy slope that became progressively soggier. I reached the building without incident, as far as I could tell, followed close behind by Stacey.

I pressed my back to the wall and heard a squish. I felt a slimy object creep down my neck and sent a hand grasping for it down my collar. What I held before my eyes was a spotted slug as long and thick as my index finger. The wall was crawling with slugs.

"Look at them all," Stacey, the former wildlife biologist, said with hushed excitement. "I've never seen so many leopard slugs in one place. Tawny garden and gray garden slugs, too. It must be the humidity."

I pressed my finger to my lips. It tasted of slug.

I listened while Stacey examined the creepy-crawlies.

"Do you hear voices inside?" I asked.

"No."

"I want you to stay here while I take a peek."

I glanced around the edge of the building and saw nothing to give me pause. Keeping my head ducked, I turned the corner and slunk along the clapboards until I was inches from the casement of the first window. I saw a sliver of light around the blind, almost like a white frame. The illuminated crack wasn't wide enough for me to see through, alas.

Then I heard it: a murmur of voices.

I had no choice but to press on to the next window. It would bring me closer to the room where the people were talking. I would risk being heard myself.

This time, I found that the blind had not been fully drawn. There was a crack no wider than an inch above the sill. I tilted my head sideways.

Whatever I had expected to see, it wasn't this. Clay Markham sat at the end of a long sofa. Chris Beckwith lay, like a child on the verge of drifting off to sleep, with his head in the photographer's lap. Clay was stroking his tuft of blond hair and gazing down at the man's ruined face with an expression I could only describe as affectionate.

"It'll pass," I heard Markham say consolingly. "You'll answer their questions, and it'll be all over."

"It won't be over in my head."

"You can master your memories, Christopher."

"I don't understand."

"Your brain has the power to obscure your past. Think of it like writing over something on a piece of paper. You keep doing it until there's no trace of what was there before."

"I can never understand you, Clay. Your mind is so . . ."

"We'll do it together," said Markham soothingly. "Say it for me. 'I was never there. I was never there.'"

A tear ran down Beckwith's scarred cheek. "I was never there."

"Keep repeating those words, and one day, I promise you, it'll be the truth. No one will be able to convince you otherwise."

Out of my peripheral vision, I saw Stacey creeping toward me. She had been right about Markham. She had seen through the gentility in which the fiend cloaked himself.

Absently, I took hold of the sill to help myself to my feet. It was a dumb move. The rotten wood crumbled in my fingers.

"What's that?" I heard Beckwith say.

I rushed to the nearest door and, not knowing if it was locked or not, announced myself, "Police! Don't move!"

I kicked the knob, the bolt gave way, and the door broke apart.

Both Markham and Beckwith had jumped to their feet. I sighted my Beretta on the sternman's center mass: the area around his heart and lungs where a bullet strike would be fatal.

"On your knees, Beckwith," I said. "Hands on top of your head."

Markham gathered himself to his full height and stepped in front of the other man, color rising to his cheeks. His furor was almost demonic to behold.

"What the fuck are you doing?" he huffed. "What the fuck is the meaning of this?"

"Markham, stay where you are!"

The photographer refused to comply with my command. Instead, he continued to advance, blocking my shot. "How dare you! You have no fucking right to be here!"

His smooth accent was gone. His fine manners were gone.

"Markham!"

But it was too late. Beckwith lunged for a walking stick leaning against the wall.

I sidestepped the photographer. "Drop it, Beckwith!"

Markham made a lunge for my left arm. He didn't have the strength to wrestle me, but I was forced to abandon the two-handed grip on my Beretta. I lifted my elbow to ward off the old man and caught him in the face with my forearm. The blow to his jaw sent him spinning. He dropped hard to the floor.

Seeing Markham collapse, Beckwith let out a snarl and hurled the cane at my head. I had a split second to raise my arm. The black stick hit me squarely on the wrist. The wood was heavier than it looked. The pain went all the way to the bone.

Before I could take aim again, Beckwith darted through an open door behind him.

Stacey crouched over the prone form of Clay Markham. The knife lay in the doorway where she'd dropped it. Her shoulders blocked my view, but I heard wheezing coming from the photographer and got a glimpse of his face, as red now as a balloon.

"I think he's having a heart attack," she said.

From farther in the building came the sounds of doors flying open, sometimes with splintering force.

*Is there a firearm in the studio? Is Beckwith making for it?*

"I'm going after him."

"I can't believe this. I can't fucking believe this!" The anguish in Stacey's voice sounded as if she were in excruciating physical pain.

"Stacey?"

"Go, Mike!"

"What are you going to do?"

"I'm going to save his miserable life."

She leaned over Clay Markham's rib cage to begin a series of chest compressions.

# 44

I peeked into the next room before entering. It was an office with overstuffed bookcases and a shelf lined with the skulls of large mammals. At a glance, I identified a bear, a bobcat, a seal. A trestle table faced a half-open window with a view of the pond. During the day, the vista must have been magnificent. But with the lights on inside the room, the panes had become black mirrors that showed not just the room in reverse but me in reverse as well.

My reflected self wore a murderous mask.

Having cleared the office, I continued into the next chamber of the disjointed building. It was like moving through train carriages after a minor derailment. A narrow hall took me past a darkroom with a closed door and a red light to signal when it was in use. Strong chemical odors seeped through crumbling drywall and left a metallic taste on my tongue.

Beckwith could be waiting with a firearm inside that darkroom. He could shoot me dead through the plaster wall. I assumed the door had a lock to prevent some idiot from intruding while Markham or Speer was developing their grotesque images in alkaline baths.

I stood to one side of the threshold and with my free hand gripped the knob.

Just then, I heard a massive splash.

*Son of a bitch.*

Beckwith had dived into the quarry pond.

I barged through a kitchen toward a wide-open door leading to the dock overlooking the pond. I was on a high from the adrenaline in my bloodstream, but I wasn't so mindless that I failed to notice something was amiss.

Three chairs surrounded the rectangular kitchen table. It looked . . . wrong.

*Shouldn't there be four?*

The question wasn't enough to stop me in my tracks. But the hesitation slowed my forward progress as I stepped onto the swaying dock.

Beckwith tried to grab my gun as I came through the door. Having thrown a kitchen chair into the water to fool me, he had been waiting outside with his back pressed to the wall. The microsecond I'd hesitated had saved me from losing my firearm.

He was so close I could smell the sweetness of the liquor and tobacco on his breath. I pulled my elbows back until the heels of my hands were against my sternum. The attitude was almost one of prayer. We fought for possession of the Beretta, and Beckwith was not a weak man.

My finger squeezed the trigger, and the recoil rammed the slide against my chest. Beckwith stumbled back, one hand clamped against his chipped collarbone. He lost his balance and fell into the quarry pond. He sank like a block of granite.

My younger self might have continued firing into the expanding rings where he'd disappeared. The law says a police officer must cease fire if he is no longer in danger. But when you've just been in a fight, it takes tremendous willpower to remember your training let alone the law.

Now I scanned the surface down the barrel of my handgun. I pulled out my Fenix and shined it on the water. The ripples subsided.

A full minute passed before I heard him resurface. He was farther out in the pond, beyond the reach of my flashlight. I heard him swimming. Injured shoulder and all, he dragged himself across the pond through sheer force of will.

"Shit!"

There was no way I was going to follow him into the water. My only option was to circle the flooded pit and catch him when he emerged. If only I had visited the quarry during the daytime and had even the roughest idea of its dimensions. I assumed there must be a path but couldn't be certain.

Stacey was still performing chest compressions on Clay Markham. She had managed to get out her cell phone, dial it, and pin the device between her shoulder and her ear.

"If I stop CPR now, he'll die," she told someone on the other end. "I understand the situation, but I need to get him off the island to a hospital."

She lifted her mouth away from the microphone to speak to me. "LifeFlight is responding to three other emergencies—fucking July—and can't give me an ETA."

"What should I do?"

"Did you get Beckwith?"

"I winged him in the shoulder before he went into the pond. Somehow he's swimming across."

"Then go after him, Mike. Don't worry about me."

"We need to arrange a boat to take Markham inshore."

"I've got it covered," she said. "Trust me."

My gaze fell upon the heavy black stick Beckwith had hurled at me. It was Kendra Ballard's missing shillelagh.

I stepped through the door I'd kicked in but halted immediately beside the ATV. It occurred to me that Beckwith might try to draw me away from the studio, then circle back to steal it. Stacey was preoccupied with saving Markham and would be vulnerable to an attack.

I had to focus. I had to trust my experience.

*He's going to run.*

*Where?*

*The sandbar.*

The road we had followed to the studio had skirted the ocean because the terrain along Hatchet Island's north side was relatively flat. Beckwith would choose a shorter, fast way to the other side.

Ahead of me, a narrow footpath zigzagged up the cliff face from which the granite had been excavated. My guess was that it climbed up and over the highest point of Hatchet Island. It either came out at the wire bales—we had encountered just such a path at the crossroads—or it joined another trail that led to the harbor.

The moon was finally up above the tallest trees and three-quarters full. I took it as a good omen.

As a rule, I distrust shortcuts, but it seemed a night for gambling. I holstered my Beretta to make the ascent.

The path was steep and made of rock from which the rain had washed away the already thin soil. The granite was treacherous in its smoothness. The trees were slick and slug-ridden. I found myself grasping for branches. Beneath the evergreens, the entire forest floor was blanketed with pincushion and sphagnum moss. It looked soft and inviting, but moss can hide holes that will snap your ankle. I didn't dare leave the path.

I thought of Stacey with Clay Markham's life literally in her hands. He was responsible for the death of at least three people, probably more. One of them had been Stacey's roommate and close friend. All she had to do was lift her hands from his chest—pause long enough for his stricken heart to cease pumping—and Kendra Ballard and the others would be avenged. Stacey could claim that she had done everything she could for the dying man, and who would be able to question her?

But she wasn't going to do that. She had committed herself to saving the vile man's life. I found that I trusted her absolutely. The love I felt for Stacey Stevens drove me in my pursuit of Beckwith. She was my teammate tonight. We were joined together in our shared tasks.

I found myself confronted with a ten-foot wall. The moonlight didn't show a way around the cliff face. The granite was utterly flat except for vertical furrows like troughs dug by stone-eating worms. These had been the holes where miners had driven iron spikes and used wedges to pry the blocks loose.

With no way around the obstacle, I had no choice but to leap straight up and catch the top with my fingertips. I tried bringing a foot up to locate a toehold, but my kayaking shoe found no purchase. There was nothing to do but pull hard, using every muscle in my arms and upper back.

I had just thrown an elbow over the rim, with the rest of my body hanging down the cliff, when I heard a branch crack. I looked up in time to see Chris Beckwith lurching toward me with a granite block raised to smash my brains in.

# 45

Instinctively, I let go of the cliff just as Beckwith hurled the stone. It missed my head, thankfully, but I fell ten feet and landed hard on my back. The impact knocked the wind out of me. I lay stunned and gasping on my granite bed.

Only the vague, moonlit shape of Chris Beckwith stepping to the edge awakened my survival instincts. He had raised another, smaller stone. I pulled the Beretta from its holster in a bad imitation of a gunslinger and squeezed off a round that chipped the rock at his feet.

The blast was enough to frighten him, though. He'd already been shot once, and when you're soaked to the skin and losing blood, the question of fight or flight becomes an easy one.

As I steadied my shaking arms for the kill shot, his shadow disappeared from the cliff edge. I thought I heard a kicked rock bouncing down a path. My pulse was so loud in my ears, and my breathing was so ragged, it was impossible to tell what I heard from what I imagined.

Sitting up, I waited for the rolling sensation inside my skull that would tell me if I'd suffered yet another concussion. I anticipated the surge of nausea that had accompanied prior head injuries. This time, though, I experienced none of those things. I explored my scalp with my fingertips. There was only a small bump, no bigger than a quail's egg, at the bottom of my parietal bone.

The best I could do, until I caught my breath and regained my equilibrium, was to phone 9-1-1.

I identified myself to the dispatcher and was doubly fortunate that she remembered me from my days working the Midcoast. Her emotionless affect dropped when she heard my name.

"I just got off the phone with a woman on Hatchet Island, Mike," she said with motherly concern. "She told me she's dealing with a man having a cardiac event while you were engaged in a pursuit of an armed assailant. Are you injured?"

"I'm fine, but I could use some help catching this guy."

"I've alerted the state police. It'll take at least twenty minutes to get backup to you. The Coast Guard is sending a response boat in case your suspect tries to flee by water."

I had a fleeting image of that team of postadolescent Coasties speeding into the channel with their fingers on the triggers of their M4 carbines. The last thing I wanted was to escalate the situation.

"As long as their commanding officer knows he doesn't have jurisdiction on the island itself."

"You want me to call them off?"

"Hell no."

It would take ages for state and local law enforcement to get their act together. In the meantime, I would take whatever armed assistance I could get. Beckwith might be heading off to find a firearm. There was no shortage of innocent civilians on Ayers Island, including children, if he wanted to take a hostage.

I asked the dispatcher, "Did the woman you spoke with say how her heart attack patient was doing?"

"He's experiencing agonal breathing. She doesn't dare stop CPR. She was going to call some of the islanders to arrange to transport him to one of their boats for evacuation."

*Smart thinking, Stacey.*

"I'll keep my cell on," I told the dispatcher. "Maybe have the Coast Guard call me on arrival."

"Will do. And be careful, OK?"

I turned and squinted down the cliff behind me. It seemed much steeper than when I'd ascended. Moonlight touched the green-gray lichen in the dark branches of the spruces.

I needed to capture Beckwith alive, to get the full story out of him. I had to find out what had happened on Baker Island and how the Markhams were involved. Before everything came my primary responsibility as a sworn officer of the law. I must not allow Christopher Beckwith to hurt another soul.

I managed to get myself up the sheer rock face after two more attempts. I had been correct in thinking that Beckwith wouldn't be waiting in the shadows to blindside me again. Having failed to ambush me twice, he wasn't going to risk a third attempt on someone he knew to be armed.

When I'd reached the bare ledges of the summit, I had a view of Ayers Village across the shallow channel. More and more lights came on in the houses while I watched. I couldn't see the sandbar from this vantage point, but I caught the sound of voices rising from below. The island's rescue team was en route to Stacey.

I began my descent, using my headlamp to guide me through the trees. I stepped carefully through the wet roots of the spruces, on the shallow layer of soil above the bedrock, and the layers of moss that sloughed off beneath the soles of my shoes. Slugs were everywhere. Hatchet Island must have spent half its year cloaked in fog.

As I neared the bottom, I heard an engine roar to life in the harbor. It sounded to my inexperienced ears like the *Persuader*.

*Does Bear know what his sternman did?*

*Was he an accomplice?*

*Should I consider him dangerous, too?*

The goat trail dumped me onto the shore path south of the land bridge. I found myself gazing out at the deeper water where the Markhams' two yachts and the island's two lobsterboats were moored. A white radiance rose from arc lights along the wharf. People were gathering there.

I was starting for the sandbar when I heard a splash ahead. It might have been squid rising to the dock lights or a striped bass rising in pursuit of the squid. But the sound caused me to hesitate.

I shrank back into the shadows to avoid being seen. From my hiding place, I scanned the channel and saw a round shadow detach itself from an unoccupied mooring. It disappeared beneath the surface like a seal's head. Thirty seconds later, it reappeared near the *Persuader*. I could only imagine how hard it must have been for Beckwith to swim without the use of both shoulders.

I cupped my hands around my mouth and called to the people on the wharf. "He's in the water! Beckwith's in the water!"

Did the islanders even know what I meant?

Would they take action if they did?

I debated plunging into the channel in pursuit of my fugitive.

The water was bubbling behind the *Persuader*'s inboard engine. Beckwith's head popped up near a gunwale. Bear Goodale hadn't seemed to hear me over the sound of his motor. He stood with his back to the transom. I had no idea if the lobsterman would be Beckwith's next victim or his getaway driver.

"Goodale!"

Bear couldn't hear me.

With his good arm, Beckwith reached up from the water to grab the gunwale of the lobsterboat. He had almost pulled himself aboard when the sound of a gunshot jolted my heart. Beckwith's body jerked and then, very slowly, slid backward into the channel.

A second shot exploded from across the passage. The way the water sprayed around the floating man told me he was being targeted by a shotgun. Each of the pellets raised its own splash.

"Stop firing! Stop firing!"

Without thinking, I waded out into the channel until the bottom dropped off, then swam toward the now motionless body of Chris Beckwith. I prayed that whoever was shooting at him would see me and take their finger off the trigger.

Only the face and hands of the wounded man were visible above the surface of the water. Even before I reached him, I saw there were red holes in the unscarred half of his face. His lips were parted, and seawater sloshed into his mouth. He made no effort to spit it out.

Chris Beckwith was dead.

Like a lifeguard, I towed the corpse across the channel to the dock, where Justin Speer and the old fisherman I'd seen on the *Frost Flower* helped haul it onto the boards. Skip Ayers extended a calloused hand to pull me out of the channel. He just about lifted my two-hundred-pound body into the air.

All the motion caused the dock to shimmy and shake. The hulls of our kayaks knocked hollowly against the float. Soaking wet, with a puddle forming at my feet, I stood over the limp, lifeless thing that had been Christopher Beckwith.

I didn't notice that Bear Goodale had followed in his dinghy. The barrel-chested man leaped onto the dock—causing another tremor. He fell to his knees beside his friend.

"No, no, no."

Bear leaned over his former sternman as if to begin artificial respiration, but old Skip Ayers squeezed his shoulder.

"It's too late for that," he said. "Don't waste your breath."

"We need to do something, Skip," said Goodale, his voice breaking.

"He's above or below now, Bear. The one place he ain't is here with us."

I directed my attention up the ladder to the wharf above the floating dock. White faces looked down. I had trouble speaking between in-drawn breaths.

"Which one of you shot him?"

"I did!"

Alyce Markham stood under the arc light with a shotgun tucked under her arm and her face full of scorn.

# 46

I did not arrest Alyce Markham, but I convinced her to hand over the shotgun: a sixteen-gauge Holland & Holland. Beckwith had been silenced. The weapon had served its purpose.

I gestured at a tarnished bollard. The nautical hitching post looked antique but was probably just another faux-historic decoration that Alyce had chosen from a catalog.

"Mrs. Markham, I need you to sit there."

She had regained control of her facial muscles to show mere displeasure instead of active hate. She could have taught classes for actors in assuming feigned emotions.

"You can't hold me, Warden. My husband needs me. I have a right to be at Clay's side."

"You forfeited your rights when you killed that man."

"This is *my* island."

"If you move, Mrs. Markham, I will put you in restraints."

Alyce Markham worked her thin lips, as if preparing a rejoinder. But she thought better of it. The woman's self-discipline was both amazing and terrible to behold.

I directed Bear Goodale and Skip Ayers to carry the corpse up the ladder to be laid under a tarp until the medical examiner arrived. Out of the corner of my eye, I caught Justin Speer skulking around the scene, snapping flash photographs with his camera. I should have known he couldn't resist.

"What else can I do for you, Warden?" asked Skip. I realized he had the first and only Maine accent I'd encountered on the island. "Jonathan and some of th'others are helping your Stacey get Markham to the *Persuader*."

"I don't want Bear on the boat with Markham."

"Hard to keep a man off his own vessel. I'd take Clay in the *Frost Flower* if she weren't slower than stock-still."

"Can you help me keep an eye on Mrs. Markham?"

"Her ladyship won't be going anywhere."

"You sound confident of that, Mr. Ayers."

"Why should she want to escape? She's not worried about what will happen if she stays."

"Why do you say that?"

"Because there's no trouble people like the Markhams can't buy their way out of."

Spoken like a man who'd watched his ancestral island be turned into a wealthy woman's folly.

"I remember the day Chris Beckwith arrived here as a lad," the lobsterman added ruefully as he studied the tarp. "He thought he'd been given the key to Eden."

Just then, a John Deere Gator UTV emerged from between the wire bales carrying the stricken photographer in its bed. Jonathan Goodale was at the wheel, and his wife, Lisa, was beside him. Stacey crouched over Clay Markham's chest, unwilling to surrender CPR duties. Several of the Goodale children trailed behind the four-wheeler like so many lambs.

I dearly hoped Skip Ayers could convince Bear to give up his keys to the *Persuader*. But I was rescued from my worries by the arrival of the Coast Guard. It was the same militarized vessel that had been first on the scene at Baker Island, with the same petty officer commanding.

The Coast Guard officer said his team was trained in first aid and even had a defibrillator on board in case Markham flatlined on the race to Damariscotta. When one of the guardsmen finally relieved Stacey, she staggered from weariness. It had taken unreal endurance to keep up chest compressions for as long as she had.

I wrapped my arm around her waist to steady her.

"I have never wanted to wash my hands so badly in my whole life," she said.

"I'm sure we can find some wet wipes."

"I'd prefer bleach. I wanted to let him die, Mike. I really did. But it was you who saved me."

"Me?"

She raised her face to make eye contact. The exhaustion showed. "I didn't want to disappoint you."

"That's not why you saved him, Stace."

She touched my face. "I heard gunfire. Is Beckwith dead?"

"He is, but I wasn't the one who killed him. It was Alyce Markham. She used an expensive pheasant gun from their cabinet."

"Why did she do it?" Stacey asked. "Did she tell you?"

"She hasn't and won't. But I expect her lawyer will claim she was trying to protect Bear Goodale from a killer and fired wide. My belief is that Alyce Markham didn't want prosecutors flipping Beckwith and getting him to testify against her husband. Maybe she was protecting herself, too. For all we know, Alyce might have masterminded the mission to send Beckwith to Baker Island."

"I'm ready to collapse after everything that's happened today. But you probably have to wait for Cruz and the others."

"We're going to have to find a place to spend the night," I said.

"I'm sure Skip and Dorothea Ayers would take us in."

"That would be perfect."

The Coast Guard boat was ready to leave, and I noticed that Derrick Ridge had finally made an appearance, creeping into the light to confer with Alyce. I needed to split those two up before they could collude even more than they probably had. Before I could move a muscle, Skip Ayers had scared Ridge off with a raised fist.

Stacey went off to clean herself up while I returned to the wharf.

I informed Alyce Markham of her husband's condition and the plan to rush him to the hospital in Damariscotta. She received the information silently. Then I called my colonel, only to find he'd received the news from the state police. Because we hadn't spoken since the morning, Colonel DeFord expressed his shock at Klesko's bizarre brush with death. He also said he would personally be coming out to Ayers at first light to relieve me as Warden Service representative.

"I know how exhausted you and Stacey must be," he said. "You both need time and space to grieve the loss of her friend."

I was experienced enough in agency politics that I knew the real reason behind this seemingly generous act: Clay Markham was an internationally known artist whose alleged participation in a double homicide would make news around the globe. The killings of the researchers on Baker Island had been a bombshell. Markham's involvement would be a thermonuclear explosion.

Alyce Markham called to me: "Can I get a bottle of water at least?"

"Sure."

I beckoned to Juniper Goodale, who, with the other island children, had taken up a position beyond the wharf to watch the drama unfold, and asked if she could find some water for Mrs. Markham.

She returned in minutes with a stained coffee mug filled with water.

"I asked for a bottle."

I ignored the complaint and crossed my arms. "You know, Mrs. Markham, I should have realized that Beckwith had been one of your husband's houseboys. It was the injury to his face—and that punk haircut—that threw me off. How old was he when Clay hired him?"

She smiled as if the reminiscence gave her pleasure. "Actually, I was the one who hired him. He was working as a bagger at a supermarket in Waldoboro. Christopher was seventeen and full of life."

"And he didn't have disfiguring scars yet," I said. "I don't suppose you'll tell me how he got them?"

"Why shouldn't I?" she asked with convincing innocence. "It was a year after he came to work for us. I was at our house on Bequia at the time, and Clay was off in Thailand. Christopher did it to himself with a box cutter when he was high on some drug or other. Clearly, he was more troubled than we'd realized. Ridge had to let him go, obviously."

"Obviously."

"I have to admit we were surprised when Christopher returned to the island after he left the psychiatric hospital. I can't say I approved, but I wasn't so heartless as to run him off. It hasn't escaped me that you've concluded Clay and I are monsters. I can assure you we're both very human."

"Maybe he had nowhere else to go."

She readjusted her extravagant glasses as if to indicate she was done talking about the late Christopher Beckwith. "Is it necessary that we sit here until the police arrive, or can we at least wait back at my house?"

"We'll wait here, I think."

"I don't know why police officers feel like they have to assert dominance in every situation. I'm sure a psychologist could explain it."

"Something about our being secretly insecure."

"If I'm not under arrest, you have no right to detain me."

"Would you like me to put you under arrest?"

The way she grinned, I had the uncomfortable feeling she was enjoying jousting with me. "If you did, I would have to call my lawyer, and he would advise me to remain silent pending his arrival. That would be the end of our little conversation. I've always said the best investment a person can make is in attorneys and accountants."

"You and your husband will both be needing the former."

"For a short time, until they make this go away."

"I wouldn't be so confident of that."

Her eyes drifted away from me toward a clutch of islanders, Speer with his camera, and some of the Goodales, whispering together at the end of the dock. Her expression became smug.

"Don't assume you'll get anything out of them," she said. "They've all signed nondisclosure agreements. We'd never have allowed them to settle here, given them housing and livelihoods, if it meant exposing ourselves to some tell-all book about the *real* Clay Markham."

"An NDA doesn't apply with regard to a murder investigation, Mrs. Markham."

"I acted to defend Bear Goodale from a man you yourself had announced was armed and dangerous. Ridge heard the alert go out over the police scanner."

"I was speaking about the women on Baker Island."

She gestured with her foot to the shape lumped beneath the blue tarp. "The man who murdered them is there."

Alyce Markham thought she had everything in hand. Her lawyers would gum up the works for the attorney general. She believed there was no direct evidence linking her husband or herself to the homicides at the seabird colony. And as for her assassination of Beckwith, her attorneys would force the state to bring lesser charges or forgo prosecution altogether out of fear of losing in court.

"When Stacey and I were on Hatchet Island, we saw something disturbing through your husband's studio window."

"Private property, posted in accordance with state law—you and your girlfriend had no legal right to be there."

"I'm a game warden. That gives me the right."

"Only if you're on duty, actively investigating a crime under Title Twelve of Maine statute. I did some Web browsing after you left the house."

I tried to remain calm. "I saw Beckwith with his head in your husband's lap."

"Clay is a kind, gentle man. Despite everything, he's remained a father figure to Chris."

"I happened to notice a distinctive blackthorn walking stick in the studio. Beckwith hurled it at me. It belonged to Kendra Ballard. I'm curious how your attorneys will explain its presence there."

"Obviously, Christopher brought it."

"And if the state police discover Clay's fingerprints on it?"

Alyce seemed unfazed. "If only you'd had probable cause to enter the studio, Warden."

"You seem to know a lot about criminal law, Mrs. Markham."

"My husband has been unjustly accused before." She was practically gloating now. "By the way, I saw the press conference the sheriff did outside the hospital in Damariscotta. I imagine the police still have to treat that Black boy as a suspect. It's certainly suspicious that he escaped in a boat with barely a scratch."

In her arrogance, she had provided me with a missing puzzle piece.

Clay had *told* Beckwith to leave Garrett alive. If investigators ever got close to the truth, the Markhams' attorneys would need an alternate suspect to blame for the killings. Sheriff Santum's press conference must have been an unexpected windfall for the conspirators.

"I think the state police are confident they know who killed Kendra Ballard and Hillary Fitzgerald." I gestured at the human form beneath the tarp. "And I suspect they'll even be able to prove why Beckwith did it."

She raised a knee, wrapped both hands around it, and began to rock back and forth. "You have my complete attention."

"Have you ever heard the name *Evan Levandowski*?"

"Of course I have," she said. "Maeve brought him over last summer because he was desperate to meet Clay. My husband doesn't usually do any teaching, but he indulged Maeve. As I told you before, he is generous to a fault. The young man may have stayed in our guest quarters for a night or two."

"A night or two?"

"It might have been longer. I can't recall. I never exchanged more than a few words with the young man."

"Did you know he jumped off the Penobscot Narrows Bridge this spring?"

"Really? How tragic."

"It's what Maeve McLeary came to Ayers Island to discuss with you two days ago. You're obviously a very careful planner, Mrs. Markham. You think everything through, as you've demonstrated in our discussion about criminal law. And you'll do anything to protect your husband."

A furrow appeared between her eyebrows.

I continued: "Clay, on the other hand, is all impulse and spontaneity. I'm guessing Maeve found him after she left your house last night. She'd gone there to blackmail you with incriminating information she'd claimed to have received about your husband from Evan. But you called her bluff."

She ceased rocking.

"Having failed with you, Maeve went in search of Clay. She repeated her blackmail threat. This time, she got the response she wanted. She provoked Clay, and he acted without consulting you. He sought out Chris Beckwith and ordered him to take the *Spindrift* to Baker. But Maeve wasn't there. You've been doing cleanup and damage control ever since. Legally speaking, your husband conspired to commit murder and made you an accessory after the fact."

She clenched her eyelids, let out a deep breath, inhaled, and then opened her eyes again.

"Please don't think you can trick me, Warden."

"I doubt I could, Mrs. Markham. You're too smart to be provoked into incriminating yourself. Unlike your husband."

She jumped to her feet, but I didn't back down.

"How dare you talk about him like that. Clay Markham is a genius and an icon."

"He's also an amoral narcissist who grooms and preys upon vulnerable young men. However this plays out in the courts, the first paragraph of Clay Markham's obituary will now include the massacre on Baker Island."

She waved her hand dismissively. "Maybe you should arrest me after all. That way I won't have to listen to you anymore. And I can enjoy watching your life fall to pieces after my attorneys hammer you in the press."

"I'm not going to arrest you, Mrs. Markham."

"Oh, darn."

"And as for listening to me, I have only one last thing to say. Earlier tonight, you said that you and Clay have lived a very strange life. Don't think I missed the regret in your voice. You made a devil's bargain when you chose to remain married to a man you knew to be a monster. You voluntarily chose to spend your life stuck in this hell loop. And for that, Mrs. Markham, I pity you."

## 47

Chris Beckwith had lived in the back room of a barn. The islanders used the building to store a tractor, a hay rake, chain saws, limb pruners, shovels, axes, and other tools used to maintain the perfect fields and gardens of Ayers Village. The air smelled of ammonia-based fertilizer and the methane gas that comes from the decomposing grass caught in the blades of machines. I followed Delphine Cruz through the barn while nesting phoebes, awakened by our predawn visit, voiced their displeasure.

"No shortage of potential murder weapons here," observed Cruz.

"Beckwith didn't need them. He picked up what he needed on the island."

"I can't understand why he brought that black walking stick back to Ayers."

"It was a gift to Markham," I said. "Maybe it was as an apology for not having found and killed Maeve McLeary. Clay and Alyce Markham like their trophies, and I doubt Beckwith ever imagined being linked to the murder. They all assumed the blame would fall on Garrett Meadows."

"Klesko was right about you and your imagination."

Bear Goodale had provided us with the key to Beckwith's apartment. We were both wearing nitrile gloves to keep from contaminating any potential evidence. The first thing we noticed, even before we'd cracked the door open, was the stale smell of Swisher Sweet cigarillos. I expected to find a mess inside. But the worn carpet had been recently vacuumed. The shower drain contained no hair. There were no dirty dishes in the sink.

"It's cleaner than I'd expected," I said.

"Sociopaths are neater than normal people," she said. "You should read the studies."

"I wouldn't have labeled Beckwith a sociopath. At least he didn't start out as one from what I've heard."

"You're a psychologist, too?"

"I think being regularly raped by Clay Markham when he was seventeen is what ripped out Chris Beckwith's soul."

Cruz dropped to her knees to look under the bed and dragged out a Pelican hard case designed to store guns, cameras, watches. The case was unlocked. From inside, she removed a Leica camera that must have cost thousands of dollars.

"How much do you want to bet this was a gift from his kindly rapist benefactor?" she said.

"Stacey thought the killer had posed the bodies on Baker Island to throw suspicion on Justin Speer. But maybe Beckwith did it himself in imitation of Markham. He just happened to be a crap photographer with no eye for composition."

"Let's hope he kept the SD card with the pictures on it."

"The proper term is *photographs*. Derrick Ridge told me it was déclassé to call them *pictures*."

"I need a dictionary to understand some of the words you use, Bowditch."

Meanwhile, I was examining a shelf that held all of five books. One was *The Perfect Storm* by Sebastian Junger. Another was a study manual for Coast Guard basic training. Two were guides of the photography for beginners variety. The last was a high school yearbook from Lincoln Academy in the town of Newcastle, just up the river. I paged through until I found Christopher Beckwith, a sophomore at the time, in a group shot of the photo club.

"What a beautiful boy he was," Cruz said. "Do you know what happened to his face?"

"Alyce Markham said he took a box cutter to it when he was high. It had the ring of truth to me. Like how abused kids sometimes gain weight in the hope it will disgust their abusers. Beckwith disfigured himself to stop Clay from inviting him to Hatchet Island."

My phone made a noise that I'd customized for texts that came from Stacey. It was an osprey's high-pitched cry.

I'd left her at the cozy home of Skip and Dorothea Ayers with a plea to get some sleep. Clearly, she'd been unwilling or unable to take my advice.

> *Dorothea just told me that her niece is a teacher at Lincoln Academy and knew Beckwith when he was a student there. She said he was the prettiest boy in school. But also a camera geek. Mike, one of the old tricks photographers used to use for softening portraits was to stretch a nylon between the camera body and the lens! Look around the place for panty hose.*

I didn't mention Stacey's hunch to Cruz. But I made straight for the plastic garbage can in the kitchen. It contained nothing but a new trash bag, one of those white ones with the red drawstrings.

Cruz had remarked on a communal dumpster we'd passed on our way to the barn. I left her inside while I went to pry up the lid. Flies descended on the stinking trash as soon as it was open.

I spotted a white bag and lifted it carefully out of the bin. Beneath a mass of coffee grounds, I found a piece of ripped plastic with a label that read *L'eggs Sheer Energy.*

I showed it to Cruz.

"Faceless."

"Or maybe he just enjoyed wearing them," she said with an approving grin. "You never can tell with certain guys."

"My overly active imagination tells me that the piece of black nylon we found on Baker Island will have come from a pair of L'eggs Sheer Energy."

Afterward, I texted Stacey to tell her what I'd found.

> *I can live with you being an amazing bush pilot. I can live with you being a better hunter than I am. And a better*

*kayaker. And more knowledgeable about flora, fauna, geology, and science, in general. But I'm not sure my fragile ego can take you becoming a kick-ass investigator, too.*

The screen showed me an ellipsis to indicate that she was typing a response. I waited with a smile on my face.

*I'm coming for your job, Mike Bowditch!*

"What's so funny?" asked Cruz when I burst into laughter.

"My girlfriend. What do they say about buying an engagement ring? That you're supposed to spend two months' salary on it?"

"My ex spent more on a custom paint job for his Harley than he did on my ring. When I saw the box came from T.J. Maxx, I should have known we wouldn't last a year. Go slow is my advice. Don't leap into anything with a girl you just met. Now you're laughing again."

*If Stacey and I had gone any slower, we would have moved backward,* I thought.

"What's so funny?" Cruz asked.

"Nothing," I said.

By the time we made it up to the Markhams' house, the sun was riding up the eastern sky, and I had begun to lose the last of my energy. Derrick Ridge had demanded to see a warrant before he would allow the detectives and the forensic technicians inside. When Cruz presented the document, his manner changed to one of obsequious submission. He began making espressos for the police while they searched the manse.

I circulated through the rooms, looking at the photography on the walls. I hadn't had an opportunity to get a close look at Markham's masterworks before. All I saw were his dramatic and eerie seascapes. He must have kept the photos of children playing dead on the walls of his bedroom.

Ridge dogged my heels the way a store detective might trail a suspected shoplifter.

"Afraid I'm going to plant evidence, Ridge?"

"God, no! But you won't find evidence of any crimes in this house."

"You realize Cruz and her partner will be interrogating Heath and Finn this morning. The detectives will want to know the specific services they performed for Clay Markham."

He gave me his awkward "say cheese" grin. "Everyone who works here has signed an NDA. I guess I should, maybe, call a lawyer for those guys. And maybe a lawyer for myself."

Followed by his annoying little laugh.

"I can't advise you on legal matters," I said. "Whatever happens, it seems like Heath and Finn will have a story the tabloids would pay good money for. An intelligent person might consider getting out ahead of them."

"I could never betray the Markhams after they've been so generous to me over the years."

"I witnessed the generous way they treated you."

"Laugh if you want, but Clay and Alyce have made me a trustee of their estate. I'm not just some servant."

I raised an eyebrow. "Then all this might be yours someday soon."

"Soon? Clay's condition is already improving. And Alyce will outlive us all out of sheer spite."

"That's not what I meant. Both Markhams are facing potential criminal charges that will keep them far away from Ayers Island."

For the first time in our brief acquaintance, Derrick Ridge dropped the nervous affect. The man standing before me looked serious, composed, and older, which is to say, he looked his real age. He had mustaches made for villainous twirling, but he resisted touching them.

"Of course," I continued, "if the Markhams are found guilty of being involved in the murders, it'll open the door to a civil suit."

"Who has the legal standing to bring a civil suit?"

"I'm no expert, but being attacked in the night, set adrift, left for dead, and set up as a potential suspect in a double homicide—I would imagine Garrett Meadows will be looking for a multimillion-dollar settlement."

Cruz appeared in the doorway behind him. She beckoned me over by curling her index finger.

"One of the techs just called to say he found a stash of prints under the floor of Markham's studio on Hatchet. Nudes and more . . . graphic images. Some of the pictures are of Evan Levandowski. They say the kid looked drugged in them. And there are older nudes with Beckwith before he went shopping for razor blades."

I addressed Ridge across the spacious, sunlit gallery. "I wouldn't start redecorating the place yet if I were you."

# 48

After Kendra's funeral in Portsmouth, New Hampshire, we returned to my house on a wooded hillside above the Ducktrap River, 140 miles north of the state border. As usual, Charley Stevens had suggested that the four of us—himself, his wife, Ora, Stacey, and me—fly down in his Cessna. It made for a quick trip down and back.

It was the second ninety-degree day of a projected heat wave and, wouldn't you know, the air-conditioning inside the church had conked out that morning.

Now that we were home, Charley and I were quick to jettison our jackets and ties. The old pilot rubbed a damp hand through his shock of white hair, which always reminded me of a horse brush in its enviable thickness.

"Your house isn't much cooler than that church," he said. "And that church was hotter than a skunk."

Sometimes I thought he invented these colorful expressions for my benefit. Then I'd hear some other old Mainer use them. I bet Skip Ayers would have recognized the saying.

"It might actually be cooler sitting on the porch," I suggested.

"I've had my fill of confined spaces for the day," said Charley.

"Here or there," said Ora, looking as beautiful as ever with her pale green eyes and snow-white hair. "I'm fine with whatever the young people decide. And no, Charley, you don't get a vote."

"And you wonder why I call you *Boss*," said her husband.

"If we sit outside, we can watch Shadow," said Stacey. "Maybe we can even let him inside."

"He's still holding a grudge because I left him alone for a couple of nights. I think he's planning some revenge."

"He's a wolf," said Charley, sticking out his significant chin for emphasis. "Of course he's planning revenge."

Even dressed for a funeral in a black cotton shift, Stacey looked breathtakingly beautiful to me. She had made it through the service with the assistance of one of my handkerchiefs, plus a few tissues provided by Ora.

*Be good to her.* Those were Maeve McLeary's last words to me. I heard her voice almost every time I looked at Stacey now. *Be good to her.*

I only hoped I could.

I served Charley and Ora sun tea on my porch—I'd built a ramp just for Ora's wheelchair—while Stacey visited with my wolf dog in his fenced enclosure.

"How often are you letting him in the house, Mike?" asked Ora. "When he's not planning revenge, I mean."

"Once a day on average. But only when I'm home. I made the mistake of leaving him indoors when I ran to the market for groceries, and I came back to find he'd devoured that ten-pound Atlantic salmon I caught on the Miramichi River with Charley. I paid a taxidermist fifteen hundred dollars to mount that fish. Most of the stuffing ended up in Shadow's belly. He even swallowed the glass eyes."

Charley Stevens slapped his knobby knee. A man of his age and folksy affect could get away with gestures like that.

"You always say he's more wolf than dog. I guess he wanted to remind you of that fact."

Ora reached out to touch the back of my hand. "You must have been glad to see your friend Steve Klesko at the service."

I had been thrilled to see him, in fact. And not just because of how healthy he looked.

Steve had informed me that Clay Markham was confined to a bed in the manse with a new pacemaker in his chest. The photographer was being attended to by Ridge and Alyce, who had easily made bail after her arraignment on a manslaughter charge. The gristmills of the justice system would slowly grind out their fates, but Klesko was hopeful. Kendra Ballard's blackthorn had been covered with Markham's fingerprints, he said.

Another bright note was the grassroots movement on social media to force museums and galleries to take down Clay Markham's work. Already the publisher of *Children in Their Caskets* had announced they were taking the catalog out of print. If ever someone deserved to be "canceled," it was Markham.

"Who was that big man you were talking to, Mike?" Ora asked.

"Rick Spinney. He's the Marine Patrol officer we told you about. He's fighting a suspension for assaulting a lobsterman from Friendship. I don't think he's going to win his case—there have been too many other incidents. But it was kind of him to attend Kendra's funeral. He had a good heart once, and I like to think it's still in there somewhere. But he shouldn't be a law enforcement officer anymore. That much I know."

"A cop who's in hot water once will take a lot of baths," agreed Charley.

Besides the Stevenses, Spinney and Klesko had been the only people I had known at the memorial. Stacey had the support of her classmates and other wildlife biologists who'd worked with Kendra.

"It was awkward, meeting Mr. and Mrs. Ballard," I said. "I felt like they blamed Stacey—and maybe even me—for what happened to their daughter."

"That's just grief," said Charley. "It'll pass."

"I'm not so sure," said Ora. "The Ballards never much liked Stacey. They saw her as a bad influence on their daughter."

I rattled the ice around my empty glass. "It's a shame they haven't gotten to know the woman she's become."

"'Tis," said Charley.

I'd been waiting for a moment alone with Stacey's parents. I realized this was my chance.

"Ora, Charley, there's something I'd like to ask you."

"Mike Bowditch, don't you dare!" said Ora, slapping my hand.

"How do you know what I am going to ask?"

Then I remembered she was Stacey's mother, possessed of the same second sight as her daughter.

"This is the twenty-first century," Ora said, leaning toward me. "Permission is not ours to give. I know you think you're being respectful and chivalrous, dear, but I wouldn't mention to Stacey that you almost asked us to give her away. I believe I remember her using the term *chattel* to describe how daughters were pawned off by their families in days of old."

"You can still show us the ring," said Charley impishly.

I produced the box and flipped it open to reveal a platinum band inset with a green tourmaline stone that had been mined in the western Maine foothills.

"Oh, it's beautiful, Mike!" said Ora.

"Do you think she'll like it?"

"No," said her father.

"Charley!" said her mother.

"I just mean, she doesn't like to wear anything on her fingers, being so active outdoors. But she'll treasure the ring, even if she keeps it safe in a box."

"When are you planning on asking her?" said Ora.

I felt the electricity humming in my nerves just as I had in bed that morning. Soon nothing would be the same.

"Not tonight."

"Why not?" said Ora.

"I thought I'd wait on account of the funeral," I said. "It's been such a sad day."

"There's still time to redeem it. I think Kendra would be glad to see the two of you find happiness after so much grief."

"She won't be expecting it, either." Charley raised a knobby finger. "So you'll have the element of surprise."

He made the proposal sound like a sneak attack.

"You're wrong about that, dear," said Ora. "She knows. I'm sure she knows."

The three of us fell silent while we watched the activity inside the pen. Shadow was stretched out in the late-afternoon sun on the lichen-covered ledge that was his throne. Stacey sat beside him, scratching the massive animal behind the ears. The wolf's eyes were closed as he indulged in her worshipful attention.

"She's the only one I'll let in there," I said. "In fact, I'm beginning to think Shadow likes her better than he does me."

The two of them together—the wolf king and his noble lady—made such a fun image I decided to get out my phone. I had to stand atop my chair to get a shot that didn't include the fence. Stacey noticed my precarious position, threw back her head, and laughed with real laughter just as I pushed the button. I wasn't much of a photographer, but I managed to capture her beauty in that unguarded moment.

As I inspected the image on the digital photo roll, I noticed that the last one I had taken had been inside the Markhams' house. It was that snapshot of *Shipbreaker*. The photograph of the photograph looked so drab and gray on my camera screen. Dislocated from its setting and tainted by everything I had learned about Clay Markham, the seascape had lost whatever interest it once held for me. I no longer cared to learn its secrets. I no longer cared about the *picture* at all.

I deleted it.

# Author's Note

Over the years I have been fortunate to visit a number of Maine's seabird islands and see firsthand the work researchers are doing to study and protect some of the most charismatic avian species on the planet.

I am especially grateful to Dr. Stephen W. Kress, who in 1973 began the reintroduction of North Atlantic puffins to Maine. My wife and I were fortunate to once spend time with Dr. Kress in the observation blinds of Eastern Egg Rock, where his pioneering Project Puffin began.

Thank you to Brian Benedict, Director of the Maine Coastal Islands National Wildlife Refuge, for introducing me to the terns, sheep, and monstrously huge garter snakes of Metinic Island.

My friends Derek and Jeannette Lovitch, birding guides and owners of Freeport Wild Bird Supply, continue to teach me something new every time we venture off the Maine coast to watch seabirds.

And thanks to Maine Audubon for the many pelagic and island trips they have sponsored and continue to sponsor, bringing amateur and professional naturalists out to see the birds that call the Gulf of Maine home. I owe many of the first species on my decades-long life list to Audubon programs.

Judy Camuso, commissioner of the Maine Department of Inland Fisheries & Wildlife, I appreciate the important work you do for the state, your willingness to entertain my many questions, and your friendship.

Having thanked the real people who study and advocate for

Maine's seabirds, I must reiterate the note on the copyright page; the characters in this novel are altogether fictional, as are most of the story locations. You will find actual islands named Baker, Ayers, and Spruce on maps of Maine, but they are not the islands mentioned in this book.

I am, however, appreciative of the staff of the Hurricane Island Center for Science and Leadership for spurring me to create fictional islands inspired by the history and geology of Hurricane Island.

As always, I am indebted to my excellent team at St. Martin's Publishing Group and Macmillan Audio, including Charlie Spicer, Andrew Martin, Kelley Ragland, Sarah Melnyk, Paul Hochman, Joe Brosnan, Sarah Grill, Robert Allen, Katy Robitzsky, Dakota Cohen, and my ever-ready audiobook narrator, Henry Leyva.

Ann Rittenberg, I couldn't ask for a better agent.

Mat and Nancy McConnel, your friendship and feedback mean so much to me.

I have no greater boosters in the world than my parents, Judy and Richard Doiron.

When I met my wife, Kristen Lindquist, twenty-five years ago, she told me I would need to take up birdwatching if I wanted to date her since it was her abiding passion. I can say without reservation that was one of the best decisions I ever made.

Turn the page for a sneak peek at
Paul Doiron's new novel

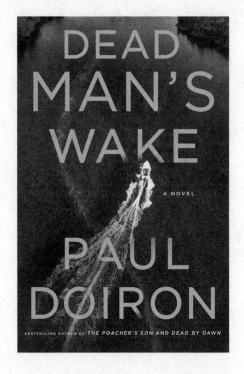

Available Summer 2023

# I

"It's a wonder that all marriages don't end in murder-suicides," said my stepfather's new wife, Jubilee.

Neil, my stepdad, nearly spit out his decaf.

It was the evening of Stacey's and my engagement party.

In the five years since my mom had died, Neil Turner and I had drifted apart. We had never been close to begin with, but he and his Jubilee had decided to have a celebratory dinner for us at their lake house in central Maine, over the Labor Day weekend. They had invited Stacey's parents, Charley and Ora Stevens, who had flown down from the North Woods in their Cessna 182 bush plane. Now the six of us were gathered in the great room, enjoying our blueberry pie and coffee while a warm breeze ruffled the curtains.

"You might want to have another look at your will, Neil," Ora Stevens said apropos murder-suicides.

"He has nothing to worry about," said Jubilee. "I told him, after he proposed, that I wasn't after his money *or* his last name."

Jubilee Batchelder had been christened Julie, but the name hadn't been fabulous enough for her adult self. (It was a judgment with which I happened to agree, based upon our brief acquaintance.) And so, in college, she had become Jubilee.

She worked as a yoga teacher and massage therapist—she had met Neil on her table—and was closer to my age than his: a fact that had troubled me at first and still did to some degree. She was an attractive if not conventionally beautiful woman, lean from hot yoga and a pescatarian diet. Her most striking feature was a mass of honey-blond hair that would not be contained.

I guessed that Jubilee had been the creative force behind the design of this modernist mansion, as my stepfather was a bright but thoroughly conventional man, a graying tax attorney who dressed in ironed polos and pressed chinos and played a lot of golf.

Somehow the topic had gotten onto the dreaded 9-1-1 calls that cops termed *domestics*. Jubilee hadn't realized that Maine game wardens—which Charley had been before his retirement and which I still was—had the same arrest powers as sheriffs, that we served as an off-road police force when no other officers were available in rural corners of the state. We saw a lot of shit, in other words. When a warden rolled up on a house fully involved in a conflagration of violence, you could never predict the outcome.

"Finish your story, Charley," Ora instructed her husband.

Stacey's mother sat, as always, in her wheelchair, cupping a tumbler of scotch on her blanket-draped lap. She wore her snowy-white hair cut in a shoulder-length bob. Her daughter had inherited her high cheekbones and almond-shaped green eyes that, in Ora, were even paler and more captivating.

"It happened just up the road when I was a tenderfoot warden," said Charley, who never needed encouragement. "The Belgrade Lakes region was my first district, you see."

Stacey's dad was a wiry man with white hair clipped close to his head and a rugged face I'd heard described as "halfway between handsome and homely." As usual, he was dressed from head to toe in green, as if he'd spent so many decades in uniform—first as an army pilot in Vietnam, then as a warden in Maine—that it was impossible for him to imagine wearing any other color.

"One night," he continued, "I got a call from the dispatcher that a man was beating up his new wife over in Skunk Hollow. He gave me some lip when I arrived, but I wrestled him to the ground easily enough. But as soon as I slapped the cuffs on the husband, the wife began punching *me*!"

Neil was still off-balance from Jubilee's joke about all marriages going bad. "I'm not sure this is an appropriate conversation for an engagement party."

"I haven't reached *le dénouement*," said Charley, who had learned French from Quebecois loggers when he was a boy in the lumber camps. "The kicker was that the wife hit harder than her man! And then, when I had them both restrained, the newlyweds began making out."

Everyone but me laughed at the punch line.

I was distracted by an intermittent noise coming through the screen doors. Some idiot on a Jet Ski was still buzzing about the lake. There were other boats racing around, too, but the whine of the two-stroke engine annoyed me as when an unseen mosquito is moving about a darkened room.

"You're not working tonight, babe," my fiancée whispered knowingly.

"It's illegal to run a Jet Ski or WaveRunner after dark."

"This isn't your district. It's not your job."

"If he crashes, it will be."

Sensing the need for a change of subject, Jubilee said, "I'd hoped you'd bring your wolf with you tonight, Mike. I'm so eager to meet him."

"Shadow isn't the best houseguest," Stacey said, tucking several strands of long brown hair behind one ear.

I felt obliged to add, "He's actually a wolf hybrid."

"A high-content wolf hybrid," Stacey said, "meaning he's basically a wolf. You'd never know looking at him that he has any domestic dog genes in him."

"Who's watching him while you're away?" Neil asked.

"A son's friend who wants to be a wildlife biologist. They get along great."

"Shadow has another new friend," said Stacey. "A raven's started visiting his enclosure. It just perches in a tree and *quorks* at him conversationally. We don't know if it's a male or a female, but we're calling it 'Gus.' Show them the cute picture, Mike."

I was reaching for my cell phone when the Jet Ski revved its engine not fifty feet from Neil and Jubilee's dock.

"I need to step outside," I said, rising with difficulty from a sectional sofa that looked and felt like a roasted marshmallow.

Stacey sprang up, too. "I'm coming with you."

The night was humid. The smell of the lake wafted across the blue lawn and through the towering pines. We crossed the patio and proceeded down the granite steps between fading viburnums until we'd entered the shadows beyond the house lights.

The Jet Ski had zoomed off by then. But I could still hear its motorcycle engine up the channel.

We had made it to the end of the dock and were gazing at cottages strung like Christmas lights along the far shore. I fancied that above the odor of the pines and the lake, I could smell the smoke from the fireworks that had been exploding at irregular intervals in celebration of summer's last hurrah.

The lake had served as the inspiration for the play—and later the movie—*On Golden Pond,* and it retained some of the quaintness that summer people treasured and lobbied hard to defend against the realities of modern life. For instance, a mail boat continued to deliver letters and packages (now mainly from Amazon, I suspected) to mailboxes at the ends of docks.

"I have to say," Stacey said, "Jubilee isn't what I expected. When you said she was only forty and taught hot yoga—"

"I expected Neil had found himself a trophy wife, too."

"Instead, she's perceptive, funny, and altogether awesome. Oh, Mike, I know how much you wanted to hate her."

"I have it on firsthand authority from the Brothers Grimm that all stepmothers are supposed to be wicked."

Stacey affected her father's Maine accent. "Well, Jubilee *is* wicked—wicked cool!"

A loon announced itself in the near darkness. Its yodeling was at once comical and haunting. Farther out, several watercrafts were racing about as if the lake were paved with wet black asphalt. One of the speedboats sounded positively rocket-powered. There were very few shoals or ledges at the center of Great Pond, but a fast-moving boat always risked striking a submerged log, especially when the vessel had the horsepower to outrun its own headlights.

The Jet Ski was coming back. In the weak starlight, it was utterly invisible except for the pale, shimmering rooster tail ejected by the impeller from the rear nozzle. I feared for the loon we'd just heard.

But the personal watercraft turned sharply before it came within range of the dock lights, made a tight ninety-degree turn, and zipped off toward deeper water. It was headed for a humpbacked shadow a half mile or so out. Neil had earlier identified the wooded islet as Mouse Island.

I held my breath, waiting for the wake to arrive. When it finally reached us, the waves caused the floating dock to buckle so that we staggered against each other like the drunken newlyweds from Charley's story.

The fenders cushioning the pontoon boat from the dock rubbed and squeaked. In my peripheral vision, I saw Charley's moored floatplane rocking. It was an amphibious model equipped with both floats and retractable wheels that could land as easily on water as on land.

"Let it go, Mike," Stacey said as I glared at the retreating Jet Ski. "For me."

"OK."

She took my arm as if we were preparing to walk down an aisle. "If we don't go back inside soon, they're going to wonder if we're *shtupping*."

"*Shtupping?*"

I allowed myself to be pulled back to our party. We'd made it down the dock and had reentered the festive glow of the house when we heard the collision on the lake.

# 2

The noise was more of a percussive thump rather than the explosion of fiberglass and metal you might expect from a motorboat striking a hard object at fifty miles per hour. If Stacey and I hadn't spent so much time on the water, we might have failed to read significance in that vague thud.

She turned back toward the lake. "One of them hit something!"

"A log, maybe?" I began striding toward the end of the dock. "I just hope it wasn't a loon."

The Jet Ski was nowhere to be seen, but it had no running lights to reveal its location. As far as I could discern, there was only a single motorboat in the middle of the lake, due south of Mouse Island. Its headlights and navigation lights were barely visible, but I could tell it was slowing to a stop.

"Could that boat have hit the Jet Ski?" Stacey asked.

"The crash would have been louder. Both boats would've gone spinning, and the Jet Ski would have broken apart."

I worked in the Wildlife Crimes Investigation Division of the Maine Warden Service. My cases involved everything from busting poaching rings to solving hunting homicides to reconstructing boating accidents.

But before I'd become a warden investigator, I'd patrolled Sebago Lake, and one of my responsibilities was to police the considerable boat traffic that clogged the waters in the summer. I spent July and August writing dozens of tickets for speeding, safety violations, and boating while intoxicated.

Once I'd watched an Allison Grand Sport go airborne after it crashed into a swimming float off Frye's Leap. This was in broad daylight: visibility unlimited. The driver tumbled into the water, none the worse for wear, being as loose as a marionette from drink. But his speedboat lodged in a stand of pines on Frye Island. It hung suspended in the branches ten feet in the air, with the engine still running. I remember looking up at the spinning prop and the vibrating bottom of the V-shaped hull. The state didn't pay me enough to climb up there to switch off the ignition. That damned boat took forever to run out of gas.

I squinted now at the distant speedboat. "They're turning around to have a look at whatever they hit."

"Your eyes are so much better than mine."

"There it is," I said. "Proof of guilt."

"What?"

"They just turned off their running lights. They know they hit something. They're hoping to slip away in the dark."

I took off at a sprint toward the house, my footsteps loud on the aluminum-framed dock.

"Where are you going?" Stacey called.

"To fetch the keys to Neil's boat."

When I slid open the door to the great room, I was met by four startled, slightly puzzled faces.

"We heard a noise out on the lake," I explained. "One of the speedboats struck something. It circled back and immediately turned off its lights."

Charley just about vaulted from the chair. "I'd call that suspicious."

I looked at my stepfather. "I need to borrow the Leisure Kraft."

"I'll take you out there," he said, smoothing his polo as he rose to his feet.

I could hardly kick Neil off his own boat, especially after he'd given us a tour of the pleasure barge earlier, showing us its many amenities. The rectangular vessel reminded me more of a floating living room than a proper watercraft. It had padded seats, a dry bar, a sound system, even a refrigerator.

"Do you have an idea where the crash happened?" he asked.

"Half a mile due west of us. Near Mouse Island."

"That rock is no bigger than a fleabite—barely enough acreage for a house and a fishing cabin," said Charley.

Ora pulled a phone from the pocket of her white cotton. "I am going to call 9-1-1 to tell the dispatcher to alert the local warden."

Neil was an attorney and cleared his throat as if preparing to address the court. "We don't have a warden here, I'm afraid."

"What's that?" Charley asked.

"This district doesn't currently have a game warden assigned to it," I explained. "The last one retired unexpectedly in May—throat cancer. And we couldn't get a deputy warden up to speed in time."

"And neither Belgrade nor Rome have municipal police officers," said Neil, meaning the neighboring municipalities, not the great cities of Europe. "The elected town councils pass ordinances, but no one enforces them. That's why the lakes association came up with the money to hire a constable." He, too, now reached for a cell phone. "In fact, I think I have Galen's private number in my contacts."

"Galen?" I said.

The name was unusual enough that I knew I'd encountered it before. I couldn't recall the circumstances. But the initial association was negative.

"Galen Webb, the lake constable we hired," Neil said. "The Kennebec County sheriff made him a part-time deputy so he could enforce state laws on the pond. If you call 9-1-1, he'll be the one they send out to investigate. Galen's a solid young man. Very polite and responsible. We've received few complaints about him all summer."

The Warden Service brass talked a lot about the importance of practicing courtesy, but it was my belief, having dealt with dozens of Maine's worst scofflaws, that a law enforcement officer who receives no complaints can't be doing their job responsibly.

"I need to get some things from my Scout," I said.

Before I could exit the room, Jubilee arose fluidly like the yoga teacher she was. She was wearing loose-fitting pastels and had a gardenia tucked behind her left ear.

"Is it possible someone was injured out there?" she asked with blunt perceptiveness. "A swimmer, maybe?"

She had given voice to a fearful possibility I hadn't permitted myself to speak aloud.

"We need to go," I said, leaving the question unanswered. "I'll meet you all at the boat."

"Are you staying here, Ora?" asked Jubilee. "If so, I'll stay with you."

"They don't have room for extra ballast, dear."

I was grateful that Stacey's mother recognized this was potentially a rescue—or worse, a recovery—mission and not a moonlight cruise. I had been afraid the whole party might want to tag along.

As I headed out to my vehicle, a vintage International Harvester Scout, I assessed the situation. The Leisure Kraft was propelled by a single 115-horsepower Suzuki engine. We wouldn't be engaging in any high-speed pursuits in that party barge.

I almost literally ran into Stacey in the dark outside. She was returning from the Scout with her medical backpack. She was an emergency medical technician, among other things, and always traveled with her trauma kit in case we came upon an accident.

"I would have brought your sidearm, too," she said. "But I don't have a key to the lockbox."

"That's all right. Can you see if Neil has a mask and snorkel? Flippers, too?"

"Will do." Light from the house touched part of her face. "I'm having a bad feeling about this, babe."

Kristen Lindquist

A native of Maine, bestselling author PAUL DOIRON attended Yale University, where he graduated with a degree in English. *The Poacher's Son,* the first book in the Mike Bowditch series, won the Barry award; the Strand Critics Award for Best First Novel; and has been nominated for the Edgar Award, the Anthony Award, and the Macavity Award in the same category. He is a registered Maine guide specializing in fly-fishing, and lives on a trout stream in coastal Maine with his wife, Kristen Lindquist.